INTO THE LIONS' DEN

ALSO BY STEPHEN FRANCIS

An Act of God

A DANIEL MILLER THRILLER

INTO THE LIONS' DEN

STEPHEN FRANCIS

First published in Great Britain 2013 by Titan Publishing

2nd edition published in 2014 by Endeavour Press

3rd edition republished in 2019 by Unicorn Publishing

Kindle edition published by Unicorn Publishing

Cover and printed matter formatting by Design for Writers
Inset photography by Simon McDermott

ISBN (HB)   978-1-9162361-0-3
ISBN (TPB) 978-1-9162361-1-0
ISBN (E)   978-1-9162361-2-7

ABOUT THE AUTHOR

Stephen lives in Ratoath, Ireland, with his wife and two children.

'*Into The Lions' Den*' is his debut novel. To find out more, visit Stephen's website at www.stephenfrancisbooks.com

Follow Stephen on   Twitter @sfrancisbooks
Instagram stephen.francis.books
Facebook @StephenFrancisBooks

For Duane

'Beware the fury of a patient man.'

- JOHN DRYDEN

PROLOGUE

BRONSON BROWNE THREADED HIS WAY along the streets of Whitehall, oblivious to the hundreds of workers pushing their way through the crowded thoroughfares. Overhead, Big Ben's chimes let everybody know they were late for whatever work they were headed. If the weary official hadn't left his office a mere four hours before, he would have considered himself tardy also.

He was a tall, refined man with a handlebar mustache of snow-white hair that drooped across his top lip, the sort 'Great War' Generals used to wear. As always, he was immaculately dressed in a suit of dark, mustard-colored tweed, which concealed his ample waistline nicely. Although only wispy clouds peppered the sky, he was prepared for all eventualities with a light, beige-colored, knee-length overcoat draped loosely across his arm; at no time was the English summer to be trusted.

He climbed the steps of the War Office, his hands shoved in his pockets and walked inside. He ignored a Military Policeman's warm greeting as he strolled across a foyer that bustled with pristinely-dressed soldiers, folder-carrying secretaries, and drawn-faced civil servants. His deep blue eyes burrowed a furrow into the tiled, marble floor as he headed towards an elegant, spiral staircase that wound up to his office on the fifth floor.

He placed one hand on the banister but hesitated. Turning slowly, he sat heavily on the steps. He closed his eyes with his elbows on his knees and hands clasped tightly under his chin. Entering his sixty-third year, his face bore the hallmarks of a man a decade older. He'd devoted more than two-thirds of his life to the service of his country, but now he was at breaking point. He wondered how long he could continue, how long this bloody war would continue.

He didn't know how long he'd been there when the guard touched his shoulder.

'Are you okay, sir?'

Browne looked up and blinked. He peered into the man's youthful, bright eyes.

'Yes,' he said, his voice quiet.

'Ms. Kendrick called down. A man is waiting to see you.'

Browne shook his head. Like every other day, his first meeting was always the 10 a.m. progress briefing with the PM. The last thing he needed now was the intrusion of an unwanted visitor, so why the bloody hell had Kendrick seen fit to squeeze in another appointment? He stared at the guard for a moment and climbed to his feet unaided, a deep rasping sigh escaping from his lungs.

He entered his outer office a few minutes later and scowled at his secretary as her fingers clacked across her typewriter.

She didn't look up.

He grunted a 'good morning' before focusing his disdain on a scrawny, pimple-faced young man pacing a path across his carpeted floor. Despite the undernourished, spotty appearance, Browne guessed he was in his early twenties. He wore a dark, navy suit, maybe a size too big, covered with creases and chalk dust, making it look like it had been bought in a second-hand store. Browne's eyes narrowed. He had seen him before – sometime last year, he remembered.

The young man stopped and turned to face him, removing a fist of chewed fingernails from his mouth. He took a cautious step forward and stuck out a saliva-coated hand. Browne glanced down before brushing past and opening his inner office door. The young man followed as though he was picking his way through a minefield.

Browne hung his overcoat on an ornate, wooden coat hanger. He walked to the other side of his desk and sat on a worn, cracked-leather chair. He leaned back, the chair creaking under his weight.

'Refresh my memory?'

The man looked at him oddly.

'Your name.' Browne's face began to redden; he had no time for this nonsense.

'Welchman, sir. Harold Welchman.'

'One of those code-breakers,' Browne said, recalling their only previous meeting.

'Cryptanalyst.' Welchman said. His face turned pale as though he regretted making the correction.

'And?'

'Sir?' the man said. He fidgeted with an untidy, black fedora.

'What do you want?'

'Oh… yes.' Welchman fumbled inside his jacket pocket and retrieved an envelope. He handed it to Browne, who didn't move to accept. Welchman dropped it gently onto the desk and began to turn around.

'Wait.' Browne slapped the arm of his chair.

His eyes moved from message to messenger several times before he snatched up the letter. Staring at the man, he plucked a small letter-opener off a green felt pad. He sliced through the envelope smoothly, shaking its contents onto the desk: a single white page, folded in two.

Browne flicked it open and twisted it around for a better look. As his eyes scanned the words, his annoyed face grew darker. Out of the corner of his eye, he could see the young man switch uneasily from one foot to the other.

'Turing sent this?' Browne asked.

'Yes, sir.'

'Have you read it?' Browne looked up, his eyes focusing on Welchman.

'I deciphered it this morning.'

'How many have seen it?'

'Just me and Alan.'

Browne let out a low growl. He knew damn well that was a lie; he could see it on the young man's face. A message of this importance would have scaled the Bletchley hierarchy.

'I thought Turing decrypted naval correspondence?'

Welchman nodded.

'So why has he seen this? This has nothing to do with the Navy.'

The blood drained from Welchman's face to the point where he looked like he would lose his breakfast over Browne's rose-red, Qalin rug. He stuttered to find an answer.

'Damn it, man, spit it out.' Browne planted an elbow on his desk, gripping his head in his open hand. He could barely look at the young man.

'He used to be my mentor.' Some spittle splashed on Browne's desk, and Welchman's face turned a sickly grey.

'So what? Don't you people have procedures for this sort of thing?'

Welchman mumbled a reply that Browne couldn't make out.

'Pardon me?' Browne's eyes flamed.

'I trust him.' Welchman shifted uneasily, looking like a startled gazelle trying to evade a predator.

'Good. So do I.' He pushed the letter to one side and fished a pocket watch out of his waistcoat. He glanced at it before snapping it shut, the click resonating like a low-caliber shot.

'Ms. Kendrick.' His voice boomed.

'Please contact the Colonel,' he said as she entered the office. 'Tell him to drop whatever he's doing and come here immediately… an important message has been delivered to us. And pass on my apologies to the PM. Unfortunately, I cannot attend this morning's briefing, but do insist that he fit me in at his next available slot.' He was almost going to add, 'even if he has to postpone a phone call with Roosevelt.'

Ms. Kendrick hurried out without comment, closing the door behind her.

If a picture was a thousand words, then Browne's expression spoke volumes of encyclopedic proportions. He sat deep into his chair and stroked the side of his face, the sparkling eyes of the morning dulled by the latest burden weighing heavily on his mind.

'I would have expected a message of this importance to have been delivered by Turing himself,' he said.

'He's waiting to see if we can intercept anything further which might be related.'

Browne looked as though he didn't believe that either. He shook his head solemnly and silently wondered what sort of place they were running up there.

'So, no further problems after those experienced last year?' He pointed to one of the leather-backed armchairs on the other side of his desk, his eyes never shifting away from the young man.

'No, sir,' Welchman said, sitting down.

'You can relax now. Your job here today is almost done. The Colonel may have some questions for you once he's read this. You can head back to your Hut once he's satisfied.'

Beads of sweat appeared across Welchman's brow. It was apparent he'd rather be anywhere else than there.

Following a sharp knock, Colonel Cumming swung the heavy oak door inward as though he was swatting away an annoying insect. He marched boldly into Browne's office, spotting his superior chewing on a cigar in front of the fireplace. He immediately detected a pervading anxiousness before his eyes settled on a young face peering from behind an armchair. A momentary lapse of recognition was followed by a sudden glare of disgust, which forced the young man to recoil from view.

The Colonel scowled at him as he plopped himself into the other armchair and, within seconds, had assumed he was nothing more than an errand boy, a lamb to the slaughter, sent by Bletchley's code-breaking cowards.

Cumming was a tall, robust man with a swathe of bristling coal-black hair. His chest was as broad as a royal carriage door, illustrated by the fact that the buttons on his tunic strained to keep it all in. He was generally a softly spoken gent with the stoic heart of a lion and the cunning intellect of a master chess player. For those reasons, Browne had requested he be transferred to his staff, reporting directly and only to him.

Welchman nodded a greeting to the Colonel, sitting precariously on the edge of the chair as though he was balancing atop Nelson's Column on a breezy day. Browne walked to the other side of the desk and sat down with an emphatic thud. He slid Welchman's message across to Cumming, who, almost reluctantly, moved his suspicious eyes away from the young man.

Cumming inspected the document for over a minute, a sickening, greyish pallor washing across his face.

'What do you make of it?' Browne said.

'Authentic?' Cumming's voice was barely a whisper.

'It would appear so.' Browne's eyes shifted sideways to Welchman.

'And you're that code-breaker fellow from last year?' Cumming said, without looking up.

Welchman nodded.

'How many know about this?'

'A handful,' Browne said, throwing his eyes to the ceiling. He tapped the desk and shot Cumming a questioning look. The Colonel shook his head almost imperceptibly.

'You can leave us now.' Browne said, dismissing the young man with a crisp flick of his hand.

The codebreaker jumped as though a switch had been flicked and electrified the chair. He hurried towards the door.

'Tell Turing we'll be paying him a visit *very* soon.' Browne's voice growled like a predatory mountain bear.

Welchman didn't turn to acknowledge Browne's promise. Instead, he quickly disappeared out the door, almost knocking over Ms. Kendrick, carrying a tea tray. She snorted her disapproval before placing the early-morning refreshments on Browne's desk and shutting the door behind her.

'Ideas?' Browne said.

'We've considered several for similar scenarios.' Cumming looked off through the window, careful to use the term 'we' instead of 'I'; he wasn't about to land himself in any more hot water.

'Similar?'

'We never considered this a possibility.'

'It's your job to consider all eventualities and have a contingency in place for every one of them.' Browne's response was as biting as the North Sea wind in winter.

'Yes, sir. We just don't have a strategy for this exact scenario. We can probably merge a couple of existing plans. I mean… we never considered anyone was this close to a breakthrough.'

'Well, the Russians are, and worse, the Boche knows about it. You need to fix this… quickly.'

'I'm well aware of the gravity of the situation,' Cumming replied evenly. 'If this communiqué is to be believed, it could be over for us. Maybe it's a fake. Have you considered that?'

Browne glared at him, his face swelling like an over-ripe tomato at a country fair. Cumming exhaled gently.

'Okay. So it's genuine. That means whatever we've done in the past, our plans for the future will count for nothing.' Cumming dropped his head.

'How could this have been missed?'

Cumming felt the question was more an accusation aimed directly at him.

'I mean, it's not just any bomb. It's *the* bomb.' Browne paused and drew a deep breath. 'We have people over there, don't we? How the hell could the Russians have kept this a secret? This sort of research isn't like baking a bloody cake. It takes time, effort, resources.'

Browne turned and walked to the window. 'How far behind are we?' It seemed as though his anger was slowly receding.

Cumming closed his eyes thoughtfully and tapped his forehead lightly.

'A few years. We're having trouble getting everybody to agree. The project is slow getting off the ground.'

Browne glanced at the mantelpiece clock. 'You have twenty-four hours.'

Without being dismissed, Cumming stood silently and marched out of the office, clutching Welchman's message in his fist. By the time he passed Ms. Kendrick, the color had returned to his face, indicating his surging adrenaline.

This was, after all, his talent. Tight deadlines, a near-impossible task, a ruthless superior, and the choking cloak of disaster hovering over him, imploring him to fail. A watertight strategy was required to avert a course of history that he had neither predicted nor desired. Resources were scarce, time was tight, and, somewhere in the back of his mind, he knew that whatever plan he could conjure up would eventually be filed away in some 'Top Secret' archive, never to see the light of day. But that was irrelevant. Hitler had diverted his armies south, away from Moscow, with the sole intention of snatching some new atomic weaponry from beneath the Allies' noses. Preventing that was the only thing that mattered.

CHAPTER 1

Daniel Miller stared at a disinterested, fingernail-painting secretary; he'd been waiting for more than twenty minutes.

Without a word, she pointed an unpolished forefinger toward the closed door before resuming her decorating.

He turned and sized it up before dropping his rucksack next to a tall, drooping, potted plant that looked as though it hadn't seen water in well over a week. He checked his uniform in a full-length mirror for stray debris, straightened himself, and knocked once. He still had no idea why he'd been summoned and was troubled because he'd been instructed to pack all his belongings before reporting to the Camp Commandant's office.

'Enter,' a deep voice called from the other side.

Once in, Daniel spotted the Commandant perusing a large map pinned to one of the walls. He took a few steps forward and snapped out a salute.

'At ease,' the Commandant murmured without diverting his gaze.

Daniel relaxed and, locking his hands behind his back, regarded his superior. He was a tall man, just over six feet, with a slim, athletic build, the result of a daily exercise routine that would put any recruit to shame. In that way, he painfully reminded Daniel of somebody from his past, but he forced the memory away. Instead, Daniel allowed his eyes to scan the room. Very basic: a modest-sized wooden desk, a hard-backed chair, one slightly paint-chipped filing cabinet (second-from-top drawer slightly ajar), and a cleaned blackboard, duster, and chalk held in a tray beneath. A large, rectangular window faced him, which afforded an excellent view of the camp and a large portion of the Warwickshire countryside.

'How long have you been with us, Private?'

'Just over two years.'

The Commandant turned slightly and glanced at him. 'Do you know where this is?' He tapped the map.

'Soviet Union, sir,' Daniel replied without hesitation.

The Commandant nodded. 'The man behind you has a few questions.'

Daniel turned slightly and saw a man sitting in an armchair, which, judging by what looked like new marks on the lino, had been pulled back from the desk to provide cover behind the door.

'How are you?' the man asked in fluent German.

Daniel replied in kind, saying he was okay.

'Any ills or sores?'

'Only my feet, sir.'

'From marching the countryside, no doubt?'

'Yes, sir.'

'No need to call me 'sir'. I'm not an officer.'

Daniel didn't respond but was curious as to why the man hadn't yet spoken a word of English. The man wore a stylish, crinkle-free navy suit, a spotless white shirt underneath, with a bright blue necktie completing the ensemble. He guessed the man was older than him by about twenty years. Streaks of gray ran through his shoulder-length, dark-brown hair, a length which wouldn't have been tolerated at this camp; very unmilitary-like. Although seated, Daniel estimated they would have been about the same height, at five-foot-nine.

'Taking everything in?' the man asked, this time in fluent Russian.

'Yes.' Daniel's response was in the same language, without even noticing the sudden switch. He spotted a wooden cane leaning next to the chair on the man's left.

'A war injury?'

The man grinned.

'My name is Christopher, but everyone calls me Chris,' he said, ignoring the question. 'How long have you been speaking other languages?'

'As long as I can remember.'

'That long?'

Daniel didn't respond.

'You're the quiet sort,' Christopher said.

'Something I picked up in the army.'

'Have they looked after you?'

'By 'they', I assume you're not one of us.' Daniel's eyes flitted to one side. He glanced at the bemused Commandant.

'I was a long time ago. I do different things now.'

'Interpreter?'

'Sometimes.' Christopher smiled, which brought a look of consternation from the Commandant. 'I do consultancy work now.'

Daniel watched as the man studied him. He tilted his head to one side. Judging by the way Christopher had mastered the transitions between Hamburg and Leningrad accents, Daniel guessed his work now resided in the area of counter-espionage and, as such, knew that asking what kind of work wouldn't elicit a revealing response.

After a few awkward moments, Christopher turned to the Commandant.

'This must be boring you,' he said in English. Crow-feet creases appeared at the corners of his eyes as he smiled. 'Perhaps we could have some privacy for a few minutes?'

Daniel thought his tone humble yet forceful, a trait no doubt honed from the years in his *consultancy* role.

The Commandant glanced at Daniel and then nodded before leaving the room with a sigh, clearly glad of the opportunity to be able to converse with somebody in a language he understood, should he have wished.

Christopher waited until the door had closed before turning back to Daniel. He struggled to his feet and, with the use of the cane, shuffled across to the map. He prodded an area in the south-eastern section.

'It was cold there last winter.' Back to Russian again.

'Hot now, though,' Daniel said, his eyes fixed on the man's movements and behavior, trying to figure out what he wanted; to see through the intrigue.

'Extremes in weather, I suppose, unlike our little island.' Christopher glanced back at Daniel. 'You're well educated.'

'My father encouraged me.'

'Did he also teach you languages?'

Daniel said nothing but wondered why a man rooted in the world of secrets didn't already know all there was to know about him.

'Of course, you don't have to answer my questions,' Christopher said, 'but it might help if we could get acquainted.'

'Help who?'

Chris smiled. 'Well, everybody, really.' He walked behind the Commandant's desk and, using the cane, pulled the blinds aside to look out the window.

He reverted to German. 'I come with a proposition.'

Daniel remained impassive.

'News has come recently of a move by the German High Command, which, if successful, could mean a rather abrupt end to the war… in their favor.' He paused. 'Hitler is sending his 6th Army to Stalingrad.' He paused again as though waiting for a response. Daniel didn't let him down.

'To capture the city named after the Russian leader before moving on to the oilfields beyond.'

'That's what we thought too.' Christopher's eyes lit up. 'Until we intercepted a communiqué a couple of days ago.'

'Bletchley?'

Christopher's smile evaporated instantly, his tone changing dramatically. 'How do you know about that place?'

Daniel silently cursed himself for saying too much, feeling like the headmaster had scolded him.

'I suppose some secrets are difficult to keep, especially with your connections.' Christopher's slight grin reappeared.

'Anyway, taking the city and the oilfields beyond is of secondary importance. The primary objective is the capture of a scientist.' He continued to look intently at Daniel before carrying on. 'We'd like to get to him before they do.'

Daniel's stomach flipped as he read between the lines. A stony silence enveloped the room as both men regarded each other for several uncomfortable seconds.

Daniel eventually spoke. 'That explains why you're speaking Russian, but German...'

'The armies of the Third Reich are moving with an all too familiar swiftness. They've penetrated further east than we would like. It's just a precaution, you see.' Christopher's face exhibited a deadpan grimness. 'You understand that although the Russians are our allies, we can't just arrive at their doorstep and expect to be welcomed with open arms. We need a different approach. Perhaps somebody with a military background, with the ability to blend into the surroundings, speak the language, and so on. Whoever goes in will have to be innovative and show tremendous resourcefulness if he's to pull it off without being detected.'

Daniel felt his skin prickle as an eddy of excitement rushed through his body. He could hardly wait to ask a question.

'Am I the only one to be approached?'

'The number of people who've made my short-list is... small.'

Daniel doubted it was in double digits.

'For most overseas missions, we usually select the most suitable candidate, and that would be it. However, this isn't like any other mission. We're looking for somebody willing to go rather than somebody ordered to go.' He tapped his cane gently on the floor. 'You have a couple of days to make your decision. There's a car waiting outside to take you home.' Christopher paused. 'Understand, you're under no obligation to accept. As I said, there are other candidates.'

Daniel looked away for a moment, his mind a frenzy of questions without answers and a hollow uncertainty. His gaze returned to Christopher.

'Why is this fella so important?'

'I'm afraid I can't tell you.'

Daniel understood only too well the 'need to know' instruction.

'I can see you're quite eager,' Christopher said. 'This isn't a decision you should take lightly. You shouldn't allow past events to sway you either way.' He picked at a fingernail, his eyes never leaving Daniel.

Daniel's mouth suddenly went dry, and he felt compelled to look away for the first time since he met the man. He knew what Christopher was alluding to and stifled a swallow.

'You're well informed.' Daniel slipped a glance towards an open file on the Commandant's desk.

Christopher followed his eyes. 'Yes, it's in your file. I had to be sure.'

'And are you?'

'We'll see,' Christopher's grin returned. The two sized each other up for several seconds before Christopher added. 'How's your foot?'

Daniel's face clouded over, and his voice turned cold. 'Fine.'

'No permanent damage then?'

Daniel tried to shake his head firmly but felt himself hesitate.

'We need to know that you're not going to break down physically if we drop you into Stalingrad.'

'I'm sure there's a fitness assessment in there.'

Christopher's tongue licked his bottom lip.

Daniel could feel the man's eyes scour his face, following the scar from the corner of his right eye to his cheekbone, a small, permanent and personal reminder of the hazards of war.

'That'll do for now,' Christopher said. 'Although I must admit, I'm very impressed with your accent. I've been in the company of native speakers most of my life. You would certainly have them fooled. Remarkable.'

Christopher turned smartly on his good leg and lurched towards the door.

Daniel glanced down at his own foot. He had been a great deal luckier than the older man. By the time he looked back up, Christopher was gone.

CHAPTER 2

'And you don't need any help?' the man said.

Anatoly Yermakov shook his head from beneath a large metal hood, trying desperately to ignore the latest intrusion. He grunted as he tried to tighten a stubborn bolt. It had been almost a year since Anatoly had set foot inside the lab. Since then, numerous students, scientists, and lecturers had paid a visit, and he had treated each one the same way, with wary skepticism.

The bother had introduced himself as Professor of Cosmology and, as such, had been the second grey-haired scientist Anatoly had met to have offered the lofty title of Department Head. The first had proclaimed himself 'Head of Modern Physics', but Anatoly had believed him to be anything but modern. It hadn't just been the piercing eyes that had unsettled him, but the complete lack of academic savvy, coupled with extreme indifference to the answers to questions that the Professor had fired at him. Anatoly had felt like he was educating the older man. It was almost as though the educator couldn't have cared less about the dawning atomic age, worrying behavior given current scientific understanding. Naively, Anatoly had initially given him the benefit of the doubt, believing the Professor had wanted to discover what caliber of researcher he had been forced to recruit. In the end, though, the man had looked and behaved more like a government official with an agenda. But despite the man's educated deportment, Anatoly wasn't taking anything anyone said as fact, not anymore.

'Got everything you need then?' the Cosmologist asked.

'Sure… could do with that screwdriver, though.' Anatoly waved in the direction of a miniature tool that had scuttled out of arm's reach.

The middle-aged man flicked the screwdriver with the edge of his shoe, sending it skidding across the floor into Anatoly's outstretched hand.

'Thanks,' Anatoly mumbled. 'What'd you say your name was again?'

'Korolev.'

'Oh, right.' He paused. 'I read some of your articles.'

'Really? Which ones?'

'Dark Matter, Gravitational Lensing. You confirmed some of Einstein's theories.'

Korolev nodded appreciatively. 'One of the few to do so.'

'I particularly liked the calculations you completed on General Relativity.'

'Further confirmation that was all.'

'No. There was some good stuff in there. I read it a while back.'

Korolev shook his head. 'When was that?'

'A few years ago.' Anatoly tightened the bolt as well as he could manage within the confined space.

'Okay...' Korolev slid Anatoly's feet a dubious smile. With his hands shoved in his pockets, he surveyed the scientific hieroglyphics scrawled on a large blackboard pinned to one of the walls. He strolled closer for a better look.

'How old are you?'

'Nineteen next week,' Anatoly said, his head appearing from beneath the giant machine for the first time.

Korolev turned and stared at a blackened face that looked as though it should belong in a coal mine. His jaw dropped slightly, a common occurrence when anybody came face to face with the youthful double doctorate for the first time.

Anatoly was no ordinary scientist.

For years, whispered rumors had fizzled throughout the academic fraternity of a physicist to rival, if not surpass, the best the West had to offer. He could talk before he could walk, read before he was three, and write complex sentences a month after his fourth birthday. By the time he had reached ten, he was studying Applied Calculus and Number Theory, while other kids his age were still mastering their fairytales. A prodigious talent with an unquenchable thirst for knowledge had led his teachers to fast-track his education, skipping him through the regular curriculum and changing classes every semester rather than at the end of each year. He had been accepted to the University of Kyiv before he reached twelve, where he studied and eventually tutored in Advanced Theoretical Physics and Complex Mathematics, making him, at the age of fourteen, the youngest ever alumna to graduate from the university. His doctorates swiftly followed a couple of years later.

However, his talent hadn't gone unnoticed.

Several years ago, a malevolence had begun to meddle with his life, which, following tragedy and deceit, had coerced him into relocating hundreds of kilometers from his home in Kyiv. The cloak of a youthful naivety had been violently stripped away, exposing a scared soul terrified at the prospect of delivering what had been demanded of him. The alternative was losing what little he had left to hold dear: that was simply something he couldn't begin to contemplate.

'Nice overalls,' Korolev said. "I can see why they've got you hidden away in the university basement.'

'Been down here since I moved from Kyiv,' Anatoly said. 'I guess it was the only place Stalingrad Technical had available.'

'Right,' Korolev said. He turned quickly back to the board. 'Interesting dilemma.' He wagged a finger.

'It was when I was in Kyiv. It isn't now,' Anatoly said, standing next to him. He picked up a cracked porcelain cup. 'Didn't have the budget or space there. Here I've got an abundance of both.'

'And you're working on the best extraction method?' Korolev nodded towards the monstrosity that Anatoly had been buried beneath.

'It should give me what I need.'

A smile appeared across Korolev's face as he scanned the blackboard again. Anatoly watched him closely between sips. The man wore long, white-grey, shoulder-length hair. He had a wrinkle-free, sallow face, which lent itself more to bright outdoor activities than the darker indoor type generally associated with those engaged in his niche of nocturnal studies. His clothes would be considered fashionable by those he claimed to teach. Although he had been in the lab only a few minutes, Anatoly could discern an almost indifferent and nonchalant swagger.

It was time to put the Professor to the test.

'Notice anything?'

Korolev turned back to the derivation. His eyes roved from one side of the board to the other. Finally, he said. 'Several logical steps are missing. The integral here and… shouldn't this be squared?' Korolev tapped the board.

Anatoly shrugged. 'Maybe…' He had deliberately included the mistakes so that he could weed out any visiting impostors. But Korolev had seen through them and, for now, seemed to be the genuine article; only time would tell.

'Just haven't got around to correcting them yet,' Anatoly lied. 'Doesn't matter. I know they're there. I've compensated near the end. The result is correct.'

'Wouldn't it be easier to write it out in full? I'd fail an undergraduate if they submitted this as an answer to one of my exam questions.'

'An undergraduate wouldn't have written that in the first place,' Anatoly said beneath a mischievous grin. 'Besides, it's safer in here.' He tapped the side of his head.

'Secrets of the universe for the enlightened few.' Korolev stared wide-eyed.

'What are you working on at the moment?' Anatoly asked.

'This and that,' Korolev said, adding a hint of mystery. 'Nothing that would interest you.'

'Everything interests me.'

'So I've heard.' Korolev's voice was barely a whisper.

Anatoly sipped the cold, sugarless tea but didn't make a face. Over the years, he had become used to leaving hot beverages around, as he had allowed his research to distract him. But it remained a mystery how the cups appeared to replicate as if by some kind of pottery meiosis.

'You've certainly got the Physics Department talking,' Korolev said, glancing across at him. 'Phrases like 'Wonder Boy' and 'Boy Genius' are on the tips of everyone's lips.'

'I'm no longer a boy,' Anatoly fired back. A crimson cloud of anger flashed across his face. He glared at Korolev, who looked as though he was trying to restrain himself from laughing.

'I think it's meant as a compliment.'

'I'd sooner be treated as an equal and nothing special.'

'Equals in this world don't get the royal treatment conferred upon you.'

'Royal treatment? I've been stuck down here for weeks working on this. I eat, sleep, and drink down here.' He pointed to a few crumpled blankets and a pillow tossed in one corner.

Korolev didn't bother to look. 'Who brings you your meals?'

'Students drop in, ask if I need anything.'

'As I said. The royal treatment. The rest of us mortals have to suffer the ignominy of the canteen queue.'

'I'm sure you don't line up with the undergraduates.'

'Actually… no.' Korolev grinned. 'But I do have to get my food, and worse, I have to dine with the rest of the staff. At times I wish I could hibernate in my lab like you.'

Anatoly's anger receded. 'You don't dress or behave like a typical Professor.'

'My disguise.' Korolev's eyes sparkled. 'Whenever I'm among the student body, I like to pretend I'm still in touch with their world.'

'I'll bet they adore you?'

'And reviled by my peers, you know how it is.' Korolev laughed. 'Being my own person helps keep me sane.'

Anatoly tilted his head to one side. He had never met a physicist like this before, and he had met plenty over the years. The majority were old in age and spirit and closer to their last day than their first, but Korolev was filled with the same youthful exuberance of those he taught and was more like Anatoly than he would like to admit.

'Anyway, it'll be getting dark soon. I've got work of my own to be getting on with. I'll leave you two alone.' Korolev nodded towards the machine.

He strolled toward the lab door, his hands returning to his trouser pockets. He stopped and turned slightly.

'I'm happy I passed your test,' he said with a wry smile. 'Don't think Evgeny would have.' He pushed the door open and went outside.

Anatoly stared after him. He concurred with Korolev's assessment of the Head of Modern Physics' mental acuity: more an administrator than a scientist.

CHAPTER 3

It seemed to Tom that the only refuge from the war was to be found at the back of the newspapers in the sports pages, and there were precious few of those. It was inescapable. Along with its citizens, the war had consumed the nation's psyche. And after three torturous years of stalemate, he was sick of it. He even dreaded running the gauntlet of his local for a jar where, generally, the main topic on everybody's lips was what had been covered on the front pages of the day's broadsheets.

He dropped the paper on the kitchen table and slid his glasses to the top of his head, sighing as he rubbed his eyes and stroked the bridge of his nose. He gazed absently out the window and focused on the tool shed in the yard. He smiled and remembered more peaceful times when pitch-perfect melodies had escaped from there. Back then, it seemed that even the birds had stopped singing. This evening, a male Bluethroat whistled away in search of a Yorkshire mate.

Behind him, the front door opened. He glanced up at the clock.

'That you back already?' he called. 'Fancy a cuppa?'

Using the table, he pushed himself to his feet and skirted across to the stove. He turned when he heard something drop in the hallway. The sight of a smiling, uniformed soldier made his heart ricochet inside his chest. He dropped the kettle, raced out of the kitchen, and draped his arms around his youngest son, clutching him so tightly he was in danger of creasing Daniel's sharp, green uniform.

Daniel spoke after a minute. 'Okay, dad. Take it easy.'

But Tom couldn't let go. His eyes had welled up. He didn't want his son to see such an outpouring of emotion. After a few seconds, he regained some composure and moved back with an enormously proud smile and glistening eyes.

'You shoulda called?'

'I wanted to surprise you.'

'You certainly did that. It's great to see you. Seen your Ma yet?'

Daniel shook his head with a smile. He'd always loved how his dad referred to his mum in his thick Dublin brogue. Daniel had found it amusing that his dad had never lost the accent despite a flair for languages and their associated inflections.

'She's out shoppin'.' Tom didn't take his eyes off him until Daniel peered around his father.

'You said something about tea?'

'Yes.' Tom patted Daniel's arms and went back to fill the kettle. 'Sit down. Throw those 'aul papers outta the way. We've so much to talk about, so much to catch up on. How long are you home?'

'Not long.' Daniel removed his cap and, sitting down, fidgeted with it. He regarded his father for a moment: average height, average build, average all over, really, except in heart and mind. And apart from a small scar embedded in his right eyebrow, he carried no other distinguishing marks. Some stray grey hairs meandered their way free of his dark brown hair when the light shone on them just so. But his face told a tale. It was older than his years, like a man who had lived in it twice over.

'Have to go back to camp in a few days.'

He watched Tom slow his actions, knowing his dad had started to weigh things up. That was a part of what he did in London: thought about things, how they came into being, and how they could be manipulated for the greater good.

'Bit short that?' Tom said. His voice had dropped to a whisper.

'Something's come up.'

The kettle in Tom's hand hovered over the lit stove for a moment before he set it down on an unlit ring.

'And you've come for my blessin'?' he said, without turning around.

Daniel didn't respond.

'You just had to go 'n follow your brother.' His head shrunk back into his shoulders.

'I haven't exactly followed him,' Daniel said hurriedly. He desperately wanted to prevent an awkward moment but knew one was looming.

Tom gave a regretful but grateful nod. 'Maybe this is a conversation to be had somewhere else. I don't want your Ma comin' into the middle of whatever it is you've come to say.'

Daniel stood.

'Why don't ya drop your bag up to your room first?' Tom said.

Daniel nodded in agreement and disappeared into the hallway. He grabbed his holdall and, with his head hanging slightly, plodded up the stairs.

Placing his fingertips on his old bedroom door, he paused before pushing. The door swung inwards with a slight squeak. He smiled at the thought that, two years on, his dad still hadn't oiled the hinges. He stood in the doorway and scanned his old bedroom.

It was a medium-sized room he and his brother Alex had shared all their lives. Two single beds lay parallel to each other against opposite walls. At the far end, a small dresser with an oval-shaped mirror stood between them. A free-standing wardrobe faced it and completed the furniture: simple but effective.

Daniel threw his bag onto his bed and sat down slowly, testing the mattress. He couldn't recall it being so soft, softer, indeed, than the army provided.

He ran his hand across the fresh linen and wondered how often his mother changed it. He hadn't been home for so long, yet she had maintained a mother's state of preparedness. That was typical of her. Just because there were no longer any children to fuss over didn't mean she had sat idly by. She was the homemaker and carer, and this was her territory.

He glanced sidelong at the dresser with its three drawers. He and Alex had used one each and fought tooth and nail for possession of the third. It had been a constant source of argument, some of which had spilled into battles of sibling proportions.

His gaze moved to the other bed: Alex's bed.

He leaned forward and gently touched it before placing his elbows on his knees and hanging his head. Memories of their childhood had been bottled up since news of his brother's death had been delivered, but now they flooded back with a searing, biting reality: the years since slipping into an unconscious blur.

He remained motionless for several minutes, allowing his emotions to effervesce, experiencing them all over again. He wondered if he had ever actually grieved but couldn't quite remember. He had been upset, of that, he was sure A family death always caused tremendous sadness and distress for those closest, but there hadn't been a body to mourn or a grave to pray over. Alex's death still held an aura of un-realness about it, as it probably did for the families of thousands of men and boys who hadn't returned from the European mainland in the summer of 1940.

After a little while, he stood and reached for the zipper on his bag. Peeling it back, he removed his belongings and placed them in the bottom dresser drawer. He tossed the empty bag on the floor and glanced at the windowsill above his bed. He smiled again.

He tilted his head and reached for the old, battered, black cornet case. He undid its clasps and ran his hand over the cold, polished brass instrument, still pristinely clean even after years of non-use. Daniel had been the youngest principal cornetist to play with the village brass band, but his music career ended the day he enlisted; his life had taken a new direction. He lifted the cornet out of the case, fixed the mouthpiece, and raised it to his lips. But he hesitated. Fingering the valves, he lowered the instrument and placed it on the bed next to him.

He stepped onto the landing, closed the door, and strolled down the stairs to Tom, who was waiting at the bottom.

When they stepped onto the pavement, they didn't turn right, the quickest way to the pub, but instead turned to the left.

A stiff, June chill came out of nowhere that tumbled down the terraced street as they headed up the slow incline to the top of the hill that overlooked the village. Hundreds of similar communities pockmarked the undulating Yorkshire Dales; all touched in some shape by the ravages of both this war and the last.

While Tom slouched, pushing against the breeze, Daniel was bolt upright as though a steel skewer had been shoved through his spine, helping pull his shoulders back into perfect alignment. The army had done for Daniel's posture what twenty years of constant paternal correction hadn't, adding almost two inches to his son's height in the process. He also noted that Daniel appeared to have lost inches laterally but gained vertically.

Heel to toe, they strolled up then down the other side of the hill, the sun disappearing behind them. A low, light haze stirred up from the surrounding fields; the gentle bleating of sheep carried on the wind.

'You still working in London?' Daniel asked, kick-starting the conversation.

Tom nodded. 'Been run off our feet these past few years.'

'I thought they might have got you something closer to home.'

Tom shrugged.

'How come you're here at this time of day? You never used to get back until late of a Friday.'

'Ah, sure, other than the weekends, I haven't had a day off in four years. The Head of Foreign Office sent me a note, insisted I take a few days this week. Said he'd noticed a deterioration in my work, told me to get myself off home to the wife, come back refreshed next week.'

'Sounds like somebody pulled a few strings to make sure you were here today.'

Tom nodded. 'I was thinkin' the same.'

'Isn't Mum tired of your traveling?'

'Hasn't been easy, if that's what you're gettin' at. Think I'll resign my post after the war, try and spend as much time with her as I can. Any idea when that'll be?' He offered a half-hearted smile.

'I'm sure you know more about that than I do.'

Tom pursed his lips. 'A few more years, I reckon. We haven't the strength to get across the Channel. But, the Americans are in now; maybe there's a chance…' He bent down to retie a shoelace that had come undone.

'Are they treatin' you alright?' he said.

Daniel could feel the conversation was about to turn towards its inevitable destination and the reason he was here.

'Yeah, it's been tough. Training is hard. They need us to be ready to *defend our island* should it come to it.' It was a throw-away comment since he knew the country had seen off the worst the Germans had thrown at it.

Tom glanced across at Daniel.

Over the next twenty minutes, their conversation idled between the army of yesteryear and its current incarnation. Tom was amazed to learn how training methods had changed since his military career ended almost three decades before. Daniel quickly pointed out that the Ministry of Defence had been forced into a radical overhaul of its education techniques since Dunkirk.

Dunkirk.

The very mention of that place turned Daniel's blood iceberg cold. He felt his chest tighten. Nobody could imagine what kind of hell the British Expeditionary Force had gone through over there; nobody, that was, except those who had returned to fight another day. Unfortunately, Alex had been one of those who hadn't made it back.

With each man immersed in his thoughts, they stopped outside the village football ground. Together, they pushed on the small, squeaky, and rusting iron gate and walked up onto the main stand.

'Get much play these days?' Daniel asked.

'Young ones mainly. They jump the gate,' Tom said quietly.

'I suppose everyone else has joined up?' Daniel said.

'Not everybody. You know, we can't afford to put every young fella into uniform. Factories need to be manned so we can produce for the war effort. It's not all about brawn.'

Daniel nodded thoughtfully as he placed his hands on the cold pitch-side rail.

The two remained still and watched the slow gloom deepen as the rising mist consumed more and more of the pitch. After some time, Daniel broke the silence.

'I have to train for a mission.'

Daniel could see a creeping dread moving through his dad's body: eyes shut, muscles tensed, as though bracing himself before jumping naked into a frozen lake.

'Where they sendin' you? France?'

'A little further away,' Daniel said, his tone hushed as though he was trying to keep a secret from some spy lurking nearby.

'Africa?'

'Russia.'

Tom turned quickly, the blood draining from his face. 'Christ. What business have you goin' there?'

Daniel patted him on the shoulder and smiled.

'I don't have to go. They've given me time to think about it. That's why I'm here.'

'Then don't, god-dammit. Hasn't this family given enough to this feckin' country already?' Tom said through gritted teeth.

'You've been talking to too many Yanks.' Daniel maintained an uneasy smile.

'It might be a bit of a laugh for you.' Tom's voice had descended into a growl. 'But this is too much… far too much.'

Daniel grabbed Tom close. He whispered next to his dad's ear. 'It's important.'

'Ah, they always say that.' Tom took a step back.

'No, dad,' Daniel said, shaking his head. 'This is *really* important.'

'Like what? You off to get at Gerry through the backdoor? Isn't there an entire Russian army tryin' to do just that?'

'If that's what they wanted, then they'd send more than just me…' He winced as soon as he let it slip.

Tom's eyes bulged. 'What? You? On your own? Is this some kind of joke?'

'Calm down, Dad.' Daniel looked around anxiously at nobody. 'I might not make it through the training. Besides, they haven't briefed me on everything, just the location, and a few minor details.' A little white lie, which he hoped might bring Tom down from the treetops.

'What good can one man do in a war that's consumed the entire civilized world, huh? You tell me that?' Tom's face was getting redder by the millisecond.

Daniel didn't have an answer, at least not one that would satisfy his dad. He kicked at a loose stone, watched it bounce down onto the grass, and then decided to fill his father in on what little he knew.

'The target is one man. Find him, neutralize him, then come home,' Daniel said, refusing to let his emotions run as high as his dad's.

Tom stopped breathing for so long that Daniel thought he had a heart attack. When they finally came, the words exploded from Tom's mouth.

'Neutralise? What the fuck does that mean?'

'Modern war, a new language, I suppose,' Daniel said ruefully.

Toms' shoulders sank almost to his waist. He turned back to the pitch. His mind descended into a murky incomprehension, mirrored by the chilling, oozing haze spreading across the grass. Daniel followed his father's eyes into the fog as the deafening silence encompassed them.

'I never wanted anythin' like this for you or your brother.' Tom's voice was hoarse. 'Never wanted either of you to enlist. I taught you the languages I knew 'cos I saw this war comin' years before it was declared. I'd hoped you'd join me at the 'Office.''

Daniel bowed his head. He had always known that his father had been grooming them for the relative safety of the civil service. 'Education,' Tom had told them umpteen times, 'will prevent you from following in my footsteps, having to do what I did, see what I witnessed.' But neither son had opted for the 'safe option'.

'I just want to do what's right,' Daniel said, eventually.

'Do what's right? None of what's goin' on over there is right. This isn't a school pantomime.' Tom slapped the rail. His lips tightened like an elastic band. 'You fuck up over there, and you die. Is that what you want? Your Ma grievin' over another dead son?'

Daniel closed his eyes. He hadn't come to look for an argument. Actually, he didn't know what the hell he was doing here in the first place. He turned away and kicked at the ground.

'Look, Dad. It'll be a quick trip. In and out.'

'How do you know that? You don't even know all the details. You said it yourself. Where is it anyway?'

Daniel hesitated for a moment.

'Stalingrad.'

He looked at his dad and guessed he was visualizing a mental map of Russia, pinpointing the city that bore Stalin's name in relation to the creeping German advance.

'Well, they better sort it out fast. At the rate the Germans are eatin' up the steppe, I don't think you've more than a couple of months before they're all over it.'

'I'm sure I'll be prepared for every eventuality.'

'Yeah, well, you'd like to think so.' Tom shot him a skeptical, sidelong glance.

Daniel ran his tongue over his parched lips. He didn't know anything about timelines. All he had was a sketchy mission overview. But there was something else that had gnawed at him all day. He wondered why Christopher had interviewed him in both Russian and German. If the Germans hadn't arrived at the city, why had it been vital that he be fluent in both languages?

'Times change,' Tom said after some time. 'Fighting remains the same.' His voice held a yielding tinge, allowing Daniel to breathe an inaudible sigh. 'We shouldn't waste our time out in the cold. Let's get ourselves indoors.'

Less than fifteen minutes later, the two men stood over two large glasses of ale. As father and son toasted, Tom and the other approving patrons were oblivious to the decision Daniel had already made. His primary goal was to complete the training and be selected. Then, if he could get to the Russian scientist before the Germans did, that'd be a job well done. If not, the opportunity to get back at an enemy who had killed his brother had been handed to him on a plate, and he wasn't about to turn that down.

CHAPTER 4

Anatoly stared lovingly at his latest creation. The culmination of eight months of near-constant and exhausting hard work had finally paid off. It was an invention he had yet to test, but one in which he was supremely confident would work first time. He ran his hand across its cold, shiny steel surface as he walked around it.

To the ordinary passerby, it looked like a giant porcupine with several long cylindrical rods sticking out of it. If he were forced to explain, however, he would say it was merely a reservoir for atomic fissile material. What he wouldn't tell them was that the only thing saving them from witnessing a self-sustaining atomic chain reaction firsthand were the six Cadmium rods jutting out from the core. That nugget of information would be disclosed only to the most trustworthy within the scientific community: Anatoly felt that there were precious few of them here at Stalingrad Technical University.

Of course, he didn't have any fissile material yet. That would be delivered under armed escort later today. Another massive invention simmered in a different lab on the city's outskirts, creating the essential ingredient: Uranium 235. Separation of the Uranium isotopes from the raw materials in which they were contained was the critical path to the creation of unlimited power, and he prayed for a plentiful harvest to feed the beast before him.

But a cloud of concern weighed heavily on his mind. He needed help for the next phase of his experiment and felt he couldn't trust any of the university postgraduates; he couldn't risk them making a mistake. An error at this point could cause a catastrophe of apocalyptic proportions, and he certainly didn't want to be anywhere in the vicinity should that happen.

He had toyed with asking some of the more knowledgeable staff at the University and the other facility to help him before eventually settling on Korolev. Given the risks, though, he wasn't sure if the Cosmologist would come to his aid. He reasoned there were three possible outcomes: continued success, the end of a dream, or annihilation. Even the choice of Korolev held both illogical and logical facets, ruled as always by heart and head, respectively. He'd only met the man a few days ago but oddly felt like he'd known him all his life. His relaxed demeanor and outgoing nature made Anatoly feel he could be trusted; there was no hidden agenda. Maybe it was because he'd seen through Anatoly's little test when nobody else had.

However, if Korolev was anything other than the scientific companion he portrayed, then that didn't matter either. His skills were undoubted. If he could help Anatoly complete the project a little faster and safer, he would be one step closer to seeing his second true love again and leaving his first behind.

Anatoly pursed his lips, considered the most compelling argument to convince Korolev, and gathered himself. Less than a minute later, he strutted away from his lab.

The summer sunshine illuminated every square inch of the campus, but this wasn't the time for sunbathing – there was some serious persuading to be done.

Anatoly believed himself to be a good judge of character and, from this, had guessed that the cosmologist was only ever likely to be at one of three possible locations. It wasn't yet dark, so that ruled out his laboratory. The end of term had been a few weeks ago, thus ruling out any of the lecture theatres. Hadn't Korolev said that his students worshiped him, perhaps the adoration went both ways. That left only one other place to search.

Budem was the university cafeteria, but most of its trade centered around the bar. It served food three times a day and drinks around the clock. It was one of the oldest buildings on the campus. A renovated barn with a rustic décor that Anatoly suspected was a relic from its previous function. With a ceiling almost nine yards above the floor, the noise created by a handful of drunken students was enough to reverberate through the wooden rafters and echo off the walls. When the place was packed, as most nights, Anatoly wondered how anybody could understand a single word another person was saying, let alone engage in any meaningful academic conversation. But then, that was one of the reasons he rarely visited the place. The debonair scientist, however, might be attempting to satiate his middle-aged sexual appetite in the company of some undergraduate females who, instead of sequestered in their dorms studying for their impending examinations, were busy losing their inhibitions.

Anatoly leaped some steps to the cafeteria doors and pushed through. He stopped just inside and scanned the interior. The bar stood proudly in the center of the room, an assortment of tables and chairs radiating outward like a spider's web to the exterior walls.

It took Anatoly only a breath to spot the man surrounded by a giggling gaggle of girls. Judging by their laughing faces, there was no doubt; the man was on the hunt. Korolev held a captive audience, regaling his prey with stories of the wondrous night sky, the cosmos beyond, and the forbidden nocturnal activities that might be indulged beneath.

Anatoly started to move toward them but hesitated. He had always been anxious around the opposite sex. Even talking to one girl made his insides complete somersaults. Here, five wide-eyed and smiling beauties clung to Korolev's every word. He couldn't just go across and interrupt. He wouldn't know what to say, even if he could manage to stammer anything at all. He began to turn away.

'Anatoly.'

He gasped and shut his eyes.

After a moment of indecision, he turned to see Korolev beaming and beckoning him with a frantic wave of his glass, wine spilling over the side. Worse, though, were the five pairs of feminine eyes that had turned their focus to him. His heart thundered, and he felt sure anybody close enough would hear it. He smiled weakly, sighed, and shuffled over.

'Ladies, this fine gentleman is the cleverest man I've ever met, probably the smartest man in Russia, if not the world.'

Korolev's proclamation was greeted with disbelief as the girls shot the scrawny Anatoly little more than a cursory glance. If the ground had opened up, Anatoly would gladly have leaped in.

'Join us.' Korolev motioned to the bartender, who dutifully nodded and prepared another round of drinks.

Anatoly inched closer, his mouth parched and his hands coated in a nervous sweat. Maybe a drink was exactly what he needed, but he shook his head. He needed to keep a clear head for what he had to do next.

'Can you spare a moment?' he said, his voice barely audible.

Korolev was too busy looking at one of the girl's ample breasts and appeared not to hear him. Anatoly drew a little closer.

'I need your help,' he said, a little louder.

Korolev glanced back at him. 'It is I who needs your help, young man. Grab a chair. I can't handle these fine things by myself.'

Anatoly scanned the group, but all eyes had returned to Korolev, who had begun to orate another humorous anecdote. Anatoly was about to open his mouth when the bartender slid a tray of drinks onto the table in front of him.

'You're way behind,' Korolev said without looking in Anatoly's direction. 'Drink up.'

Anatoly reached across the table and tapped Korolev's arm.

'I *really* need your help.'

Korolev's eyes breezed across him. He seemed only now to have noticed Anatoly's sense of urgency. He gazed at Anatoly for a few seconds before glancing at the tray of drinks.

'Not before you have a drink.' A corner of his lips slowly creased into a smile.

As before, Anatoly could feel all eyes on him, but he didn't return any of their looks. He eyed the glasses reluctantly.

Vodka.

Anatoly had never touched a drop in his short life, but he knew he wouldn't get the older man out of the bar unless he acceded. He reached out and fingered one of the glasses.

'Jesus.' Korolev said. 'You'd swear he was a virgin.' He glanced at Anatoly and immediately corrected himself. 'An alcoholic virgin.' The comment elicited a burst of laughter from the girls, followed by a massive grin from Korolev.

Anatoly exhaled deeply as though preparing to dive off a cliff. He lifted one of the vodkas, shot it a scowl, and downed it in one go. He hadn't anticipated what would happen next. A numbness, then a sour taste, followed by a burning sensation as the alcohol blazed a trail along his esophagus. He gasped and half-stifled a cough through a haze of teary eyes. Whatever gastric gymnastics had gone before was nothing compared to what was going on now. He closed his eyes and tried desperately to prevent the foul liquid from bouncing back up, along with whatever else had been lying in wait.

After a few seconds, he drew breath as though it was his first. He waited a moment before squeaking. 'Can we go now?'

Korolev beamed. 'Of course.' He pushed his chair away from the table amid a chorus of groans. 'Don't worry, girls, this won't take long,' he said as he stood up. He shouted across to the bartender. 'Another round for these fine ladies.'

The groans quickly turned to cheers as the two men left the bevy of beauties clinking their glasses.

They were halfway to the door when Korolev grabbed Anatoly's arm.

'Have to make a quick stop first.' He turned suddenly and hurried off. Anatoly clenched his fists, his eyes shooting to the ceiling.

Korolev pushed through the toilet door and headed for a urinal before changing his mind and detouring to one of the stalls. After entering, he locked the door and slipped down his pants. He rested his elbows on his knees and thought about the students he'd left behind. Another hour or so, and he was sure he'd have been able to get at least one, if not two, to return to his lodgings.

Damn Anatoly.

He smiled, though, at the young physicist's innocence. Surrounded by such a voluptuous array of femininity, all he could think about was his science experiments. He wondered if that was the single-mindedness somebody needed to possess to be truly great. Perhaps that was the sign of true genius: to ignore life's physical pleasures and see beyond them. Maybe, for Anatoly, what he did was pleasure enough.

He reached out to grab some paper and heard the toilet door open and the sound of two laughing men entering. He listened to their footsteps clink off the tiles as they headed for the urinals.

'Imagine the nerve of the guy. I mean, he must be twice their age,' one of them said.

'You're generous. More than twice, I'd say, old dinosaur,' the other replied.

'Still, he should be going for somebody his own age,' the first said, over the sound of two jets of piss splashing off the porcelain.

'There's nobody else his age in this shithole. Not any of the students anyway, and have you seen some of the staff? They're as old as the crap they're teaching.'

The two laughed again. On the other side of the stall wall, Korolev didn't. He knew they were talking about him.

'Fuck. Stop making me laugh. I'm wetting myself,' one said.

'Yeah, too old to fuck the students and too young to fuck his colleagues,' the first said. 'Although, he's trying his best. Did you see how many girls were over at his table?'

Korolev snapped off some paper, and the conversation on the other side of the wall abruptly stopped. He quickly tidied himself up, pulled up his pants, flushed, and opened the stall door. He walked casually toward the wash-hand basin without looking toward the two men to his left, who had momentarily stopped relieving themselves. In his peripheral vision, he could see them look over their shoulders before glancing at each other. He ran the cold tap and dipped his hands under the water, interweaving his fingers.

He patted his face and ran his hands through his hair as the two young men, probably first-year students, pulled up their zippers. He stole a glance at them in the mirror and saw them nudge each other. Both of them were over six-foot, not that it mattered to Korolev. He breathed slowly and gripped the sides of the basin. His head bowed as each student stood in front of the basins on either side of him.

They eyed each other in the mirror and fired looks down at Korolev's hunched back.

'Enjoying yourself,' one of them said.

'Very much,' Korolev answered. He didn't look up.

'Looks like you've got a way with the ladies,' the first one said again.

'Girls, you mean,' the other laughed.

'You could say that,' Korolev said. 'Plenty to go around, though.'

He straightened up and turned to face the one to his right, exposing his back to the other. 'But then, you need to have balls to be able to fuck them, something you both lack. So you can think about me when you're alone in your dorm room tonight and wonder what might have been.'

The smile disappeared from the student's face. Korolev could see him clench his fists. Out of the corner of his eye, he saw the kid to his rear make a move.

Korolev pushed backward, catching both by surprise. His momentum drove the student into the urinal wall. Korolev quickly turned and grabbed the kid's hair, smashing his head into the wet urinal, splitting it open. The boy screamed as blood spurted onto the cracked porcelain, the wall, and the floor. Korolev snapped his head backward and tossed him onto the floor, writhing in agony.

The second kid charged forward, screaming: his face red, his eyes bulging. Korolev glanced to his left and saw the punch coming before the kid had even thought about throwing it. He took a short step back and felt the air rush past his cheek as the kid's fist slipped by and crashed into the wall. The student doubled over and screamed in pain, clutching his hand to his stomach. Korolev had heard the cracks and knew the guy had broken a couple of bones, but it didn't stop him from delivering an elbow to the back of the kid's head. The screams stopped immediately as the student crumpled to the floor, unconscious, beside his friend.

Korolev looked down at the two boys lying on the stinking, piss-stained floor, one whimpering, the other out cold. He stepped back and admired his handiwork. It'd been a while since he'd had to engage in hand-to-hand combat, and he was genuinely pleased that he wasn't out of practice.

He turned to the basin and quickly ran his hands through the running water. Giving himself a quick once over in the mirror, he walked calmly to the door and disappeared into the bar. He spotted Anatoly pacing near the exit.

'Sorry about the delay.' He patted his bum.

'I don't want to know,' Anatoly said. He stopped and pointed. 'You've blood on your sleeve.'

Korolev glanced down, not alarmed. 'Nosebleed. I get them from time to time. I'll wash it out later. Let's go and see whatever you think is so damn important.'

The two scientists left the building; his heart rate increased at what he was about to do, the other, his heart rate returned to normal, despite what he'd just done.

*

Anatoly's hands trembled as he scribbled illiterately through the rivers of sweat that dripped onto the notepad. He rechecked his calculations; he had to be sure.

Korolev sat on the floor a couple of yards away, his back against the wall, now completely sober. He realized what this was, what he was witnessing: a unique moment in history and no time for a foggy memory. He looked from Anatoly to the porcupine and back again. All of his scientific life, he had followed in the footsteps of genius, and now he was staring at it, knowing he was participating in a scientific revolution.

Anatoly's taut, frantic expression slowly developed into an enormous grin and spread across his boyish features. He shook his head, staring at his scrawl through a waterfall of tears. Goose-bumps, the size of walnuts, had covered his skin as he neared the end of his experimental determination. His body tingled like the first time he made love to a girl, except this was better. This wasn't a lingering moment that dissipated as quickly as it had arrived. This was earth-shattering and groundbreaking all at the same time. Geophysicists would have called it seismic!

He had been sitting in the same crossed-legged position on the laboratory floor for so long that the numbness made him feel as though he was floating on air. The first run hadn't been a fluke. Neither had the second nor the third, for that matter. But the fourth verified the validity of the three previous experiments.

He launched the loose-leaf pages wildly into the air and, yelping with delight, fell backward onto the cold concrete amidst the falling ticker-tape of mathematical formulae, derivations, and chemical equations. He punched the air with both fists and covered his tear-sodden eyes. He had come a long way from skimming stones across the ripple-free Dnieper River as an eight-year-old, wondering what made them skip across the surface rather than sinking.

Since then, he had achieved more than all the theoretical and experimental Professors at either Kyiv or Stalingrad universities. Now, he had done what the rest of the scientific community hadn't, including those holed up in America who were allegedly hot on his trail of scientific discovery. At least, that had been the rumor. They would come a close second and, by their actions, verify his results.

He, a spotty Ukrainian teenager, had been the first to demonstrate precisely what interdisciplinary knowledge could achieve. No longer would subjects be placed in academic silos and labeled accordingly.

But, despite winning the race, he knew he wouldn't receive the plaudits and accolades the scientific community usually bestowed on such momentous events; the present Soviet regime would never allow it. So he, Anatoly Yermakov, would remain anonymous.

The experiment itself had been both simple and beautiful in its conception but incredibly difficult in its construction. He had to determine the specific components to make it work. Even more challenging was acquiring the 'special' ingredients. Still, over the past year, he had sourced the constituents and performed the purification process himself, which was vital to ensuring the breakthrough. After that, the rest had been a cinch.

It had been a new-age alchemist's dream.

He thrashed his arms and legs wildly and rolled around like a spoiled toddler on a shop floor.

He raised himself onto his elbows and surveyed his lab. The place had been his home for the past year. Usually scrupulously neat, a trait inherited from his mother, it now resembled the devastation left in the wake of a hurricane, a natural occurrence when an experiment was nearing completion, with the person frantically engaged in simultaneous thoughts and actions. He looked at Korolev.

The Professor's mouth was half-open, speechless. Anatoly knew the man would have understood the significance of what had just happened. Equally, he knew the older man had never experienced anything like the adrenaline rush flooding his body. Anatoly had back in 1938. Back then, he had detected Krypton and Barium atoms after bombarding Uranium 235 with neutrons and was the first to induce nuclear fission. Subsequently, Hahn and Strassmann verified his success in the Autumn.

But he looked past it all. His eyes focused on the blackboard at the far end of the room. Amid the chalk dust and scribbles was written the single most significant mathematical equation of the 20th century, perhaps the most important ever.

He had read Einstein's three 1905 *Annus Mirabilis* papers before his ninth birthday and had been fascinated with physics ever since. He had even derived the equation himself and was delighted that he had confirmed the former postal clerk's workings. The beauty of this particular equation was its simplicity, and you didn't have to be a scientist to remember it. He imagined it would be on the tips of everyone's lips for years to come.

He glanced down at the sheets, scattered about like confetti after a wedding. He realized that if he could produce results like this on his own in a university lab, imagine what could be done if a government put its substantial monetary muscle behind it. As with every major scientific discovery, he was sure there would be a legion of applications for the new physics.

But he knew there was one application that would supersede all others and the reason he'd been brought so far eastward, away from prying eyes. The history of humanity was littered with political and economic lust. He knew the implications would be grave if his research were further developed.

The time he'd spent devising and conducting his experiment had been mottled with a desire to pursue his dream, fear of where it might lead, and desperation to escape. The physical act of leaving would have been easy had it not been for the regime's emotional grasp over him. Hope had, for over a year, obscured what was now apparent, and he'd allowed himself to hide it.

He felt a chill drip down his spine. Finally, he understood the profound meaning of what he had achieved: mankind's first-ever self-sustaining atomic chain reaction. But two questions were seared onto his consciousness: what would his government do with it? How would his research shape global future events? Deep down, he knew the answers to both.

He felt a wave of nausea sweep over him and, rolling over to one side, vomited on the floor.

CHAPTER 5

Shortly after midnight, three men came together at the foot of the War Office steps. Brief introductions followed firm handshakes and courteous nods. They stuffed their bags into the boot of a government-issued car, hopped in, and began their journey north. The car meandered through the twisting Whitehall streets, dodging dog-tired fire crews and exploding buildings; the aftermath of yet another German air-raid. They had witnessed German bombings for almost two years and had thus grown used to them if such a thing could be said of any aerial bombardment. But that wasn't what was on their minds. Each was immersed in his thoughts as the car snaked its way through the heart of rural England.

To a man, they wore somber expressions. They knew that although the task at hand was critical, within the timelines they had been set, it was also damn near impossible. However, those timelines had not been established by some card-punching bureaucrat at the Ministry of Defence but by an evil tide sweeping away to the East towards the Volga and the city that sat next to it.

Each man in the newly formed team was a specialist in his field, and their job was frighteningly simple: to create a fearless killing machine from one of the four candidates they would meet later that morning.

'I've been thinking about this,' one of them said eventually, breaking hours of silence. The man turned the page in the file he'd been reading and stroked his chin.

Christopher's gaze moved away from the rolling Warwickshire countryside. He regarded Ethan Markovic for a moment and smiled to himself.

Ethan was a thin, wiry man in his late forties. Always impeccably dressed, he had dark brown hair that matched his creaseless suit. A Jewish nomad, he had arrived on British shores in the mid-1930s as his family fled the rising Reich, having fled Russian persecution more than a decade earlier. With a Cambridge doctorate in European Culture, he was highly educated and would be the man who would groom the candidates' linguistic skills. He thumbed another page and frowned.

'I'm just not sure we can do this.' His eyes scanned the last page before he closed the file, set it aside, and opened another. 'We haven't got the time.' He shook his head. 'Just not enough time.'

Christopher sighed gently and closed his eyes, all too aware of the difficulties.

'I mean, honing one language is possible, but two… just not enough time.' He shook his head then suddenly looked up, his eyes bright.

'Actually, why not just one language? The Germans haven't reached the city. Why not just improve the Russian, then send the man in before the Germans get there – complete the mission and get out before the first bomb falls?'

Christopher smiled knowingly, as a father would to a young, questioning son.

'We can't take the chance. The speed of the German advance is quick, lightning quick. Yes, they get bogged down from time to time, but on the whole, they're racing across the Russian steppe almost quicker than the Russians can retreat to set up new defensive positions. With the training our men have to receive, I'd rather not take the chance that the Germans won't arrive there before our man drops in, hence the need to improve both languages.'

'Then it's impossible,' Ethan said, adjusting his tie under his shirt collar.

'Jesus, you're so bloody negative,' the other man sitting next to him said.

Ethan fired a sidelong glare at Chester Leatherby.

Chester was, when standing, a towering, athletic man well over six-foot, with a fresh, sun-tanned face that belied his fifty-plus years. His grey hair was neatly cropped, a style that lent itself to that worn by the younger enlisted men. In a previous life, he had been selected to participate at the 1916 Berlin Olympics as part of a rowing coxed pair. But the outbreak of the first major European skirmish had put paid to any dreams he had of returning with a gold medal. Recruited as the team's physical instructor, his job was to weed out the weak of body.

'Please don't use that language in my presence,' Ethan said, his eyes lighting up fiercely.

'Sorry old boy. Forgot with whom I was speaking,' Chester mocked, then grinned at him.

Ethan returned to the file. 'I'll bet you haven't even read these.'

'Don't need to,' Chester snorted, turning away to look at the brightening sky above the countryside rumbling by. 'I'll know what I need to know after a couple of days in the open.'

'There's a lot more to this than making sure the men can run five miles without breaking into a sweat,' Ethan said evenly. 'One false move, one misspoken word, and that's it. Shot as a spy, or worse.'

Chester looked back at him and scowled. 'That doesn't make any sense. What the hell is worse than being shot?'

'Many things.' Ethan's voice was hollow.

A shiver tingled up Chester's spine.

'Yeah, well, anyway. Being able to say 'shit' in seven languages won't do any good if they don't survive the parachute drop and pick their way through the city.'

Ethan bowed and shook his head. 'Barbarian,' he mumbled.

Chester's grin returned.

'You are both correct,' Christopher said. 'The man we send will have to be all of those things, be able to *do* all of those things and a lot more.'

Both men looked solemnly at the older man.

It was a moment before Christopher spoke. 'This is a hazardous mission, possibly the most dangerous I have ever had to prepare for. The candidates have been briefed. They know some of what's involved and some of what they have to do.' He paused. 'Yet they still volunteered.'

Ethan and Chester glanced at each other.

'Doesn't it strike either of you as odd that even one person, let alone four, should volunteer for what can only be described as little more than a suicide mission?'

He scrutinized each man's face for any sign of understanding. He'd planted a seed of curiosity and watched intently to see if it would take root and blossom.

Ethan broke the silence after a couple of minutes. 'You believe there to be ulterior motives at play?'

Christopher remained silent, his face impassive.

'You're wondering if we're going to train a young man and deliver him to the front line so he can exact revenge on the enemy.' Ethan continued.

'Partially,' Christopher said. 'I'm more concerned that whoever we send doesn't place his own goals ahead of the mission, thereby putting everything we're working so hard to achieve in jeopardy.'

The only sound inside the car was the noise of the tires grinding off the road outside. Ethan moved the file he'd been reading and placed it on the neat little pile next to him. 'We need to be watchful,' he said.

The grin long gone, replaced by a grim comprehending, Chester nodded his agreement.

The three men stared out the same window as the sun peaked above the horizon.

CHAPTER 6

A STEELY-FACED DANIEL CLIMBED ABOARD the bus, just as he had done almost two years ago. His gaze washed across the edgy faces of the raw recruits already onboard. Some looked oddly at him, probably because he was wearing a uniform.

His country had set about strengthening its military machine to cope with the fascist threat: volunteering had peaked a couple of years ago, so the government had looked to alternative means of swelling the ranks of enlisted men. Daniel could tell by their faces that these fellows' numbers had come up. Fortunately, he wasn't one of them. But then, that depended on your point of view.

He slid into a vacant seat in the middle of the bus, forcing himself not to make eye contact with the others. He didn't want to get involved in any banal conversations. He had to think about what the military might have in store and prepare his mind as best he could. At a guess, it wouldn't be anything that resembled the necessary training the rest of the lads on this bus would have to endure.

As promised, Christopher had contacted him a couple of days after their meeting to learn of Daniel's decision. For Daniel, he'd made up his mind before he'd left the commandant's office.

He was in.

He would be one of four to receive specialist mission training, after which the trainers would decide who drew the short straw. Those weren't Christopher's exact words, but they amounted to the same.

It was nearing midday when the bus eventually trundled up a lonely road, dust spewing off its tires. It came to an abrupt, drunken stop outside a set of imposing wrought-iron gates. Daniel glanced at two armed soldiers stationed on either side of the entrance and smiled at the irony: at least they would be safe from attack.

The group of twenty-two wide-eyed civilians filed off and herded into the center of the camp, some clutching their bags to their chests as though they were protecting their lunch money. The air was warm and still and thick with irritating insects, the crackling crickets keeping time with an unseen, lone bugler playing away in the distance.

Daniel appreciated the welcome.

With only a handful of long wooden barracks finished, the place looked more like a construction site. Others were in various stages of completeness, while some had only their foundations dug. The smell of fresh paint clung to the air. Daniel was impressed with how the builders' tools were neatly stacked at several locations; obviously, an 'army thing'.

He surveyed the rest of the camp from left to right, looking for any sign of his welcome party.

A salivating officer appeared from behind one of the huts and bawled at them, ordering them to line up in two rows. The men shuffled into two lines, glancing at each other to see if anybody was doing it right. Lots of them looked in Daniel's direction and copied what he had done: bag at his feet, legs together, stiff, straight back, staring directly forward.

Once the group had stopped fidgeting, the officer, by screaming at the top of his lungs, introduced himself as the section sergeant, which got a few sniggers because he could have whispered, and everybody would still have heard him.

Daniel was mildly amused to see that the man had almost the same physical attributes as his first training officer: slim waist, broad chest, shoulders pulled back further than could be considered humanly possible. He wore a tight, thin mustache and held a small cane under an armpit. A mountain of a man, he was the very embodiment of the British stiff-upper-lip.

'Throw your bags in there,' the sergeant said, pointing at one of the finished barracks with his cane. His eyes betrayed the dismay he must have felt in his heart. 'Dismissed.'

Daniel leaned down to pick up his bag.

'Private Miller, a word.' The sergeant stepped toward him. 'You don't bunk with the new men. Take your things and go to the mess. The rest of your lot is already there.' He pointed behind Daniel.

'Yes, sir.' Daniel flashed a salute, which was reciprocated. He was annoyed that he hadn't been the first to arrive, but it couldn't be helped. His superiors had arranged transport to the camp, and they hadn't exactly rolled out the red carpet.

Daniel glanced behind as the sergeant moved off and spotted a much larger, stable structure. There were a couple of vans parked away to one side. Daniel assumed they were delivering the muck that would be later fed to the men. He grabbed his bag and made a beeline for it.

As he drew closer, he strained his ears to hear anything from inside, but all was quiet. He reached out and pushed through the door, his eyes taking a moment to adjust to the sparkling brightness inside.

The camp 'mess' was anything but, with a glisten and fragrance that would have made his mother proud. Five parallel rows of connected wooden tables stretched from the entrance at one end to the kitchen at the other. Long wooden benches lay partially obscured beneath both sides of each table. In all, Daniel reckoned it could comfortably seat over two hundred hungry men. Large rectangular windows ran the length of both sides of the room: shafts of angled sunlight shone through from one side.

At the other end, he spied three men sitting on separate chairs, facing the kitchen. They each turned around to get a better look at who had entered. Judging by their youthful appearance, he guessed they were the competition. His grip tightened on his bag as he walked between two rows of tables towards them. Other than his shoes clicking off the hard wooden floor, the room was silent.

He dropped his bag next to the last remaining unoccupied chair, sat down, and stared straight ahead. After a few moments, he glanced at the other three men. They all appeared to be older than he, but not by much. All wore their dress uniforms, just as he had. On examining their insignias, he immediately realized that as a private, he was the most junior rank in the room.

Two of the men sat motionlessly, their eyes now closed, while the third, a navy captain, sat back with his legs crossed, reading a newspaper. Daniel frowned, hardly believing that anybody in the military could adopt such a slouched posture. Seemingly the more relaxed, the seaman held the highest rank of the four. Daniel sighed quietly to himself and turned away.

They didn't have to wait long as the mess door behind them squeaked open only a few minutes after Daniel had taken his seat. They turned in unison to see three well-dressed, middle-aged men enter briskly, breaking through the shafts of sunlight as they approached. Daniel recognized only Christopher. The three men stood before the group. None of the candidates stood to attention. Christopher's eyes swept across them, his lips tightly closed. The three standing scrutinized those seated as though trying to make an initial assessment of their charges. Christopher eventually broke the silence of anticipation.

'We have only a short time together and much to cram into it,' he said in flawless Russian. 'You may have thought that your first day would be relatively easy with us breaking you in slowly.' He stamped his cane into the hard-wood mess floor, eliciting a slight jump from everybody in the room, including the other two men. 'We don't have time for that.' He paused. 'Gather your belongings and leave them next to the vans outside. You won't need them or what's in them.' He pointed towards a kitchen door to their right. 'There is a bag outside for each of you. Inside, you'll find the only clothing and equipment you'll need for the duration of your training. Nothing else is permitted.'

He scanned the group again, but only for a moment. 'This is not the regular army or navy. There will be no order to dismiss.'

Daniel and the other three candidates glanced at each other, unsure what to do. This hadn't been what he had expected; he guessed the others felt the same. No introductions. No agenda. No information on how long they'd be training or even the kind they'd receive. Other than the fact that whatever possessions they'd carried into camp would be effectively confiscated, there was nothing.

The navy captain sitting at the end folded away his paper and leaned down to pick up his bag. Daniel and the other two men followed suit. They all stood awkwardly and started slowly for the kitchen door.

'There is only one rule you must obey while you're here,' Christopher said, switching to German. The four candidates turned to face him. 'No English is to be spoken, ever. Breaking this rule is followed by instant dismissal, and you will be transferred back to your units.'

'Jawohl,' three of the men responded. Daniel said nothing.

Without waiting for further instruction, the group turned back to the door. As they walked away, their bags either slung over their shoulders or hanging loosely by their sides, Daniel pushed away a growing apprehension that had begun to niggle at him. He had important things to think about. He was here for one reason. To learn the skills needed to complete his mission and return home safely. And if he were to kill some Germans along the way, that would be a bonus. He owed that much to his dead brother.

CHAPTER 7

Anatoly had never played with any of the children on the 'collective', and why should he? Constant ridicule for being smarter than they had alienated him from those both his age and older. As a result, he had become an academic hermit. And for the duration of his short life, he'd lived that way; why should he change now?

Anatoly looked again at the door, debating whether he should leave and return to his lab. The last thing he needed right now was friendship. Worse still, he wasn't even sure he knew how to forge a meaningful relationship anymore, let alone if he could be bothered. Such was the maelstrom swirling about his mind that he hadn't realized he had already knocked until Korolev answered.

'Come in. Let me get your jacket,' the Professor said. He held out a wine glass full to the brim.

Anatoly stepped in and slipped off his coat as Korolev shut the door behind him. Korolev thrust the glass into the birthday boy's hand.

'Drink up. You're already a couple of glasses behind.'

Anatoly took a sip and made a peculiar face.

'Not to your liking?' Korolev said with a mischievous grin.

'A little bitter,' Anatoly admitted. He looked a little embarrassed.

'Too fond of that cheap vodka, I'll bet.' Korolev grinned. 'Don't worry. It's an acquired taste. But you're in luck. There's more where that came from.'

They made their way from the short hallway into a large living room. A tattered sofa stood limply as the room's centerpiece. There was a small kitchen area at one end of the room, with a table and two chairs cloistered in one corner. Korolev leaned toward a nearby shelf and grabbed a full glass of his own. He inhaled the wine's bouquet and sipped.

'Magnificent.'

Anatoly surveyed the rest of the room. It was even more sparsely decorated than his own. The walls were an unpainted grey and, except for several stacks of books haphazardly piled on a sideboard, there were no other adornments. A plethora of end-of-term exam papers lay strewn about the hardwood floor. He picked his way to one of the chairs and set his glass on the table.

'I thought there'd be others?' he said.

'God, no. I haven't asked anybody else,' Korolev said, not affording the exam papers the same courtesy as he tramped across them. 'The rest of the staff are either too busy, stuffy, or stupid. Besides, I wanted to get to know you a little better, especially after what we did… I mean, what you did the other day.' His eyes sparkled as he set his glass down.

This hadn't been what Anatoly had bargained for; he didn't want to divulge anything about his personal life. Try to keep things on an academic, professional level – wouldn't that be best for everybody? But how to get out of the place without insulting the host? He gulped back some more wine as his eyes rested on the columns of books nearby.

Judging by the fine and even coating of dust that had gathered on them, it was clear that some academic topics had remained untouched for quite some time. The mess was something Anatoly's mother would never have approved of and would have gone to great lengths to remedy.

He missed her.

Korolev followed the line of Anatoly's eyes. 'You like my collection?'

'You have interests in areas outside your field?' Anatoly's voice was curious but guarded.

'Ha.' Korolev shouted. 'I don't believe in the segmentation of knowledge. It's far more important to understand all facets of human learning. It helps one excel in one's own chosen field. We must examine and evaluate our work from different perspectives, don't you think?'

Anatoly looked at him oddly but didn't respond straight away. 'Isn't that a contradiction?' he said at length.

'A scientist's noesis. I challenge anybody to dispute the validity of my argument.' He glanced to one side.

'No argument here,' Anatoly said, holding his hands up defensively. He sipped from his glass again. 'You like wine?'

'All gentlemen should indulge themselves.' Korolev skipped across to the kitchen and opened a cupboard. He bent down and slid something out.

'I've never tried it before.' Anatoly leaned to one side, trying to see what Korolev had in his hands.

'Well, don't worry,' Korolev said. 'You'll be a connoisseur before we finish the lot.' He turned around and handed Anatoly a large, neatly wrapped, square-shaped package.

'For me?'

'Better open it,' Korolev said. 'It won't keep.'

Anatoly squeezed it and tested the weight. He slipped a finger into a gap in the wrapping and ripped gently at the brown paper. He removed the packaging and set a large leather pouch on the table. He glanced up at Korolev, who, by now, looked as though he could contain his excitement.

He flipped the flap open and removed a brown and cream freckled bone chessboard. Korolev stepped forward and, placing a hand on top, pressed on one side. A compartment slid silently out from beneath, revealing a set of beautifully crafted, ornate chess pieces. He picked up a knight and held it up to the light.

'Hand carved from African ivory.' His eyes sparkled.

'This must have cost a fortune,' Anatoly said. He surveyed the other thirty-one pieces, each sitting comfortably in its own little felt-covered recess.

'Yes… maybe… I don't know,' Korolev said. 'Let's play.' He tossed the leather pouch to one side and sat down.

'How do you know I can play?'

Korolev smiled. 'You're a Soviet scientist. Of course, you can play.' He reached across and, picking up two pawns of white and black, placed them behind his back. He looked expectantly at Anatoly, who sat opposite and tapped Korolev's right arm.

'You're white.'

They quickly set up the pieces and studied each other. Anatoly's eyes dropped to the board. He raised a hand and, hovering above his pieces for a moment, moved a pawn to E4. Korolev responded in kind, with pawn to E5.

After a couple of moves each, Korolev said. 'You know this opening is named after a Spanish priest who analyzed it in 1561.'

'Ruy Lopez,' Anatoly said quietly, without looking up.

Korolev glanced up at him. 'Knew you could play.'

'My father and I played all the time.'

'Did he beat you often?'

'He never beat me.' Anatoly tapped the table. 'Your move.'

The first couple of games didn't last more than a few minutes, with Anatoly winning each comfortably.

Having polished off their second bottle, Anatoly had lost only a handful of pieces to Korolev's handful of games. In one, Anatoly appeared to toy with Korolev as he picked off each of his pieces one by one until only his King remained. He chased it about the board for a few more moves before Korolev finally knocked it over.

'I'm a pretty decent player,' Korolev said, 'but I can see why your father had such difficulty.' He opened another bottle and set out two fresh glasses, pouring them two-thirds full. He stood the glasses to one side and allowed the wine to breathe.

'Have you read *The World Set Free?*' Korolev asked.

'H.G. Wells?' Anatoly nodded loosely.

'Then you're aware of the power that could be unleashed if you continue your research?'

Anatoly shifted uneasily in his seat. It had been the first time the subject of his work had cropped up this evening.

'Wells is a true genius,' he said eventually. 'Recognising the power contained within the atom.'

'He was quoting Einstein?' Korolev said with a tinge of cynicism.

'But he spread the idea and got people thinking about the possibilities.'

'Dangerous possibilities,' Korolev replied. He sipped his wine without taking his eyes off the young man. 'Have you considered the moral implications of what you're doing?'

Anatoly's taut expression indicated that he had tormented himself with that very issue.

'I suppose if it weren't you, it'd be somebody else. Research on this is taking place all over the world. I've even heard the Reich is hard at it; now there's something to be truly scared of.'

'I know I'm not the only one in the world doing atomic research,' Anatoly said, his voice rising. 'Besides, I was the first to split Uranium 235. Otto and Hahn only validated my results.'

'But they were unaware of your experiments.'

'Irrelevant.' Anatoly's voice was getting louder.

'History will document them as first.' Korolev said, remaining calm.

'So what? I don't give a damn what the history books will say.'

'But you won't receive the credit you deserve.'

'I'd rather not take the credit for setting the human race off on a road that could ultimately bring about its demise.'

'*A change in human conditions that I can only compare to the discovery of fire.*'

'Look who's quoting now?' Anatoly gulped back a mouthful of wine.

The two scientists eyed each other as if they were prizefighters stepping out to face each other in the last round of a bout; tension choked the air. Korolev eventually broke the deadlock.

'So if not that, what are you going to do with the rest of your life? You're so young.'

Anatoly swayed slightly, appearing at first not to hear the question, clearly still agitated with his host.

'Age is an illusion, a state of mind. I'll continue my work,' he replied, his anger abating. 'What about you?'

'Yes, I too suffer from the same illusion. Some may call it a delusion.' The Professor grinned. 'Somewhere inside, there's a little boy who yearns to stare into the heavens. The nighttime summer sky offers much.' He arced an unsteady hand above his head.

'Where'd you say you came from?' Anatoly said, suddenly realizing he didn't know anything about the man.

Korolev studied the young physicist for a moment before answering. 'Burgas.'

Anatoly had heard of the Bulgarian coastal town on the Black Sea. He stared intently at the man opposite.

'You're not Russian?'

Korolev laughed. 'Not a drop of that Red blood in my body, just like you.' He emptied the last of the third bottle into his glass.

'But your name?'

'A deterrent against the curious,' Korolev said, gulping back another mouthful and dragging his sleeve across his face. The time had long passed since both drunks exhibited the manners of gentlemen.

'But your accent… it's so perfect, I could've sworn…'

'It's the complete deterrent,' Korolev grinned through a hiccup. He gazed stupidly at Anatoly. 'What brings you to Stalingrad?'

That was a good question, which Anatoly had ruminated upon ever since the train departed Kyiv last year. The simple answer was that a confluence of wretched events had brought him to Stalin's city.

'I'll bet it was a girl.' Korolev prodded.

Anatoly grew silent, lost in a memory.

'I'm right.' Korolev beamed. 'I can see it in your eyes, the love of a girl. Who is she?'

Anatoly looked up, his face drawn by a sudden and bitter sorrow. 'I don't want to talk about it.' He knew he sounded pitiful.

'Ah, she broke your heart. They all do in the end. Maybe it's just as well. Damn Germans have taken the city anyway. You're better off away from her… and there.'

Anatoly knew that to be untrue. He had lost the love of his life, the only real friend he ever had, more than thirteen months ago, albeit temporarily, he hoped. The emotions felt then began to surge again when news had reached him that she'd been taken by the Narodnyy Komissariat Vnutrennikh Del or NKVD, the Soviet state's secret police. He tried desperately to suppress them. He wasn't about to show Korolev the torment he still harbored. It was part of the reason he worked so hard. His research had become a distraction and a necessity if he was ever to see her alive again.

But Anya's abduction hadn't been the only thing that had driven him from his home. Daryna, the NKVD messenger, had complicated his life to the point where he didn't know what was real anymore. Both women commanded polarising images in his mind. While he tried to forget the heartbreak of losing Anya, he knew he should always keep Daryna at the forefront of his thoughts. Relocation had been her suggestion – an eloquent word for what had happened.

Korolev must have seen the anguish because he quickly changed the subject. 'More wine?'

Anatoly nodded thankfully.

'You're doing some interesting work.' Korolev poured another couple of glasses. 'When did you discover your love for science?'

Anatoly sat back in the seat. 'Can't remember.'

'Yeah, you're a lifer, alright. You'll be doing this 'til the day you die, I'll bet.' He eyed Anatoly. 'How old were you when you discovered fission?'

Anatoly stared at his glass for a moment. 'It was the summer of '38, so... fifteen. I was completing my doctorates,' Anatoly said. A slight grin slid across his face as he remembered. He swirled his glass.

Some wine dribbled down the side of Korolev's face.

'Students don't usually get their qualifications exploring new areas.'

Anatoly shrugged. 'I've always worked on new stuff. No point in experimenting with things others have mastered. That would be a waste of time.'

Korolev didn't hide the wide-eyed look of amazement. He dragged his sleeve across his mouth again. 'So, what's next?'

Anatoly considered the question for a moment as he sized him up. 'Take the next step.' He hesitated. 'Build a bomb.' His voice croaked with guilt.

Korolev leaned forward, and it seemed to Anatoly that everything in the world had stopped to listen to their conversation. 'Nobody is even near doing that. How close are you?'

'Closer than I'd like to be. If I moved out of the university, I'd be much closer.'

Korolev whistled and fell back in his chair.

'I don't want to talk about it anymore. I thought I was here to celebrate my birthday?'

Korolev reached for the wine and topped up their glasses.

*

When he eventually stirred, Anatoly found himself in a crimson room. At first, he thought he was squinting through a pair of bloodshot, ruby-red eyes until he realized the empty wine bottles on the table were acting like a monochromatic filter on the shafts of sunrise piercing through gaps in Korolev's dirt-covered window. He lifted his head and peered over the top of an uncorked bottle before immediately returning to the optical gloom of the stained glass.

Lying still for a few moments, he struggled to gather his thoughts, slowly recalling snippets of the previous night's babblings. Despite the raging inferno that would have sweltered Beelzebub, cremating the inside of his skull, he smiled and remembered. The black night had matured into the dark morning as he and Korolev had considered centuries of human comprehension and deliberated over decades of man's ingenuity. Emotions had ranged from furious shouting to tearful laughter and everything in-between. Conversation had never invigorated him so much.

After a couple of minutes, he had collected himself sufficiently to raise his head again, a little slower this time. He scanned the room.

He spied the top of Korolev's head, peeping over the back of the sofa. Another half-empty bottle grazed the floor as it dangled loosely from his limp-wristed hand. A strange gurgling noise resonated from below, swiftly followed by a short, sharp snort and the grating sound of a parched throat.

Anatoly rose unsteadily and went to the outdoor toilet, balancing himself against the wall. If he had learned anything about Korolev, it was never to try and keep up with the man while he was drinking.

CHAPTER 8

From beneath the shelter of his hand-made, leafy bivouac at the edge of the woods, Daniel stared out at the rain teeming down from the gun-metal grey clouds that seemed to cover the entire county of Warwickshire or wherever on earth he was. Cowering undercover in various locations for the best part of three days, only moving at night, wasn't exactly how he thought things would pan out when he agreed to undertake the training. He was cold, hungry, and wet, and if he didn't know better, he'd have thought the tutors had enlisted the bizarre June weather to help reduce their already small list of mission candidates. Watching the steady curtain of fine drizzle pock the surfaces of the hundreds of growing puddles was hypnotic, and Daniel felt his mind drifting back to Monday afternoon.

The four candidates had been escorted to the van outside the mess, where they swapped their holdalls for another, much smaller, canvas bag. Inside they found, among other items, a new set of clothes: hard-wearing, brown trousers, an old cream cotton tunic, a pair of dark and heavy woolen socks, a loose collection of underwear, one pair of ill-fitting boots, and a grubby knee-length overcoat. They had been instructed to change where they stood. That had come as a shock to them all, especially the Captain, who seemed annoyed about having to show his privates to the Privates. Daniel attributed his irritation to rank and his lack of close-quarter interaction with enlisted men over the years. Once done, they carried their near-empty bags to one of the camp classrooms, where they sat in silence, their tutors having abandoned them for the time being.

After more than thirty minutes, only Christopher returned. He laid out the timetable in a medley of flawless German and Russian, which reminded Daniel of his dad.

'As soon as we're finished today, you'll be blindfolded and taken from the camp to different locations. Once you arrive at your destination, you'll be given a crude, hand-drawn map of the area. You won't be told where you are. That's for you to work out. Your objective is to get back to camp before sunset on Thursday. If you don't make it, you're out.'

He paused as though waiting for a question before continuing.

'One thing to note: all human interaction is forbidden. You mustn't be seen by any of the locals. Don't test us on this. We'll be watching. We may even *be* the locals.'

Daniel thought he glimpsed a grin form on Christopher's lips, but it disappeared just as quickly.

'You'll have to forage for food and water as none will be supplied. If you need it, you'll have to find shelter wherever you can. You've been trained for this, so it shouldn't be a problem. I expect to see all four of you back here before the deadline expires. Once you return, you'll move to the next task.'

Daniel glanced at the Captain to gauge his reaction, but the seaman didn't seem all that concerned. Perhaps, the guy had anticipated some field-work and had prepared accordingly. Daniel hadn't, but then, it hadn't been that long since basic training, where he had become an expert outdoorsman.

'At this point,' Christopher continued, 'I'd usually ask if you have any questions. On this occasion, you don't get that opportunity. The rules are simple. Follow them, and you pass, don't, and you fail.'

He leaned forward and stared into each man's eyes, lingering slightly longer on Daniel. 'Only the best candidate will make it through this process. We will not play favorites. If at any time we believe you are not up to the challenge, then you leave the program and return to your unit.'

He walked to the door and opened it wide. 'If at any time you feel you can't carry on....'

Daniel watched Christopher scan the faces for a moment and wondered if the man was trying to determine who would be the first to throw in the towel. He wondered where he figured in Christopher's reckoning but didn't dwell on it because it didn't matter. It was clear that the training program was not so much a test of ability but a test of one's mind. Only the strongest in both would succeed. That's the way it had to be. That's the way Daniel wanted it to be.

A gunshot ripped Daniel away from his daydream – a farmer taking a pot-shot at vermin, perhaps. He wiped the condensation from his watch. Sunset wouldn't be for another two hours if he could see the sun. He wondered if any of the other trainees held the same view he did.

The camp lay no more than a mile away, partially obscured by a blanket of trees and the odd hedgerow. He had been staring at it since he had arrived earlier that morning. Unfortunately, he'd also been scowling at a farmer plowing the field that lay in his way. He couldn't believe how long it had taken the farmer to furrow the ground and had grown increasingly suspicious of the man as the day progressed. He could understand making a mistake and having to re-plow a patch here or there, but the man had plowed the entire field a couple of times.

Daniel wondered if this was part of the test: a disguised sentry to be avoided if the objective was to be achieved. He wondered if similar barriers were scattered around the camp's perimeter to make access difficult for the candidates. His eyes followed the farmer as he began to plow the field for the third time. Daniel made up his mind. He'd have to devise a plan to bypass him. The man beside him groaned and rolled his head to one side. Daniel glanced sidelong at him.

He had recognized Robert Blake immediately as one of the other candidates. He'd stumbled across the midshipman crawling through a forest's undergrowth a few miles behind. At first, Daniel thought it was some devious trap devised by the trainers to lure an unsuspecting candidate out into the open. But, from his hiding place, Daniel could see that Blake was distressed enough not to be faking. Blake came to a panting and whining stop, his face dropping into the mud.

Faced with either tending to or leaving the man, Daniel quickly chose the former. He slipped out and cautiously approached the unconscious man.

Even before he leaned in for a closer examination, he could tell that Blake's lower left leg was broken and not just in one place. He pulled Blake's trousers up, revealing a grotesquely crooked leg. Bruising had started to develop, and his leg was swollen. Owing to the absence of blood, he could tell that the fracture was closed and not open; Blake had been lucky if one could call him that. Infection wouldn't set in.

He quickly moved the injured candidate into a recovery position, carefully minimizing the movement of the damaged leg. The last thing he wanted was for Blake to choke on his vomit. He wondered how long it had been since the injury had occurred. Maybe he'd gone into shock. Daniel would have to keep him warm nonetheless. He removed his heavy overcoat and wrapped up the unconscious man. He groaned.

Daniel's eyes scoured the wooded terrain for fallen branches that might be used to splint the injury. Seeing none, he scurried away and found several that looked as though they might do the job. He selected the best two and rushed back. The midshipman was still out cold, which was a good sign for the moment, but Daniel knew he had to stabilize the leg quickly. He had to be careful or risk compressing a nerve or a blood vessel that could cause permanent damage. He whipped off his tunic and set about ripping it into strips. Moving Blake onto his back, Daniel grabbed hold of his knee and ankle.

'No,' Blake said, his voice barely a conscious mutter.

Daniel looked into his eyes and saw something he'd seen on many faces before; fear. He raised a finger to his lips and shook his head. Picking up a small branch, he placed it between Blake's teeth before looking back to the leg. Again, he put his hands on Blake's knee and ankle and prepared to pull. In his head, he counted to three. Blake's muffled scream masked the grating of bone. The scream stopped. Blake lay unconscious on the sodden ground.

As happy as he could be that he'd succeeded, Daniel covered up the straightened leg. He placed the two larger branches on either side of the leg and secured them with the strips of the torn tunic.

By now, naked to the waist, Daniel was getting cold. He knew he had to keep himself warm; otherwise, neither of them would get out of the forest alive. He scanned the trees around and, not seeing more than ten yards past a blanket of greenery, guessed they were deep enough inside the woods to risk lighting a fire without anybody noticing. His intention was still to win the competition, but not at the risk of losing his life; there would be other opportunities to get at the Germans.

He gathered the driest twigs he could find, along with some dry leaves to act as kindling. He rummaged in his pocket and retrieved the flint set, one of the other items they'd been given.

It took him less than a minute to light the fire. He fanned the small flames into a warm glow, watching as a thin column of smoke ascended, thankful that the green canopy overhead captured and dissipated it before it escaped. Daniel drew in closer and settled in for the day.

Later, just after twilight, Daniel retrieved the water that had collected in a hand-made reservoir of large leaves and found some large edible Oxes Tongue mushrooms at the base of an Oak tree. He decided to skip feasting on the numerous insects hopping, skipping, and jumping about.

After he and Blake ate, he extinguished the fire, carefully removing all traces of human habitation. He pulled his coat from Blake and slipped it on. Once comfortable, he lifted the injured man over his shoulders and traipsed off in the general direction of the camp.

Now, he leaned across and pulled the sleeping man's coat lapels tighter to help keep in the warmth. He looked back at the farmer, re-plowing the field.

All the traveling to get to this point had been done under cover of darkness, but now he had to find a way of traversing the last furlong in daylight with the burden of Blake over his shoulders. Being so close to the camp, he toyed with the idea of leaving Blake where he lay and making the last leg of the journey alone before dispatching somebody to fetch him. It would be easier to succeed without lugging the injured man the rest of the way.

He mulled it over for twenty minutes, the clouds overhead darkening, the constant drizzle becoming a torrential downpour, the unseen sun creeping towards the hilltops somewhere to the west.

Then, a stroke of luck. Either under instruction or sick and tired of getting soaked, the farmer gathered his plow and other equipment before heading off toward a distant farmhouse. Through the fading light and rain, Daniel watched him depart the field. He didn't know how long it would keep raining, but he wasn't about to sit around and wait for the only cover he had to evaporate. He had to move quickly.

He stood and buttoned up his coat to the neck. Dragging Blake out from under the bivouac, he braced himself, bent down, and strained under the man's dead weight.

Blake groaned as Daniel set off across the plowed field, splashing through puddles and floundering over furrows.

Panting hard, he reached the hedgerow on the far side and stopped. While in the open, he'd had to hurry; now, he was exhausted. Every muscle in his body ached, and his heart thumped as though he'd run a mile at full speed. He took a few minutes to regain a stable breathing pattern, trying to stretch out his legs. With Blake's sodden body sagging across his shoulders and water dripping down his neck, Daniel pushed on, all the time scanning the area for any sign of activity.

He pushed through the hedge and stumbled onto a muddy, tire-tracked road. He twisted and looked to the right before turning and heading off to the left. Out of sight, obscured by the drizzle, he knew the camp gates lay only a couple of hundred yards ahead.

As he neared, he could make out the stony, silhouetted sentries. He stopped. They hadn't seen him yet. Had he to make it past them unnoticed to achieve the objective, or only get to the gates? He wasn't sure. He was so tired and miserable that he didn't care. Blake needed medical attention, and he was near the point of physical disintegration himself.

Daniel stepped out of the haze and shuffled through the open gate. The sentries, eying him curiously, remained motionless.

He staggered towards the 'mess' and fell to his knees at the door. He turned to one side and laid Blake down carefully. The last thing he heard was hurried footsteps drawing closer before he collapsed unconscious.

*

It was close to midnight when the triumvirate of trainers gathered. They pulled their chairs closer to the table, above which a solitary light dangled. They re-studied the four files in front of them.

Ethan drew gently on his pipe as Chester flapped at the ensuing smoke. He shot the linguist a look of displeasure and turned back to Robert Blake's file.

'One down,' he said, his voice a gentle murmur. 'Three remain.'

He closed the file and, setting it aside, reached for another. As soon as Blake's condition had been ascertained (a compound fracture of the lower left tibia and fibula), they immediately reached the same conclusion. With time running out, he wouldn't have been able to complete the training and so couldn't continue.

'Webb will be the one to watch,' Ethan said, commenting on the navy Commander's file. 'Made it back with a full day to spare, even got under the wire without being seen.' He shook his head. 'Impressive.'

Christopher leaned forward and carefully re-examined each word of the file he held, glancing periodically at the attached photograph. He sighed.

'Simmons too,' Chester said. 'The guy strode through the gates at lunchtime, in broad daylight, and headed straight for the mess before ordering a plate of scrambled eggs. Cheeky bugger.' He smiled. 'I like him. Confident, self-assured, audacious.'

'Reckless and arrogant,' Christopher said. He ran two fingers along his ridged forehead.

He'd committed to memory everything the file had to offer and stared intently at the photograph, Daniel's photo, hoping it would surrender some unwritten secret. But only the face of an expressionless young man looked back. Christopher struggled to find a word accurate enough to describe the emotion that lurked beneath the blank gaze. He settled on melancholic.

Chester looked up. 'Who's that? Uh, Miller.' He leaned back in his chair and sipped on a glass of beer: overlooked contraband that had been smuggled in from the outside world. 'He cut it fine, but he did drag Blake's broken backside into camp. Gotta give him credit for that.' He smiled to himself as the alcohol dulled his senses.

Christopher pursed his lips and shook his head. 'I'm not sure.'

Ethan and Chester both looked at him.

'There's something not right. It might reveal itself over time.' He placed Daniel's file on the table and sipped some tea.

'You're on tomorrow,' he said, nodding towards Ethan.

'Until training is complete,' Ethan said, a smile emerging. 'Six hours a day, every day. By the time I'm finished, they'll think their mother was from Bavaria, and their father was from Leningrad. I'll be watching to make sure they don't start to drift off after being in the wilderness for the past few days.'

'What have you planned?' Christopher asked.

'They'll assume their new identities immediately. One German, one Russian. They'll become completely familiar with both. I'll merge what they know about themselves and their experiences with their alter egos. Their British pasts will be systematically replaced but not destroyed.'

Christopher nodded in appreciation. He knew how much effort Ethan had already put into creating the characters the three men would play, and he knew of no man alive better suited to ensure that every nuance of their new lives would flourish.

'And you?' He looked at Chester.

'I'll have them for four hours each day, some before breakfast, some before lights out. I've planned a rigorous exercise routine to get them into peak physical shape. We'll kick out anybody who doesn't cut it.'

'Anything else?'

'Air and water training,' Chester said ambiguously. 'Parachutes and submarines. No good learning all those languages if they can't get there in one piece.'

'Good.' Christopher closed his eyes. 'I'm monitoring the Russian retreat against German progress daily and praying for a change in fortune. I want to make a 'go, no-go' decision by the middle of August at the latest.'

The three men nodded in agreement and silently sipped their beverages. They knew their job was tough but not nearly as challenging as what lay in store for the remaining three candidates.

CHAPTER 9

ANATOLY FLEXED HIS FINGERS BEFORE wrapping them around the wrench. He gritted his teeth and braced himself: this bolt was giving him more trouble than the rest put together. With straightened arms and on tippy toes, he pushed down with all his body weight. His eyes clamped tightly shut, he exhaled and let out a low rasp. After a few seconds, he felt it begin to move. He stopped for a moment, beads of sweat trickling down his face, and scowled at it.

He'd removed more than half the nuts and bolts that held the giant porcupine together, but it was like somebody had welded this particular one more tightly. He looked at his hands and rubbed them gingerly: the welts had started to develop.

He surveyed the laboratory – the junkyard.

Pieces of his invention lay scattered on the concrete floor, resting where they'd been thrown. What had taken years to conceive and weeks to build had been dismantled in less than a few hours. Seeing his creation lying in ruins hadn't given him any pleasure. Instead, happiness came from knowing that his research would end right here in the basement of Stalingrad Technical University. If the world wanted to blow itself apart, he wouldn't give it a helping hand.

Even though he knew that on the outskirts of the city lay the much more extensive, custom-built facility, with all its chemists, mathematicians, physicists, and technicians, he was delighted that confusion reigned in that place. He'd always worked alone and had never learned to work alongside other scientists, let alone coordinate the activities of almost three hundred of the most brilliant minds Russia could offer. But he knew they'd take years to see the fruits of their disorganized labor if they ever did. And by then, the war might have run its course without the necessity of creating an abomination.

His thoughts idled on Anya for a moment. He loved her; there was no question of that. But for once, he'd forced his head to rule his heart. He couldn't allow his desire for her to be responsible for arriving at his work's inevitable destination. At the same time, he felt in his heart that she wouldn't have allowed that of him.

The time had come to leave the city. Leave Russia. He didn't have a plan: a first for him. He didn't know where to go and, even if he did, how he'd get there.

He'd toyed with the idea of escaping under cover of last night's darkness but had felt compelled to destroy his invention first. He was reasonably sure that Korolev wouldn't be able to recreate the atomic chain reaction, but he couldn't take the chance. Knowledge alone might bring NKVD persecution upon the Cosmologist, but not without the appropriate apparatus.

He turned back to the wrench to try one last time.

'I was told, but I didn't believe it. So, I had to come and see for myself.'

He froze. Every time he heard that voice, it made his skin crawl. The sweat excreted through exertion, becoming a prickly and frosty coating.

'I'm pleased you've decided to relocate with the rest of the science faculty. They can certainly do with your expertise. A beacon of shining light, illuminating their path of discovery.'

He closed his eyes. He could hear the smirk in her voice.

'You should have told me. I could have had somebody come and help you move your equipment,' she continued.

His mind searched for a response, something witty, something other than the truth, but he drew a blank. She'd caught him; now he had to confront her. He turned slowly.

'I've done all I can here.' He wondered if she'd be able to see through the half-truth before secretly cursing himself for believing that she wouldn't.

She moved closer, her footsteps silent.

His eyes were drawn to her curling lips.

Like a frustrated adolescent, he began to take in the rest of Daryna's beauty, the same as he always did. From head to toe, he traced her curves – an easy thing to do when she wore such tight-fitting clothes. She wore a black knee-length skirt and matching trim-free jacket that no doubt mirrored the blackness of the soul concealed beneath. He latched onto her smiling eyes and wondered how she'd been able to creep up on him, especially wearing those heels. He quickly looked away, feeling a sudden flash of heat across his face. He tested the jammed bolt once more.

'Yes, this place is rather small.' Her fingers touched the fission chamber lightly as though she was inspecting it for dust; her eyes scanned the room, pausing briefly on the blackboard at the other end of the lab. 'You can accomplish far more when engaging with other like-minded people.'

He felt her circling behind him and felt trapped, just like always.

'I can't do this anymore,' he said finally, his back still turned to her.

Maybe she would see his agony, see that his heart wasn't in it, and release him. Over the past few years, his dream turned into his nightmare. But equally, he knew that his nightmare had become her dream. His head fell. Depression sloped off his shoulders like rain pouring out of an over-flowing gutter.

'Look at you,' she said, her voice as cheery as a nightingale. 'You'd think you just lost your favorite puppy.' She came around to face him. 'Whatever it is, I'm sure we can fix it… together.' She placed a comforting hand on his arm.

She tilted her head slightly to one side and stared into his eyes. He'd have thought she was concerned if he didn't know better. But he knew her only interest was in what he could give her, which at that moment was nothing. He stepped back, broke contact, and looked anywhere except at her.

'I want to go home.' He spoke as though he was admitting to throwing a stone through a window.

'You can't go home.' She spoke as though she was telling a toddler why he shouldn't put his hand in the fire. 'You know that.'

Of course, he knew that. Did she think he wanted to return to a Kyiv with the swastika fluttering overhead? He wanted everything to return to the way it was before he had met her and before he'd left his home where his father worked the commune, his mother kept the house, and he taught physics to undergraduates. It wasn't so long ago that his life was so much simpler.

He shook his head.

'I want to leave Stalingrad,' he said, still not looking at her. He could feel her face harden.

Silence.

He waited.

Despite the campus roasting above ground under a mid-summer sun, the temperature in the lab seemed to have dropped to single digits. He felt the bristle of a shiver slip across his back when she eventually spoke.

'On your own?' Her voice was still sweet, but there was an underlying menace.

'No.'

More silence.

The air closed in around him, crushing him, dulling his senses. He felt dizzy. A low, dense humming grew louder in his ears. It hadn't been there before. Maybe he imagined it. His heart rate increased steadily, and his breathing became shallower.

'I want Anya with me.' He forced the words out.

Daryna moved before him and placed her hand on his arm again.

'There's nothing I'd like more than to see the two of you reunited.'

His heart rate increased again, and a spark of hope sizzled inside.

'But you know that's not possible.'

The spark suddenly vanished, a lone firework disappearing into the deep night sky.

'Many powerful people have invested heavily in this project and in you. They want to see this through to the end.'

'But this has nothing to do with Anya.' He was close to tears.

'I know that.' Her lips tightened. She shook her head and sighed. 'But the people I work for don't care.'

He looked into her eyes.

'I've pleaded with them on your behalf to release Anya, but they want assurances. They want your research to yield the results they're seeking. They need to make sure you're not distracted. Having Anya flit around the campus would put everything in jeopardy. You need to focus on what you're doing.'

He couldn't tell whether she was lying or not.

'Besides, we have a deal. You finish what you started, then you'll be together again. Placing a hand on her chest, she offered a little smile. 'You have my word.'

Anatoly stared at her, empty. He had questions, hundreds of them, but no answers, and by the look of her, even if he asked, Daryna wasn't going to offer any. He looked around. Another layer of cold sweat washed across his face, where, underneath, the blood had drained away. What could he do now? Leave as he'd intended and condemn Anya? Stay against his will and damn humanity. Maybe the answer lay somewhere in between.

He slowly nodded and glimpsed the hint of a smile teeter at the edges of her lips.

'I'll leave you to pack up,' she said. 'And I'll get word to Anya of your progress. I'm sure she'll be delighted. Maybe I can return with some news from her.'

He didn't look at her. Deep down, something bothered him; it had for several months, but he hadn't been courageous enough to think openly about it. He had no way of knowing if Anya was even still alive. He wondered if he should ask Daryna but thought the better of it. Better to live with hope than to learn the truth by seeing through the lie.

He heard Daryna's footsteps for the first time as she slinked away behind him, the lab door opening and closing with a low hiss that he'd never before noticed. The room fell silent. He walked across to a bench and laid his hands on it. His head hung loosely. His eyes filled up, and tears dripped onto the worn wood.

CHAPTER 10

'Ahoy there.' The voice echoed through the doorway.

Anatoly closed his eyes and gritted his teeth, refusing to turn around to face the latest interruption. The bother approached.

'Nice way to greet a friendly face.'

Anatoly recognized the dulcet tone. His eyes lit up, and he sparked to life. He leaped off his chair, turned, and threw his arms around Korolev.

'Not the reaction I was expecting.' The older man grinned.

'Take me away from here,' Anatoly said. 'I can't work under these conditions.' Desperation and frustration draped across his body like a funeral gown.

He drew back and looked pathetically at Korolev, who simply laughed it off.

'What are you talking about? You've got state-of-the-art equipment, more qualified assistants than an entire physics department, and more funds than several universities put together.'

Anatoly shook his head. 'That's not it.' He took a step back and crept away slowly, his hands finding their way into his pockets, his back hunched. 'I just don't want to be here anymore.'

Behind him, Korolev said nothing, only observing and waiting.

'I love science, you see,' Anatoly said. Korolev could barely hear him. 'The learning, thinking… the process of creating a new science.'

'And you can't do that here?'

Anatoly shook his head. 'I don't have the freedom to use my talent.'

'I'm not sure I understand?'

'Back in Kyiv, I had room to experiment.' Anatoly turned around. 'Here–'

'You're not a student anymore, Anatoly.'

'That's not the point.'

'Of course, it is.'

Anatoly stared at Korolev, open-mouthed. 'Of all people, I thought you'd understand.'

Korolev smiled. 'I do.'

Anatoly tried to turn away.

'If you weren't as gifted, then maybe you'd be able to do more of what you'd like to do. The truth is that you can't. You're an asset to the government. Do you believe Moscow would let you run around on your own fool's errands, especially with so much at stake?'

'I know what the government wants.' Anatoly's voice grew louder. 'I just don't want to do it.'

'Don't say that out loud.'

'Why not? It's how I feel.' Anatoly took a step forward.

Korolev glanced down at Anatoly's clenched fists and raised his hands, palms outwards.

'I only came to see how you were doing.'

Anatoly stopped, his eyes fixed firmly on the older man. Time stood still as they stared at each other, each refusing to balk.

Behind, the lab door squeaked open, and a clipboard-carrying, lab-coated engineer entered a couple of steps. Anatoly's head shot around. He glared at the man, who must have realized he had interrupted a private moment. He gave a quick bow and retraced his steps, closing the door. Anatoly turned back to find Korolev laughing.

'What's so funny?'

Korolev placed his hands in his pockets and turned away, tapping the floor lightly with his heels.

'Oh, Anatoly, if only you knew how good you have it here. Your undoubted genius is protecting you from being sent to the frontline with thousands of men your age. Is that something you'd jeopardize?'

He flicked a wry smile Anatoly's way. 'Where would you rather be?'

'Anywhere else. I'd prefer to be doing something else.'

'Like what?'

Anatoly thought for a second. 'Like maybe locking myself away in some observatory so I can stare at the stars all night.'

Korolev stopped tapping his feet. 'You know, I'm not sure I know how I should take that.'

Anatoly didn't reply.

Korolev bowed his head and ran his fingertips gently across his clean-shaven chin. He stepped forward slowly.

'What we do, our areas of expertise, are opposites, Anatoly. You're breaking the boundaries of physics, laying down the foundations of future scientific discovery. I look into the heavens and see science that has already happened. Some of what I study doesn't even exist anymore. I'm little more than a student of scientific history.'

He paused.

'I'd swap places with you in a heartbeat if it was possible.'

He looked away.

'We don't always get to choose the path of least resistance. Sometimes our lives take a particular direction simply because it's for the greater good.'

Behind him, Anatoly dropped his head and sat squarely down on a stool. He clasped his hands and locked his fingers together. He closed his eyes and sighed. Korolev suddenly whirled around, his thoughtful frown replaced by an excited exuberance.

'Maybe we can work together.' He clapped his hands together.

Anatoly looked up. 'But you've got your work to be getting on with.'

'Cutbacks.' Korolev waved his hand. 'Budgets have been slashed across the board to help fund the war, which is getting closer to us each day, I might add. The heavens and their mysteries will still be there once it's all over, even if we're not.'

Anatoly's face started to brighten.

'You'd do that?'

'I'd sooner be down here than up there.' Korolev pointed to the surface. 'Anyway, you look like you could do with a friend.' He placed a comforting hand on Anatoly's arm.

'I suppose I could do with some help.' Anatoly scratched his head.

'Go on.'

Anatoly thought for a moment. He didn't want to mention his recent encounter with Daryna or that the woman was effectively blackmailing him. He tried a different tack.

'There are so many people to co-ordinate. If I want something done, it takes longer for me to show them what to do than it would have taken me to do it in the first place.'

He got up from the chair and turned away.

'And they bicker like you wouldn't believe. They all seem to know what's best. They know nothing.' His face had turned strawberry red.

'And… I think they're afraid of me,' Anatoly said, under his breath, eyeing another passing white-coated lab rat suspiciously.

'I doubt that,' Korolev said with a hearty laugh. 'You're not exactly the intimidating type.'

'It's not that.'

'So, what is it?'

'I just don't fit in.'

Korolev looked around. 'Why? Because you're the youngest one here?' He stared at the young scientist for a couple of seconds. 'You're in charge, and you think because you're so young, the others don't value or respect your decisions.'

Anatoly took a couple of seconds to reply.

'I've always worked alone, never as part of a team. I'm in over my head.' He looked as though he might start crying.

'Is the work you want getting done?'

'Don't get me wrong. There is essential work being done –'

'Just not as quickly as you'd like?'

'Not as quickly as the government would like.'

Korolev snatched a lab coat off a clothes hook on the wall. He slipped it on and ran his hands down the front.

'While you're off searching for your sanity, I'll help sort out this mess.'

Anatoly's face brightened even more than before.

'But first, you can start by showing me around.'

'I suppose I can spare a few minutes to give you the grand tour.'

'I'd be honored.' Korolev bowed dramatically.

As the two scientists strolled through the warren of well-lit underground corridors, Anatoly explained how the entire facility was, in fact, two separate functional units in which independent activities were simultaneously run. He told Korolev the importance of building the place underground was to enhance security and provide secrecy from prying eyes above.

'When I arrived, I was surprised at how far my plans had progressed,' Anatoly said. 'But I hadn't envisaged building everything in one location.'

'All our eggs in one basket?'

'Something like that,' Anatoly said. 'Although it has had its advantages,' he quickly added.

Korolev glanced at him but didn't say anything.

'Having everybody in one location is good for communication and for the speed with which I can get things done –'

'I sense a 'but'.'

'It's led to increased NKVD presence and protection not only of the secrets but of the personnel.'

Korolev nodded. 'I had to jump through hoops to get down here.' He flashed an annoyed look, which told Anatoly what he thought of the beefed-up security.

'When I first came here, I was delighted to see so many people working on the project but less pleased with how they'd been deployed. Theoretical and experimental physicists, chemists and mathematicians, undergraduates and post-doctorates, technicians and lab assistants running around all over the place.'

'I see.'

'I've tried my best to get them to work in harmony, but it's taking away from what I should be doing. I'm not an administrator. I'm a scientist. I've been trying to coordinate everything. Assembling teams, scheduling their tasks and objectives, and analyzing their outputs. It's more than a full-time job. I do more reading now than I ever did, and it's nothing I need to know. But if I don't, something gets missed, and mistakes are made. We can't afford any mistakes down here.' He shot Korolev a worried glance. 'It's far too dangerous.'

'I'm beginning to see the extent of your problems.'

'It gets worse. Most of the people down here are quite intelligent, but the vast majority have spent their lives, lives considerably longer than mine, studying their respective fields and little else.'

They rounded a corner and stopped next to two large metal doors. Anatoly stared at the floor for a moment and exhaled a long sigh through vibrating lips. He took a deep breath, slapped the shiny surface, and launched himself into the detail.

'This is where we separate the Uranium isotopes. As you know, in its natural state, Uranium comes in at just over 99% of the 238 isotope and slightly less than 1% of the 235 isotope.'

'… And it's the 235 Uranium isotope that's fissionable when bombarded with neutrons.'

'Exactly.' Anatoly said. 'I'm impressed.'

'Don't get carried away. I read one of your articles.'

'Good.' Anatoly couldn't recall that he had written any, but he persevered.

'I need quite a bit of uranium 235, so I've to filter it from the rest. When I was in Kyiv, I considered a few ways to do that before deciding that gaseous diffusion was the best. At a constant temperature and pressure, the gaseous form of the lighter isotope's molecules travel faster than the heavier ones, which means that in a confined space, the uranium 235 molecules collide more often with the sides of the container they're in.'

'You hardly vaporize solid uranium?'

'No. We use uranium hexafluoride. It's solid at room temperature, but it's easily vaporized.'

'Where do you get that?'

'It's a long process, but I take a milled uranium ore and dissolve it in nitric acid. That yields a uranyl nitrate solution, which I obtain by solvent extraction. I treat it with ammonia to produce ammonium diuranate, which I further reduce using hydrogen. That gives uranium dioxide. Then, I treat that with hydrofluoric acid to give uranium tetrafluoride, which I oxidize to produce uranium hexafluoride.'

'Glad I asked,' Korolev said with a low whistle. 'Explains why you've so many damn chemists running wild around the place. You know you shouldn't let them do that.'

The two men grinned at each other before Anatoly continued.

'As I mentioned, the lighter uranium collides with the container walls more often than the heavier one, so statistically, over time, more uranium hexafluoride molecules with the lighter uranium 235 isotope pass through a special membrane at the end of each container. I repeat this process a couple of hundred times and concentrate the mixture to the level I need.'

Anatoly pulled on a long metal lever sticking out of the ground; the two doors parted noiselessly. They took two paces forward, and Korolev gasped sharply.

They had stepped into a low-ceilinged room the size of a small footb1all pitch. Several evenly-spaced, round pillars bisected the room, preventing whatever was above from caving in. Dim, staggered lighting illuminated a myriad of small, shiny, cylindrical canisters arranged in neat, parallel rows.

'We pump gas into the first container, a diffuser,' Anatoly said, pointing to the far end of the room, 'which is fed from one cylinder to the next through nickel-coated pipes. There, the gas is repressurized before it enters the next container to compensate for the pressure loss across each diffuser.'

'Nickel?'

'Oh, yes.' Anatoly smiled. 'Uranium hexafluoride is corrosive to most metals. I had to make the pipes leak-free because it reacts poorly with water.' He paused. 'It can get quite damp down here.'

'I presume you've to cool the gas once you've repressurized?'

Anatoly nodded.

'That explains the electrical cables going through that wall.' Korolev pointed towards a wall on the right that sprouted tens of heavy rubber cables.

'Anyway, that's the concentration process.' He sighed. 'The next step is a little trickier, but you've already witnessed a self-sustaining, atomic chain reaction.'

Anatoly allowed Korolev to survey the room one last time before they turned and walked back into the corridor. He pulled back on the long lever, and the steel doors slid silently back into place. The two men continued their walk along the corridor before Korolev interrupted his thoughts.

'You said the next part was trickier. How?'

Anatoly didn't reply immediately. Instead, he tried to decide how best to answer. Eventually, he said, 'What you need to understand is that what we do down here is cutting-edge science. None of this has been tried before. It's as if we're stumbling in the dark, feeling for a light switch while wearing a pair of oven gloves.'

'But *you* know what you're doing?' Korolev looked a little apprehensive.

Anatoly nodded. 'I've thought about this for years. I know what to do, the risks to mitigate, the hazards to avoid, and the difficulties to overcome. The problem is that everyone else is learning all this for the first time. It's like teaching children the fundamental laws of physics, albeit brilliant children. They're learning quickly, but time is against us.'

'The Germans?'

'The wolf howling at our door.'

'And you're worried that our house isn't built of brick.'

'They've managed to overrun every defensive position we've put in front of them. Who's to say Stalingrad will be any different?'

Korolev stopped and stared off down the corridor. 'They're coming here.'

Anatoly stopped and cocked his head to one side. 'Why would they do that? Surely taking Moscow, cutting off the enemy's head, and ending the war is more important. Why come all this way?'

'I think you know.' Korolev shot him a sidelong glance.

Anatoly grew silent. The only reason to risk everything in diverting an entire army hundreds of miles into southern Russia stood pensively in the underground facility, contemplating, yet keeping secret, how he could delay his inevitable breakthrough.

CHAPTER 11

Arthur Webb, Kevin Simmons, and Daniel Miller wandered about the pier, glancing silently at each other, sizing up the competition. They wore loose-fitting navy fatigues, which indicated where the next part of their training would take them.

The last three weeks had been the most physically grueling and intellectually challenging time of their lives, its toll affecting each of them both differently and the same. If they weren't role-playing in a classroom, they were running the roads and dirt tracks of Warwickshire, existing solely on a diet of foreign languages, minimal sleep, and fear. It had become a continuous re-evaluation of what they had done, never knowing if they were the competition front-runners or on the verge of being booted out of camp – the lack of feedback from their tutors keeping them on their toes.

As promised, the regular military dress code had been relaxed to the point where they sported hair far longer than any of them preferred, brushing their collars whenever they turned their heads. They also had a generally grubby look, as though they had slept in the middle-England wilds since coming to the camp. Each of them had varying degrees of facial stubble – a consequence of shaving only every other day, although Daniel's beard didn't compare favorably with those worn by the other two. None of them saluted a passing superior anymore, a deviation from standard etiquette and a habit Daniel had found incredibly difficult to break. Overall, they looked a lot less like the soldiers they had initially been groomed to be.

They stopped their pacing and turned at the sound of an approaching car.

A dusty, dark-green Humber Snipe pulled up a few yards away, the engine cutting out a moment later.

Daniel shielded his eyes against the setting sun and craned his neck to see who would emerge.

The sound of lapping waves against the quay filled the void between the candidates and the car before Chester Leatherby eventually stepped out. He wore the same colored hard-wearing fatigues. A snappy wave of his hand commanded the three men to follow him.

They walked past a row of buildings that were in various stages of re-construction following a recent bombing. As they drew closer, the clanging hammers and whirring machinery reverberated through the blown-out walls as weary workers fleetingly appeared and disappeared from view. Daniel thought it must be heartbreaking for them to continually have to rebuild the following day what had been destroyed the previous night: how they found the motivation to continue was beyond him.

They rounded a corner at the end of the pier and stopped. Bobbing gently to the sway of a tranquil tide lay a submarine.

From his vantage point, it looked quite small, but Daniel knew that, like an iceberg, most of its bulk lay hidden beneath the surface. He gritted his teeth and scowled at the floating tin can, the next part of his training.

He was an intelligent man and understood how such a contraption could sink and hide beneath the waves, but it remained a mystery as to how the damn thing could re-emerge at a Captain's whim. Surely, such witchcraft was against all commonsense.

Bringing up the rear, Daniel watched and waited before stepping onto the narrow, wooden walkway that bridged the gap between pier and sub-marine. He grasped the rope handrails and tiptoed as lightly as possible to avoid plunging into the water below before making an exaggerated leap and landing on the metal hull with a thud. He steadied himself and straightened upright.

He followed the others to the base of the two-meter conning tower, noticing that Leatherby didn't reach for the rungs that clung to the side. Instead, he walked right past it. From the back, Daniel peeked around the others and spotted an open hatch a few paces further toward the stern.

They stopped a few feet from it and peered into the blackness below. Without speaking, Leatherby pointed downwards, and, one by one, the candidates silently eased themselves into a seated position before disappearing from view.

Daniel slipped in last.

The compartment was warm, stuffy, and stank of diesel, despite the fresh July air ventilating through the hatch they had just dropped through. Daniel could feel the presence of other people, but it took his eyes several seconds to adjust to the relative gloom before he put a shape on them.

A group of four clean-shaven young men prodded a line of engine pistons with various tools. None passed more than a tired glance at the three men who had dropped in on them.

Leatherby appeared next to Daniel and moved past the sailors, his vast bulk climbing awkwardly through a circular hatch into another room. The three candidates followed.

Inside, they found another three men, each operating various controls, but Daniel's eyes were drawn to a short, slim, cap-wearing man, hunched over a table, staring at a chart. The man whistled a nondescript tune as his finger traced an imaginary line across the sheet. He twisted his head, leaned forward, and squinted. His lapels bore a Captain's insignia.

He continued to survey the chart for several seconds before turning around.

'You must be pretty damn important.' He sized them up and down.

It'd been the first English words Daniel had heard since the training process had begun, the Captain's accent charming yet bizarrely foreign. However, he could tell by the Captain's well-punctuated, public school accent that he was of aristocratic lineage and wondered what kind of person would willingly command one of the most dangerous and terrifying instruments of war. Surely, there were far safer positions on dry land that could better utilize his undoubted skills. Then again, the same might be said of him.

'We've been rushed off our feet making sure we're ship-shape in time for your arrival,' the Captain said, with the disdain of someone who had just had mud splashed on a new pair of shoes. Then, his tone changed. 'I hope you like what we've done with the place.'

He slipped a smile at Leatherby, who fired back a frown.

'Welcome aboard. I'm Captain Melville.' He offered his hand to each man. His grip was firm but not painfully so.

'I'll show you around.' He turned. 'This is the Control Room. You'll find me here most of the time or in the Officer's Mess further on that way.' He flicked a hand towards the bow.

'You passed the radar operator's station when you came through the hatch. Through here…'

He slipped through a small doorway.

'My cabin, cozy, eh?' Melville didn't wait for a reply before grabbing hold of a short horizontal bar above another hatch, diving feet first into the next compartment with an agility that Daniel found hard to believe.

Daniel sucked in a breath and followed the others through in the same manner.

Melville pointed out the Ward Room, several tiny Messes that would accommodate only a handful of men at a sitting, and eventually the Torpedo Compartment to the front. He rested his arm on one of six torpedoes.

Daniel glanced at them, suppressing his apprehension.

'Not much to her. 276 long, 25 across. We've two 2,500 brake horse-power diesel engines at the back that'll get us nearly 16 knots on the surface, slightly less when we're under. She has a range of around 4,500 miles, which is plenty if we need to travel a distance without stopping.' He laughed again, adding to the general feeling of awkwardness that had begun to take hold.

Daniel would have settled for any other form of transportation. Still, planes didn't have the range, and all the ships were either busy protecting the transatlantic conveys or patrolling the Mediterranean. This was, unfortunately, the only option left to the British Army and, therefore, to the competition's victor. Being submerged at anything up to 90 meters wasn't all that appealing, but there wasn't much he could do about it.

He glanced sidelong at Webb. The naval commander couldn't have been more delighted if he had just been offered a commission on one of His Majesty's Ships; behavior Daniel half-expected once they'd been dropped off at the docks. He tilted his head in the other direction and looked at Simmons.

He didn't look nearly as relaxed as Webb, a sheer veneer of sweat skimming the infantryman's face. In fact, he appeared uncomfortably edgy. Simmons' nervous glance back was all the assurance Daniel needed to realize that the competition had just become a two-horse race. The only question was how long would the Second Lieutenant last.

'You know why we're here?' Leatherby said. He shot Melville a stern look.

Melville nodded and clapped his hands as if he were a Maharaja summoning his servants. He bustled past them and retraced his steps back to the control room. They followed in single file.

Once there, he barked a few orders to the other submariners who scurried away to do whatever it was they had to do to get the boat underway. Daniel watched Simmons, who had grasped a protruding section of the bulkhead.

'We'll go topside until we get out of the harbor. It's always a nice view from up there,' Melville said with a wink. He grabbed hold of a vertical ladder rail. 'The real fun begins once we get to diving depth, though.'

The whole boat shook a moment later as the engines sparked to life behind them. Melville craned his neck over the seated sailors, giving the controls a cursory glance, before scampering off into the conning tower.

Daniel was last up but noticed that Simmons had led the way, no doubt relishing the prospect of gasping fresh air again.

The view from the conning tower was beautiful in one direction but ugly in the opposite. Ahead, a sliver of light floated on the horizon for a moment before eventually sinking from sight. Behind, the last of the builders were heading off, leaving a trail of partially restored buildings in their wake. They would return tomorrow to resume their chores. Up and down the pier, dock workers continued to unload shipments from cargo ships while the light allowed.

Out on the bow, a lone submariner untied the last rope from a mooring ring and flung it back to a docker who tiredly tidied it away. A second docker joined him. They silently placed long wooden poles against the boat's hull and leaned downwards, the rods bending under their exertion. Daniel was surprised that the efforts of a couple of men were enough to move the submarine sufficiently far away from the pier so that Melville could shout the order 'all ahead, half-speed' through the conning tower hatch.

A few moments later, the engines roared back from below deck, the twin-propeller shafts whisking up the water's surface behind them. Daniel ran his hand along the conning tower's rim as the submarine eased away from the pier. He glanced across at Simmons, staring beyond the mouth of the river, his eyes seemingly hypnotized by the darkening horizon.

The boat only took a few minutes to enter open water before turning to port.

Ahead, there was only the expanse of a seemingly empty Irish Sea. In peacetime, running lights would litter the surface; tonight, there was nothing. Daniel looked back toward the land, cast into a thickening twilight by the disappeared sun. The absence of house lights made it look like an enormous, uninhabited, dark-purple sprawl stretched as far as his eye could see. It all made for an eerily lonesome yet enchanting experience.

The three candidates stood silently, listening to the engines drive the submarine forward as the rising and falling bow forged a path through a sensually rhythmical spray of seawater. Beside them, Captain Melville again hummed the same non-descript tune through a smile and a loosely hanging cigarette. His fingers tapped out an irregular beat on a pair of binoculars dangling from his neck.

It started quietly, a low discordant drone floating on the offshore breeze. Daniel was the first to turn. Having experienced it before, he recognized it immediately. One by one, the men switched their gaze to the land and then to the sky above. They scoured the broken clouds but could see nothing.

Then, small pockets of light began to mottle the landscape below, soundless explosions. The peaceful atmosphere atop the conning tower immediately evaporated, replaced by foreboding electrification. Melville pointed away to the right.

Darkened outlines of an attacking flock of enemy aircraft, most probably Junkers 88s, were illuminated periodically by an array of powerful searchlights that began to crochet the panorama. Flak from unseen gun emplacements on the ground dusted the sky, while iridescent tracer rounds arched through the air, seeking a target.

'Prepare to dive,' Melville yelled down the hatch.

Instantly, the pitch of the submarine changed in concert with the screaming of the engines.

'Everybody get below.' Melville scanned the heavens, his binoculars sweeping an arc over the city they had just left.

Webb was the first to slide down the ladder. Daniel followed, his eyes adjusting immediately to the changed alizarin crimson hue in the Conn. He grabbed hold of the edge of the map table, his head pivoting back and forth as he watched the submariners perform their duties without panic or hesitation. That impressed him.

A few seconds later, Simmons landed on his backside on the floor next to him. Daniel thought he must have slipped off the ladder in haste to get below deck. It was followed by the metallic clunk of the steel hatch slamming overhead and the feline-like drop of Melville into the control room. Melville glared at Simmons briefly before shouting course corrections to his crew.

Daniel could feel the submarine pitch further forward, the hull creaking as though it was bending. The contents of his stomach flipped, and he desperately tried to keep whatever was in there from re-surfacing. He took in a massive gulp of stale air and held on to the bulkhead.

Simmons remained sitting on the floor, his arms and hands splayed against the wall and floor. His head tilted forward, his eyes wide, staring at the Conn ladder.

Silence descended after the initial burst of crew activity; the only sound was that of engines driving the propellers, which, in turn, steered the submarine deeper.

Daniel caught a teacup as it slid gently across the inclined map table. He wondered if an enemy plane had spotted the vessel leaving the harbor and would follow her out to sea. He wondered if, from beneath the surface, he'd be able to hear the splash of a bomb or the rapid plops of machine-gun bullets spraying the water from above. Oddly, he looked up to the submarine's ceiling as if he'd be able to see any of that through the hull. He noticed everybody did the same, except the helmsman, Melville, and Simmons.

Simmons began rocking gently back and forth, making a strained, pithy, whimpering noise. Daniel glanced down at him; nobody else did.

The submarine's pitch remained the same for another minute, but the creaking increased, and it wasn't confined to one place either, seemingly moaning from all sections of the hull along the boat's length.

The deeper they went, the louder Simmons' whining became. He'd stopped rocking and had started shaking. Daniel stared at him, ignoring everything else that was going on. He flashed a look across at Webb, who'd been standing with one hand in his pocket next to Leatherby. The Commander grinned back and gestured a 'thumbs down'. Daniel glared and mouthed a 'fuck you'.

He squatted next to Simmons and slowly placed a hand on Simmons's knee.

'Take it easy,' he said, in German, Simmons' preferred language. Daniel wasn't going to break one of Christopher's rules by speaking English.

Simmons didn't look at him. His eyes were clamped on the Conn ladder as though glued in place. His breathing had become rapid as sweat drenched his hair and face.

'Concentrate on my voice,' Daniel said. 'Keep listening to me. Ignore everything and everybody else. Listen to my voice.'

Although Daniel was terrified, he began to sing the opening bars of 'Abide with Me', his favorite hymn, as he gently touched Simmons' hand, tapping out its slow rhythm against the backdrop of submarine groaning and Simmons' weeping. Without knowing, he imagined the other occupants of the Conn looking at him, wondering what the hell he was doing, as if he'd lost his mind. Right now, the only thing that mattered was Simmons. Daniel had no idea what the man would do in the confined space, like maybe making a dive for the ladder and hatch above. Everybody on board was in danger unless he could be calmed.

The submarine had leveled out by the time he'd gotten midway through the second verse, but he kept going. He'd no idea how deep they were or how long they would have to stay submerged. He didn't want to take his eyes off Simmons to check any of the gauges, even if he'd known which ones to look at.

'Look at me,' Daniel said, 'Sing with me.'

Daniel started singing again, and Simmons slowly diverted his eyes away from the ladder and stared at Daniel. Daniel could see the savage terror in his eyes; the man's mind had strayed beyond lucid sanity.

Eventually, Simmons started to mumble the tune. For Daniel, that was good enough; it didn't matter if he didn't know the words. Keeping Simmons occupied on something other than being inside a hollow, metal cylinder, surrounded by a couple of thousand tons of water, was all he had to do until they could get him out and onto dry land.

Daniel had sung the hymn almost twenty times, his voice rasping by the time Melville gave the order to surface. Daniel felt the submarine push against his feet. He stopped singing and took Simmons' hand.

'We're going up. Won't be much longer.'

Simmons half-smiled. Even some of the tension Daniel had seen in his shoulders had disappeared, his eyes now relaxed.

'Count backward with me,' Daniel said. He started at two hundred.

'Wait here,' Melville said by the time Daniel and Simmons had reached twenty-three.

Melville scaled the ladder and opened the hatch, allowing a blast of fresh air to flood into the Conn.

Simmons's eyes flicked away from Daniel. He closed his eyes, feeling the rush of fresh air on his face.

'All clear,' Melville called out, his voice echoing down the tower.

Leatherby walked across to Daniel and looked down pitifully at Simmons. 'We'll stay surfaced until we find some other place to dock. I'll get a call through for a field hospital unit to come to pick up Simmons. We'll resume our training once he's gone.'

With that, he turned and walked back toward the radio operator.

CHAPTER 12

Evgeny Popov was, at the best of times, a dour man of few words, matched by a complete lack of compassion for his fellow man. If he could stand upright, he would measure only a lowly five feet and four inches. But, an abnormality had curved his spine and pulled his shoulders forward, depriving him of another couple of inches. Not that his physical appearance mattered. Only a fool would view him with pity; the wise would regard him with fear.

Today was Tuesday, and he was anxious: it was the same every Tuesday when she came to report to him at the enormous NKVD Headquarters in the center of Stalingrad.

He stopped pacing his office long enough to squint at a dusty clock that hung lop-sided above a row of four locked filing cabinets. He snorted; she was always late. He'd demanded that she report to him once a week, but, like a wedding day bride, she always set the timetable. He shuffled across the room and snatched a half-crushed packet of cigarettes from his desk. Fishing one out, he rummaged in his pocket for a box of matches.

After lighting up, he closed his eyes and inhaled deeply. He held his breath for a few divine seconds before releasing a cloud of light grey smoke. He watched it disperse as it rose, knowing it would further deepen the shade of the yellow-stained ceiling.

Then he heard it. Faint at first, the double click of boots echoing along the corridor outside. Her boots. He glanced at the clock again and ran a sweaty hand across his greasy, hairless scalp. He stubbed the cigarette into an overflowing ashtray of similarly discarded half-chewed butts, some ash spilling onto his desk.

As she neared his office, the footsteps grew louder, less muffled, and more staccato. Then silence. He held his breath. The knock still made him jump. He waited a moment before calling her in, making his way behind his desk as she entered. He slunk into his chair, his eyes trailing her feminine movement as she drew closer.

An outsider might believe that the emotions he tried desperately to hide were an unrequited love. That wasn't the case, not with her. He cleared his throat before speaking.

'Good news, I hope?' He knew he didn't sound all that menacing.

'Better than last week,' Daryna said. She didn't offer a smile but gazed with dark eyes at the oversized portrait of their leader that hung behind her boss, obscuring a window that she guessed presented, at one time, a wondrous view of the Volga.

Evgeny waited for her to continue, his eyes coveting her like a pubescent teenager. Always dressed in black, her flaming red hair flowed gently off her shoulders, accentuating her snow-white, blemish-free skin. He'd heard rumors that everywhere she went, masculine eyes followed; they couldn't help themselves, and he wasn't surprised. However, he wouldn't be ensnared. Beauty was, after all, only skin deep, and he was aware of the hideous beast beneath her magnificent exterior. Only others, no longer living, knew how horrible. He looked up from her breasts and caught her staring at him. One corner of her lips turned up in a satisfied smile.

'Better than last week, how?'

She took a moment to answer. 'We had something of a breakthrough.'

Evgeny leaned towards her. His hands clasped tightly together. 'Go on.'

She smiled, which made Evgeny's face light up.

'How far away are we?' His voice a whisper of anticipation.

'How should I know?' She scowled at him. 'He's doing things nobody else understands.'

Evgeny wouldn't have tolerated that kind of rebuke from another subordinate, but then, Daryna wasn't like any of them.

'But we are closer,' she added. 'Ever since Korolev joined him at the facility, he's been behaving like a child on his birthday.'

That was the best news Evgeny had heard since she'd convinced Anatoly to move away from Kyiv if convinced was the right word to use. He fell back and slapped the armrests of his chair, a broad grin lining his face. Getting Korolev to agree to bond with Anatoly had been his brainchild and, it would appear, had yielded a positive result.

'I am concerned, though,' Daryna said.

Evgeny's eyes flicked back to her.

'I'm pretty sure he doesn't want to finish what he's started.'

Evgeny's face clouded over.

'He seems fearful of where his experimentation will lead. He understands more than most the implications of taking the next step.'

'You've spoken with him?'

Daryna hesitated a moment. 'Yes.'

Evgeny's piercing eyes settled squarely on her face. 'A challenge indeed,' he said, at length, providing her with the opportunity to offer a solution. He waited.

'I'll make sure he doesn't let us down,' she said.

A chill rippled along Evgeny's spine, leaving him no doubt she would make good on her promise.

'How…?' Evgeny started, then a smile glanced across his face. 'Surely he doesn't still believe she's alive?'

'He believes anything I tell him.'

'But she *is*… dead?'

Her face didn't reveal the answer either way. She merely glanced toward Stalin's portrait.

Evgeny lifted a pair of spectacles off his desk and played momentarily with the temples.

'There's only so many times you'll be able to use her to manipulate him, especially without proof that she's alive. Eventually, he'll figure out you've been lying to him and know she's gone.'

'You underestimate the power of young love,' Daryna said, a wicked grin flicking her lips. 'Especially a first love. As long as he thinks he'll see her again, he'll do whatever I ask.'

Evgeny nodded, his lips pursed. He slipped on his glasses and, standing up, pointed to the seat opposite him. She sat as instructed and crossed her legs as he strolled across to a filing cabinet. He rifled through the top drawer until he found what he was looking for.

'I understand that you can't be aware of the timelines regarding this project, but there are forces at work that require it to be moved along.'

He handed her a slim, beige folder; his eyes fixed on her breasts again. Putting his hand over his mouth, he gave a slight cough and retook his seat.

Daryna opened it, her eyes immediately settling on the date: today's date. Even though the report was brief, her face darkened further as she moved from line to line. She snapped the file shut once finished.

'Is this accurate?'

Evgeny nodded blandly.

'The Germans have changed the focus of their attack?'

'Completely.'

'They're after our natural resources.' Her anger was all too evident.

Evgeny smiled. 'That's one way of putting it.' He glanced at her hands, crushing the folder.

Daryna stared at him, her eyes unwavering.

'Anatoly Yermakov,' she said. Her head dropped, but only for a moment

Evgeny didn't respond but was bemused by her disappointment. He'd known her less than a year, and, during that time, she had never come close to displaying anything that might resemble affection. He watched her, knowing her brain was nibbling at the possibilities and probabilities while calculating the contingencies.

'Can we hold out?' she asked, eventually.

He shook his head.

'How long have we got?'

Evgeny looked at the clock as though that would help him determine the arrival of the Nazi threat.

'A few weeks at most.' He slid a hand across his scalp. 'Can he finish in time?'

Daryna set her jaw and stared at him.

'Then find out,' Evgeny said. 'If he can't complete what we brought him here to do, then we need to decide what to do with him.'

'Move him east to start again?'

Evgeny could hear the exasperation in her voice, although she didn't show it.

'We do whatever it takes. Do you understand? I think you'll be having an interesting conversation with our protégé very soon.'

Daryna stood and was about to turn when Evgeny spoke again.

'I want a full report on his efforts next week. I don't care if you don't understand it. He does. Get him to write it down. After all, we're providing him with the capability and resources to complete his life's work and see out his dreams. Impress upon him how terrible it would be if his worst nightmare were to come true.'

He turned away and opened a hard-backed notebook, a sign that she was dismissed to get on with ensuring Anatoly delivered or face the consequences.

CHAPTER 13

THE AIR INSIDE THE WAR Room was chokingly dense and still, leaving even the most promiscuous smoker gasping for air. If the number of columns of smoke rising from the hands of the seated committee was anything to go by, then it seemed as though chain smoking had become the new national pastime.

With the heavy drapes closed and a couple of dull lamps at one end of the conference table, the only source of illumination, one would be forgiven for mistaking the scene for a modern-day religious inquisition. Browne ambled from the darkness behind the assembled military brass and, following the customary courtesies, introduced a confident Colonel Cumming.

Cumming began with another brief bout of platitudes.

'Gentlemen, let me begin by thanking you for joining us today. Our time is precious, so I won't beat around the bush.' He surveyed the somber heads and dove right in.

'Following the Third Reich's successive failures to overrun our nation, first with Operation Eagle and subsequently Operation Sealion, its attention has turned East, where they have attacked Russia with the launch of Operation Barbarossa. After numerous devastating victories on their way through the Russian steppe, they stalled at the gates of both Leningrad and Moscow. Thankfully, the current Nazi preoccupation with the East has meant that they've left us untouched for the most part.

A few heads bobbed grimly, knowing Britain was through the worst of the German siege on the island.

'Recently, however, Hitler has ordered a large portion of his army to head south, away from Moscow, to attack Stalingrad. Military strategists on both sides of the Atlantic had believed the objective was a move on the Crimea, aiming to swing through the Caucuses to capture the oilfields there. The initial assessment was that Germany was running low on the natural resources required to sustain a long military campaign. So, we believed that, if successful, Army Group South would merge with Rommel's Africa Corp somewhere around Palestine. That is if Monty doesn't give them a roasting on their way through North Africa.'

That got a little laugh, and Cumming smiled. He was about to launch into the next part of his pre-rehearsed speech but was interrupted.

'Are we to understand that this assumption is incorrect by your use of the past tense? That the solicited advice from military strategists and consultants is inaccurate?'

Cumming shaded his eyes with a hand to see who was asking the question but couldn't discern a face. He took his time before answering.

'Yes.'

A low growling swept around the room, which he did nothing to stop. Hidden from sight at the back, Browne smiled at his subordinate's calmness.

After a few seconds, Cumming took a step to the left and pointed to the back of the room. A few switches were flicked, the desk lights went off, and a projector displayed a map on a white screen behind him. The room dropped into silence again, and all eyes focused on where Cumming had planted his pointer.

'Stalingrad. The new focal point of Hitler's anger but not for the reasons we had previously suspected.'

He let the statement hang in the air for everybody to consider. He had long since discovered that the illusion of a compelling presentation lay partly in its content but primarily in its delivery. His audience needed to understand the gravity of the message he was about to deliver, so he dramatically changed tack.

'Since the early 1930s, scientists across the globe have strived to harness the power contained within the atom.' Cupping his hand as though he was holding a cricket ball, he paused and noted some bewildered expressions.

'It's a well-documented fact that atomic power will be the guiding and shining light that will allow the human race to leap into a new technological age, much like our ancestors did when they discovered fire and stepped out from the relative safety of their caves. The brightest minds say that if done correctly and appropriately, we will be able to light and heat our cities, run our motorcars, explore the greatest depths and heights of this planet, and beyond using this power, the key phrase being, 'in an appropriate manner'.'

He swung his pointer like a conductor would a baton.

'Unfortunately, we find ourselves, and not for the first time this century, in the throes of war. As is the case with every technological advancement, there is a growing fear that this newfound source of energy will be used for destruction rather than invention. Indeed, you are privy to a top-secret project in the United States whose sole objective is the production of an atomic bomb.'

Cumming could have paused to allow his audience a moment to digest what he had said, but he pressed on, not wishing to give them a breath.

'We've received information from one of our agents in Stalingrad that the Soviets are pushing ahead with a similar bomb program.' Cumming's eyes glinted as he surveyed the room. Everybody was hanging on each word he uttered.

'Every scientific resource available to the Russians has gathered in one location. Stalingrad.'

His wooden pointer cracked off the map. There was an audible gasp as his words slapped those present like a school teacher's cane.

'They kept this little secret very well, but unfortunately, not well enough.'

'What does that mean?' A voice called out from the dimness. Cumming continued.

'Bletchley intercepted a top-secret communiqué from German High Command to General Paulus, commander of their 6th Army. He's been ordered to drive his forces south towards the newly settled scientific community. Gentlemen, Hitler is aware that he cannot now win the war by conventional means. He realizes his Reich will not last the one thousand years he so fervently promised without an overwhelming technological advantage. As of…' Cumming checked his watch for effect. 'June 5th, Germany's 6th Army has but one objective: to capture the greatest Russian scientific minds and build an atomic bomb for themselves.'

A silence permeated the room, which intensified as the seconds ticked by. Cumming strolled in front of the seated dignitaries, his footsteps echoing throughout the room. He felt their eyes following his every movement as an audience would a tightrope walker without the protection of an under-hanging net.

Finally, he stopped.

'The communiqué was a little more specific than that. Hitler is sending in a small contingent of Waffen SS under the protective umbrella of the 6th Army. It's their objective to capture the Russian brains.'

He smiled. 'Actually, and you may have difficulty believing this, they have only to capture a single scientist, a man named Anatoly Yermakov.'

Some sniggering broke out, which Cumming half-expected, so he carried on undeterred.

'Yermakov is to the Russians what Einstein is to the western world. In fact, and this may surprise you, he is now considered by most in his field as the finest physicist who has ever lived.'

'Rubbish,' an exasperated voice called from the room. 'The greatest scientific minds are working on the Manhattan Project in America, as you said.'

'I'll tell you what's rubbish,' Cumming shot back. 'That Hitler thinks so highly of this one man that he's willing to send an entire army into the heart of Russia to locate and capture him. What's more, at nineteen years old, the man in question is barely that.'

Scattered chatter broke out as the select group of men huddled together, each talking over the other about the very notion of some youthful Soviet scientist who was unlocking the mysteries of the atom, while they in the West merely sat around and discussed it. There was quite a bit of head-shaking and frowning directed for the most part toward the patient,

Colonel. But that was nothing to what he expected after finishing his presentation. All he needed was his cue, which he had carefully planted.

'What are we going to do about it?' Browne asked from the back, glancing absently at his fingernails. It would have been evident to everybody that he knew what was planned had they bothered to turn around.

'We're going to get to him first,' Cumming said soberly.

Another sharp intake of breath was followed by a few seconds of silence that one could have driven a coach and four through.

'And you've got a plan?' a voice asked.

Cumming smiled and continued to prowl before them. 'We do. We've spent over two months creating and assembling a mission that best suits our needs. I should point out that it is a long shot, but its one which we are quietly confident will deliver the desired result. Gentlemen, I present to you Operation Chameleon.'

The expectant faces urged him to stop dangling the carrot.

'Shortly after we discovered what Jerry was up to, we took several similar contingencies and molded them into the plan, which I'll present here today. I'm not going to bore you with the finer details, but, in short, we intend to send a team of our own to Stalingrad.'

'How many men?' another voice asked.

Cumming stopped walking. 'Just one.'

'Excuse me, did we hear you correctly?' the voice asked. 'One man?'

Cumming glared at his inquisitor before repeating himself.

'We're going to send a soldier, yes… one man to Stalingrad. His mission will be to seek out and destroy Yermakov by whatever means necessary. To accomplish this, he'll have to blend in with the indigenous population and the defending and attacking forces as the need arises. He'll have to be fluent in Russian and German, be of fighting age, and be supremely fit. He'll have to possess cunning, composure under pressure, and a commitment to the objective.'

'And you've found somebody who fits that description?'

'We have.'

'Apart from the required skills, is this man also insane? Surely, he realizes this is a suicide mission?'

'No, he understands that desperate times require unorthodox solutions and sacrifices by everybody.' Cumming couldn't have cared less whether he had just snapped the head off a five-star General.

The room plummeted into silence once more as several pairs of anxious eyes searched each other in the dimness. It was clear that Cumming hadn't convinced everyone. He took a deep breath and began to justify himself.

'We've examined this from every conceivable angle. This is the only option. A single soldier will be anonymous, impossible to detect, a needle in a haystack of needles, if you will. Sending in more will attract unwanted attention from both the Germans and Russians.'

'Why not just ask the Russians to move their man?'

Cumming smiled. 'Because we like the idea of them making the bomb just about as much as we like the Germans doing it. We need to be the only game in town.'

'What about the fine print?'

'The details are unimportant at this time.'

'On the contrary, if you are to get the backing of this committee, then the devil is very much in the detail. I suggest you dig a little deeper,' the voice said, with an ominous tone of finality.

Cumming nodded slowly. He sipped on a glass of water to relieve a sudden onset of dry mouth. He had hoped he wouldn't have to delve into the particulars of the operation, especially given the time frames available, but equally had known that if the plan were ever to see the light of day, there was the chance he might have to divulge a lot more.

'Following a thoroughly comprehensive personnel search, we selected four candidates to undergo a rigorous training program created by some of our top men, a competition to determine who would 'best fit' the mission selection criteria. Particulars of the program included extensive linguistic classes, the creation of two aliases: one German and one Russian, parachute and submarine training, and outdoor fieldcraft.'

'Parachutes and submarines?' The question emanated from the gloom.

'Transport requires a submarine from Portsmouth to Egypt, followed by plane to the outskirts of Stalingrad, or as near as we can get without being shot down. He parachutes in once there.'

'Why are we only hearing of this now? If the threat is so great, why haven't we been approached before? You said the communiqué was delivered to us from Bletchley over two months ago.'

Cumming had anticipated that question.

'Gentlemen, a great many missions are devised and discarded. You have the privilege of seeing the viable few that make it safely through several stages of intensive planning. Chameleon is one of those. Your time is precious. I wouldn't have wanted to waste it two months ago when we had nothing except a threat.'

'Okay. We've seen your slides and understand what's at stake. Who have you selected?'

Cumming motioned to the back of the room with a wave of a finger.

Ms. Kendrick appeared, carrying a stack of thin folders. She circled the table, laying one in front of each committee member, before returning to the darkness. The lights suddenly came on.

Once their eyes had adjusted to the glare, the committee flicked open the files and came face to face with the mug shot of a smartly uniformed young man. Cumming allowed them to gloss over the file for a few moments before continuing. 'As you can see, this man meets all the pre-requisites outlined before.'

A momentary silence hung in the room before one of the civilian members spoke.

'What made him stand out from the others? You said there were four?'

Cumming shook his head. He was getting tired of stupid questions.

'He passed every test we threw at him. His linguistic skills are excellent, his ability to adapt to hazardous situations exemplary, his courage beyond reproach.'

'Anything else we should know?'

Cumming thought for a second before adding. 'He's ruthless, and that's exactly the person we need on this mission.' He paused and took another sip of water.

'When do you plan on going?'

'If this committee approves, then he leaves in three days.'

'What happens once the mission is complete?'

'Excuse me?'

'Extraction…'

'We can get our man to Stalingrad, but it'll be up to him to get himself out. This may well be a one-way trip.'

'Good God! And there's nothing we can do for him?'

Cumming shook his head. 'We've discussed it at length. It's hoped that once he has achieved his objective, he can either make one of the daily Dakota drops or that he'll be able to blend in with the indigenous Russian population. Once the war is over, all efforts will be made to repatriate.'

'What if the Germans win the war?'

'We're hedging our bets.'

'That's a big gamble. A man's life hangs in the balance.'

'Sir, I believe you're missing the point,' Cumming fired back. 'I've already explained the ongoing Anglo-American effort to create the atomic bomb. You're now aware that the Russians are trying to develop their version. What makes you think the Germans aren't? We're receiving reports confirming that they are. Do you know if they're ahead of us or behind us? We either roll the dice with one man's life or the entire country's. The scientific community believes whoever develops the bomb first will win the war, with the other countries facing either submission or annihilation. What else would you have us do?'

Cumming's speech was impassioned, but it drove the nail of reality home. It was some time before the most senior member spoke.

'I believe I speak for us all when I say that we will give you the green light on this, but with the proviso that you make every attempt to develop a better extraction plan to get Commander Arthur Webb out safely.'

Cumming bowed graciously, despite having no intention of acceding to the demand. Commander Webb would be on his own. If by some miracle he managed to get to one of the daily departing Dakotas once he was done, great; if he didn't, fine. All that mattered was that he hunt and kill Anatoly Yermakov. Everything else was irrelevant.

CHAPTER 14

Daniel sat alone on the side of his bunk in an empty barracks. Shouts, swears, and groans: the noises of men enjoying evening football as they waited out the war drifted in through an open window. He'd allowed his mind to wander; his boots polished well beyond the point where a Sergeant-Major would have deemed them acceptable.

He shook his head, hardly believing that he hadn't been selected. He couldn't understand it. Linguistically, he was the best in a class, which, incidentally, included his tutors. His fitness was supreme and unmatched, and his ability to improvise was superior to the other candidates.

He'd proved it. So why hadn't he been selected?

Instead, that arrogant son-of-a-bitch Webb had been preferred while he'd been returned to his camp: why? It didn't seem to matter which way he looked at it. He couldn't understand why he'd been turned down. He struggled to find in himself some flaw, a blemish, a weakness but came up empty. Maybe they'd based their decision on who they felt had the most combat experience, who'd proven himself, stared the enemy in the face. But he'd done that too. They knew he had first-hand experience of the war; he'd been wounded and almost died, for Christ's sake. As far as he was concerned, they'd made a monumental mistake and chosen the wrong man.

Outside, a whistle blew, which was followed by a chorus of cheers.

Daniel stared at his boots before storing them neatly under his bunk. He gathered the polish, brushes, and cloths and put them away just as the first of the rowdy men entered behind him.

The soldiers, most undressed to their waists, started to remove whatever clothing they'd left on and head for the showers amid an exchange of jeering and laughter. Some of them glanced Daniel's way and quieted down.

'Missed a great game, Dan,' one of them said. 'Don't know why you'd want to be stuck in here when it's so warm outside. It won't last much longer. Indian summer, isn't that what they call it?' He rubbed Daniel's hair and jumped onto the top bunk. 'You need to get that cut before the SM sees you.'

Daniel didn't reply. He lay back on his bunk and wondered how much longer he'd have to wait before he could get at the Germans and how much longer he'd have to endure the joy of the rest of his company. Instead of staring at the bump in the mattress created by his bunkmate's backside, he should be preparing for a two-thousand-mile journey.

'Hey, you listening?'

Daniel could do nothing but.

'You been quiet since you got back from wherever it was you were.' The other soldier waited a few seconds before adding. 'Ah, suit yourself. It could be a long war. It'd go quicker if you talked once in a while.'

Daniel rolled his eyes. He had no intention of stewing away in some dusty camp with the other enlisted men. The time had come to take matters into his own hands and fast-track his entry into the war. He knew what he had to do, but equally, he knew his plan might dramatically backfire and end up costing him his life unless played absolutely correctly.

*

Browne woke to the sound of knocking on his bedroom door.

'Yes,' he said, his throat as dry as ashes. He gave a slight cough and reached for a glass of water. He didn't get home often, but when he did, he savored the time away from the office and the politics.

'Phone call, sir.'

Browne uttered an inaudible profanity and threw back the covers. He stretched out his legs, his feet finding his slippers in the dark. He stood, slipped on a dressing gown, and walked to the door.

His landlord stood outside, looking as though he was about to apologize. Browne held up a hand and waved him away. He tramped down the stairs and lifted the receiver off the hall table.

'Yes.'

He didn't bother to ask who it was; he didn't care. If somebody had dared bother him at this hour of the morning, whatever time it was, then they must have had a damn good reason. Introductions were, therefore, irrelevant.

For the next forty seconds, he listened to the voice on the other end before saying, 'I want Cumming and Christopher in my office in the next thirty minutes. Get a staff car to my house in ten minutes.'

He replaced the receiver in its cradle and stood motionless in the darkened hall for several seconds. Upstairs, the landlord peered over the banisters.

'Everything alright, sir?'

'No… it bloody well isn't.'

*

Browne glared at Christopher and Cumming, although it was hardly their fault. Even though he'd had the journey from home to office to digest the news, he was still seething.

'Two days.' He thumped a clenched fist so fiercely on the mantelpiece that it made the Victorian 'Oak Tree Train Mantel Clock' shift slightly.

'We should have had him wrapped in cotton wool.'

The two men knew he was right, but even this turn of events was unfortunate, if not unexpected.

Browne thundered across his office floor, stopping at his taped-up window. He surveyed the scene outside as fire crews battled the remnants of another bombing raid, trying to douse the mini sunsets that mottled the city. He laid his hands on the window sill and hunched forward, his forehead resting against the pane.

'So that's it.' It wasn't a question.

The other two men glanced at each other. Christopher nodded to Cumming, who cleared his throat.

'Not quite, sir.'

Browne didn't stir.

'There is another option.'

Browne raised his head. His eyes traced the water stream that gushed high into the air from a nearby hose before disappearing into the burning building it was trying to save.

'You said it was *dangerous*,' Browne said.

Cumming shifted uncomfortably.

'It's all we have left,' Christopher said, speaking for the Colonel. 'We might as well prepare our terms for surrender if we don't at least try.'

"Independent thinking… reckless… emotional…' Those are just some of the words in the report. I know because I've read it several times.' Browne turned and clasped his hands together behind his back. 'Are you saying you were wrong?'

Christopher shook his head. 'He's all of those things. He's also a great deal more.'

'But, your initial fear still stands?' Browne's eyes scoured Christopher's face.

'It's a possibility. Nobody can ever be certain.'

'The fear that, if push comes to shove, he might not carry it out, that he might do something unexpected?'

'Battle makes everybody behave differently than they or their commanding officers can predict. We know there is no substitute for actual frontline experience. It's the same every time we send an agent into France or Belgium,' Cumming said.

'But if this goes wrong?' Browne shifted his attention to the Colonel.

'Then at least we'll have done something. I'd rather go down swinging than whinging.'

Browne stepped casually across to a bookcase that rose floor to ceiling and spanned wall to wall. He ran his hand across the spines of some of the hundreds of books stored there: Moore, Pope, Milton, Dryden, Wordsworth, Byron, Dickens. His hand hovered over a leather-bound copy of Henry V. He stared at it before his eyes swung from side to side and took in the entire Shakespearian collection: a gift from Lloyd George.

'Once more unto the breach,' he whispered. He bowed his head. 'Get Miller in here. Make him ready.' He turned around and, from beneath two bushy eyebrows, stared unwaveringly at the two men. 'And make damn sure *he* doesn't drop an aftershave bottle on his foot like Webb.'

*

Browne hadn't bothered to return home. Instead, he suffered the indignity of the staff canteen, which, thankfully, remained open twenty-four hours a day. Although the War Office posted a round-the-clock rota, the place was unusually deserted, which pleased him no end.

While he perused the early morning briefings, he sipped from a steaming china cup of Darjeeling. Today though, his interest lay in only one location, which didn't make for good reading. The Luftwaffe had been bombing Stalingrad for almost 48 hours, leaving the city in a sea of flames along its entire 40 km length. Oil storage tanks were pouring their flaming contents into the Volga. Civilian casualties were rising and counted in the thousands so far.

He stared at the report for over a minute before sitting heavily into the chair. He wondered if there was any point in going ahead with the mission; had they left it too late, was the report accurate? He caressed the cup in his palms and raised a warm hand to his forehead.

His thoughts were disturbed by a small group of administrative staff who had burst through the canteen doors. He glanced behind him. They looked like they'd been up all night and had come down for some end-of-shift refreshments. That was all the encouragement he needed to head back to his office. He placed his half-empty cup on the table, grabbed his small bundle of reports, and headed for the exit.

Once outside, he walked across the lobby and launched himself at the staircase. He'd only got a little over halfway up the first flight when he heard his name called out. He turned and looked down on a flustered Colonel Cumming, who brushed aside the Home guardsman with a dismissive glare. Judging by his expression, he bore only bad news. Browne closed his eyes and sighed.

Cumming charged the stairs and, with one hand on the rail, stopped next to his superior.

'He's gone,' Cumming said, between gasps of breath.

Browne's face wrinkled into a frown, waiting for the Colonel to elaborate.

'After we met, I sent word to his Commandant that Miller was to be awoken and dispatched to us immediately.' Cumming took in a massive gulp of air before continuing. 'He wasn't in his bunk.'

'Did they try the toilets?'

'They searched everywhere.'

Browne's mind clouded over, and he closed his eyes. He waited for an idea to spark, anything at all, but nothing came to him. He grabbed hold of the banisters as he felt his head begin to swoon. He felt Cumming place an arm around him to steady him further.

'Let's get you to your office.'

They took the elevator from the first to the fifth floor, by which time Browne had recovered sufficiently to walk unaided. He hadn't said a word the entire journey, though.

As he slipped a key into the lock, the outer office door swung noiselessly open. He paused and quickly checked his timepiece. Odd that Ms. Kendrick should have arrived so early. Stranger still was the silence: no clacking of the typewriter, no leafing sound of papers, shutting of metal filing cabinet doors. Kendrick must not yet have arrived. His mind raced back to when he'd left for the canteen. Perhaps he'd forgotten to lock up; after all, he'd had a bit of an early morning shock.

He shook his head and entered, flicking on a light switch. He stopped again.

Ahead of him, the inner office door stood ajar.

'Everything-'

Browne cut Cumming short with a chop of his hand. He glanced sidelong at the Colonel.

Cumming padded across to Ms. Kendrick's desk and snatched a letter opener. He looked back at Browne and shrugged: any weapon was better than none. He turned and moved towards the open door, stopping to regulate his breathing before entering. Browne was only two steps behind him.

Once inside, Cumming's eyes swept the office for anything that might be out of place.

However, Browne's attention had been drawn to a thick tuft of dark-brown hair that peaked over the back of one of the leather-backed chairs. He pointed.

Cumming started to walk across.

'Put down the knife,' a voice said from the other side.

Cumming stopped as the intruder rose and turned to face him. Time suddenly seemed to stand still before Cumming blurted out.

'Miller. What the devil are you doing here?'

Daniel stepped out from behind the chair. 'I want another chance to prove myself.'

'I'm calling the MPs and have you arrested,' Cumming said. Daniel could hear the disdain in his voice. He turned to leave, but Browne drew up alongside him. 'One moment, Colonel.' He cocked his head thoughtfully. 'We've been looking for you, young man.'

Daniel didn't respond, but a slight questioning flickered across his face.

Browne walked quite casually around his desk and sank into his chair. 'The Colonel's right, of course. You should spend the rest of the war in the stockade for what you've done.'

Daniel didn't flinch. He'd anticipated a verbal reprimand and threats; so far, it was living up to expectations. He knew military justice, knew the risks he'd run.

'I want to know what I did wrong, sir?'

Browne glanced down at his desk and brushed away a speck of dust. 'You're not in a position to make demands, nor am I in a position to divulge Top Secret information to anybody who just happens to stop by my office.'

He folded his hands across his stomach and leaned back. Gently bobbing back and forth, his eyes studying Miller from head to toe: medium-length, unwashed hair, twenty-four-hour stubble, a glisten of sweat across his brow, long dark coat, civilian clothing underneath; nothing that readily identified him as military.

Daniel remained quiet but resolute while he awaited his fate.

Cumming circled Daniel and dropped the letter-opener on the mantelpiece. He placed his hands behind his back and stalked, never once taking his eyes off the young private.

'How did you get in here?' Browne asked after a few moments.

That one question allowed Daniel to breathe easier for the first time.

'Up the stairs, like everybody else.'

Browne shook his head, the corner of his lip curling beneath his mustache. 'You know what I mean.'

Daniel did. He eyed the Colonel briefly.

'The MP on duty believes you've got a nephew going off to war.'

Browne scowled. 'Impossible. I'm an only child and unmarried.'

'Yes, sir, but he doesn't know that.'

'You expect me to believe that you told one simple lie and gained access to the entire War Office, especially given your appearance?' Browne flashed a stern look at Cumming. 'Security needs to be beefed up around here.' He looked back at Daniel. 'And what about the doors? I know I locked them.'

'Picked.' Daniel said.

'What about your trip from Warwickshire?' Browne asked.

Daniel shifted uncomfortably and hesitated before answering.

'I borrowed a fire truck from a town near the camp and drove to London. Told the station chief that equipment was being commandeered from all over the country after another bombing. Wasn't stopped on the way either. I guess nobody stops an essential service when there's a crisis.'

Browne remained quiet. He sat forward and placed his arms on the desk, his fingers interlocked.

'Whatever about breaching our seemingly inept security measures.' He leaned in. 'How did you know to come here?'

'Sir?' Daniel looked confused for the first time.

'You don't know me, shouldn't even know I exist. You've only met your tutors, and I trust them not to have told the candidates anything they didn't need to know. So, why come here?'

Daniel pursed his lips and debated the merits of letting Browne know how bad security really was. After all, that part of his plan had been the easiest to carry out. But, in for a penny…

'A couple of phone calls, sir.'

'Excuse me?' Browne's face almost turned to solid granite.

Daniel cleared his throat. 'I knew somebody was pulling strings throughout my training. The tutors had to take direction from somebody and plan their activities per the mission objectives. It stands to reason that the person involved was in London. I arrived here just over an hour ago and headed straight for the Ministry of Defence.'

Daniel paused. Browne waited patiently. Cumming stopped circling, his face turning a beetroot shade of purple.

'I guessed that most public phone boxes would be out of action, broken phone lines, and so on. But there is a phone just inside the doorway of the MoD. It's before you get to security, so it's accessible to the public and the building's staff. Because it's on government property, it's got a direct line to the Ministry's operators…'

He eyed Browne, whose stony expression had changed to utter disbelief.

'I told the operator I was Sir Christopher's assistant and that he needed to speak urgently with the War Office.'

'Were you asked for security identification?' Cumming asked through gritted teeth.

'No, sir.' He glanced at Cumming, who looked like he might keel over, before turning back to Browne. 'So, after a couple more phone calls and using the information I picked up from each, I got your name and location. I didn't know for sure if you were the one in charge, but given the available time and your seniority in the War Office, I took a gamble. I guess I was right.'

The room descended into a frosty silence, with only intermittent noises from outside causing any interruption. Browne suddenly stood up.

'Colonel, call for an MP and have Private Miller taken away. My immediate concern is plugging the gaps which allowed him to get here.'

Although he didn't show it, Daniel's heart sank. Had he blown it? Was court-martial now the only inevitable outcome?

Browne turned his focus back to Daniel and stared at him quietly as Cumming headed for the door. He returned a moment later with an MP.

'I can't decide if you're clever or lucky,' Browne said. 'Perhaps a little of both. In any event, you will require both where you're going. The Colonel will give you further details during your debriefing and subsequent re-briefing.' He glanced at the Colonel, who nodded his understanding. Browne held up a finger.

'To answer your question, you didn't do anything wrong not to be selected. You just weren't the best fit at the time. But, circumstances have changed.'

Browne turned away and stared out the window as the new day dawned over the city. His mind shot back to Miller's personnel file and training assessment. Maybe they had got it wrong. Maybe he should have been picked instead of Webb. He'd shown incredible resourcefulness and daring to end up in this office but, more worryingly, had demonstrated an outrageous ambivalence for the rule of military law. Throughout history, that sort of independent thinking had been systematically eliminated, as it only caused instability among the ranks. However, as he'd said, things change with time. Maybe there was a need for new ways of getting the job done.

CHAPTER 15

'Welcome aboard, *HMS Temerity*,' Melville said, an enormous grin spread across his face.

The name had caught Daniel's attention as he had boarded and had eased some lingering fears, but not them all.

'We'll be underway within the hour.' Melville turned back toward the Control Room. 'Oh, your bags arrived ahead of you. They're on your bunk.'

'Bags?' Daniel was expecting only one.

He walked behind Melville, who stopped beside a row of bunk beds.

'Normally, the crew shares these; two men rotate their rest times. We've trimmed down for this trip, so there's a bunk for everyone this time. I don't have to tell you how that lifted the men's spirits. This one's yours.' He patted a mattress. 'I'll let you get settled in.'

Melville headed off, barking an order at some sailor, leaving Daniel staring at two medium-sized green holdalls.

Daniel unfastened the clasps of the first and dumped its contents onto the bunk. One pair of scuffed, dark-brown boots, one pair of crumpled, dark-beige trousers, one heavy, cotton tunic (complete with elbow holes), a ragged, brown, woolen sweater, and a scruffy and worn, black, knee-length coat. As with his training attire, each item had seen better days, much better days. Daniel checked the attire for distinguishing marks and labels, but aside from an abundance of additional pockets attached to the inside of the clothes, there were none.

His disguise.

The clothes were creased, but Daniel folded them anyway and placed everything neatly back into the bag. He turned his attention to the other holdall. It wasn't as bulky but heavier than the first and rattled when lifted. He thought it prudent not to upend its contents onto the bed as he had the first.

Undoing the clasps, he reached inside, his fingers touching a small cloth pouch. He retrieved an emergency first-aid bag and eyed it curiously, opening it and laying its contents on the bunk. The inventory was an amalgamation of items found in numerous types of kits, ranging from those used by parachutists in Europe to jungle soldiers in the east.

After a few seconds, he moved the dressings, gauze, tapes, and bandages to one side and set about removing the labels from the Fraser's Solution, Atabrine, Sulfadiazine, and Halazone tablets. He examined a small pair of scissors and, retrieving a pocketknife from his britches, began to scrape off other identifying marks.

Once finished, he returned everything to the pouch except for two tubes of ointment that could be used to treat burns, cuts, and scrapes. They were labeled in English, and he knew it would be suicide to carry them once he had reached his destination: an oversight perhaps, by whoever packed the bag.

Dipping into the holdall once more, he fished out a gun holster, his hand skimming across the smooth leather. He popped the clasp and slid out a Tokarev TT33, admiring the dark, silvery-grey Russian handgun. It was light and short and could be stored relatively discreetly on his body. He glanced back into the holdall. Six 8-round magazines accompanied the pistol. He laid them out on the bed in a neat row next to the first aid kit.

Next, he retrieved a long body-strapping that contained six Russian F-1 anti-personnel fragmentation hand grenades. The strapping was designed to be wrapped around his body and concealed beneath his jumper and coat.

Daniel shook the bag and took a last look inside. That was it: no documentation, no last-minute mission details, nothing.

He replaced the weapons and redid the clasps before slipping the emergency kit into the first holdall. He sat opposite the lower bunk and, holding his head in his hands, stared at the two bags.

What the bloody hell am I doing?

Tales of eccentric and downright ridiculous British ideas had been spoken of before, but this one took the biscuit. Worse, he had willingly allowed himself to become the focus of another potentially hare-brained scheme. He was about to be thrown into the midst of a raging war between two gigantic armies, and all he had for protection was a handgun, a couple of grenades, and some second-hand clothing.

He lowered his head and stared at the grills of the submarine floor. His thoughts were interrupted by footsteps and the playful tone of Melville's voice.

'Forgot to mention, old boy, this arrived by dispatch rider earlier. The miserable devil wouldn't hand it to anybody on board other than me. He even requested that I show him my identification.' He snorted.

He passed Daniel a large, sealed, brown envelope and bent down to whisper in his ear.

'It's obviously important. You can use my quarters if you need some privacy.'

Daniel broke the seal and peered inside. He could make out two large words etched across the document. Standing up, he grabbed one of the bags off his bunk and offered it to Melville.

'Captain. Can I ask you to store this in your small-arms locker? It wouldn't be right for me to retain possession while onboard.'

'You'll get it back when you disembark.' Melville flashed a knowing grin. He led Daniel back toward the Control Room and dropped him off at his quarters. With a swipe of his hand, he closed the privacy curtain.

Sitting on the Captain's bunk, Daniel slowly emptied the envelope's contents onto a small side locker.

Over the next twenty minutes, Daniel's understanding of the mission was copper-fastened. He examined and frowned at some last-minute updated intelligence the mission planners had assembled. This was going to be much more challenging than he thought.

*

Browne stared out across London and raised his half-full brandy snifter. He took a sip before resuming a swirling technique honed over years of contemplation.

'Time of departure?' His voice was barely a whisper.

Behind him, Colonel Cumming revealed a gold-plated watch from beneath a pristinely-starched cuff. 'They cast off ten minutes ago.'

'Off the record.' Browne half turned. 'I think this plan is foolhardy, with no chance of success. Miller will be lucky to survive the drop into Russia if he gets that far.'

'We've been through this before. There is no other way.'

'There's always another way. We just haven't thought of it.'

'You mean me?'

Browne noticed Cumming's annoyance.

'This isn't about you. For once, can you put aside your ego and think of the men?' He paused. 'For years, you've devised plans for this and that, sent men away, men who will never come home.' Browne turned and faced the Colonel.

'Yes, I create the plans. Plans that you and others sanction at the War Office. Damn it, Bronson. We've got a war to win.'

'Don't you think I know that?' Browne started to raise his voice but caught himself in time. He sighed and turned away. He despised this part of the job. Both men stared silently southwest across the city at a magnificently natural crimson sunset that had, thankfully, replaced all those artificially created by the Blitz.

'Into the lions' den, Daniel goes.' Browne swirled his brandy one last time before polishing it off.

*

Daniel watched *Temerity's* bow dip gently beneath the waves as it plowed a westerly path parallel to the English coast. He glanced behind him at the Isle of Wight and then to his right at the coastal town of Bournemouth.

He turned to his left and looked past Captain Melville. Somewhere to the south in occupied Europe were Normandy and the Cherbourg Peninsula, but they remained hidden beneath the horizon. The Captain glanced across at him.

'The minesweepers have been out most of the day, clearing a path for us. Not that the Germans would dare lay anything this close to home. We should be clear to the Atlantic.'

Daniel didn't say anything but continued to stare straight ahead.

'You okay?'

Daniel shrugged.

'Seasick?'

'Homesick.'

Melville nodded. 'I get the same whenever I go on a mission, but it fades, although nothing beats the feeling of returning home.' He glanced at Daniel and winced, realizing the young Private may never see his homeland again.

CHAPTER 16

Dressed in the warm, native Russian attire provided and, with a parachute strapped to his back, Daniel stared at the plane's hull opposite. His nerves tingled tempestuously as the Dakota gobbled up the miles across Russia, the drop-zone nearing. He had tried to relieve himself several times since boarding but was empty.

Following ten days above and beneath the waves and a day-long hop from Port Said to Mosul, he'd spent a week sweltering on an Iraqi airbase, waiting for Whitehall to give him the green light for the last leg of the journey: the flight to Stalingrad. Above, the Germans, it seemed, were launching wave upon wave of bombing sorties, while below, their infantry held the city in a deathly stranglehold, closing in from the north, west, and south. With the river at their backs, it appeared as if the city was lost. If the Russians were to escape destruction, then they'd have to get their feet wet and relocate to the eastern side of the Volga. In London, the powers that be had said it was too dangerous to drop beforehand. Daniel asked himself: what made now any safer?

The plane jolted slightly, and Daniel tensed. He listened for flak but heard none. With only dim moonlight for illumination, he looked along the line of supplies secured to the hull of the modified Dakota with holes cut into it's sides to allow machine-gunners offer a modicum of protection from the smaller, more maneuverable enemy aircraft.

As part of the allied liaison, an agreement had been reached to ferry supplies, armaments, and sometimes personnel (Daniel being the human cargo on this occasion) from various locations in the middle-east via numerous transport drops, the frequency of which depended on the level of danger to the allied aircrew. He'd been told there would be at least one drop a day.

Everything seemed peaceful. Two of the four crewmen slept on a makeshift bench near the cockpit, their heads leaning on each other like lovers at a late-night movie.

He watched them for a few minutes and thought about the circumstances that had conspired to bring the two young men together. Had it not been for the war, they probably would never have joined the RAF, never met, and never used each other as pillows.

Daniel's brow furrowed. Had it not been for the war, he wouldn't be flying by the seat of his pants to some godforsaken city, and Alex would probably be playing professional football with a first-division team.

He patted himself down once more to ensure he had everything; he'd already checked himself more than half a dozen times. Stored discreetly in several pockets were rations to last two days: he would have to scavenge after that. He had debated carrying any weapons, eventually opting only for the Russian-made handgun. Against orders, he had left the rest in Iraq. He knew damn well that ingenuity and quick thinking would be his most effective weapons.

He carried two sets of identification in pockets hidden inside either side of his rumpled, brown coat. He just had to remember which side kept which set, but he had worked out a system to help him remember.

One of his alter egos was Dmitri Guskov, a Russian who had embraced the Communist philosophy and joined the NKVD at the ripe old age of nineteen. The other was a card-carrying member of the Nazi Party named Dominik Brandsa. Brutality and butchery garnished each man's lives to date. During the siege of Moscow, Guskov had infiltrated German lines and taken prisoners back to Lubyanka, where he'd been able to practice his brutal skills in its basement. Brandsa, on the other hand, had received specialist training in 'actions of deception'. His role was collecting enemy information by any means necessary; generally, that meant his prisoner's torture and subsequent death.

That had been something that had gnawed at Daniel's psyche: if these two characters were anything like the people he was likely to meet during his mission, then he was beginning to have doubts about whether he was suitable at all. Even during his training, he'd found it difficult to identify with both, but the psychotic Russian persona had been the worst.

Despite what he knew of armed warfare, the weeks of preparation, and his near-death experience two years before, he didn't know how exposure to sustained battle conditions would affect him. He had listened to several first-hand accounts, described to him in graphic detail by soldiers who had returned from France but was worried it hadn't been enough. That had been another cause for concern and a source of great annoyance.

He thought back to the dossier he had been given on *HMS Temerity*. Details of the scientist Yermakov; his upbringing, what the NKVD had done to his parents and his girlfriend, his undoubted genius. It was all there, in striking black and white. In a way, he felt sorry for the chap. Yermakov had been manipulated all his life. Nobody deserved that kind of intrusion, but then he remembered what kind of regime ran Russia. Manipulation was probably the least of his worries; he had a life for now.

He felt a pat on his arm. A crewman stood over him and pointed to a red light.

Daniel stood and clipped on. The crewman checked his chute and, nodding soberly, tapped Daniel's helmet. Daniel didn't return the man's gaze. He was staring at the two little bulbs above the door. The red one lit, the green not. He felt the plane descend and reduce its speed before leveling out.

The crewman opened the door, and a rush of cold air blasted into the cabin, almost knocking Daniel over. Looking out across a pitch-black landscape, the only thing he could make out was a thread of silver meandering away to the northeast.

The Volga.

The thread grew larger until it passed underneath. Out of the corner of his eye, the red light extinguished, and the green light shone.

Without hesitation, he leaped and, after a few seconds, looked up, breathing a sigh of relief.

What an incredible wasted effort if the mission ended abruptly had his parachute failed to deploy. He looked down and counted the seconds as the ground raced towards him.

Nine, ten, eleven, twelve.

He braced himself and hit Mother Russia much harder than he would have liked.

CHAPTER 17

'Time to go.' Korolev slapped the door. The thud reverberated around the room as if somebody had dropped a hammer into a ship's empty hold.

Anatoly didn't budge.

Korolev smiled. He had witnessed this self-induced, catatonic state many times; the young man oblivious to everything around him. Korolev stood before him and gazed in awe at true genius in action. Not a single hair moved on Anatoly's body. The only signs of life were his almost imperceptible shallow breaths and a trancelike rapid eye movement associated with deep sleep.

Korolev's eyes dropped to the large sheet splayed across the table of penciled schematics of what appeared to be varying types of bomb assemblies. Scribbled around the edges were hundreds of formulae and calculations. Most of the schematics had red lines crossed through them: all, that was, except for two.

Korolev reached out and gently shook him. 'Wakey, wakey.'

Anatoly moaned and raised his head.

'I almost had it. I'm so close.' He leaned back and let out an exasperated sigh.

'So are the Germans. Evacuation orders have been given. We've got to leave. They're going to blow the place once everybody is out.'

Anatoly stared at Korolev for a few seconds and groaned like a child being asked to complete his chores. He rolled up the schematics and slipped them into a thin metal tube, sealing it fast at both ends.

Before leaving, he paused and looked back at the place that had been his home during his time underground. Of all the rooms, this one was special. It was an addition, custom-built in less than a week, under his specific instruction. Isolated from the rest of the facility and made with six-meter thick concrete walls, floor, and ceiling. But Anatoly had known that had things gone awry in here, then no amount of concrete would have saved the entire installation from complete destruction.

That's why nobody else was allowed to work in this particular room.

He had digested the Top Secret memos and briefs, a bounty from Russia's spies. The Americans and British had finally started to take things seriously and were at advanced preparatory stages, but they were months behind him, maybe even years. He had heard persistent rumors that Fermi and Szilard were about to create the first artificial, self-sustaining, atomic chain reaction – perhaps before the New Year dawned. First, that was in the West. Since Korolev took over the administrative duties, Anatoly found that he could indulge in his fantasy, ignoring his ethical misgivings. Success followed success, which almost matched the breakneck speed of the German advance, but Anatoly hadn't quite been able to overtake it.

His eyes scanned the room one last time before resting on a large cylinder almost identical to the one he had used at the university. He smiled fondly at his creation, the uranium removed long ago. All that remained were several cadmium rods protruding from one side. He felt a tug on his jacket, turned, and ducked through the door.

By the time they emerged from the complex, most transport trucks had already moved off with their scientific brains safely onboard, replaced with Russian military and armaments.

The 'dig in' had begun.

They hurried to one of the last remaining trucks, bypassing a row of T-34s grinding their way along the road, leaving flying gravel, newly formed potholes, and choking diesel fumes in their wake.

The last time both men had been to the surface, the scene had been so different, with long stretches of trimmed grass, colorful flora, and tweeting birds frolicking in the air. All that was now replaced. War, it seemed, placed an indescribable toll.

Autumn was approaching and with it a chill. The further the Germans had advanced, the more the temperature had dropped from the soaring mid-summer heat only a couple of months ago. Nevertheless, Anatoly removed his lab coat and tossed it onto a nearby scrapheap. Both men were pasty-faced, a consequence of their self-imposed, scientific hibernation.

They hopped aboard the truck that would take them to safety. Korolev nodded to a security guard, who barked an order at the driver. Anatoly stared at the lines of infantry, trudging along the way he had come.

He looked toward the nearby slopes and spotted artillery placements in various states of construction and camouflage. Each gun barrel pointed in a westerly direction at forty-five degrees. Female troops, carrying ammunition boxes, plodded up and down the slight inclines like streams of ants carrying food to the nest. All around, civilians requisitioned from the city furiously dug deep anti-tank ditches.

There was something secure and yet unsettling about the panorama. The military was there to protect the civilian population from the Nazi threat, like a warm blanket of firepower, yet they recruited them into their ranks.

Was the threat that menacing? All the time he'd been working and researching, Anatoly had never given the German advance more than a cursory thought. Now, above ground and in the cold light of day, seeing the thousands of soldiers and armaments creeping towards the frontline, he felt a sense of foreboding cleave through what might have been a child's sense of security. His breathing became shallower and faster, and somewhere in his chest, a tinge of anxiety threatened. He shook his head, trying to dismiss the panic.

The truck rumbled past the deafening roar of machinery and the endless lines of men, but something didn't seem right. He turned toward Korolev, but the Professor was sprawled across one of the truck's benches, his eyes closed.

A wave of exhaustion suddenly crashed over Anatoly's body. At first, he couldn't believe just how tired he was. He glanced at Korolev again and adopted a similar supine position. Not long had passed since he had been forced to relocate through intimidation. And, he was on the move again, this time because of invasion. His mind drifted back to the hours he had spent on the stinking and cramped train carriage as it wound its way across the Russian steppe.

For hours, he had stared blankly at the passing scenery, barely registering its subtle change. Acres of bland meadows, sparsely populated by an odd tree, had given way to small clusters of tiny villages. As the lumbering train nibbled up the miles, the distance between the communities lessened until there were no more gaps. Single-story huts gave way to multi-story houses and, eventually, some large industrial buildings.

He had only been able to catch a few hours of intermittent sleep since he had boarded and had eaten even less. He felt his body move forward as the train began to slow. A high-pitched whistle sounded ahead, letting the passengers know their journey was almost at an end.

And, as if by magic, the view of a vast, bustling industrial cityscape changed to one of smoke-stained, cracked glass. The station's platform became visible once the train's belching had dispersed. It screeched to a halt. Anatoly waited patiently until the last passengers had collected their baggage and alighted. He rose cautiously, slipped a worn, brown suitcase off the rack above, and followed the other exhausted travelers onto the platform.

The station was thronged with jostling people, some rushing for connecting trains, others pushing for the exits.

Minutes later, following a crowd seemingly headed in the direction he had just come, he found himself standing outside on an equally busy avenue.

The scenes to the left and right were identical, with a myriad of crusading trucks, horn-blaring cars, and eager, chattering people. A large strip of finely cut grass bisected the wide, tree-lined boulevard. Trams tore along invisible tracks and swung around corners onto new streets. White suits and knee-length dresses were the fashion, and the aroma of different coffees filled the air. This modern city was excitingly vibrant, a place where maybe he and Anya could settle down once he'd done his masters' bidding. He thought of Anya.

Suddenly, he was jolted forwards and snatched away from his memories. The truck's brakes screeched, and the driver pounded the horn, shouting obscenities. Anatoly stared out the back and watched as they moved again past the endless column of troops, marching in the direction he had come.

What a mass of men.

The sons and daughters of Mother Russia striding to her cry for help. She had to be protected from the evil that crept from the West.

Anatoly knew that many of the students and technicians at Stalingrad Technical University had been transferred to more 'beneficial' projects, their efforts redirected towards securing victory for the Red Army. He knew the word 'beneficial' meant anything the NKVD wanted it to mean. Promising students could find themselves wearing a lab coat on an assembly line or a trench coat on the front line; it all depended on Mother Russia's needs.

His thoughts drifted back to the place that had been his home for a little over a month. He had grown to love and hate it in equal measure. A facility of his design that could have spawned his most celebrated achievement had the war not intervened. But it had, and now he was leaving. He thought of the vast number of personnel who had devoted their time and energy to helping him complete his wonder.

He had been so close.

If only Daryna and her cohorts had built the facility on the far side of the Volga. Maybe the Red Army could have kept the Germans at bay long enough to allow him to finish the job. But then, life was full of 'maybes'.

CHAPTER 18

Daniel stirred and opened his eyes with a groan. He had no idea how long he had been unconscious. It was still dark, so it was a good bet it hadn't been for too long. He instantly became aware of his new surroundings and lay perfectly still, listening for sounds he thought might be out of place on the lush, green Russian steppe. Aside from the gentle rustle of his chute playing in the night-time breeze, all was as he expected, or rather hoped, it would be: quiet.

He raised his head slowly above the grass, surveying the horizon in all directions, but saw nothing other than a copse of trees to the south and the odd terrain undulation and orange glow to the northeast that wasn't the rising of a mid-September sun.

He had landed about ten miles southwest of the city's outskirts. Although he could only discern some of the more significant explosions, he was beginning to have second thoughts about proceeding further. He stared at the spectacle ahead: the attack in full swing.

Of course, he knew of the German preference for a Blitzkrieg attack, but he had hoped the Red Army would have been able to hold their own, especially on home turf. An amalgamation of intelligence reports had said that the Germans had started carpet bombing the city almost into oblivion on 23rd August. That had been a few weeks ago. But yesterday's decrypted German report indicated that Yermakov still hadn't been captured, which meant that his mission was still on.

Reluctantly, he unbuckled the chute and slipped out of the harness. Pulling the risers and lines towards him, he gathered in the canopy as noiselessly as possible. Once the parachute was compacted and buried beneath some underbrush, he held his breath and listened again.

Satisfied that he hadn't attracted the attention of a passing patrol, he stood. He righted his coat and checked his pockets for his packed essentials. He peered into the darkness ahead and set off towards the city.

His first stop, and the only one he hoped he'd have to make, was the atomic facility not far from where he'd landed. If his jump had been timed correctly, it was directly in line with the city that followed the contours of the Volga.

As he walked, he glanced periodically at the clear sky. Despite the waning moon, he was amazed at the intensity of the starfield on show. But for the fact that he was working against the clock, he would have stopped to take in the wondrous celestial canvas. Thoughts of home returned, reminding him of evenings spent stargazing as he walked along the Yorkshire country roads.

The ground underfoot crunched where he tread, and a light frost glistened off the grass. He could see the vapor from his breath, and his clothes were damp from where he had lain. It surprised him. The weather report he had received in Mosul was that Stalingrad would be warm and dry.

He walked for a couple of hours, stopping to drink from a canteen several times and listening out for patrols.

As the hours went by, he could pick out waves of Heinkel 111s and Junkers 88s against the brightening sky. Messerschmitt 109s danced about, protecting the bombers from Russian aircraft. He was still so far away that only the loudest explosions could be heard, but he could feel the damage being inflicted as the ground shook slightly under his feet. The bright orange glow climbed above the horizon like another rising sun, gaining luminosity with every bomb that dropped and every step he took.

He trudged on.

'*Halt!*'

He froze, rooted to the spot. With his eyes flickering across the meadow in front, he didn't dare move. Was the command directed at him? He wasn't sure.

'*Hande hoch.*' Another command barked from somewhere to his left.

He raised his arms very slowly and interweaved his fingers behind his head, still scanning the undergrowth. Then he saw the slightest movement, as first two figures, then a third, followed by a fourth and fifth climbed out of the grass. The metallic sound of a couple of rifles being cocked behind him made his blood freeze and his heart pound. His mind swirled.

He had been trained for this very scenario over and over again. Still, training and being faced with the real thing were two entirely different propositions, especially as the slightest step out of place could mean both his mission and life would be terminated. Even with an icy sweat sliding down his back, he had never felt more alive than he did right now. He could almost feel the adrenaline, being secreted by the bucketful, gush through his arteries and leak into his muscles. A trained, automated response kicked in.

'Take it easy,' he replied in German, as calmly as he could.

Three of the five figures to the front approached him, their rifles raised and pointed at his chest and head. He could hear footsteps rustling behind, but he dared not turn. He would find out soon enough how many had him surrounded.

'Who's your commanding officer?'

The men in front stopped and glanced at each other.

'I asked you a question.' Daniel could feel his heart rate slow as his confidence grew. After all, they still hadn't killed him.

'I am.' The voice was no more than a couple of feet to his right.

Daniel turned and saw a young man, not much older than himself. He glanced at the insignia.

'Don't look at me.' The German looked like a starving Alsatian eyeing a plate of chopped liver.

'That's no way to speak to a superior officer,' Daniel replied evenly and with a hint of agitation.

A rifle muzzle smashed into his ribs, and he stumbled sideways. He straightened himself and frowned at the insubordination.

'I have papers.' He started to reach his left hand into his right outside pocket only to have the muzzle jammed harder against his body. He put his hands back up. That had been his trick – lefthand: *links*, righthand – *Russian*.

'Check for yourself,' he said, happy he had hinted at where they might look for his documentation.

The officer didn't disappoint.

He stood before Daniel and stared into his eyes as the other men fanned around him. Daniel could see they all had their weapons trained on him. He counted eight. The German officer reached into Daniel's right pocket and withdrew a Soldbuch. He flicked through it for a couple of seconds but seemed to find it difficult to read in the semi-darkness. Daniel decided to help him out.

'My name is Captain Brandsa.'

The officer looked from the book to Daniel and back again. He tapped it on his rifle, thinking.

'What are you doing out here? Especially dressed like that.' He threw Daniel a bemused look.

'I could ask the same of you, Lieutenant. Aren't you a little too far south?'

The young officer ignored the question and eyed Daniel curiously. 'Where did you say you were from?'

'I didn't, but as you've asked, Danzig.'

Daniel hoped none of the octet hailed from the same city and that his accent would hold. He waited patiently as the Lieutenant slowly circled him, his eyes never leaving his captive.

'You still haven't said what you're doing out here?'

This was the part of the story Daniel could tell almost truthfully. 'I've been sent to infiltrate Russian lines. I'm to gather intelligence on enemy formation and strength.'

'What, on your own?'

'No,' Daniel said. 'There are many of us. I'm surprised you haven't seen any others already.' He twisted his head around, glancing at the other soldiers. They had already lowered their rifles and were breaking out the cigarettes.

'They must be better spies,' one of them laughed.

Daniel smiled and glanced at the Lieutenant.

The officer paused before handing Daniel back his identification. 'You should be more careful. This place is crawling with Ruskies. We've had to take out a couple of enemy patrols ourselves.'

Daniel dropped his hands to his side. He suddenly wondered how deep inside German lines he was. Maybe there weren't any clearly drawn lines at all. If the Lieutenant was to be believed, it seemed as though patrols were practically tripping over each other, even if he hadn't come across any others yet.

'A wonderful sight.' Daniel beckoned towards the raging inferno only a few miles away. 'Won't be long before we can claim another city and another victory.'

That got a few hearty grunts and nods. Daniel glanced at the glow of their cigarette tips and shook his head. On the flat steppe, they might as well be waving a red flag at a bull.

'When do you expect to be back?' The Lieutenant spoke to Daniel as though they were long-time friends. Daniel could have dismissed him for attempting to discuss ongoing operations with a superior but instead tried to elicit some information of his own.

'Unknown. I've to find the location of a Russian underground complex. Perhaps you know where it is?'

The Lieutenant shook his head. 'We've only come across small tunnels and trenches.'

'No, this would be quite large. If you knew what I was talking about, you'd recognize it immediately.' Daniel's heart sank a little, knowing he'd have to navigate his way there alone.

'Why is it so important?'

The officer asked too many questions for Daniel's liking, so he diverted the conversation. 'Maybe you can direct me to your command. I can ask there?'

'Keep going on that way. You'll stumble across it very soon.' The Lieutenant flashed an air of superiority that made Daniel want to kill him. But he forced another smile instead.

Without a word, the Lieutenant motioned for his squad to move out. Daniel turned and watched as the group spaced out and began a lazy, single-file stroll further southwards.

Once out of earshot, he exhaled as if it had been his first breath. He looked back to the city and resumed his trek.

He had only been walking a couple of minutes when he heard the staccato sound of distant, rapid gunfire and shouts to the rear. He paused and stared back across the brightening plain. He couldn't make out anything besides a couple of muzzle flashes. But who had destroyed whom?

With a bit of luck, a Russian patrol had taken out the Germans and eliminated any chance that his encounter would be relayed along the chain of command back to headquarters. All he needed was a Russian good deed to help envelope him in an anonymous cloak of invisibility.

The firing stopped almost as quickly as it had begun: a trap sprung and snapped shut. Daniel waited a full minute before continuing.

He closed his coat around his chest to protect him from a sudden icy blast that plowed its way across the steppe. The direction of the wind had changed, flowing south along the Volga, carrying with it a light flurry of ash and soot. He looked into the sky ahead and could make out more squadrons of German planes moving in from the west and dropping their payload before banking and returning to their airfields.

Stalingrad was taking a pounding, and it didn't look as though the Russians were putting up much of a fight, certainly not in the air anyway. Perhaps his nonchalant premonition of a German victory would come to pass sooner than anyone could have imagined.

He carried on, vividly recalling the sand tables and maps he'd studied back in England. He knew the complex was approximately three miles outside the city's limits to the southwest. He recalled there being a ring of earth surrounding the entrance. He had no idea whether it was natural or man-made, but the feature had made for an excellent defilade. The circle would make for a good artillery position, with supplies protected on the land behind. Unfortunately, it meant that the entrance was obscured from the ground. So Daniel scanned the land for a flat-topped hill, something other than the undulations created by nature.

He stopped to sip from his canteen, his eyes fixed on several pillars of smoke that looked for all the world like chimney smoke escaping clusters of houses that sat atop a rise not too far away. It was worth a shot, and at least he could chalk one possible location off his list, should it prove incorrect.

He headed in that direction, his eyes switching between land and sky. Other than the patrol he'd bumped into and the visible air sorties, there was no other sign of a German presence. They were hammering on the city's front door and close to driving the Russians out of the back.

As he drew closer, he realized that what he'd thought looked like smoking chimneys were smoldering artillery emplacements. The high ground had offered the Russians an excellent view of their killing zone but equally rendered them prone to aerial attacks. He climbed a steep incline, eventually reaching the top.

Standing on the crest, he was awed by the devastation that assaulted his eyes. An array of field, divisional, and anti-tank guns lay upturned, twisted, and destroyed as though Hell's own fire and brimstone had swept across along their unstoppable path toward the city. Daniel inched, almost timidly, through the waste, disgusted by the view. He approached a 42mm anti-tank gun and squinted at the charred bodies of its crew, the acrid aroma and heat intensifying with each step. Staring at them, although difficult to tell, he believed most to be women. He backed away and looked along the line, horrified at the slaughter. Nothing had been left untouched by the attack. From what he could tell, there were only dead Russians and horses; destroyed from the air, the German infantry spared for the ground assault into the city. He turned away and looked down the hill.

Standing at the end of a dirt track was a concrete entrance, its double doors hanging loosely, partially blasted off its hinges. His heart skipped a beat. This had to be the place. With some luck, the indiscriminate bombing had done what he'd been sent here to do.

He ran down the hill, bypassing even more grotesquely twisted corpses of bodies and animals. Reaching the bottom, he slowed to a trot and knelt in a tentative crouch. He withdrew his Tokarev and hurried to the side of the entrance. He breathed heavily for a few seconds, listening for any other sounds, before peering slowly around the corner.

Inside was a tunnel sloping underground. He couldn't see more than ten yards before blackness consumed the inside. He would be exposed if he went in, his body clearly outlined against the bright sky, but he hadn't got a choice. He had to learn for himself if Yermakov was hiding within or, better still, already dead.

He dipped around the corner and, hugging the wall as though he were clinging to a cliff precipice, inched along, his eyes slowly growing accustomed to the darkness.

It took him several minutes to descend deep into the facility before it leveled out. The air inside was warm and stale, making it difficult for Daniel to breathe. Beneath his clothing, sweat oozed from his pores. The corridors weren't completely dark, partially illuminated by regular low-level lighting, most probably run from some backup generator installed in case of emergencies – Daniel didn't think this was the kind of emergency the Russians had in mind when they built the complex.

He crept along what appeared to be the main corridor, stopping from time to time to glance through doors as he came upon them. Each one looked as though it had been ransacked by looters, with tables and chairs tossed about, cabinets opened, and papers and folders scattered everywhere. Numerous pieces of what Daniel believed to be scientific equipment lay discarded on the floors.

He tiptoed down several other corridors, the rooms off them in a similar state of disarray. He listened for any sound, no matter how minute, but aside from a low electrical hum, there was nothing, not even the faint scurrying of a lone rat.

He'd been searching for almost an hour before he decided to return to the surface. There was nobody down here. It stood to reason that the invading German infantry would have searched the whole place carefully, especially as they were looking for the same thing he was. But he'd had to go down; he'd had to see for himself.

His trip back was relatively straightforward. Initially, Daniel had thought he might get lost in the mosaic of tunnels, but, in their wisdom, the Russians had placed maps of the complex at each emergency light, so he knew where he was in relation to the exits.

Soon, he felt the floor incline and started climbing to the surface. Before he left, he threw one last scornful glance back into the abyss, listened for signs of life outside, and emerged into the blinding mid-morning sunlight.

Accomplishing his mission would have been relatively easy had the Germans not beaten him to the underground research laboratory. Now, he faced two possibilities: the Germans had Yermakov already, or he'd been evacuated with the rest of the scientific community. Daniel couldn't do anything about the former, so he knew he had no option but to believe in the latter.

He gazed along the track that headed northeast, Yermakov's most likely escape route. Daniel returned his handgun to his pocket.

Throughout the morning, he'd noticed that the city's explosions had gotten louder and more frequent – making him think. It would be tough enough to find somebody in a city at peace. How difficult would it be now the place was in chaos? Was there any point in going on? Maybe he should head for the airfield on the eastern side of the Volga and wait for the Dakota to return and pick him up. He could always say he tried and failed, and nobody would be any the wiser, but that wasn't an option, not for him, anyway. He might not be able to find Yermakov, but he would at least give it his best shot.

He crouched and drank again from his canteen.

His parents had instilled in him a deep sense of right and wrong, a sense of pride in oneself and one's work. Throughout his short life, he had worn that Miller family value on his sleeve like a company insignia.

Despite the impossible obstacle in his path, not attempting to complete his duty was as much a foreign concept as he was a stranger in this land.

So, what was his next step? It was obvious, really – the pooling of resources. Locate the one other group of people who were also searching for Yermakov. It was time to search for the Waffen SS, who'd been sent here for precisely that reason.

He replaced the canteen in his jacket pocket and, almost reluctantly, started to follow the trail into the city.

CHAPTER 19

THE BACK OF THE TRUCK was incredibly uncomfortable. Riveted to its sides, two long, narrow, wooden benches ran their length. Both Anatoly and Korolev faced each other, having tried to rest. Towards the back, a couple of armed NKVD guards chatted idly about how, between the pair of them, they would stop the Germans dead in their tracks.

Anatoly glanced nervously at Korolev, who just smiled back. The older man seemed more relaxed than he had been in the lab. Now that he had time to think about it, Anatoly felt annoyed and grateful for the evacuation. To him, it was an abomination to leave anything unfinished, but at the same time, he wouldn't have minded if he never got to complete his project.

'What now?'

'We continue our work somewhere else.' Korolev flicked some dust off his trousers with the back of his hand.

Anatoly stared at him open-eyed.

'But it'll take months to get us back up to speed and achieve the same work rate, and even then, only if we have the same concentration of supplies and manpower. The front is soaking up a lot of resources. Not to mention that we can't just build another laboratory out of nothing.'

Korolev was about to respond but became distracted by a commotion outside. They both turned to look.

Columns of soldiers were breaking ranks, some diving into the hedge-row and ditches on either side of the road, while others aimed their rifles into the air, shooting off a few harmless rounds. Then they heard it; the high-pitched whine of a flock of attacking Stuka dive-bombers, screeching louder and louder until it became unbearable.

The truck picked up speed. It swerved and bounced along the road, the driver hammering furiously on the horn. Anatoly gripped the side of the bench to keep from falling off. He looked across at Korolev; his smile had disappeared, his face turning a ghostly grey. His eyes flitted from Anatoly to the road and back again.

Several surrounding buildings exploded, spewing bricks and mortar onto some soldiers as the truck hurtled into the Stalingrad suburbs. Anatoly shot a glance backward and saw soldiers fall by their dozens, blood spurting from their bodies as their limbs were severed, mowed down by a Stuka's machine guns.

Another explosion. Closer this time.

The truck shook, and some debris smashed off the side. The men outside screamed as they tried to organize themselves, firing helplessly back at the enemy. Eruptions of earth and plumes of black smoke billowed into the air, leaving massive craters behind. The noise was incredible, deafening, terrifying.

Pieces of bodies littered the side of the road: arms, legs, heads, broken and bloodied, scattered everywhere. Amid the screams of pain, there were very few shouts of courage. Anatoly's muscles went rigid, his fingernails digging into the bench like a vice-grip. He found himself breathing rapidly. He closed his eyes, praying the driver would go faster.

More whines and more planes dove, dropping their payload while spraying bullets indiscriminately at anything that moved.

Then, an enormous blast lurched the truck into the air. Anatoly felt as though he was floating and, through squinted eyes, saw the two soldiers at the back vanish into thin air. The truck came crashing down and dove into the ground, its wheels buckling as it flipped over.

Anatoly and Korolev were thrown around the inside like rag dolls in a washing machine, their bodies smacking painfully off the canvas walls and each other. The truck skidded sideways into a wall and abruptly stopped, enveloped in an enormous dust cloud.

When Anatoly eventually came to, his mind was groggy, and he found it difficult to get his bearings. He coughed, blood spluttering from his mouth. Patting his gum gingerly, he yanked a loose tooth before tossing it away. Rubbing his head and checking his hand for blood, he surveyed the damage.

The noise of the attack had dissipated, leaving only cries and moans in its wake. Anatoly guessed he must have been knocked unconscious, maybe from clattering off Korolev. He took another look around, but his friend had disappeared, hopefully, left in search of help.

The truck had ended on its side with his left leg caught between the canopy's stanchion and the ground. He tried to move, but every joint and muscle in his body ached. He tugged his leg, yanking it free and ripping his trousers on some twisted, jagged metal in the process.

Using the bench for support, he slowly stood. He checked himself for broken bones, but he seemed in good shape apart from scratches, scrapes, and some newly forming lumps.

Hunched over, Anatoly half-walked, half-staggered out of the truck and into Hell.

Soldiers littered the road as far as his eyes could see, their screams of agony reverberating throughout. Some men twisted grotesquely in obvious suffering, but many lay still where they had been cut down.

In every direction, columns of black, choking smoke rose from burning corpses, mutilated horses, and burning houses. Mercifully the Germans had broken off their attack, although there had been nothing merciful about it.

It had been a slaughter.

Some men crouched or stood, holding their heads in horror, hardly believing what had happened. They may have been the lucky ones, but they would have to endure the memories of their incinerated comrades for as long as God allowed them to live.

Anatoly sluggishly walked around the truck, searching for Korolev. He stooped and checked beneath the wreckage for any signs of life; there were none. The driver was dead, his head half-caved in by some flying shrapnel. He looked back along the road for the two soldiers who had been dumped when the bomb had hit but couldn't make them out amidst the carnage.

All the dead looked the same.

Still dazed, he didn't know what to do other than turn east and trek past the confusion towards the center of Stalingrad.

*

A couple of hours later, struggling in the dank September air, Anatoly found his pace had slackened to a shuffle. Along the way, he noted that the attack he had survived hadn't been an isolated incident. He passed several pockets of similar chaotic destruction, interspersed with areas of peaceful bliss.

It was at one such island of calm that he decided to rest. He helped himself to a couple of water canteens he had retrieved from some dead soldiers, figuring they wouldn't need them anymore. Sitting on the side of the road, his back against a low wall, he removed his shoes and socks. He wasn't made for wandering around like a lost soul. He poured water from the canteen on his hands and splashed it over his face before massaging his feet. He wiggled his toes to relieve the burning sensation that had plagued him for the last mile. Closing his eyes, he let his mind drift away from the noisy military machine that continued to march past.

He must have dozed off because when he awoke, he caught a soldier rifling through his pockets while two others looked on. Anatoly let out a roar that made them all jump backward. They must have thought they were scavenging from the dead.

The three, only boys really, backed away and, without so much as an apology, started to rejoin the tide of human traffic, heading out to defend the city. Having gotten over their initial fright, they looked back, joking and laughing.

Anatoly could see the funny side of it and imagined he would have felt the same if one of the soldiers he had relieved of a canteen had suddenly opened his eyes. He slipped on his socks and shoes and resumed his march.

Before long, the small, shrapnel-splattered cottages became two-floored, terraced houses that eventually grew into more extensive, industrial-type premises.

The deeper Anatoly went into the city, the slower he walked, not because he was tired but because he had to pick his way through the utter devastation around him. Some buildings were utterly demolished, while others had roofs and walls caved in. Unusually, some structures didn't bear the scars of the aerial bombardments.

On he walked past thousands of soldiers heading out of the city. The thought suddenly occurred to him that he had seen very few civilians. He imagined he should have at least seen those who had lost their homes trudging about, laboring beneath whatever possessions they had left in an attempt to escape the nightmare. Instead, he caught only fleeting glimpses of the natives dodging in and out of buildings or running across one street only to disappear down another. Those he did spot seemed apprehensive at best. If the civilian population had any sense, they should have been heading to safety on the other side of the Volga and not hanging around here.

It was then that he spotted a young girl strolling toward him. She didn't seem to be in a hurry to go anywhere. When she drew closer, she smiled and put a hand out to stop him.

'Are you lost?'

'Excuse me?'

'You're not from around here.'

Anatoly shook his head. 'I'm from Kyiv,' he said without thinking.

He tried to gauge her age. She had a scruffy face surrounded by short, brown, scraggly hair.

'Are you?'

'What? Lost?' She laughed.

He thought it strange that somebody who looked as young as she should be so cheerful, especially given the situation. But she had such an infectious smile and a delightfully pure laugh that he couldn't help but smile.

'From around here, I mean?'

'Oh, yes. From over there.'

She turned and pointed towards an area that hadn't been hit as hard as the rest.

'Why are you out here?'

'I'm out looking. Isn't it exciting?'

Anatoly was staggered that anybody could believe that an attack on their city, the massing of troops, and a near-death experience could be described as exciting. Petrifying and soul-numbing, maybe, but definitely not exciting.

CHAPTER 20

THE YOUNG GIRL HAD INTRODUCED herself as Nina, a thirteen-year-old Stalingrad local, although Anatoly thought she might have been a little younger. At just over five feet, she was short, slim too, and hadn't developed as a typical early teenager should have. But then, who was he to judge.

By the way she led Anatoly through the maze of debris-strewn, potholed streets, he could tell she hadn't lied about being from the neighborhood. She gave him a running commentary on who lived in which houses and owned which shops, or at least what was left of them. She even went so far as to let him know who she disliked and, seemingly more important to her, the reasons why.

During her excited monologue, Anatoly thought he had made a mistake in befriending her, thinking he might have been better off letting her go on her way while he tried to get to a ferry point and cross the river. But the more she gabbled, the more he succumbed to her amiable and naïve nature and so had become happy to have made her acquaintance. Who better to guide him to a safer location than this young street urchin?

'Have you lived around here all your life?'

She nodded. 'I was born in my house, same as my two brothers.'

'Are they younger than you?'

She shook her head. 'They're older. They're in the army. They promised they'd keep me safe from the Germans.' Her eyes lit up innocently.

Anatoly wondered if any of the destroyed bodies he had passed on the road had been one of her brothers, or perhaps even both. He drank the last drop from the stolen canteen, his stomach aching with hunger.

'Do you know where I can get some food?'

A wide grin appeared on Nina's face. 'You can come to my house. We've plenty.'

'Really?' His voice did little to hide his skepticism. 'How far is it?'

She pointed up the road. 'Fourth road on the left. Ninth house on the right.'

He surveyed the immediate neighborhood and winced. 'Is it still standing?'

'Yes. Most of my street is okay.'

Anatoly quickly weighed his options before taking Nina up on her offer. It would be good for him to sit with a regular family for a change; it'd been so long since he'd done so. Once refreshed, he could resume his march to safety.

'Why aren't you in the army?' she asked after they had walked further.

'I'm a scientist.'

She stopped abruptly, her eyes wide. 'What do you do?'

Anatoly thought about how best to broach the topic before settling on a half-truth. 'I'm trying to develop a limitless source of energy.'

She looked like she didn't believe him

'To power our cars and planes, light our homes and streets. It'll be quite the thing once I've achieved it.'

'So you haven't done it yet?'

'I'm nearly there.' He shook his head. 'Only for this.' He looked into the air and clenched his fist.

They turned a corner.

'You must be clever?'

'I've been to university, if that's what you mean.'

'My dad doesn't want me to finish my schooling. He said I need to get a job instead.' Her smile disappeared, and her head dropped. 'I suppose it costs a lot to go to university?'

Anatoly's heart melted. He didn't know who to feel sorry for most.

'I wouldn't worry about it too much. When all of this is over, nobody will have any money, and everybody will start from scratch. It'll be a great time for you and your family to prosper.'

'What's 'prosper'?'

'It means flourish… progress. You know what I mean?'

She didn't look as though she did, so he didn't push it.

'Here we are,' Nina said, her face brightening up.

Anatoly stared at a three-story house sandwiched in a row of similar dwellings. By the looks of it, Nina's parents weren't that poor after all. The damage in the area wasn't as bad as he had seen in other parts of the city; almost all of the buildings here still retained standing walls, some even had roofs, although not one of them held an unbroken window; an oasis of creation amidst a raging sea of destruction.

Nina walked up and pushed on the hall door, which swung stiffly inwards. She turned back and bade him follow.

Once inside, they walked through to the kitchen at the back. Anatoly took a quick look around. Aside from some kitchenware on the floor and an upturned chair, the place looked as though it had experienced a moderate earthquake.

Much to his surprise, Nina didn't stop there. Instead, she opened an adjoining door that led to a small but empty pantry. Anatoly groaned. She walked in and, pushing a shelved wall to one side, revealed a hidden door and stairway to the house's cellar. Without looking back, she walked down the stairs. Anatoly paused for a moment before following.

A fine layer of dust covered the steps, leaving a footprint on the creaking boards after every step taken. He squinted after Nina in the near darkness as she started to light the first of several small candles.

He was surprised at how homely the cellar appeared. In his experience, they were a waste depository for objects with which people refused to part. Despite the prevalent musty odor, a cooked food smell lingered, only serving to enhance Anatoly's hunger pangs. Scattered about were several aging, floral-cushioned chairs that looked as though they could do with some new upholstery. A gas cooker stood in the corner underneath a thin, partially boarded-up, street-level window. Next to it was a cupboard and a rusty steel sink. On an adjacent wall were several shelves laden with various canisters of paints, brushes, and an assortment of handyman tools. The makings of a couple of beds were stowed neatly underneath the stairs they had just come down.

'Are you still hungry?'

He nodded.

She opened the cupboard next to the cooker and revealed an array of tins of different sizes and shapes.

'Beans?'

'Sure.'

She emptied a tin into a small saucepan and lit the cooker.

'Where are your parents?' Anatoly scanned the cellar.

Nina shrugged.

The cellar grew quiet.

'Are you alone?'

The young girl's head dropped.

He didn't have to see her face to know she was getting upset; he decided not to ask any more awkward questions for now.

They sat opposite each other a few minutes later and, using their knees as makeshift tables, tucked into a couple of plates of steaming hot beans.

'How come you're walking around the city?' Nina asked between mouthfuls.

'I was on a truck leaving the place where I was working. It must've been too close to the frontlines. We were attacked. I walked for miles before I bumped into you.' He suddenly remembered that his feet were raw with pain. He slipped off his shoes and looked at his blistering feet.

'Where were you going?'

'I hadn't thought about it, but I suppose anywhere away from where the army was heading was a good idea.'

'I'm not sure about that. The Germans started to bomb this area a few days ago. Today was the quietest. It was the first day I left the cellar.'

'Have you been on your own since the bombing started?' Anatoly asked, his curiosity finally getting the better of him. He hoped she wouldn't break down.

She nodded again.

'I was doing my chores upstairs when I heard the air raid sirens. Father went to dig trenches for the army a week ago, and mother went out for more food. They told me to come down here if the alarms went off, so I did exactly that. I waited over there for them to come back.'

She pointed under the stairs.

'Your mum might've taken shelter in a neighbor's cellar until it was safe to come home.'

'Do you think so?' Nina's eyes widened.

'Sure. I mean, who'd want to be walking on the streets when the Luftwaffe is dropping their bombs?'

'And daddy?'

'If he's helping dig trenches, he's probably a long way from here. He probably won't come back until he's finished. I saw lots of people digging around my research lab.'

The relief on Nina's face made Anatoly's heart lighten, and the mood in the cellar lifted a couple of floors. It didn't matter that he couldn't be sure what had happened to her parents, but he knew he had to make her believe and hope. It appeared that that was all she had left.

They had just about finished their grub when the distant sound of air raid sirens sounded. Nina's head shot up.

'Come on, let's take cover.' She said it like she was asking him to play a game of chasing.

She quickly blew out the candles before hurrying under the stairs. Like a couple of nervous children afraid of some non-existent monster lurking in the closet, they threw a large rug over themselves and snuggled close. This time though, the beast was very real.

At first, all they heard were each other's shallow breaths. Then slowly, from outside the psychologically impenetrable safety of their shield, they began to hear several dull, low thuds and the higher-pitched return fire of the sputtering Russian flak guns.

As the explosions' frequency, intensity, and loudness increased, Nina gripped Anatoly tighter.

The bombs were getting closer.

With each blast, he could feel her body stiffen even more until her grip became painful, but he didn't complain. Ground vibrations and the droning of overhead airplanes intensified synchronously. Anatoly could hear nearby buildings taking a pounding and wondered how close they were.

Then, as quickly as it had begun, the sounds faded until all that remained was the sound of their breathing. Nina maintained her vice-like grip, only relenting after several minutes of comforting words.

He pulled back the cover and was thankful for the cooler basement air. It had become uncomfortably hot beneath their makeshift woolen armor, and he had built up a sweat. He surveyed the cellar but found it difficult to make anything out. He glanced across at Nina, curled into a tight fetal position, her eyes clamped shut.

He got to his feet and fumbled with the matches that Nina had used to light the stove. He lit a couple of candles and scanned the room for damage. Except for a tin of spilled paint, he was amazed that everything was as it had been before the attack.

He could hear shouting outside and the grinding sound of tank tracks on the road. The voices were Russian, so he breathed a low sigh of relief.

He blew out the candles and returned to sit next to Nina; she looked as though she hadn't budged an inch since they had taken cover. Anatoly had read accounts of soldiers who had been shell-shocked after exposure to enemy fire. He feared what prolonged bombing might have on somebody as young and fragile as Nina. Touching her head lightly, he stroked her straggly hair. He lay down next to her and, exhausted from his first full day in the war, fell asleep.

CHAPTER 21

Daniel began to encounter German patrols with increasing regularity the closer he got to the city. He had been stopped and forced to identify himself four times since leaving the facility, passing each inquisition with ease.

As a result, confidence in his ability to blend in with the enemy had grown to a point where he believed he would be able to trick almost anybody. But, his trainers had warned him repeatedly against the perils of over-confidence, which ensured he maintained a degree of caution. Operating within both German and Russian armies were detachments of dangerous personnel with specialized skills whose job was to ferret out and deal with the spies lurking in their midst. He wondered what they would make of him should he be uncovered.

The last patrol he met had decided to send a couple of men back to Battalion HQ to report their status in the field. They informed Daniel that somebody there would probably know where the Waffen SS unit was and offered to escort him the rest of the way. Daniel felt he had to accept their offer as it might otherwise arouse suspicion. He knew a slip, a misspoken word, and he'd be uncovered. So, with great apprehension, he made the trek through the heart of the German Wehrmacht with a pair of Kraut soldiers for company.

At first, his mind ran riot at the thought that they might have smelled a rat. He couldn't understand why they hadn't just radioed back. He considered maybe the reporting was a rouse, they were suspicious, and they wanted him to reveal more about himself. Their insignias indicated they were a part of Hoth's Panzer Corp., so he went along with the assumption that they were genuine. But, should the situation change, he was prepared to take lethal action.

'Seen much combat?' the soldier named Karl asked.

Daniel stared at the ground ahead and shook his head, reluctant to tell them anything that might later catch him out.

'We've been in the advance since we crossed the Don, stationed out here since the end of August. Damn communists are running so fast we're finding it hard to keep up. Putting up a hell of a fight in the city, though.'

That gave Daniel pause for thought. If the Russians had lost Yermakov, why would they continue to fight so stubbornly?

'Shouldn't be too much longer,' the other one said. He had introduced himself as Ben.

'Be home before Christmas.' Karl laughed.

Daniel gave them a sidelong look. Judging by their demeanor, he guessed the pair were roughly the same age and maybe a year or two older than he, but he sensed something else that their jovial nature couldn't hide. It was difficult to say what exactly that was, but if he were to guess, he would have said they were 'uneasy'.

'I hope you're right,' he said. 'Wouldn't want to be stuck out here after October.'

The two glanced at him.

'Gets cold. You can already feel it in the air in the morning.'

'We've been in the cold before,' Ben said.

'Not cold like this, you haven't.' Daniel was surprised at their naivety. 'How long have you been in the army?'

'Joined the Hitler Youth a few years ago,' Karl said. 'Then the army last year, to serve my Führer.' His face beamed as he swatted at an annoying insect. Ben nodded his head vigorously.

Daniel found that interesting. Karl hadn't said he was serving his Fatherland but his leader, Hitler. He'd heard that devotees had flocked to the Wehrmacht in their thousands, some as a result of their sparkling victories in Western Europe. When momentum like that is established, it tends to drag everything along with it. But what if things changed? What if the advantage of Blitzkrieg was taken away? Getting embroiled in inch by inch street-fighting might prove a dispiriting test of their resolve and devotion. Maybe that was why Hitler had forbidden his troops from entering Leningrad and Moscow last year. Stalingrad was different for many reasons, and one in particular.

Chit-chat was frequent as they walked, but in truth, Daniel didn't offer much. He couldn't have cared less about which young Fräulein was waiting for Ben back home or what Karl did during his last rest and recreation. The sooner he was rid of them, the sooner he would be able to get on with the business at hand.

His mind turned to his brother and the girlfriends he had left behind, and he found it increasingly difficult to control the rage festering within, so he had to force the memories of Alex away and allow the anger to subside.

Daniel noted the number of soldiers and armaments increased rapidly the closer they got to the southern section of Stalingrad. He spotted an artillery redoubt with tens of 88mm canons firing practically non-stop into the city. Even in the cold mid-morning, their shirtless, muscular gun crews continually reloaded once a spent shell-casing was spat out. A couple of columns of Panzer III's, IV's, Panthers, and Tigers slowly moved north-eastwards, tearing up the grassless ground. Their pennants vibrated, and commanders rocked in their turrets, pointing and barking orders at their drivers. Most carried foot-weary, hitchhiking soldiers. Then there was the infantry marching in their thousands to the frontline somewhere. It didn't take a genius to figure out that something big was in the offing, maybe one last push to drive the Soviets out of the city for good. There was something macabre about the entire scene. It was a breathtaking, intimidating, and utterly disgusting sight.

A mile or so further on, Daniel saw something he immediately recognized. Exhausted nurses and doctors, their uniforms splattered with congealed blood, lumbered lethargically about a large field hospital trying to take care of the hundreds of broken and moaning men arriving at its doorstep by the truckload. Rows of stretchers laden with young men, their heads, arms, and legs wrapped in blood-soaked bandages, lay in the cold open air. Some had lost limbs; lots didn't move at all. He glanced across at Karl and Ben; they'd become quiet. They stared at the ground until they'd bypassed the misery.

After another fifteen minutes of meandering through the heart of the 6th Army, Daniel was glad of the escort. Nobody looked in his direction anymore. It was almost as though Karl and Ben provided him with a cloak of invisibility, and he had been accepted as just another nut in the Wehrmacht's war machine.

As the density of military might intensified, Daniel began to think it might not be a bad idea to loiter around HQ for a while. His cover had proven airtight so far, so maybe he could learn something that would help him, like finding out where in Hell this Waffen SS squad was. But he knew he ran the risk of being detained should he bump into somebody who knew more about ongoing operations than Karl or Ben, which was probably every-body else at HQ. And so, he decided against ditching them for the moment.

They eventually came to the most prominent building he had seen since he'd met them – a large, detached, two-story farmhouse. Several Schützenpanzers were parked haphazardly out front, with sentries standing either side of the main door that had been adorned by a long, red canvas banner with a black Swastika emblazoned on a white, circular background. Daniel reckoned it looked like a crooked target.

He felt the atmosphere in the area had changed. Nobody shouted here, and transports moved slower and less noisily, which was odd. He noted that, by and large, the soldiers appeared cleaner shaven, their uniforms less dusty and dirty than those of the infantry he had seen along the way.

The three stopped outside. Ben slipped a crumpled pack of cigarettes from his pocket. Pulling one out with his teeth, he offered the pack to Daniel, who declined. Under a forced façade of calmness and with hands thrust in his coat pockets, Daniel followed Karl into the building. In reality, he was shaking like an autumn leaf.

He entered a small foyer that had several open doors leading away to other rooms on either side. Near the back, a rickety wooden stairway ran up to the next floor. Smartly dressed Adjutants silently crisscrossed in front of him, clasping thin bundles of folders firmly to their chests. Several weary-looking and dusty officers emerged from a room further along. They were engaged in a heated exchange as they brushed past. Daniel tried to figure out what they were saying, but they moved out of earshot too quickly. Not one had taken any notice of him.

Karl went into the same room, but Daniel hesitated. Instead, he peeked in and saw several older men hunched over a table; all Colonels and one Lieutenant General. Karl saluted and approached the most superior officer. Daniel strained his ears to hear what was being said but still couldn't make out anything.

Then, as though from nowhere, an overwhelming panic gripped him, and he felt a layer of sweat exude across his entire body. He could feel the blood drain from his face and drop into his feet, making them feel like they'd been dipped in concrete. What was an enlisted man doing reporting to ranks of this level? Had he been deceived by the young soldiers' and willingly walked into a trap?

He quickly scanned the lobby, searching for an escape route. There was a back door a few meters away, partially blocked by a handful of chatting Adjutants. He needed to make a decision quickly. Remain and risk exposure, while flight might attract attention and get him shot. He looked back to the front door and spied the sentries still in position. Meanwhile, Ben stood outside, flicking dirt with his toe, the cigarette hanging limply from his bottom lip.

No easy exit that way.

He heard footsteps above and turned toward the stairs. Maybe he could hide up there?

'Captain Brandsa?' a voice called.

Daniel didn't respond, momentarily forgetting his German alter-ego was being summoned.

'Captain Brandsa?' Karl called a little louder.

Daniel, wrenched out of his thoughts, twisted sharply toward the room to see Karl beckon him. He drew a sharp breath, tried his best to compose himself, and entered.

'Captain, I'd like to introduce you to somebody.' Karl's eyes sparkled. *That's it. Done for.*

'This is Lieutenant General Mayer.' Karl looked toward the oldest man in the room. 'My father.'

Daniel automatically turned and saluted. Mayer returned a flippant wave and resumed his discussion with the Colonels.

'Gentlemen, the plans you've brought me are excellent. Just be sure we've coordinated both infantry and Luftwaffe. It's the only way we'll push the Soviets across the river.'

He gave a curt nod, dismissing the other officers. He waited until the door closed before he turned his attention to Daniel.

'Aren't you a little young to be a Captain?'

'Yes, sir.' Daniel could feel his blood simmer, hoping it didn't show on his face.

'Care to elaborate?'

Daniel shifted on his feet and immediately launched into one of his well-rehearsed responses.

'Promotion due to specialized skills, sir.'

'And what are they?' Mayer walked around the other side of the table and sat heavily on an old wooden chair that didn't look as though it could take his ample weight. Daniel stared at the man's balding head as the General removed his boots and began to massage his feet.

'Information gathering, sir.'

'So, you're a spy?' Mayer spoke into his chest. 'No need for them out here… only fighting men.'

'I can fight too, sir.'

Mayer looked up. Daniel felt the man's eyes fix on him, run the length of his scar, and examine his muddy clothes.

'No doubt.' Mayer eyed him curiously.

Daniel glanced at Karl, who was staring at a large map of Stalingrad on the table. He looked back at Mayer and wondered what a Lieutenant General was doing this close to the frontline. Come to think of it, he didn't know how close *he* was to the frontline.

'And what's a spy doing out here? Shouldn't you be on the other side of the frontline?'

'I'm not at liberty to say, sir,' Daniel replied, knowing that Mayer might take great offense to him not answering a direct question. Instead, Mayer cocked his head to one side and squinted.

'Yet you can tell my son that you're looking for some Waffen SS squad in the middle of all of this?'

Daniel hoped that the mistake hadn't cost him. He remained tight-lipped.

'You don't say an awful lot.' Mayer frowned. He leaned back on the chair, which creaked to the point of collapse. 'A lot of people come and go on the field of battle and in the staging areas. It can be difficult to keep up with it all. I know we've infiltrated the Russian ranks with spies, as have they ours. You don't look like anything I've seen before from either side.' His face was deadpan; his eyes were simply dead.

Daniel's stomach began to swirl and gurgle like the last water disappearing down a plughole.

'I don't like it when people unknown to me come in unannounced. I don't like that you're not where you're supposed to be. I don't like it when I don't know everything that's going on in *my* theatre of operations.' His eyes suddenly lit up like the Blackpool Illuminations. He joined his hands, weaving his fingers across his stomach.

Daniel felt his mouth turn dry as though he had swallowed a mouthful of budgie grit. He felt like he had to respond

'I'm with the Einsatzgruppen .'

'A Jew-hater?' Mayer suddenly sat upright

'Sir?' Daniel asked, clearly not understanding.

'Here to catch and deport Jews back to some labor camp?' Mayer scowled. 'We don't have time to be rounding up, deporting, and shooting Jews, Gypsies, and Slavs. Win the war. Then our Führer can do whatever he damn well wants with them. I'll have no part of it, though.'

'No, sir,' Daniel said, not understanding what Mayer was talking about and trying to gloss over it. 'It's a special mission devised in Berlin.'

'Aren't they all?' Mayer's expression did little to disguise his contempt for the Berlin bureaucrats. 'And you've come here for my help?'

'No, sir.' Daniel wondered if the Lieutenant General was merely putting on a show for his son.

'Then what?'

'I'm looking for somebody. But I can leave if you can't help,' Daniel said. He tried not to sound like a petulant child.

Mayer smiled and shook his head slowly. 'No… not yet. You have all the hallmarks of a soldier who's been out here for months: the unkempt hair, the scraggy stubble. You've even got the obligatory stare. You've seen some action. But where, and on what side?'

'As I said, sir, I can leave and get on with my mission without your help.'

'I didn't say I was going to help you. I'm curious to know why a man dressed like you wants to find anybody in this shithole.' He stared unwaveringly into Daniel's eyes. Daniel didn't flinch; he had been through much fiercer interrogations.

'You're with some special SS squad on some secret mission,' he said. He slipped his boots back on, the air escaping with a *pfh* sound. He appeared to have grown tired of his little game of cat and mouse.

'Not with… have to meet up with them, sir.' Daniel said, relieved that the topic of conversation had returned to his lie.

Mayer turned to his son. 'You can return to your patrol.'

Karl saluted and headed for the door without saying goodbye to his father.

'There are some things that must remain secret, even between father and son.' Mayer paused and waited for Karl to shut the door. 'There are

SS all over the place. But I feel you're looking for one unit in particular.' He eyed Daniel expectantly, who shrugged. He walked around the other side of the table and twisted the map so it faced both of them. He exhaled.

Daniel could smell a mixture of stale cigar smoke and too-strong coffee. It did nothing to curtail the noises coming from his belly.

'I understand your reluctance to divulge what you consider sensitive information, but I know quite a bit of what's going on. Maybe I can prompt you. You've seen a map before?'

'One like this, sir, yes.'

'So if I were to point here and here.' Mayer fingered two locations that interested Daniel greatly: Yermakov's atomic research facility and Stalingrad Technical University.

'It seems I underestimated you,' Daniel said. He felt the blood return to his face.

'I make it my business to know what's going on on my battlefield,' Mayer replied. 'That's why I've asked every patrol to report to Battalion HQ in person at least once daily. Lines of communication can so easily be breached. Radio messages can be misinterpreted. You never know who's listening. Wouldn't you agree?'

Daniel could have sworn the General was looking at him with the suspicion of a man who never allowed himself to be crossed.

Daniel forced a tight-lipped smile.

'Very good,' Mayer said at length. 'The squad you're looking for has already been to the Soviet research complex. It was deserted. Odd that it hadn't been destroyed, something I would have done. Anyway, they've pushed into the city, towards the university, but have been bogged down by severe resistance along the way, just like the rest of us.'

'Sir, how close are they?'

'Well, we're here.' Mayer's fingers staked the map.

That close.

Mayer walked across the room and opened the door. He collared a passing Adjutant.

'Prepare the necessary papers so Captain Brandsa can safely pass to the frontline. Safe from us, that is.' He glanced back at Daniel and added, 'And make sure he's got something in his belly before he goes. It could be a long time before he gets a decent meal where he's going. You should find somewhere to bunk for the night. It'll be dark soon and too late to look for your friends.'

The Adjutant waited, which Daniel took as a sign that he should leave. He stood bolt upright and saluted the Lieutenant General, who merely nodded and walked back around the table.

'I'd love to know where you got your tan,' Mayer said before Daniel had left the room.

Daniel turned and stared after him, but the General had resumed scrutinizing the map.

'Dropped in from a warmer climate, perhaps, maybe with Rommel in North Africa?' He looked up and stared at Daniel intently.

'I hope your mission is a success. It would be a disaster if your quarry fell into the wrong hands.'

Daniel nodded, turned, and followed the Adjutant out, realizing he had hardly taken a breath since he'd walked into the building.

CHAPTER 22

ANATOLY WOKE WITH A JOLT. He raised his head slightly and tried to scan the cellar. Although seeing anything in the almost complete darkness was difficult, he had heard something. Then, he remembered Nina.

He reached out and felt her lying next to him and could hear her slow, rhythmic breathing. He stayed still for a moment before silently getting to his feet. He felt his way to a small shelf, fumbling in the dark for a water canteen. Gulping back the stale water, he was reminded not so much of the thirst caused by dehydration but of the fine grains of dust floating in the still air, clogging his nose and lungs. As quietly as he could, he coughed a glob of thick mucus and spat it into where he thought the sink was.

Behind him, Nina stirred.

The only source of light was the small slit window high on one wall, which, had it been daytime, would have revealed a restricted view of the street outside. Anatoly could see nothing now, so guessed it was late evening. Through the partially shattered glass, he could hear a constant rat-a-tat-tat of raindrops pelting off the pavement.

But that wasn't all.

Hushed and hurried German voices followed the unmistakable sound of scuffling jackboots on the debris-littered road. He froze, realizing that the rat-a-tat-tat was machine gunfire. He glanced to where Nina lay but couldn't see her. That was good. If he couldn't see her, anybody looking through the small window couldn't either. But could they see him? He inched his way back towards the stairs and dropped to the floor. With his heart pumping ice-cold blood, he pulled the heavy blanket over him. Under there, he was protected from the monster that had emerged from the west and freely roamed the city to feast. He lay still, hardly daring to breathe.

He tried to dismiss his fear by forcing himself to believe it was an illusion caused by what he had witnessed on the road into Stalingrad, but he found himself falling. The fear was real and growing. He closed his eyes and gripped the blanket more tightly.

Nina moved next to him.

'Anatoly, what's wrong?'

He didn't reply.

Feeling him shivering, she cuddled close to him and asked again.

'The Germans are outside.' His voice was a high-pitched, muffled squeak.

This time Nina's body stiffened. They clung tightly to each other, jolting when they heard bootsteps on the kitchen floor upstairs.

They stayed underneath for what felt like hours before they dared to peek over the covers and look towards the stairs. It was beginning to brighten outside, and the dull light from the window cast an eerie, navy illumination across the cellar. They looked at each other, knowing they both had the same thought.

Would the Germans find the secret door in the pantry?

The footsteps had stopped, and several strained German voices sounded, maybe orders being dispensed. The sound of metal scraping along the floor, followed by dragging furniture, made Anatoly and Nina tense even more.

Their eyes followed the sound of rushed footsteps retreating into the hall before they darted back to a foot tapping directly above. The tapping stopped, then came the sound of feet strolling through the kitchen, moving closer to the pantry and the hidden door. Nina and Anatoly's hearts started to beat in unison… faster. Their adrenaline-filled bodies began to ooze another layer of sticky sweat on top of other, older layers. They stank, but neither of them cared. Neither of them could smell anything anymore. Soon they would be discovered, and then…

Then the quiet morning air was filled with a rapid burst of crackling machine-gun fire. It seemed to be coming from the back of the house. A heavy thud followed a brief silence. Several more footsteps raced across the floor to the hallway and stopped, maybe having come from the back garden.

Nina and Anatoly heard muffled shouts followed by more short bursts of fire. They sighed with relief as they recognized a thick eastern Russian accent. They heard frantic shouts and screams of anger and pain in German and Russian, followed by another burst of machine-gun fire. A few small explosions sounded, sending tremors throughout the house and still more gunfire.

The frontline had landed right on top of Nina's house.

Huddled beneath an obvious bloodbath, Nina and Anatoly gripped each other, too terrified to move and attract attention.

In less than a minute, the firefight ceased abruptly. All they could hear were Russian voices and many more footsteps.

Had the Russians been victorious? Anatoly had no idea. They could be surrounded by Germans or the Germans surrounded by Russians; from the depths, it was impossible to tell. What he did know was that, regardless of who had cornered or conquered whom, it was far safer down here than up there.

CHAPTER 23

Daniel chewed on Mayer's words as he devoured a ham and egg sandwich, washed down with a steaming mug of coffee, courtesy of the Adjutant. There had been something about the old man's demeanor that had made Daniel wonder. Clearly, he was a career soldier who had devoted himself to winning whatever war his country was fighting at the time. But Daniel couldn't be sure if the General had suspected him of being something other than a loyal Reich soldier. If he did, he had shown a remarkable unwillingness to obey the very leader who had deposited him in Stalingrad in the first place. Maybe the answer lay somewhere in the middle: an old-school warhorse who played everything by the military code-of-conduct handbook.

Daniel shrugged and started to examine a small map given to him by the Adjutant, which pinpointed the last known location of the SS squad: slap bang on top of the frontline. As if that wasn't bad enough, he had been informed that only five remained alive of the original eighteen who had been sent into the city to find the Soviet physicist. A measure of the squad's desire to complete their objective was that the thirteen dead hadn't been sent back for burial but left where they had fallen.

Daniel derived both good and bad news from this. Good, in that the Germans still hadn't discovered the whereabouts of Yermakov and were desperate to continue their search, but bad in that the high casualty rate showed he would be moving into a more perilous section of the city. Memories of what he'd seen at the facility flooded painfully back. Vivid images of scores of young corpses clouded his mind. It made him consider the possibility that he might not make it out of the city alive. He tried to ignore the danger, but it gnawed at him like some flesh-eating fungus.

Adequately fed and, with new papers stashed safely away, he looked into the sky. Mayer was right; the sun had disappeared, leaving the city in shadows. He set about finding a place to shelter for the night.

*

The following morning, with no further update on the location of the Waffen SS unit, he departed Battalion HQ and continued northeast into the Stalingrad suburbs.

Over the next two miles, he identified himself to any interested parties by lifting his coat collar and revealing an SS insignia – another parting gift from Mayer's Adjutant. Daniel despised having the identification on his person, but it allowed him to move unrestricted past several troop formations that were inching their way forward to new offensive positions.

The Luftwaffe, it seemed, controlled the skies and, along with coordinated artillery strikes, continually pounded the city ahead of him. Swells of smoke filled the air while vast dust blankets hampered visibility on the ground. Unusually, Daniel couldn't hear any machine-gun fire. Nobody seemed to be firing at the advancing troops. It was almost as though the Russian infantry had deserted its post, leaving the Wehrmacht to pick its way unhindered through the city's ghostly, skeletal remains.

However, years of war experience had taught the Germans a thing or two about city fighting. He noticed all the men had begun to crouch lower, move slower, and generally doing much less than he expected of fighting men. With each step he took, more and more soldiers disappeared from view, some into buildings, others into foxholes and trenches, until he felt alone. He decided to adopt the same protective attitude. Crouching low, he slid silently into a bomb crater and took out his canteen and map.

He sipped some water and examined the position of the Waffen SS squad, but it wasn't much use to him without knowing where he was. Thanks to the damage caused by Richthofen's 4th Air Fleet, which was almost impossible to determine – the 'Red Barron's' fourth cousin's planes had destroyed so much of the city as to render most maps obsolete.

But Daniel knew the location of Battalion HQ and, using his compass, had a rough idea of how far he had to go to catch up with them. If his calculations were accurate, the squad was pinned down a couple of hundred yards north of his position.

The artillery bombardment stopped, and everything became very quiet. Daniel strained his ears for signs of movement, but there was nothing besides the sound of a falling wall. He waited a few minutes before popping his head out of the crater and glancing in that general direction. It looked safe enough. He sank back into the crater, folded the map, and slipped it into a pocket. He raised his canteen to his lips to take a last slurp before setting off when it pinged out of his hand.

'Shit!'

He slammed himself back against the crater wall, pressing his spine into the dirt, not daring to move. He flexed his hand and grimaced. The shock of the bullet ripping the canteen from his grasp had felt as if he had stuck his finger in an electric socket. The synapses in Daniel's brain were lit up brighter than a Christmas tree as he evaluated his options.

Moving to a new location was a definite no-no. If they were aiming for and could hit his canteen, he would be easily picked off before he managed to get his arse off the damp ground. On the other hand, staying put was equally dangerous. He had no idea where the sniper was, and he knew it was possible for the shooter to relocate and try to finish him off under the cover of the dusty haze.

He was a sitting duck.

Worse again, he didn't even know if it was a German or a Russian who'd fired at him. Dressed in this garb, a German could easily be forgiven for shooting somebody who looked like the enemy. Then, out of the blue, a voice called out.

'Comrade, why you have not come to our side? We have food, water, a place to sleep.'

Something wasn't right. The language may have been barely Russian, but the accent was unmistakably German.

'Comrade, I know you are alive. Surrender. We take good care of you.'

Daniel didn't reply.

'They shoot you for deserting if you go back,' the voice said a second later.

Daniel wasn't sure if getting him to show himself was a trick, but he couldn't stay put either. It might even be a diversion, with somebody else circling for a better shot. He decided to take a chance.

'How do I know you won't kill me?' he replied in flawless German.

Silence.

Daniel guessed that the sniper must be a Kraut and a confused one at that. Eventually, the voice called back in German.

'Where are you from?'

'Danzig,' Daniel replied. He stifled a sigh of relief, pleased that he'd guessed who was shooting at him but scared by the knowledge that the Germans had him pinned down. Just as he suspected, they were shooting at anything that wasn't wearing a grey uniform.

'Prove it.'

Daniel thought for a moment before replying.

'In the battle for my city, I helped our warship *Schleswig-Holstein* blow the *Westerplatte* defenders to bits. My involvement is well-documented in Berlin.'

Another moment of silence followed.

'Come out and move slowly to your left. Keep your head down. The place is crawling with Ruskies.'

It was a moment of truth. He could either trust them or not. In the end, it was an easy decision to make.

He raised his hand to the top of the crater and gradually pulled himself into view, waiting for a bullet to hit. Once his eyes were above ground level, he scanned the direction he was heading and all the ruins around him.

It was a good bet that if the Germans were in hiding, it was for a damn good reason. He crept up onto his belly and, inch by inch, slid along the ground, brushing aside bits of broken brick, metal fragments, and clumps of congealed dirt.

It took him more than ten minutes to crawl less than a hundred yards, his body flexing to the contours of the undulating ground. Where he could, he used the debris as protection against a possible pot-shot from the Russians, who he was sure were hidden amongst the ripped-up city walls.

Twice he strayed from the path, chiefly because he still couldn't see the German position, but the voice called out to correct him each time. Then, as if he'd pressed a secret button, a large piece of roofing that had been resting against some brickwork slid silently to one side, revealing a small entrance under some rubble. He moved toward it and slithered in; the roof pulled into position behind him.

Once inside, he assumed a crouched position because the height of the hovel didn't allow for standing. He was greeted by five blackened but severe-looking faces, three of whom pointed their MP40 machine pistols straight at him. A fourth man held an MG42 machine gun across his lap, while a fifth was a couple of yards off lying on his belly with one eye peering through the telescopic sight of a Mauser 98k rifle. He swept a slow arc through a tiny hole in the wall in front of him.

My would-be killer.

Daniel slowly moved his hand to his coat collar, revealing his SS insignia. The three men aiming at him didn't relax the grips on their weapons. Instinctively he knew this was the group for which he'd been searching. A glance at their uniforms verified it. On each soldier's cuff was a circular band with the barely legible words, *'Das Reich'*.

'Who are you?' One man asked. He was everything Daniel believed a stereotypical Aryan soldier to be: blonde crew-cut hair, sparkling light-blue eyes, a square, chiseled face, and a tiny scar running above his left cheekbone.

Daniel tried to disguise the contempt and hatred he felt, hoping it didn't show.

He recognized the man's insignia as that of 2nd Lieutenant and so trotted out the same lie he'd used back at Battalion HQ, adding that he'd been sent because their Russian wasn't up to scratch.

Once finished, he noticed that the men had begun to lower their weapons. He dusted the dirt off his clothes.

'We'll have to check out your story with HQ,' the Lieutenant said. He motioned to another man who started to pick up a radio.

'I wouldn't do that,' Daniel said hurriedly. He didn't know which HQ they were talking about or who they would contact.

'I just came from Battalion. Mayer told me to order you not to break radio silence.' He tried to sound like he and the Lieutenant General were old buddies.

The Lieutenant was about to say something, but Daniel had a flash of inspiration.

'Why do you think you're pinned down? Russians have been monitoring your transmissions ever since you arrived.'

The Lieutenant stared at Daniel as if deciding whether to believe him or not. Then he said, 'Mayer likes regular updates.'

'He prefers his men alive,' Daniel fired back. 'And you've lost thirteen already. I guess the rest of you don't want to add to that.'

Daniel leaned forward, his stare burrowing into the Lieutenant's face. Time to see who had the biggest balls.

'Okay, we'll .'

The sound of a shot made both men instantly recoil. They looked across at the sniper.

'Why didn't you warn us?' The Lieutenant's chiseled features were grizzled with fury.

'Had to get the shot away,' he replied, a wry smile drawn across his face. 'We can move out now,' he added.

The Lieutenant regained his composure and said. 'We've been stuck here all night while some bloody Russian sniper played games with us. Killed three of us in the last few hours, including our 1st Lieutenant.'

'Puts you in charge,' Daniel said.

He shook his head. 'You're the ranking officer.'

'I'm not taking over, just helping you get the job done. You get to keep what's left of your squad,' Daniel said, looking around. 'But like your sergeant said, let's get out of here while we can.'

They all turned to the sniper, who had resumed his systematic surveillance of the cityscape. After a few seconds, he nodded, and the squad, with Daniel in tow, evacuated their hiding place.

'How do you know where to search?' Daniel asked the Lieutenant once they were out in the open.

'We scanned Russian radio transmissions for a few days before entering the city. This morning we came across an interesting conversation which we've been monitoring ever since.' The Lieutenant's voice was barely a whisper.

He must have seen the confusion on Daniel's face because he chose to elaborate.

'It appears the Russians have lost their star pupil and dispatched a search party of their own. They've been meticulous in their search but haven't turned up anything.'

'How do you know where they are?'

'They've been sending back detailed information about where they've been and where they're going. We've pieced the information together. They've gone back into the city. Seems like their leader has to report their progress before they head back out again.'

Daniel nodded, quite amazed at the Russian stupidity.

'What's the plan?'

The Lieutenant grinned smugly. 'We move deeper into the city, and once they come back out, we let them do the donkey work, get close to them without being seen. As soon as they find what we all want, we move in and take him off them.'

Daniel marveled at the simplicity.

'And the beauty of it all is every time they radio back, they give their own soldiers' positions away, so we should know what to expect and avoid as we get closer.'

'And they're not scrambling the communication?'

'Listen, there's so much unscrambled radio chatter going on. It's a miracle we stumbled across this one. I suppose the Russians thought it'd be a million to one shot we'd hear them, but then they don't know that we're here is to snatch the poor bastard from under their noses.'

Daniel was dumbfounded. Apart from their stupidity, he couldn't believe the Russians had been so profligate with their information, but it didn't matter as it'd hopefully make his mission that little bit easier.

As the six moved slowly through the suburbs, the sounds of battle intensified all around them. Nebelwerfer rocket launchers fired salvo after salvo from their rear, only to be echoed by Katyusha rocket launchers to their fore. Sporadic machine-gun fire broke out so often that Daniel soon grew used to it.

After an hour of steadily tramping through the remains of house-lined streets, he could easily distinguish whether German, Russian, or a combination of weapons were firing. Instinctively, he also knew if he was the target. Whenever the gunfire seemed too close, the Lieutenant ordered the squad to take cover until it died down; they didn't seem that interested in getting involved in a fight, and who could blame them.

Daniel glanced up intermittently and saw, through the haze, more squadrons of Stuka bombers glide across the sky unopposed, their sirens whirring in high-pitched screeches. He knew he would be terrified should he be the focus of their attack but also knew he was safe from the aerial assault. As they made their way through the ruins, they stepped across several large Swastika flags facing skyward in some clearings. The Lieutenant told him that because of the close-quarter ground fighting, the Wehrmacht had used them so the Luftwaffe could identify their infantry positions, thereby concentrating on bombing the Russian support infrastructure behind the frontline. Neat. At least everybody knew where they stood.

It wasn't long before it began to grow dark. Huge flames silhouetted the ruins of the destroyed buildings, and the random movement of the grotesque shadows played tricks with their minds, which slowed their advance even more.

When the terrain allowed, Daniel could see the giant Mamayev Kurgan hill, which dominated the center of Stalingrad away to the north. It was taking a ridiculously heavy pounding from both sides. Massive explosions and tracer rounds from machine-gun fire along the hill's slopes were visible. It was apparent to even the most novice strategists that taking 'Hill 102', as it had been designated, was a vital objective; it offered complete control over the entire city. He counted himself lucky they weren't headed in that direction, not for the moment, anyway.

With darkness intensifying and the squad getting increasingly jumpy, the Lieutenant made a hand gesture, and they moved into a building to hunker down for the night.

Daniel looked around for a comfortable place to rest. It wasn't strictly 'indoors', but it was off the street. He scanned the area for possible escape routes and sat propped against a wall with exits a few yards on either side of him. If they were to be jumped in the middle of the night, then he would make damned sure he didn't become another '*Das Reich*' casualty.

CHAPTER 24

Browne carefully studied the man sitting before him. He had never known him to deliver anything but a truthful message, so why should he doubt him now?

'He hasn't made contact for more than twenty-four hours?'

Christopher nodded.

'Most unlike him, even given the environment where he finds himself.' Browne thought for a moment. 'You'll let me know as soon as he surfaces?'

'Of course. We both know that losing him would put our espionage program back decades.'

'And contingencies?'

'I've already started planning.'

'Somebody in the Kremlin?'

Christopher shook his head and smiled. 'You don't need to know, Bronson.' He flashed a wink.

'Fine.' Browne shuffled some loose papers and felt Christopher's eyes crawling over him. Christopher struggled to his feet and rubbed his knee.

'Still giving you trouble?' Browne asked.

Christopher nodded grimly.

'I thought the pain should've lessened in the warmth?'

'As did I. Maybe I should move to a drier climate.' Christopher grinned.

'I'm sure there's some duty we can get you to perform for Monty.'

'Hah. I said drier. I didn't mean hell on earth.' Christopher laughed.

Of all of Browne's close confidantes, Christopher was the only one who expressed his opinions openly and directly to his boss's face. Like Colonel

Cumming and Ms. Kendrick, he had earned the older man's ear through years of devoted loyalty and servitude.

Like Browne, Christopher had been in His Majesty's service during and since The Great War. It had been a stray German bullet and ensuing arthritis that visited him whenever the weather took a turn that served as a permanent reminder of his previous uniformed years.

'What's up with you these days?' Christopher said. He had noticed an apparent lack of motivation in his superior.

Browne sighed and stared absently at the fireplace for several moments.

'I feel lost,' he said finally.

'About sending another man on what probably amounts to little more than a suicide mission?'

'No, it's not that,' Browne shook his head. 'It's the whole bloody mess. Is this what we've resorted to? Sending a child halfway around the world to save the lot of us?'

Anguish washed across his face, rooted in his hunched shoulders, locked away in his clenched fists.

'It would've been much easier had the Russians moved Yermakov before the Germans got within striking distance.' Browne tried to sound as though he was feeling anything other than regret, but it was difficult. 'But they didn't. Too damn stubborn. They never thought Hitler's hand would reach so far. Now we're all in a jam.'

Furrows deep enough to plant potatoes lined his forehead. He stared vacantly at his friend.

'Maybe I should call the whole thing off, see what happens over there?' It was a half-question, spoken softly. 'Even if the Germans do get him, who's to say he'll work for them? Maybe they'll just shoot him and save us the bother. Or maybe we can send Daniel to Berlin, or wherever the hell they plan to create their bomb and put an end to it all there?'

'Private Miller.' Christopher pointed out.

'Sorry?' Browne looked distracted.

'We always refer to the men by rank.'

'What did I say?' Browne's voice was steeped in wistfulness.

'You called him by his first name.'

'Maybe we should do that more often.' Browne's voice grew louder as he emerged from his melancholy. 'Surely they deserve at least that?'

Christopher shook his head. 'No, Bronson, they don't. We wouldn't get the job done if we went down that road. We maintain our distance. It's always been that way, probably always will be too.'

Browne closed his eyes, knowing Christopher was correct. 'It doesn't make it any easier,' he said quietly.

'That's why we do the job,' Christopher said. 'That's why we've been *asked* to do the job. We don't get personally involved. We wouldn't be able to reason if we did. Anyway, Miller has already dropped. It's too late to call it off.'

He turned towards the door and said, 'A pity it had to turn out this way. Tom has given absolutely everything for this country, and it's not even his.'

'I beg to differ,' Browne said without looking up.

Christopher smiled. 'You'd do well not to argue the point.'

Browne agreed but would never have said so. The pair had had many heated disagreements without a discernible victor. They studied each other for several moments. Browne noted the concerned look developing on his friend's face and brushed it off with a flick of his hand.

'Go on. Clear out. Can't you see I'm busy?'

'As am I.'

Christopher bowed his head. He opened the door and disappeared outside, leaving Browne to contemplate the decision of sending another Miller off to war.

Once he'd closed the door behind him, Christopher was surprised to see another gentleman waiting in Browne's outer office. He spied Ms. Kendrick glancing worriedly over the rim of her glasses between bursts of staccato typing.

'Haven't seen you in some time,' Christopher said, smiling. He extended his hand towards the man he had known for more than twenty years.

The other man neither stood nor accepted the act of friendship.

Christopher's face darkened. 'I understand how you must feel.'

'You've no idea how I feel.' The man's voice was unwavering.

Christopher stood motionless for a few seconds before turning and hobbling to the door. 'Maybe we can discuss this later?' He didn't turn around.

The other man didn't reply.

'Mr. Browne will see you now,' Ms. Kendrick said, interrupting the awkwardness that had landed in her office.

As Christopher departed, the man stood and walked calmly to Browne's door, pausing before marching in.

Ms. Kendrick closed her eyes and breathed a sigh. She lifted her telephone, dialed an extension, and whispered into the receiver.

Browne stood at the window, sipping an afternoon tea. Staring across London as he pondered the fate of the Allied world had become his new pastime. The panorama had changed since the beginning of the Blitz. Some magnificent buildings were mere shells of their former splendor, and many more were damaged beyond repair. But the bombings had become less frequent as Hitler's rage had been vented eastwards.

With the RAF having won the battle in the skies over Britain, the invasion of England had become indefinitely postponed. How thankful Browne was that Hitler had become seemingly bored with his old foe and decided to go and pick a fight with the Red Army. He wondered if Hitler might regret choosing to open a new front.

He heard the door close behind him and footsteps draw closer. He drew a sharp breath. The sound of squeaking leather allowed him to exhale and relax.

'I was wondering when you would come for a friendly visit,' he said.

'I wouldn't call this friendly.'

Browne turned and stared at a man he'd known since The Great War. He set his cup down and slipped a cigar from a case on the desk.

'You haven't changed a bit,' the man said.

'My smoking?'

'Your arrogance.'

'Surely you would allow a condemned man a last cigar?'

'I'm not here to harm you,' the man said, surveying the office. It looked more like a private library.

'You're here to berate me?'

'The thought had crossed my mind.'

'Then what?'

The man studied Browne carefully before saying. 'To get answers.'

Browne rubbed his mustache thoughtfully. 'We face a threat greater than any we've ever faced before. Standing idly by and hoping that we're dealt a winning hand would be not only foolhardy but also reckless.'

'Don't you think your plan is foolhardy?' The man's voice remained impassive.

'Initially, yes. But the more I've thought about it, the more I believe it will succeed. It is, after all, the only way we can ultimately achieve victory.'

'Agreed.'

Although he didn't show it, Browne was taken aback by the man's concurrence. He moved away and rested an elbow on the mantelpiece, half-puffing, half-chewing on the cigar. The man's eyes followed him.

'If there were any other way, we would have taken it,' Browne conceded.

'We both know there wasn't.'

'So, you want to know why we're sending *him*?'

The man nodded.

'He was the best fit for the mission.'

'He was the last one standing.' The man's eyes pierced icy daggers into the side of Browne's skull.

Browne exhaled a vast plume of smoke and tapped some ash into the fireplace. The man looked away and stared out of the window. Browne glanced across at him.

'I don't know why you came here,' he said.

'I had to know it was the only way. Had to see it in your eyes, had to believe this wasn't some feckin' construct of your imagination.'

'And have you?'

The man's eyes dropped. 'I have what I came for,' he said at length.

He stood and walked to the door. Grasping the handle, he paused. 'Amazing that it came to this.'

'Quite unbelievable,' Browne said, hoping he wasn't about to have a repetition of the conversation he had had only minutes ago.

'That all the years of tuition should be wasted by this feckin' war. Those boys were never supposed to be on the frontline, never supposed to be infantrymen. Work at the 'Office'. Intelligence gathering, that's what you said. That's what we agreed. That's what you promised me.'

'We always knew this to be a possibility. That's why it was done. And you were in the best position to make this element of the plan a reality.'

The man shot a fierce look at Browne and exploded.

'But, not both. That was never part of the agreement. You were never to take both my boys.'

'It is unfortunate, but needs must.' Browne's voice held a tinge of sadness.

The two men stared at each other for several tense seconds before Tom opened the door.

'Why didn't you return to Dublin after the war?' Browne asked.

Tom stopped and stared at the floor. 'There's nothin' there for me.'

'But you've family.'

'I don't think I'd be welcome. You know how things got while we were fightin' the Boche. I don't know if they'd think I was a traitor for havin' fought for the enemy.'

'The enemy?'

'We were fightin' for our independence.'

'But the enemy of our enemy is.'

'Our friend?' Tom laughed. 'Maybe… Anyway, what's done is done. Maybe I'll go back once this war is over. Catherine might like that.'

He sighed and left.

Browne returned to his window to recast a watchful eye upon his domain, but he was troubled. Tom's unexpected visit made him think of the lies, deceptions, and propaganda spilling from the War Office. So many secrets, so many untruths disseminated as fact, an enormous interwoven web of intrigue and deceit, but it was for the greater good. In his world, the end most definitely justified the means; he had to believe that.

Operation Bedlam was well underway in France and was already bearing a fruitful crop of information. Having overcome some initial problems, the resistance movement now worked like a finely tuned engine. Sure, mistakes were made by some on the ground, but that was understandable – it was a high-pressure environment. The Germans, too, had begun to counter the Allied insurgency by shooting all conspirators. Yet, despite that, ranks within the resistance had swelled, which all bode well for the time when the Allies would return to mainland Europe and push the German war machine back across the Rhine.

But that couldn't be done without the hard work and energy of those British intelligence agents stranded after the Dunkirk disaster. Their dedication and devotion to duty had surprised even him. They had known the risks, and they had known the consequences should the enemy snare them.

Not one had been coerced.

Browne felt a swelling sense of pride in England's sons yet, at the same time, understood the pain and suffering bestowed upon the families of the men who had stayed behind.

Once more, his thoughts were of Tom.

CHAPTER 25

IT WAS CLOSE TO MIDNIGHT, and the temperature across the Dales had dropped, forcing even the hardiest of souls to throw an extra log on their fire, unusual for mid-autumn. It was no different at the Miller household.

Tom and Catherine sat apart on the sofa, staring into the dying embers within their fireplace. Their flourishing marriage of twenty years, filled with joy, hope, and expectation for their sons, had been extinguished when news of Alex's death reached them a little more than two years ago.

Tom remembered the day.

He had been listening to a BBC Radio broadcast for news on the war, followed by the Prime Minister's speech. Churchill's stirring words echoed in Tom's mind long after he had switched off the radio. A speech written and delivered to produce an adrenaline rush, increase the pulse rate, and, most importantly, give the people hope. After the obliteration of the BEF and its subsequent evacuation from Dunkirk, maintaining morale was paramount.

'*Fight them on the beaches… never surrender*'.

Tom smiled.

That was the fighting spirit he remembered from The Great War. Maybe some of that had been lost as a generation of men had also been stolen more than two decades before.

Despite every mortal's frailties, the truly great leaders exhibited many similar characteristics, but charisma and passion would get Britain through the tough times ahead. And Churchill had both in abundance. It exuded from his pores, forming around him like an effervescent and unflinching aura.

A sharp knock at the hall door dissipated the evoked emotions.

Two men, clothed in full dress uniforms, stood before him, their somber looks betraying the news they had come to deliver. Tom could tell this wasn't the only household they had visited that day. He hadn't heard their words but stared into each pair of eyes, praying they'd made a mistake.

After they left, he went absently to the kitchen and placed a near-empty kettle on the stove's naked flame. After watching it gurgle and juggle uncontrollably for a moment, he lifted it away and placed it on the countertop. He walked down the hall and out the front door.

He wasn't sure where he was going. His mind was dull and vacant. All around him was a blur. The emotions stirred a few minutes ago had dissipated into the ether like the last firework, vanishing from a night sky.

Only emptiness remained.

He was oblivious to old Mrs. Simmons's greeting; she looked queerly at him when he didn't acknowledge her. Shuffling off with hands in his pockets, he turned left at the bottom of the hill.

The early June wind was warm and carried a hint of humidity, but lethargy and a hollow numbness acted in concert as a protective barrier against the mild elements.

He had been walking for over half an hour when he found himself at the village football ground. The unlocked gates had been freshly painted in preparation for a new season, yet two months away. Tom pushed through and strolled around to the tiny main stand. When full, it could hold up to three hundred people – there was no one around today. He walked up to the fourth step and sat where he usually stood. He drew his knees up to his chest and looked across the pitch that had been reseeded at the end of the regular season several weeks ago, but there had been nothing regular about it. Along with every other local club, this had lost many players to the BEF, resulting in a lackluster league of little importance and indifferent competition.

His sorrow was amplified as his eyes followed a slight wind sliding diagonally across the uncut grass. Finally, he buried his head in his hands and, tearless, shook uncontrollably. He let out a rib-breaking scream before his diaphragm eventually contracted, forcing the air to gush back into the vacuum within his chest. Falling backward onto the stone steps, he closed his eyes and wished he could have exchanged places with his firstborn.

He wasn't sure how long he had been there, but the sun had dipped below the treetops to his right. He figured it was about time to get off home and see the rest of the family.

Catherine.

So consumed had he been with his grief that he hadn't thought about her, not even for a moment. A new and disheartening emotion overcame him.

Regret.

She had never wanted Alex to join up and, in true Catherine-esque style, had made her view known only once. He supposed it was especially tough for a mother to lose a son, but Alex was his son, too. He let out a heavy sigh and struggled to his feet. Retracing his steps along the main street and up the hill toward his home, his mind replayed the only way he could think of to pass on the tragic news.

He felt sick.

'Been down the pub?' Catherine called from the kitchen as soon as he had stepped inside. She poked her head around the doorway and smiled at her husband. Tom's head hung limply; his gait bedraggled.

'Tom?'

He didn't reply. He reached out when he got closer, drew her to him, and held her tight.

After what seemed like an age, Tom stepped back and gazed into her moistening eyes. She closed them softly in a gesture of knowing and turned away. He took a step toward her, but she withdrew. He knew she wouldn't let him see her cry. He started to mouth something, but no words came out. He turned and walked back down the hall and disappeared into the living room.

'What did you do in the war?' Catherine asked, ripping him back to the present.

He slid her a sidelong glance, still partially consumed in his fading memories. He shook himself and stood to toss another log on the dying fire. He looked at the sparks rise against the backdrop of a blackened hearth before they disappeared up the chimney and wondered why, after all these years, she was asking about now. Did she want to know what Alex had been through and what Daniel was facing? Maybe she'd seen the pain of the experience etched on his face, a permanent reminder of what he'd seen, and worse, done. Like almost all who had returned from the European battlefields, he'd kept his silence. Innocent boys had returned as broken men, unwilling to speak of the horror they had witnessed. Over the years, he'd struggled to accept the part he'd played, as deep-rooted and persistent emotions of shame and guilt lay beyond his consciousness. He had tried to forget the slaughter of thousands of his countrymen, Irishmen, at the hands of the Boche.

Maybe now, it was time to break that silence.

'Why did you join up?' She stared across at him.

He rubbed his jaw.

'I don't like to talk about it.' His voice was barely a whisper.

'That's okay,' she said, returning her gaze to the hearth. 'I shouldn't have asked.'

Tom leaned across and patted her hand. 'I said I didn't like to talk about it, not that I wouldn't.' He caught her understanding glance and forced a smile.

'I joined the Royal Dublin Fusiliers in 1914 and learned the ways of soldierin'.' He paused. 'Soldierin' the British way that is.'

His mind wandered for a second but returned quickly.

'Ireland was still under British rule back then; lots of us had joined the British Army. We were young, full a piss an' vinegar….'

She frowned.

'Sorry.' He grinned boyishly. 'Anyway, it was a strange time. We'd been fightin' you English for hundreds of years and were startin' to make some real headway into self-governance when the whole European thing started up. After Ferdinand was shot, one thing led to another, one treaty followed another, and within a few months, the entire continent was at war.'

'All because of one man.' She shook her head.

'Yeah. Silly really, lookin' back now.'

He reflected for a moment before continuing.

'I joined up with some friends. We craved adventure, a change from the mundane. We wanted to prove we were responsible men. Of course, we were invincible.' He glanced across at her. 'Nothin' was gonna stop us winnin' the war. We'd been told we'd be out there for only a few months, but two years later, we found ourselves still in the trenches, with no more than a few hundred yards of mud between the enemy and us.'

He purposely left out the part about the dying men who had been left screaming between the rows of barbed wire; she didn't need to know that part.

A melancholic smile slipped across his face.

'In some places, the front lines were so damn close we could hear the water boilin' on their fires… smell their food cookin.''

Catherine half-laughed.

'My fightin' ended in 1916, on the Somme. Fired all we had at the Boche for days. Salvo after salvo went over. The order was given, whistles blown, and we went over the top….'

He caught himself and swallowed hard, fighting back a tear.

She squeezed his hand.

He whispered. 'We'd made it just over halfway when we were spotted. The German machine-gun nests were easy to make out 'cos of their muzzle flares. They opened up, one after the other across the whole line. Lads all around me cried out and fell. Some slowed their attack… thought about turnin' back, but they shouldn't 'ave… they were cut down. Out of a whole battalion, only three of us made it to the other side. We stood on top of the trench and fired at anythin' that moved. To be honest, we were hysterical and just shot blindly. Well, I did, anyway.'

He glanced across at Catherine. Her eyes were wide, her mouth slightly open.

'The next thing I remember was wakin' up next to one of the other men who had made it with me. We were propped up against a trench wall, our hands and feet tied. The third lad lay at our feet. He… didn't have much of a face left.' He fell silent.

'What happened then?'

'A few officers questioned us.' He smiled. 'Their English was quite good.'

Then the smile wore away and was replaced by a pained expression of remembrance. 'They beat us, gave us a good hidin'. They wanted information. After a while, I think they realized we didn't know anythin', but they kept hammerin' away anyway, retribution for all the shells we'd fired at them before, maybe.'

Catherine inched closer.

'Seein' as they weren't gettin' anywhere, they sent us to a POW camp. We were thrown in with other Irishmen but kept apart from the other prisoners. That lasted for a few months. After that, with the war still ragin' and news filterin' back that the only change at the front was the number of dead and wounded, restrictions were eased, and we started to mingle. Christ, we even mixed with the guards; I was on a first-name basis with some of them, too. Prisoners from all over Europe packed the camp.'

'Is that how you learned to speak all the languages?'

Tom nodded. Languages had always come easy to him, and he had no idea why. From an early age, he'd noticed that his sons possessed the same *gift*.

'You know, I never wanted any of this for them?' he said. 'I tried my best to keep them outta harm's way, educate them so they could take up a different service. I always hoped they wouldn't get stuck on a stinkin' frontline like I had. I never wanted either of them ta see what I had seen or do what I'd done.'

'But you had an agreement with Whitehall? They didn't honor it.'

'Ah, sure, it wasn't their fault,' Tom said. 'Our boys made up their own minds. I suppose I didn't allow for that. I thought I'd be able to control them.' A wry grin crossed his lips.

'And that's what they are, boys, not men.'

Tom didn't want to entertain that argument, so he didn't respond. The simple fact was that most infantrymen were boys, barely out of their teens, some still in them.

They sat quietly, each wrestling with their memories and emotions. Then Catherine leaned across and snuggled into him. A tear appeared at the corner of his eye and trickled slowly down his cheek. It had been the first time she had embraced him since the 4th of June 1940.

CHAPTER 26

DEEP BENEATH THE CITY, IN the basement of the NKVD headquarters, Evgeny slid a sweaty hand across his skull and stared at the dust scraped from his bald head. He wiped it on a trembling wall and caught his breath sharply at another explosion overhead. Even he, a veteran of 'The Great War', had never witnessed a pounding like it before, as the Germans peppered the length of the city. Over the past few days, they'd stepped up their onslaught, indicating an imminent and final crushing blow.

He sucked nervously on an exhausted cigarette butt and paced his relocated office. The floor beneath his feet shook, and he was doused with another shower of dust. He shivered; they were getting closer.

Panic started seeping into his body from the moment he went underground: he didn't like being down here. It might have been the drop in temperature or the nervous adrenaline surge caused by knowing that a lucky direct hit would trap him forever, but he knew it was neither.

It hadn't even been three whole days since his prized asset had been lost, and he'd no idea if Yermakov was dead, alive but lost somewhere in the city, or worse, captured by the Germans. Consequently, he had deliberately withheld the disappearance from Moscow, hoping he would be able to locate the boy and avoid any unpleasantries before he had to file an official report.

That hadn't happened.

He'd ordered a search party, led by Daryna, to the massive underground complex. She'd radioed back with bad news. Like Canute, the entrenched Red Army had been unable to hold back the Fascist tsunami that had devastated the area. Annoyingly, the facility, although deserted, had remained unharmed. Contrary to orders to blow the place once the attack had begun, everything was as Yermakov had designed and left it. Somebody would pay with their life for not following that particular order if they hadn't done so already.

He'd ordered Daryna back to the bunker, knowing it would give him time to consider his options. Politically he was done for if he couldn't find a way to deflect responsibility for the fiasco away from himself. He heard footsteps in the corridor and couldn't help a delicate smirk. The scapegoat approached – a lamb to the slaughter.

The door creaked open behind him. He shifted uneasily but didn't turn around. At his side, he touched a concealed handgun with his elbow; his 'Get Out of Jail Free' card, should the need arise.

'I haven't much time to deal with you,' Evgeny growled, immediately setting the tone.

He marched in front of her and, with his face no more than three inches away, glared into her eyes, remnants of the crooked cigarette grasped firmly between what remained of his rotting, yellow teeth.

Daryna didn't recoil, which only served to infuriate him.

He turned his head slightly to one side and spat the butt onto the ground, some drops of spit sticking to her cheek. It was a man's world, and she was an outsider in it. He would ensure he delivered that message with all the force his authority allowed.

'What have you been doing since he went missing?' He took a slow step backward, firmly keeping his eyes fixed on her. He could see her measure her breathing before replying. He smiled inwardly.

'Searching, sir.'

Evgeny started to pace back and forth, staring at the floor, periodically glancing angrily in her direction. He'd heard the same thing since he'd dispatched her two days ago. He stopped and slammed his fist on the wall with a ferocity that shook a large portrait of their beloved leader, tilting it to one side.

'You get one more chance to find him.' He paused for a moment, then started walking towards her again. 'Leave no stone unturned. I want him found alive or his head brought to me, do you understand?' His eyes blazed.

Although brief, it wasn't an idle threat; the message was clear. He was exhibiting a generosity that she would never display had their roles been reversed. That's why he trusted her to solve his most critical problems.

'Yes, sir.'

'Get moving…' His voice grated through his throat.

Daryna turned swiftly and was out the door before he had time to change his mind.

Barely drawing breath, she didn't stop until she exited the bunker several minutes later, the crackle of gunfire and exploding mortar shells surrounding her. She let out an enormous sigh, feeling it was safer out here than down there with him. She stopped briefly and searched the area for an ally, finding him standing next to a battery of anti-aircraft emplacements; their all-female crews were working hard, tripping over spent shell casings and restocking for future raids – the acrid smell of cordite bit the air.

'We've got a lot of work to do,' she said as she approached.

Igor Korolev glanced back, slightly annoyed.

'How much time?'

'I don't know.'

'We should get out of here.'

'And go where?'

'Anywhere they can't find us.'

Daryna shook her head.

'We're surrounded. Germans on one side, Russians on the other. We try crossing the Volga, and we'd be shot for desertion. The NKVD has secured all the ferry points.'

'You've security clearance. Use it.'

She smiled. 'Evgeny wouldn't be foolish enough not to inform the crossing guards to be on the lookout for us. He wants us to find Yermakov at all costs, or else.'

'Or else?'

She nodded. 'If I go down, you're coming with me. After all, you were the last to see the boy alive.'

'I told you, he was unconscious when I went to look for help. When I got back, he was gone.'

'Then, you better help me find him.'

Korolev put his head in his palms. 'I can't believe you talked me into this.'

'We've all got our part to play. Yours was to foster a relationship with our protégé…'

'And I did that.' His voice oozed incredulity.

'You were to make sure that nothing happened to him.' Her voice was calm. On another day, she would have shot him on the spot for his insubordination.

He didn't reply.

'We'll give ourselves a few days. If we can't find him, we'll reconsider our options,' she said, eventually.

'In a few days, the Germans will have taken the city, and we could be dead. We should cut our losses and run now.'

'If you don't do your best to help me find Anatoly, I'll shoot you myself. At times like these, there's no room for cowardice.'

'What about sanity?'

'You won't find that here this time of year, either,' she laughed.

Korolev's head swam. He had other plans, and they didn't include Daryna or the NKVD. Even though he despised both, he was here for a reason. And, he knew he would have to stay until the time came for him to move on to his next mission.

Unlike most, he embraced the thrill of battle to the point of euphoria. It was an elixir that helped satiate an animal craving that'd been part of the reason he'd taken on this mission. Maybe it was the testosterone that bubbled like a volcano, but he thrived on it. In some ways, part of him was delighted that Hitler had thrown his eyes eastwards. But even a fool knew when to run, and that time had long since passed. He only hoped his handlers in Whitehall knew that, too. Then again, he hadn't checked in with them in a few days; Lord only knew what they were thinking now.

They hurried past company after company of half-armed and fully-scared soldiers. Some looked at the pair in disbelief that a woman of such beauty was striding through the ruins of Stalin's City, seemingly oblivious to the raging battles around their position. Korolev glanced sidelong at her. He knew he'd have to be extremely careful. If she suspected even for a second that he wasn't in this as wholeheartedly as she was, she'd probably stick the barrel of a gun to his head.

They walked a couple more blocks without taking cover and entered a half-demolished factory building. With its main walls the only parts of the building still standing, they picked their way across a debris-filled floor with the agility of a pair of sure-footed, Ural mountain lions, their feet crunching the shattered glass that had fallen from the roof.

Korolev glanced up through the chasm left by several caved-in floors. Here, the sounds of war were muffled. All he could see was a smooth, grey, cloud-filled sky. An icy wind blew through the large bomb-made holes in the walls, making the place feel isolated and surreal.

They made their way to one corner and, pulling back a creaking metal door, stepped into a dark corridor. They didn't bother to light the way — they knew the path blindfolded.

After walking down a moderate decline for about twenty yards, they stopped at another door and knocked. They waited for a moment before entering a surprisingly well-lit room.

The five armed soldiers on the other side lowered their guns and resumed whatever conversation they'd been having. Daryna and Korolev moved past them and into an antechamber beyond.

It was a Spartan room that reeked of mold and dry rot. The air inside was damp, which made Korolev shiver. A trickle of water ran down one wall, pooling on the floor. Daryna strode towards the only piece of furniture: a wooden table away to one side. On it was a high-powered radio transmitter and a map of the city.

Korolev watched her intently as she unfolded the map. Automatically, he put his hand into his coat pocket, brushing against the handgun concealed there but moving to the small box nestled beside it. He fished for a cigarette and lit up before sloshing across to join her.

Her fingers traced a line on a map from the research facility to the Volga 'What's next?' Korolev asked.

She didn't look up. 'He's a smart kid. He'll be heading for a ferry crossing if he's still alive. I'll take the patrol out again, start searching the roads and buildings between where you were attacked and the river. You,' she glanced at him, 'can stay here and monitor communications between me, our troops, and the Germans. I want clockwork updates.'

Korolev nodded, realizing the opportunity for escape, should he need it, had just landed in his lap. He stared furiously at the map. The last thing he wanted to do was display anything other than complete devotion to the task at hand.

Without another word, Daryna swiveled and shot out of the cellar, leaving a small wake in the puddles behind her.

Korolev looked after her. He'd give it a few hours. Then he was gone.

CHAPTER 27

Anatoly paced the cellar, aware that Nina was following his every move. He stopped and turned towards her.

'What?'

Pulling a stained blanket tighter around her, she said nothing.

'If you're looking for me to do something, I can't.' He stared at her and sighed. It wasn't her fault. Moreover, he should be happy she had taken him in. He had survived this long down here. Maybe he could get through the rest of the war without having to return to the surface again.

He sloped across to her, plopped himself down, and threw his arm over her shoulder, holding her close.

'I don't think it'll be much longer. I'm sure our army will be victorious soon, and then we can get back to our normal lives.'

'Do you think so?'

He nodded. 'I hope so...'

'You've got a funny accent,' she said.

He glanced at her sideways. 'So have you.'

She giggled. 'Does everybody from Kyiv speak like you?'

He shook his head, then paused. 'I don't know. I've never thought about it.'

She scrunched up her nose. 'It's a long way from here, isn't it?'

'I suppose it is.'

The pair sat with their backs against the wall and stared at the concrete cellar floor, Anatoly's eyes moving to a wooden crate behind which a hole, only big enough for Nina's hand to squeeze through, was hidden. It was from there that the first few rats escaped in search of a fresh meal.

Why the vermin had searched down here for their next meal was beyond him, given the readily available buffet on the surface. Their scratching let Anatoly know when one had returned; there were none today.

'Why did you come here? To escape the Germans?'

'No.' He smiled, although he considered himself fortunate to have moved. Kyiv had fallen to the Reich last year. Had he stayed, he might have been killed.

'I came to continue my work, away from the Germans.'

'I could never do that.'

'What?'

'Just leave my family like that to work.'

He remained silent for a while before saying. 'I don't have a family anymore.'

Nina turned to face him, her face aghast.

'It's okay.' He pulled her close, cradling her head under his chin. He kissed the top of her head.

'What was it like when you were growing up?'

Anatoly tilted his head back and thought for a moment. 'There's not much to tell. I grew up on a farm on the outskirts of the city.'

'Had you got friends?' She gave him a gentle nudge.

He shook his head, his eyes vacant.

'Really? All alone on a farm? A lot of space out on the steppe.'

'I kept myself busy.'

'Doing what?'

'Normal stuff, experimentation… finding out new things.'

'I don't do that, so it doesn't sound all that 'normal' for a kid.'

'I played chess with my father whenever he wasn't working on the collective.'

'I don't know how to play chess.' She looked thoughtful. 'Was he any good?'

'He was okay.' He wrinkled his eyebrows, thinking back.

'We've been down here a few days. You've never talked about your parents before.'

'Never came up, I suppose.'

'Tell me about them.'

He drew a deep breath and exhaled slowly. 'My father worked the collective with other farmers, and my mother looked after the house.'

'Sounds nice?'

He shrugged. 'It was pleasant.'

'So, what happened to them?'

Anatoly's face clouded over. His muscles tightened.

She felt it.

'What's the matter?'

He looked away.

'Please tell me.'

Anatoly lay down. He curled his hands into fists, resting them on his forehead. 'I haven't seen them since I joined the university.'

'How long ago was that?'

'Nearly six years.'

She sat upright. 'You've been alone all that time?'

He forced a smile.

The two remained quiet until Nina broke the silence. 'Where did they go?'

He shook his head. His eyes moistened, and a tear formed. Eventually, he answered.

'I came back from school one day, near the end of the term, and they weren't around. I looked for them all over, knocked at neighboring homes, and tried contacting their friends, but nobody knew anything. Nobody knew where they were.'

'Just disappeared?'

He nodded almost imperceptibly. 'I'd heard stories about how sometimes people were taken away by the government for questioning, so I figured that's what had happened.'

Similar stories had trickled throughout the state. The notorious NKVD, or People's Commissariat for Internal Affairs, had carte blanche when it came to abductions.

'I contacted some local government representatives. They knew nothing, or at least they were unwilling to tell me what they did know. But people don't just disappear.'

'What do you think happened?'

'I'm sure the NKVD was behind it. My mother told me what she and father did during the 1917 revolutions. The government tried to control the people, and what had begun innocently as patriotism soon turned into prolonged periods of detention and inquisition. Stories of torture and summary executions were rife, but I find all of it hard to believe. What government would do that to its population?'

He glanced across at her. His anger was evident, his voice barely a whisper.

'Others have spoken of 'detainees', being sent away to the east for 're-habilitation', whatever the hell that means. But nobody knows for sure because nobody has ever returned. I suppose deep down, my parents knew their day would come.'

A solitary tear melted along his cheek. He rubbed it away.

Nina sat up and laid a comforting hand on his arm.

'I'm sorry I shouldn't have asked.'

After a while, he sat up and wiped his eyes. 'Alright, we might be here for a while longer, so I'm going to teach you how to play chess.'

'I don't think we have a board and pieces.'

Anatoly's eyes sparkled for the first time since they'd gone underground.

'That's okay. We're going to make them.'

CHAPTER 28

A FILTHY, DANK NIGHT MELTED into an eerie, soupy morning as Daniel stirred. Despite his protestations, he hadn't completed a stint on watch, but that still hadn't allowed him an uninterrupted slumber. It seemed the darkness hadn't dulled the sounds of battle.

Since they settled down the previous evening, he'd lost count of the number of times he'd woken up, his eyes darting around the damp building every time he'd been disturbed. The sounds of battle had died away as though the two armies had called a breakfast truce before they started ripping at each other's throats once they'd been fed.

He struggled to his hands and knees and crawled over to the Lieutenant, who was tearing up some stale bread. He handed a piece to Daniel.

'Stiff?'

Daniel nodded as he chewed on the meager portion. He slipped his canteen from beneath his coat.

'Got cold during the night, dropped below freezing.' The Lieutenant pointed to the thin film of frost on Daniel's coat.

Daniel groaned. That's all he needed. An early Russian winter to further hamper his mission, and it was still only September. He chewed some more and rubbed his chin. He hadn't shaved since Iraq, partly because he hadn't had the opportunity, mostly because he couldn't be bothered. Besides, the grizzled look allowed him to blend in better.

'All quiet last night?'

'Apart from our artillery.' The Lieutenant smirked.

Daniel brushed some water droplets off his coat and glanced at the rest of the squad.

'Why do you think you were selected for this mission? Aren't you a Panzer outfit?'

'Because we're the best unit to get the job done,' the Lieutenant said without hesitation. He didn't smirk this time.

Daniel didn't respond. He had taken an instant dislike to the Lieutenant the moment they had met. The fact that the man had not sent his comrades' corpses back behind the frontline confirmed to Daniel that, underneath his rigid, unforgiving exterior lay the heart of a cold-blooded killer, capable of the worst murderous atrocities. The delight he took in his army spraying shells all over and destroying what was once a beautiful city only cemented Daniel's opinion. Even civilians caught in the crossfire didn't seem to matter to him. Daniel imagined it was a German just like him who had killed Alex, and so when the time came, it would be he who would take pleasure in exacting the revenge he craved.

Their attention was drawn by one of the other soldiers tapping softly on the brickwork. They turned as he beckoned them toward him. He had been keeping watch behind one of the bomb-blasted walls. Daniel and the Lieutenant crawled quietly to his position and peeked out.

At first, all they could see was a deserted street made up of the remnants of several pock-marked walls, but then they spied a group of men materializing out of the gloomy, grey haze. The Lieutenant tightened the grip on his MP40 as Daniel instinctively moved his hand towards his handgun.

A squad of six Red Army soldiers marched over the rough ground in a haphazard, undisciplined manner. They were led by a man who Daniel assumed to be their Commissar. He shoved another soldier roughly in front of him, slapping him across the back of the head whenever the prisoner slowed too much. They stopped in front of a bullet-riddled wall, which was covered in bloodstains dripping to the ground; it looked as though the wall itself was bleeding. The Commissar pushed the sobbing soldier against it, smacked him across the face, and screamed at him. The prisoner reluctantly started to undress.

Daniel glanced at the Lieutenant and wondered why he wasn't preparing his men to save one of their own.

After a minute and a few more solid punches and slaps, the prisoner stood half-naked in his underwear, hugging his torso, trying desperately to stave off the cold. By the time the Commissar had folded the uniform and tucked it under his arm, the other soldiers had lined up facing the prisoner. Each member of the firing squad checked their rifles as the Commissar walked off to one side. He barked another order, and the men raised their weapons unsteadily.

'Fire!' The officer called lazily before six unsynchronized, staccato shots rang out. He hadn't even bothered to say, 'Aim'.

The prisoner fell first to his knees and, with a muffled groan, toppled forward onto his head, crumpling into a distorted fetal ball.

The German sniper tapped his Lieutenant's shoulder and pointed at the Commissar, but he shook his head. Hitler's *Instructions on the Treatment of Political Commissars* directive would be disobeyed for the moment. The sniper grimaced at an opportunity lost to kill a Bolshevik.

On command, the Russian squad reformed and began a dogged shuffle back to wherever they'd come from as though what they'd just done was commonplace. The Commissar flashed a last look at the executed prisoner before taking up a position to their rear.

Once he was sure the Russians were out of eyesight and earshot, Daniel started to step out of the building. The Lieutenant grabbed hold of his coat and stared at him with a pair of piercing blue eyes.

'He may still be alive,' Daniel said with a strained whisper.

He didn't dwell on the Lieutenant's mystified look. He shook off the Lieutenant's grip and stepped gingerly out of his hiding place. He glanced up and down the street, checking the windows and holes in walls in the adjoining buildings for any signs of movement before crossing over.

Once by his side, Daniel hesitated before rolling the prisoner onto his back. Just as he had expected, the man's eyes were open, but he drew rapid, shallow breaths. Some blood trickled from the corner of his mouth.

Daniel glanced at the two punctures on the man's body. Neither was in an area that would cause him to die anytime soon. If he were to receive medical attention, the guy might live.

Daniel smiled. No wonder the Germans had advanced this far if the Russian aim was so poor. Two out of five had hit, and neither had been a kill shot.

The man started to get up, but Daniel held him back.

'Why did they shoot you?' he asked in German.

'Who are you?' the injured man replied in Russian.

Daniel's heart raced before it dawned on him. He should have recognized the brown Russian army uniform the man had taken off. Instead, he had assumed the Russians had caught a German and were exacting mortal reparations.

'It doesn't matter who I am,' Daniel snapped back in Russian, careful to keep his voice low. 'Why were you shot?'

The man tried to focus, but his eyes rolled around. 'Too much vodka….' He was beginning to slur his speech.

'You drank too much?'

The man nodded his head, letting out a groan.

'They were setting an example?'

Again, the man nodded. He tried to sit up, but Daniel continued to restrain him.

'How far is the frontline?'

The man stared at him before wiping the blood from his mouth. He didn't respond.

'I'm looking for somebody,' Daniel said, knowing the question he was about to ask was a long shot. 'A Ukrainian scientist. Can you help me?'

The man half-laughed and tried to push Daniel's hands away with a strength that belied his condition. He struggled to a seated position.

'I'm getting out of here,' the Russian said. He attempted to stand.

Daniel glanced across to where he knew the hidden German squad was watching his every move. He had a decision to make, and it had to be fast.

He slipped his hand into his pocket and took out his gun. The Russian saw what was coming and smacked it away before Daniel could get a shot off. Daniel stared at him for a moment before swinging his body behind the Russian and placing a chokehold around his neck.

At first, the man didn't struggle, but once he became aware of what was happening, he started thrashing his legs wildly, scraping at Daniel's arms and head. Daniel twisted his head away to avoid the Russian's clawing fingers.

It took less than a minute before Daniel was sure he had accomplished what the firing squad hadn't. He checked for a pulse; there was none. He slipped the man's lids over his swollen and bloodshot eyes, leaned over him, and offered a silent, penitent prayer. The man deserved at least that much.

Inside, Daniel felt empty; outside, he felt numb. Whatever about shooting a soldier at a distance or dropping a bomb slap bang into the middle of a company of men, this was different. This was personal. He had smelled the man's body odor, felt the bristles of a day-old beard as he had committed a murderous act with his bare hands. He found it strange that he had never considered how he would feel about killing another human, even though he had been sent on this mission to do exactly that. The moral implications had just never crossed his mind. Daniel looked at his hands.

They shook.

He balled his fists until his knuckles turned whiter than the clouds overhead. Adrenaline flushed through his veins, and his arms began to shake from their lethal exertions.

Nobody had told him killing somebody would be like this. Maybe they couldn't. Maybe it was different for everybody. Maybe they felt it would be better if he were forced to kill when painted into a corner; that's what had happened. He wouldn't have been able to return to the SS unit if he had let the Russian live. His cover would be blown to pieces, just like this godforsaken city.

But he had passed the test, and it revolted him. His stomach churned, and he belched: an acrid, sickly taste soured his mouth. He looked one last time at his despicable handiwork before re-surveying the street for other military transients and hurrying back to the watching Germans.

The Lieutenant looked at him oddly. 'You thought he was one of us?'

Embarrassed, Daniel nodded, which elicited a small chorus of sniggers from the rest of the squad.

'Pack it in. We're moving out,' the Lieutenant said over his shoulder. He turned back to Daniel. 'While you were playing with the Ruski, we intercepted another radio transmission from our Russian scouts. They've come back to play. We've double-checked our maps. They're not that far away. The bad news is we've strayed onto the Russian side of the line. Maybe it passed right over us in the night. Who knows. We'll have to be careful of fire from them and fire from our own Wehrmacht from here on, so watch your back.' He added the last bit with a devilish grin.

Within minutes, the squad was cautiously picking its way through the city. It hadn't taken the Lieutenant's warning for Daniel to sense that the danger had increased immeasurably. It seemed to him that the sound of gunfire had tripled since yesterday. He could feel the vibrations from artillery barrages coming from both front and rear, thankfully, for the moment, too far away to impede his mission. Overhead, the Luftwaffe looked to have increased the number of sortie attacks on Russian positions, no doubt trying to reclaim lost territory and drive them back towards the river.

On a more positive note, it appeared as though he had successfully crossed no-man's land without so much as a scratch, which had been something his father had had great difficulty doing in the stalemate of almost thirty years ago. But then, this was a very different war. Back in England, he had been briefed on the nature of urban warfare, but so far, it was nothing like what either the instructors or textbooks had described. He'd been told to expect close-quarter combat with danger lurking around every corner. But, except for a lone sniper and a Russian firing squad, he had barely seen a soul, let alone two souls slug it out to the death. Expect lulls in the fighting and discover sectors of the frontline that seemed indifferent to the raging battles on either side, they'd said. Urban warfare was a chaotic amalgamation immune to the rules of war.

Still, his mind flashed back to the soldier he had killed – another human being, a friend, not a foe. He tried desperately to remove the memory of the man's swollen face from his consciousness, but it remained. He felt sick, the slushy stale bread making its way from his stomach. He gulped in some air and tried to suppress nausea.

The wave passed a few moments later, but the memory of the soldier's face didn't. Psychologically he'd been branded with a permanent reminder of his first kill. Now he doubted whether he could carry out his mission or whether he could exact revenge. If killing one man had made him feel this bad, how would he feel if he had to kill more?

He closed his eyes and shook himself. Hadn't they also said the first kill was always the toughest? They'd said it got easier as the body count went up. The only question was, did he want it to get easier? Had he the stomach for it?

He wanted to go home.

It took them more than thirty minutes to progress the next couple hundred yards, and, as they moved, the buildings changed from plush two-story dwellings to more significant multi-story buildings forming a small industrial area. Here, the level of devastation had increased tenfold from that which they had already passed. Most structures were at the point of collapse, with only the odd supporting wall remaining intact. Many floors and roofs had wholly caved in, discharging piles of debris everywhere.

As they picked their way over shattered bricks and splintered wooden beams, they heard a voice from behind a wall to their rear. Instinctively, the squad dived for cover behind several of the larger rubble piles and waited. Daniel tried to slow his breathing but feared he was panting like an unfit, long-distance runner. He heard several pairs of footsteps pass on the other side of his sanctuary.

Slowly, he poked his head above the stones and watched a little troop of four heavily armed Russian soldiers being led by a pristinely dressed woman. Wide-eyed, he drew a sharp breath.

She was magnificent.

She had long, flowing red hair that fell halfway down her back. She wore a long, black leather coat and had black, calf-high leather boots. Her deportment left Daniel in no doubt that she was in charge. But what on earth was a woman like that doing in a place like this?

As they shuffled away, he strained his ears to hear what she was saying, but she was facing away, and all he could make out was the odd muffled sentence. Without warning, she turned around, forcing him to duck back behind the rubble pile again. That's when he heard a partially garbled sentence that made his heartbeat quicken.

'…fucking scientist…'

He looked at the Lieutenant, who, even with his limited Russian language skills, had also been able to translate. He smiled crookedly and nodded.

The woman's voice became muffled again and started to fade away. Daniel raised his head gingerly above the rocks and watched the little band trudge away and disappear around a corner.

He turned back to the Lieutenant, who was busy gesturing hand signals to the rest of his squad. Slowly they crept out from behind their hiding places and began to track their quarry.

Crouching low, Daniel followed. He couldn't afford to lose either of them now.

CHAPTER 29

GRASPING THEIR WEAPONS TIGHTLY TO their bodies, the squad hustled to the next corner and hid behind the wall. Daniel joined the Lieutenant a moment later, watching while he tried to regulate his breathing. The German edged his head around and turned back with a huge grin.

'These Russians are either incredibly brave or incredibly stupid. Three are on their knees in the open about thirty yards away, arguing over a map and jabbering on the radio. We don't even need to eavesdrop on their transmission – I can hear it from here. He glanced back around the corner. 'The fourth is scouting ahead.'

'Have they spotted us?' Daniel asked.

He shook his head. 'The woman seems to be in charge.'

'NKVD?'

'Probably. Good-looking too… for a Ruski.'

Daniel moved across him and snuck his head around the corner.

Good-looking was an understatement. She was a portrait of exotic elegance and stunning beauty. Her coat fluttered in the chilled breeze revealing a pair of toned legs wrapped in tight, black trousers. Even though he had never been, he imagined she wouldn't be out of place, sipping a glass of red wine outside some café on a pre-war Champs Élysées. But there was something about her deportment that intimidated him. The way she glanced at the three bickering soldiers was almost disdainful.

She suddenly wheeled in Daniel's direction. It took him a fraction of a second longer than he would have liked to pull his head back. Wide-eyed and frozen, he stared at the Lieutenant, who quickly signaled to the rest of his squad to get ready; he'd got the message.

Remaining hidden, they listened for any movement in their direction, but all they heard was the woman shouting at her subordinates. Daniel gambled and shot another glance.

Her troop was standing, and although he couldn't hear clearly, he could tell by her vexed expression and rapid gestures that she was furious. Once she had finished her tirade, the three soldiers fell in behind her. She followed the fourth soldier, who hadn't concerned himself with the heated discussion, further into the city.

Daniel smiled; she wasn't so stupid as to take point.

While he watched them disappear into the dust, Daniel recalled the hours he had spent pouring over maps and sand table replicas of the city, committing each topological characteristic and quirk to memory. The intention had been to instantly identify every street, avenue, and lane, every suburban, urban, and industrial center. Despite the ravages of war, he could recognize some landmarks that the Reich hadn't entirely obliterated. He scanned the area; they had been hours well spent.

'They've moved on.' Daniel shot a hopeful look at the Lieutenant.

'Then, we follow.' The German turned to his squad. 'Fan out. You two go right. We'll go left.'

They followed the Russians north into the city, their eyes moving carefully between their quarry and the ragged buildings.

Now and then, a single shot rang out from a Mosin-Nagant, the Russian sniper's weapon of choice, probably fired at some hapless German. Daniel had learned to distinguish the distinctive crack of the firing pin while cowering in a foxhole back in the Warwickshire countryside.

This place was a long way from there.

He thought it odd that he hadn't seen anybody other than the firing squad and this woman with her entourage, especially for a city under siege. Sporadic cackles of gunfire and mortar explosions seemed to come from all other parts of the city, but oddly, nothing near his position. It was almost as though a path of peace had been carved out amidst the horrors of war, which he was sure were being perpetrated a few blocks on either side of him.

And that was another thing he didn't feel, fear.

No fear of the unknown, of being captured, of being tortured, of dying. If anything, he was exhausted, but he had expected that. He knew there would be times when he would have to keep moving, unable to rest, and other times when he would have to lay low. They had trained him well; to be able to function on only a couple of disturbed hours sleep each day.

The morning dragged on, and the cat and mouse game continued. Maintaining a discrete distance, they watched the Russians sweep through numerous vacant buildings, stopping to reread their maps and radio back to their base. Judging by the woman's deepening scowl, it was clear she was becoming ever more frustrated with the ineffectiveness of their search. They disappeared around another corner, and a thought struck Daniel. What if she had seen him, and they were being led into a trap?

He told the Lieutenant, who considered it for a moment before nodding. 'Too much of a chance to take. We'll set a trap of our own.'

As the squad gathered around, he pulled a worn and partially ripped map from inside his jacket and unfolded it. After a moment, and without uttering a word, he made a series of finger movements across the map before looking at each man to ensure they understood what was to be done. 'Go.'

Daniel was impressed at how quickly the message was communicated and the speed with which the squad dispersed. The Lieutenant tapped his arm.

'Wait here until we're done. Follow once the shooting has stopped.'

His face contorted into another moronic grin, which Daniel had grown to hate. He forced a smile.

Less than five minutes later, Daniel heard several concentrated bursts of MP40 gunfire. After a few moments of silence, he left his hiding position and scampered off to the next corner. He heard shouts in German, the sound of hurried hobnailed boots trampling the ground, followed by a woman's voice speaking with an absurd calmness.

Now it was time for him to carry out the plan he had hatched while he had waited for the Germans to spring their trap. His only fear was that they wouldn't play along. He closed his eyes, took a deep breath, and called out in German.

'Don't shoot. I'm coming out.'

He raised his hands and slowly emerged from behind the wall.

Four of the squad had surrounded the woman, but only one had his machine gun pointed at her. The other three had trained their weapons on him.

Perfect.

'What's going on here?' he asked in German, mustering a casual smile.

The German guns relaxed and swung back to the woman, who had turned to look at him. Daniel shuffled toward the group, noting the horribly contorted bodies of the four dead Russian soldiers scattered on the ground. He didn't once look at the woman.

'Mind if I put my hands down? I'm afraid my fingers will fall off with the cold.'

The Lieutenant eyed him curiously but nodded and took a few steps forward, obscuring the woman's view.

'Captain Brandsa,' Daniel said, flashing a wink. 'Identification in my inside pocket.' He patted his chest.

The Lieutenant fished out the same ID he had seen before, gave it a cursory glance, and handed it back.

'Sorry, Captain. I didn't recognize you in that outfit.'

'Seems like you're lost?' Daniel said, ignoring the apology and delighted that the Lieutenant was playing his part.

The officer shrugged his shoulders. 'We're scattered all over the place.'

'No frontline?'

'Sure there is, but there are pockets where the enemy is behind us, and we're behind them. Makes us all a little uneasy.' He glanced back at the woman.

'What've you found?' Daniel asked, changing the subject and looking at the sharply dressed, shapely woman. 'Unusual to see such a thing in a place like this, you agree?'

The officer turned. 'Apart from her clothes, it isn't that uncommon. These Communist barbarians have stationed women all over the frontline. It disgusts me.'

Daniel glanced at him inquisitively.

'Women fighting men. Do they think this is some kind of joke?' the Lieutenant said.

Daniel didn't respond immediately but said, 'It's quite clever. They doubled their fighting strength and boosted the morale of the male troops. And in your own words, they've 'disgusted' the enemy. Given the option, many of our men would prefer not to fire on a woman. Isn't that why she's still alive and these four dead?' He swept his hand over the Russian corpses.

'What of their distractive nature?'

'Never underestimate the power of the Russian Commissar in coercing the men into towing the Party line. Besides, women distract both armies equally.'

The Lieutenant shrugged again, this time in submissive agreement.

'What do you propose we do with her?'

'Interrogate her. See what she knows.'

'But not before we have a bit of fun with her,' another soldier said, laughing. He grabbed her chin and slapped her across the face.

The woman's face lit up like a furnace, a mixture of rage and the force of the slap.

The other soldiers shared the joke.

'Not exactly befitting gentlemen of Das Reich?' Daniel offered a wry smile.

'No place for those out here, sir,' the unrepentant soldier replied.

A prostrate Russian soldier moaned and, clutching his belly, slowly wriggled like a dying earthworm. Daniel looked at him – they weren't all dead, after all. The soldier had been hit several times, and judging by his wounds, it would be a slow, painful death.

One of the Germans walked across and kicked him in the ribs, causing a trickle of blood to spurt from the Russian's mouth and run down his cheek. His eyes shifted uneasily as a man who knew the end was coming.

'Lend me your sidearm.'

'Don't waste a bullet on him, sir.'

'Even in war, we must have compassion for the enemy.'

Reluctantly, the Lieutenant handed over his Lugar. Daniel checked the magazine.

As Daniel walked to the dying Russian, a freezing sense of dread overcame him. He lifted his arm and pointed the Lugar at the soldier's head while trying to stave away the nerves threatening to shake it from his hand. The chilled wind gathered pace as it funneled its way down the avenue.

He paused.

A couple of the Germans sniggered – a war-time Captain struck by stage-fright.

At that moment, Daniel could feel the anger build inside. He allowed it to consume him. Now that he was so close to a hated enemy, he would smite them with the yearning of a vengeful brother. Mentally, he had prepared himself for this moment before he had enlisted. The time had come to test if killing would get any easier. And so, with a fluent swing of his arm, he turned.

It took no more than a couple of seconds to end the lives of four of the five startled Germans. They had been taken entirely by surprise – none had raised their guns. The Lieutenant jumped and tried to get off a few rounds with his MP40, but luckily for Daniel, fate was on his side. It jammed. A look of panic flashed across the young German's face.

Daniel strode up to the man who, uncharacteristically, had started shaking. Calmly, he placed the gun barrel to the German's forehead and, without hesitation, pulled the trigger; he hadn't been in the mood to hear any whelping pleas for clemency.

The Lieutenant's body flopped to the ground as a warm flow of satisfaction replaced the anger Daniel had felt moments ago. Surprisingly though, it only lasted a few seconds. He had expected to feel jubilation, maybe ecstasy, at having killed the killers of his brother or at least others who represented the same evil. Instead, a wave of remorse bathed him, not for what he had done but for what he had become. Leaving behind an adoring family, he'd murdered an innocent Russian, a squad of Germans, and ultimately betrayed the Allies, and for what? The satisfaction he desired was nothing more than an illusion. He turned and faced the woman. She had leveled one of the machine guns directly at him.

'Let's get out of here,' he said in Russian, ignoring the threat.

'I'm in charge,' she said evenly, seemingly not in the least bit surprised that he had switched languages.

'It didn't look that way a minute ago.' He pocketed the Lugar.

'Everything was under control until you showed up.'

Daniel knelt by the side of the Russian soldier with the stomach wounds and stared into his dead eyes. Death had been greedy and had come sooner than anticipated.

'Who are you?' she asked.

Daniel didn't answer. Instead, he offered a second prayer of the day.

'I asked you a question.'

Daniel stood and, without offering identification, told her the second part of a lie fabricated in Whitehall's bowels.

'My name is Dimitri Guskov,' he said. 'The Kremlin sent me to report on the fighting appetite of our comrades in defense of our beloved city.' He cocked his head to one side. 'And you are?'

This time it was the woman's turn to remain silent, clearly deciding if she should reply or just blow him away. Luckily for Daniel, he was unaware of what kind of creature he had saved. But she relented and lowered the gun.

'Daryna. NKVD.'

'Have you a second name?'

'You don't need to know.'

Daniel started walking in the direction they had come.

'This way,' Daryna said, motioning the machine gun in the opposite direction.

He stopped. 'You were heading that way before you ran into these guys. I don't fancy becoming another fatality.'

'Fine. You go your own way. I've got a job to complete.'

She bent over the radio operator and relieved him of his magic box of tricks. She fumbled with both weapon and radio with a little less finesse and poise than she had shown so far. Daniel looked at her and, in a symbolic act of chivalry, said, 'Give it to me. You carry the gun. If they shoot, they'll shoot me for carrying the radio.'

Clutching the gun, she almost threw the radio at him, but Daniel glimpsed a faint 'thank you' in her eyes.

'How long will it take you to do whatever it is you've to do?' he asked. 'I've got a mission of my own to complete.'

She shrugged. 'Could be an hour, a week, maybe never.'

'Doesn't your boss believe in deadlines?'

Daryna turned away from Daniel, not allowing him the pleasure of a twisted smile. Her boss believed in deadlines, especially in the absolute meaning of the word.

With the radio unit strapped to his back, and Daryna leading the way, only Daniel knew that his objective and the woman he had befriended were identical. Better still, his hurried plan to eliminate German and Russian patrols had been perfectly executed.

CHAPTER 30

Daniel curled up in a tight ball and settled down for what remained of the night. Deep in the belly of a bunker, burrowed into a steep slope that swept down to the Volga, the dulled sounds of war overhead imposed a soothing effect on his weary mind. His thoughts wandered to the last few hours with Daryna.

Thanks to regular updates from her communist friends, they had managed to evade every skirmish in their path on the way behind Russian lines. But their journey had been incredibly frustrating, with them having to frequently double-back to make any headway.

However, it had been Daryna's outrageously unnatural arrogance that had eventually got them through the trigger-happy frontline. Daniel had lost count of the number of times his heart skipped a bar when groups of gun-toting Bolsheviks had challenged them.

With Daryna completely ignoring their pernicious demands for identification, she flashed an indignant glare as she brushed them aside without even breaking stride. Hardly believing his eyes, Daniel had hurried a couple yards behind, ready to use the radio as makeshift armor if needed.

It had been late when they finally reached the shore, but not completely dark. A multitude of floating, phosphorous flares illuminated the night sky. That, and the omnipresent explosions from the constant artillery barrage, tracer rounds from machine-gun deployments, and flames from the burning city made for a phenomenal yet terrifying sight.

*

Later, they stood outside the bunker, surveying the mayhem of what remained of the wretched civilian population. Thousands of women and children huddled together in one enormous surviving and heaving mass while the war stormed around them. Some mothers cradled dead children, while some youngsters tried to rouse their deceased parents. Although his face didn't betray his feelings, Daniel's heart melted. The Russian situation was even more desperate than he could ever have imagined. He didn't like to admit it, but the human misery here was far worse than what he had experienced in Coventry.

Looking across at the jetty, he saw scores of frightened soldiers, fresh for the slaughter, practically fall off a bullet-riddled ferry and ushered into the city by their screaming Commissars. The corpses of those unlucky to have been hit during the crossing were pushed off the deck to make way for the severely injured soldiers who would attempt the return trip. The lifeless bodies floated away down the river like contorted branches of a fallen tree.

Everywhere Daniel looked, he saw only despair. The Germans had come to repeat what they had done in France and the Low Countries, although he couldn't have imagined they had been this brutal in Western Europe. Witnessing the repulsive horror of this place strengthened his resolve to complete his mission and get back home.

Daryna had displayed a look of complete contempt for the spectacle and vanished in a brazen rage, leaving Daniel wondering what his next move should be. His priorities were simple: water, food, and rest, and, as he glanced at those moving in and out of the bunker, he figured it to be as good a place as any to accommodate his immediate needs.

He bunched himself into a tight fetal position and drifted off.

*

'Here! Try this one on for size.'

One of Daniel's company buddies shoved a giggling girl toward him. She landed squarely on his lap and draped her arms around him. Laughing, he threw his head back and took another swig of ale. The girl rubbed her hand across his mouth, wiping the excess alcohol away before planting her lips on his.

He tickled her, and she squealed, accidentally kicking the table and sending a clink of half-empty glasses onto the floor. A huge cheer erupted as the contents showered those closest. A dance band played on the stage through the noisy and smoky din. A barman threw an agitated scowl before moving off to serve another thirsty customer.

'I'll get another round,' one of the soldiers slurred. He staggered to his feet and made his way to the bar, bouncing off everybody along the way, offering no apologies.

Over the past three and a half months, the boys of A-Company had turned into men. They had become a well-oiled fighting machine, but to look at them, you wouldn't think so. Now, they were just well-oiled. This had been the week they had been waiting for, ever since they had first stepped through their camp gates. Free to do what they wanted so long as they were back before sunset Sunday evening.

They had earned it.

'I think I love you,' Daniel hiccupped into the girl's ear. She continued to kiss and lick his neck, running her fingers inside his unbuttoned shirt.

'You told my friend the same thing a few minutes ago.' Her breath tickled the side of his neck.

'I love her, too.' He laughed.

His hand skimmed up and down her leg, touching the top of her suspenders, his fingers lightly snapping them.

'Easy there, soldier.' She moved his hand away and beamed a huge smile. 'All good things…' She tried to pull down her skirt to protect her modesty.

'Can't wait.' He groped her bum and twisted her around, planting an enormous kiss on her.

Suddenly, he pulled away and looked up: the band had slowed things down. A huge grin materialized on his face.

'C'mon, let's dance.'

They made their way to the dancefloor and joined all the other first-time lovers who were busy grappling with each other as the strains of 'Moonlight Serenade' drifted through the hall.

Her smell was as intoxicating as the liquor he had consumed, a mixture of perfume and sweet sweat. She laid her head on his shoulder, and he nudged his crotch gently into hers. She didn't pull away.

They held each other tightly, her soft breasts pressing against his firm chest, and Daniel believed he was falling in love, even if it was just for one night.

Then, he stopped dancing.

'What's the .'

'Sshhhh.' He put a finger to her lips and strained his ears.

'We've got to go.' He yanked her by the hand and hurried across to his friends.

'Sirens. We've got to get underground.'

'Ah, you're hearing things,' one of the fellas said.

The music suddenly stopped, and the barmen started shouting at everybody to clear the bar. The place exploded into chaos. Colliding soldiers and their girls charged for the exits, snatching their belongings and pushing the people in front. Although the air-raid shelters weren't that far away, nobody was about to hang around.

The drunkenness that had slowly seized Daniel immediately evaporated. He took the girl by her arm and weaved his way around some bumbling boozers before pushing through onto the street.

The panic seemed to dissipate once they were outside. People stood around smoking and staring into the sky as they pointed at the intersecting streaks of spotlights. Pedestrians walked about as they would on any other cold November evening.

But then, barely audible above the chattering, a depressed drone could be heard. One by one, people stopped talking, and everybody searched the sky. At first, it sounded like a distant wasp's nest, but another, altogether different sound soon added to the hum. Not continuous, but intermittent, like dull thunderclaps. Along with the drone, they, too, were getting louder.

Closer.

People started to shuffle away down the road as they continued to scan the sky. It was only when another more powerful blast sounded that they started running. Some started screaming.

Still, the sirens wailed.

Daniel tightened his grip on his girl, his eyes searching for the shelter. He dragged her away, following the others, assuming they knew where they were going.

He picked up the pace, but the girl was having trouble keeping up, her heels catching on the cobblestones. She stumbled after him, pulling him back, but he refused to let her go.

The rate of explosions increased, their intensity amplifying. Panic had descended on the city as everybody ran in the same direction, shoving each other out of the way. The noise from the bombs seemed to have them surrounded.

He spied an entrance ahead. Sandbags lined its brick walls. A Home Guardsman frantically waved his arms and shouted at people to get inside.

The girl's legs suddenly buckled, and she fell to her knees, her hand slipping from Daniel's grasp. He stopped and looked between her and the shelter. It wasn't even twenty yards away.

Everything moved in slow-motion. Adrenaline fizzed through Daniel's body, and he darted toward her just as the wall behind them burst open. For a moment, Daniel felt as though he was floating. He saw the girl's deformed body lying on the ground as he sailed over her.

Then everything went black.

*

Daniel woke with a bump as though falling out of a tree. He glanced around groggily. Even beneath Stalingrad, the tunnels trembled in response to the explosions impacting the surface. Aside from the fine dust that floated gently from the gaps between the wooden support beams, the bunker was probably one of the few inviolable places left in the city, but that didn't prevent him from feeling uneasy. The dust wasn't the only thing that filled the air down here. At times, the stench of close quartering was so overpowering that Daniel was glad the dust had filled his nostrils. The tunnels seemed thick with men from every corner of the Soviet Union: Russia, Georgia, Kazakhstan, Turkmenistan, Uzbekistan, and god-knows-what other 'stan'. The racket of conversation in so many languages made his head hurt.

He had settled down amongst hundreds of weary, filthy Red Army soldiers lining the bunker walls. They looked as though they had already accepted their fate. Although his sleeping companions had found temporary relief from the shelling, he hadn't been able to drift off for long periods despite the aches, pains, and exhaustion that percolated his body.

But his personal body count still haunted him. His innocence had been destroyed in the same manner as the men he had killed. He racked his brains, trying to figure out how he had become the very thing he despised. How had he allowed himself to become so cold-blooded? How had he fooled himself into thinking it would have been any different? Is this what war did to ordinary people, turning them into something less human? He tried to rekindle the feeling of satisfaction, the warm glow that had encapsulated him immediately after he had wasted the SS squad. But it just wouldn't come.

He felt hollow.

He nodded off several times, only to be disturbed by another massive blast. Increasingly, he wondered if it was really all that safe down here, or would the whole lot suddenly become a ready-made tomb.

The next thing he knew, he was woken by the shrill sound of several whistles as Commissars charged through the tunnels shouting at the soldiers to return to the surface. The Motherland refused to wait for a son's or daughter's rest.

When he staggered out of the bunker, he shielded his eyes from the sunlight and stepped to one side to allow those behind to continue their march, presumably into battle. That was when he felt a firm pair of hands shove him into a line with some other soldiers.

Daniel spun around.

'I'm NKVD, you mo…' his voice trailed off.

The man before him was a Goliath. With a height that must have been approaching seven feet and a width of similar dimensions, Daniel wondered why on earth the Russians didn't just let this guy fight the Germans all by himself.

The monster's eyes burned deep into Daniel's, whose flicker of fire had all but been extinguished. Without uttering a word, the giant yanked him forward. Daniel tried to resist but quickly discovered his efforts to be utterly futile.

He was dragged about a hundred yards along the bank and dumped into a lineup of around sixty men, facing a much larger group of boisterous soldiers that must have numbered in the thousands. A few other men were positioned next to him a few minutes later: the men facing and staring at them quietened down. He took a sidelong glance at the guy shivering next to him.

What the Hell is ?

'Attention,' an officer screamed, at the top of his lungs, resulting in an asynchronous shuffle of feet.

The officer barked a few unpleasantries at the larger group before reminding them that their duty to Mother Russia must be coveted above all else, even one's own life. He spoke about desertion and what would happen should anybody attempt it, fail to prevent others from doing it, or even talk about it. Then, he said something that made Daniel's blood run ice cold.

'I will demonstrate the seriousness of this most heinous of crimes and what we do to prevent such treachery.'

Daniel glanced across at the officer, who had unholstered his sidearm. He checked the gun, cleared the breach, and, counting aloud, started moving along the line of men in which Daniel stood.

'One, two, three… eight, nine.'

There was no ten. A single shot rang out, and a lifeless body flopped to the ground.

'One, two, three…'

Every muscle in Daniel's body strained as the officer resumed his count. He continued to walk along the line, executing the Roman punishment of decimation.

Daniel searched for a way out but drew a blank. He couldn't run. He would be cut down before he got even a few yards. Even if they didn't shoot him, they would certainly make an example of his cowardice, which might be worse than a swift bullet to the head.

A pair of hands with immense strength suddenly grabbed him; the monster had returned. It moved Daniel to the right and sneered, saliva dripping from its stinking mouth.

Every time the officer reached the count of ten, another shot rang out, and another soldier was savagely cut down, his brains blasted out the back of his head and splattered on the ground behind him.

Daniel lost count, only hearing the gunfire become louder as the officer came closer. He glanced down at his trembling hands and felt his eyesight contract until all he could make out were his dirty fingernails, seemingly miles away at the end of his tunnel vision. Like the guys next to him, he shivered, partly from the cold sweat that had bathed his body but mainly from a deepening fear.

He was powerless.

He looked up and blinked his eyes, searching furtively for any way out, but he couldn't see one. Through squinted eyes, he turned to the left and, for a moment, thought he saw Daryna standing with some military brass, observing proceedings. But he wasn't sure. Everything was blurry.

'…seven, eight, nine.' The officer stood before Daniel, his pistol raised no more than three inches from Daniel's forehead. He could smell the singed gunpowder as smoke drifted lightly from the barrel. The officer's hand was steady. His finger pulled the trigger slowly.

Daniel's mind went numb, and the light at the end of the tunnel evaporated.

CHAPTER 31

Click!

Daniel didn't blink; his eyes were already closed in anticipation of the inevitable. But it hadn't come. Very slowly, he opened them to a squint to see the officer holster his weapon and turn abruptly away before marching back along the line without so much as a 'lucky bastard' comment.

The officer bellowed another order, and the soldiers in both firing and witness lines dispersed like scampering gazelles being chased by a coalition of cheetahs.

Daniel stared after him for a moment before his gaze settled on the fiery-haired Daryna, stomping in his direction. She looked like she had been well fed and rested and, by the looks of it, had even managed to procure a change of clothes.

'You're with me.' She breezed past him.

Daniel took a half-step after her, then stopped. After his near-death experience, he felt more alive than ever, and at that moment, with his adrenaline levels spiking, he was in no mood to be ordered around.

'I'm not going anywhere. What the fuck was that all about?'

She swiveled on her heels.

'It was a demonstration of how we deal with those who fail to perform their duty against the enemy.'

'Yeah, well, that's great. But why the fuck was *I* put into the line-up?'

An evil smile curled onto her lips.

'Communication with Moscow is limited, and I'd no way of checking your story.'

'That was a test?'

She still smiled.

'I could've been killed.'

She fired a 'so what' glare at him and continued walking away.

Reluctantly, he followed, deciding he stood a better chance of finding Yermakov with, rather than without, her. He just hoped that was still her objective. The last thing he wanted was to get involved in some other fruitless aspect of the war that didn't concern him.

'What's the plan?' he asked once he caught up.

'You're going to help me find somebody.'

'I'm not a fucking policeman,' Daniel said. 'Besides, I've my own problems.'

'Like what?'

'Like I said yesterday, 'information gathering'.'

'You've been reassigned. My objective is far more important than yours.'

Daniel hoped they were identical.

'Why me?'

'Because you have skills that could prove useful. You speak German, and you've already been to the frontline and survived. You know what to expect.'

'So long as I'm not shot for desertion. I hope you've done the paperwork.'

'There's no time for paperwork. Don't worry. You'll be safe with me.' She laughed.

Daniel was reminded of the evil queen from 'Snow White'.

'Safe like the last squad you commanded? It didn't work out too well for them. Have you got replacements?'

'You're it.'

That was the best news he had heard yet.

'You and me versus the world?' Daniel said. 'Wonderful. Can I trust you not to get me killed out there?' He nodded towards the burning city.

'You can't trust anyone.' She flashed him a wicked smile.

They walked over to a large indentation in the side of the slope, which was a hive of activity. Soldiers were going in with nothing and leaving with weapons, ammunition, and other bits and pieces that those in charge believed were enough to repel the invader. Daniel stood back and watched as Daryna pushed through the crowd of clambering men.

Men. Daniel thought. Hardly. Just children, most were younger than him.

She returned a couple of minutes later, carrying a PPSh-41 machine gun, an AVS-36 rifle, two TT-33 pistols, two combat knives, and a couple of belts packed with F1 grenades.

Daniel noticed that some of the soldiers stared enviously at the haul. She handed him the machine gun, a pistol, a knife, and a handful of grenades; Daryna was obviously not your everyday female soldier. Slinging the rifle over her shoulder, she fished out several small boxes of ammunition from beneath her coat.

'Thanks. Thought I was going to have to throw the guns at the Germans. What, no anti-tank mines?'

She stared at him. 'You don't speak like a Russian.'

For a moment, Daniel thought maybe his accent had floundered and, even though it was only seconds ago, struggled to recall what he had said and, more importantly, how he had said it.

'Russians don't make so many jokes.' Her eyes zoomed in on him.

Daniel felt like a bug under a microscope. 'I guess I've discovered life is too short around here. Might as well enjoy it while I can.'

She shook her head slowly, seemingly, not understanding the sentiment, before abruptly changing the subject. 'We need to find another radio.'

Getting a working radio took even less time than it had the weapons. Daryna just marched up to a group of soldiers, reached in, and took theirs. They looked like they were about to protest, but she discharged a scowl of such intensity that they backed down without a whimper.

She beckoned Daniel over with a finger as she removed a map from her pocket.

'We've to find a scientist.'

Daniel had trouble containing his excitement. He forced a 'you must be joking' smile.

'His last known position was here.' She pointed to the map.

'Right in the middle of the 4th Panzer Army.'

'That was a few days ago. We moved him out, but his transport was attacked, and we lost him.'

'So, what makes you think he's still alive?' Daniel asked, trying to muster a little artificial incredulity.

'We don't.'

'And you're risking my neck for this man, a fucking scientist. Are you crazy? I must be crazy.'

'I can always put you back into a firing squad. Maybe this time, the chamber won't be empty. Besides, it's worth sacrificing your life for this man.'

Daniel wondered what *she* would sacrifice.

'Why is he so important?'

'That's none of your business.' She fired off another scowl.

Daniel decided it would be best to shut up before she took out her revolver and finished what the Commissar had started. He nodded grimly.

'The truck was hit along this road, here. He knows where the ferry points are, so if he continued into the city, he's likely to be somewhere between there and here.' She splayed her fingers between the two locations, separated by only a few miles. Daniel was well acquainted with the area from his training days. Expensive apartment blocks, recreational areas, shopping, it had it all.

Had…

He could bet his own life that very little of it existed anymore.

'Fucking weed is probably hiding in some cellar,' she said.

'Or a sewer.'

She ignored him. 'I've already checked these locations.' Her finger hopscotched across the map. 'Which means there's only this area to search.'

'What if he's moving around and you're missing him?'

'Let's just say he's not the sort who would venture out into the middle of a war.' Her eyes gleamed. 'This way.' She folded the map and shoved it back in her coat pocket.

They started climbing the steep ridge into the city when several deployments of anti-aircraft guns opened up behind them. Daniel's eyes shot to the sky, but he couldn't see anything.

Then, dozens of Stukas and 109s emerged from the dense black smoke that permanently hovered over the city. The noise level amplified to ear-bursting proportions as tens of bombs were dropped indiscriminately onto the Soviet positions, scattering the panicking Russians. Massive eruptions of earth spewed into the air, interring civilians and soldiers alike. Some soldiers dropped onto their backs and fired their rifles up at the low-flying aircraft; not many hit a target.

Daniel scrambled up the incline after Daryna, who hadn't stopped to look around. His legs were like jelly by the time he made it to the summit, but he tore off after her, nonetheless. His body ached as the Germans came around for a second pass, and, with bullets chopping the ground around him, he dove headlong into a freshly made crater. Lightening, Daniel felt, was unlikely to strike the same place twice.

Explosions bellowed all around, showering him with dirt. He curled into a ball, trying desperately to make himself as tiny as possible. His mind was suddenly wrenched away from Stalingrad to another city, another place that had been blown to pieces by German bombs.

*

Daniel could make out distorted figures scurrying through the fiery haze of pluming smoke. His back was drenched. He tried to raise his head but couldn't; it felt as though a grand piano had fallen on him, except this was as hard and rough as stone. His eyes moved sluggishly to one side. Everything was out of focus. Even the sounds were garbled. Amongst the cries for help were shouts for stretchers, the sparking of fires, and the sloshing of pumped water through hoses. But it was all just noise.

He felt tired.

He tried to move his arms and legs. No good. The piano, or whatever it was, wouldn't budge. He tried to call out, but his lungs didn't work. They were barely sucking in the dust-filled air. A mixture of water and ash sprayed over him.

He felt no pain, just complete paralysis, his whole body numb. He tried to call out again but only whimpered. At least that's what he thought. Everything sounded the same, a deafening high-pitched hiss.

Something came over to him. It touched him. He couldn't see. Then it all went dark again.

*

Every muscle in Daniel's body tensed tighter than ever before. It was almost as though his body was shutting down, organ by organ. He mumbled the same sentence repeatedly.

Please, God, get me out of here.

The planes broke off their attack less than a minute later, and a quietness fell, except, that was, for the agonizing screams of the wounded and dying men. Daniel forced himself to breathe again as he slowly and painfully unfurled himself. His body was as stiff as an over-starched collar, his muscles tighter than an overwound clock spring. He lay in the crater for a moment before eventually crawling up to the rim.

He scanned the area with a slow and hazy mind and spied Daryna darting from behind a pile of rubble. Despite his muscles feeling as though they had been set in concrete, he struggled out and hobbled after her. The place looked like what Daniel imagined the moon's surface to look like after being pounded by a meteor shower.

'Thought you needed me?' He panted as soon as he caught up. He watched her sip from a canteen. Oddly, she smiled and offered him a drink, which he accepted.

'We'll wait here until we're sure the attack is over before we move deeper into the city,' she said. 'The closer we get to the Germans, the safer we'll be from their air attacks. They won't be bombing their own infantry.'

Daniel wiped a dribble off his chin and tossed the canteen back to her. He looked around. There were soldiers huddled everywhere, camouflaged against the walls and ground. Nobody moved, not because they were dead, but because they were paralyzed with fear. He knew exactly how they felt.

He looked towards the river and saw enormous plumes of smoke rising from the riverbank. It appeared the focus of this attack had been the ferry crossing. The Germans were trying to suffocate Russian resistance by disrupting the city's only available supply line. He wondered how quickly they could restart the flow of ammunition and medical equipment before wondering how long they could hold out if they couldn't.

With the aerial assault seemingly over, men began to seep out of the ruins. Daryna got onto her hunkers and made a 'let's go' sign.

Although he wasn't too thrilled about it, Daniel assumed the same position, and they made a beeline for the city.

With the river a few hundred yards behind them, they found they no longer had to stoop and could walk upright through the mass of men and machinery fanning through the city. The soldiers were taking up positions in torn buildings, hurriedly dug trenches, and anywhere else that offered them some cover.

Daniel thought it unusual that there weren't many wounded moving in the opposite direction. It was all hands to the pump.

It didn't take them long to pick their way to the edge of Russian-held territory and for their stoop to return. They weren't even sure they hadn't already crossed over to the German side. The numbers of visible men had reduced notably, with most soldiers adopting a chameleon-like existence amid the desecrated city.

Daniel wasn't surprised that, given yesterday's experience, Daryna had also begun to hug the walls.

The next few hours were torturous. Searching buildings for any sign of life, uncovering hidden cellars, dropping to their knees for periodic radio communication, questioning the Russian units they came across, evading running battles, avoiding being shot by Germans, avoiding being shot by Russians. It would have been extraordinarily exhilarating if it hadn't been so terrifying.

Whether it was German time or Russian time, Daniel's stomach started to rumble, so it must have been lunchtime. Along the way, they had requisitioned rations off a few dead soldiers, so they had plenty to eat. They got off the street and settled down inside an empty ruin.

'German food is better than ours,' Daniel said, taking care to stay in character.

Daryna didn't reply, but judging by how she favored the Wehrmacht rations, he could tell she agreed. He watched her study the map as she ate. Her face knotted as though she had just swallowed an ice cube. She cursed quietly between mouthfuls and glowered at a compass as if it was all its fault.

Hope, too, was withering in Daniel. Although he had only been searching for a few days, he knew Daryna had most likely been searching since Yermakov went missing. She knew the city, knew the traps, was getting constant updates on the battle, and had so far come up empty-handed. Maybe this was an impossible mission. It would have been much easier had he arrived before the Germans began their attack. A bullet to the back of the man's head and Daniel could have returned home a hero. Even if Yermakov had made it safely to the Eastern side of the Volga, Daniel could have spoofed his way across and eliminated him there.

But no.

As in all war, events had conspired to complicate matters, and nobody knew where in this Hell they were. Daniel wondered if Yermakov even knew where he was.

They were about to resume their search when they were surprised by the grinding of tank tracks on the debris outside. Daniel poked his head out from their temporary mess and quickly pulled it back.

'Panzers… lots of them.' His voice was barely a whisper.

Daryna's reaction startled him. 'Infantry?' She asked, more annoyed than scared.

'Didn't see any, but they're probably behind.'

Her face flamed to match her hair. She cursed again and removed all the weapons she had secreted about her body.

Daniel did the same.

If the Germans came snooping, then they would go out swinging.

They crouched against the wall on either side of the doorway and waited as the grating got louder.

Before a single tank passed them, several shots rang out from what sounded like close-quartered artillery positions. Suddenly, the whole street erupted as though the battle for the city had landed outside their doorstep. The deafening noise of buildings being blasted by shells, mortar rounds dropping through the air, machine-gun fire cutting down anything in its path, ricocheting off obstacles, choking the air. Walls collapsed, men yelled and screamed in blood-curdling pain as tanks exploded, and metal fragments coated in blood bounced off whatever walls were left standing.

Complete pandemonium had ensued.

Daniel considered stepping away from the wall. One direct hit, and that would be it, but he held his ground. His knuckles turned white on the machine-gun grip. He glanced at the grenade belts beside him just in case.

But then, almost as quickly as it had started, it all died down. After the initial onslaught, each army resorted to taking pot-shots at the other. Judging by the directionality, Daniel figured he and Daryna were slap-bang in the middle of it all. A quick survey of the building told him the worst possible news. His face said it all, reciprocated by Daryna's grim expression.

No way out.

CHAPTER 32

ANATOLY WAS AT BREAKING POINT, not because he was afraid of the explosions or the screams of the dying soldiers overhead. Neither did the crunching of collapsing buildings and wondering if theirs would be next hold any fear either. Simply put, he was bored.

It had been three days since they'd descended into their hideaway, and, with the war closing in around them, they were petrified about being discovered. They had lost all track of time. Minutes felt like hours, days like weeks. Only the alternating light and dark of the slit window assured them that time hadn't stood still. He felt as though the cellar walls were closing in, suffocating him. Above, the house appeared to have changed hands several times in some bloody game of tug of war. Right now, he wasn't sure who controlled it.

He was also sick of beans. Breakfast, lunch, and dinner had been tin after tin of tasteless beans, washed down with half a mug of water. The bread had run out, and, with access to the surface prohibited, there was no chance to forage for something more edifying. The dreaded beans would have to do; they were, unfortunately, still plentiful.

Between bombing runs, he had tried to reinvigorate his dulling mind with memories of his childhood, his parents, his teachers, and Anya, but all he could think of was his latest project; he had been so close. A few more days, a week at most, and he would have made another in a long line of breakthroughs. Viewing the war from down here, he doubted he would ever get the opportunity to complete his work. And maybe it was just as well. He would have willingly grasped it if somebody had offered him a way out of it all. Conversation with Nina had dried up. There was only so much he could talk about with a thirteen-year-old girl with limited academic knowledge. He'd tried to teach her the rudiments of chess, but as she'd grown tired of his instruction, so too had he become frustrated with her lack of aptitude.

Initially, he thought it would be fun to try and educate her; at least he could keep his mind active. But he had found her lacking. Her capacity for learning was minimal, caused, perhaps, by leaving school at such an early age. And so, his role as teacher had stopped almost as quickly as it had begun.

Below street level, there was nothing that either interested or energized him; his mind had effectively switched off. It was a new and dreadful experience that he prayed he'd never have to repeat.

He gazed at her slender form, huddled beneath the stinking blankets. The poor sod still believed her parents were alive and would someday come back for her. Anatoly suspected otherwise.

Outside, there was a lull in the fighting. Judging by the deepening darkness from the window, he figured it was getting on for the evening, the day's aggressions being put to bed, only to be reawakened at first light. As darkness intensified, all was quiet except for the occasional volley of gunfire.

Internally, a debate raged. He was torn between staying with Nina and making a run for it. The former gave him relative safety until they were discovered or the war was over, while the latter might mean capture or death. It could also mean deliverance into the hands of the Russian scientific community, and therein lay the dilemma.

To stay or to go?

Standing in the center of the cellar, he listened and watched his breath in the reducing light. He hugged his body and glanced across at the young girl again. He couldn't just leave her, could he? Then again, maybe it should be every man for himself?

It was killing him.

She could become another casualty, another statistic, but then, so might he should he leave. His head drooped into his sinking shoulders. Even with all his education and undoubted genius, he didn't know what to do. These were not scientific questions that yielded black and white answers. On the contrary, he found himself staring into an abyss of morality with probable solutions of too many shades of grey. He smiled to himself. The more he thought about it, the more he likened it to the 'new' science with shades of grey comparable to the various quantum states.

His mind drifted away, and he thought of Anya.

*

'Tell me why I'm learning this stuff again?' she said, falling back on the bed.

'Because it's important,' Anatoly replied, resisting the urge to follow her.

'How can this be important? It's old and outdated.'

'Old, yes. Outdated, no.'

'But shouldn't *we* be studying the 'new physics'?'

'No. *You* should be studying this.' He patted the large, hard-backed volume on his lap, which, at that moment, was serving two purposes: to educate the young, eyelash-batting student and to conceal his growing erection, a consequence of her flirting. He was happy she hadn't pried the book away and thrown it into a corner.

'When you understand this, we'll move onto the 'new physics.'

He glanced discreetly at Anya's breasts, covered by a thick woolen sweater, but turned away quickly, hoping she hadn't noticed. He had to keep things on a professional footing, at least for now.

'But it's boring.'

'It's necessary.'

'Why?'

'Because it'll give you a better understanding of how and what the human race has learned over the millennia, why we bother to expand our knowledge, why it takes so long to discover new things, and what benefits we can reap when we put our new-found knowledge to good use.'

'I thought it was so that I could pass my exams.'

'That's the result of you learning this stuff.' He rubbed his hands through his hair vigorously and sighed. He patted the book again.

'Can't we do something else?' she asked, batting her eyes again.

He fought the temptation for his mind to wander to more carnal activities but struggled. He looked at the clock on the dresser.

'A few more minutes.' He said, conceding he wasn't going to get much further with her today. He had been tutoring a few first and second-year students whenever he had the time or needed the extra money but disliked both their lack of personal ambition and craving for the knowledge he possessed.

Anya was different from every one of them in many ways. She had curves; at least, that's what he dreamed lay beneath the folds of knitted jumpers she usually wore. She smelled heavenly and had long, dark brown, flowing hair matched in color by her innocent eyes. More importantly, she'd taken an inordinate non-academic interest in him, which had never happened to him before, mainly because he'd always been surrounded by the sort of company that others her age usually tried desperately to evade.

She swung around on the bed, lay flat on her belly, and hunched herself onto her elbows, cradling her head in her hands. 'Okay, let's get this over with.'

Anatoly followed the flow of her body from the top of her head along the curvature of her spine, over her backside, and down her legs to her ankles. He took a short, sharp breath and closed his eyes.

For the next quarter of an hour, he repeated how the most famous failed experiment of all time was arranged and carried out. He explained the profound implications of the 'null' result observed by Michelson and Morley and what effect it had on the direction of the 'new physics'.

During his oratory, he gesticulated his way around the room with a passion for the subject that would've been equaled only by a couple of rabid romantics in the throes of intercourse. From time to time, he glanced at her to see if she was paying attention, and each time she returned his persistent enthusiasm with a vacant but pleasant smile.

'Okay, that'll do for today,' he said, puffing his cheeks. She didn't move. He scratched his head and decided that the vacuum had been too great to fill in one lesson. She'd listened to the words but not their meaning, which was okay. From his perspective, he was thrilled they had spent the hour together. He stopped pacing and stared at her. She gazed into his eyes.

'You've got a lovely speaking voice,' she said. Her eyes sparkled in the mid-morning sun.

He threw his eyes to the ceiling.

'I want to hear you say something not science-related.'

'Like what?' He sat slowly beside her.

'Tell me about your childhood.'

'But I *am* still a child.'

'Not to me.' She slid across and rubbed her body against his. She eyed him expectantly, and he felt alive inside.

CHAPTER 33

Stalingrad tumbled into darkness quicker than a wake of swooping vultures, a phenomenon Daniel attributed to the depressing black smoke that lingered over the dying city. He blew on his freezing fingers and was immediately transported back to the damp tool shed in his backyard. What he wouldn't give to be blowing hot air into a cornet in a peaceful part of Yorkshire instead of cowering in some draughty excuse of a building in war-torn Russia.

Forget about autumn. Winter was coming and quick. He knew it, and he didn't want to be around when it eventually gripped the city.

Except for the odd rifle crack, the fighting on the other side of the wall had dissipated entirely. Unfortunately, neither he nor Daryna knew if both sides had entrenched or dissolved into the city to do their killing elsewhere. Neither of them felt inclined to stick their heads above the parapet to find out.

They set about turning the building they occupied into a fortress to be held. Moving into one corner, they huddled against a wall, close enough so they could whisper to each other but far enough apart so they could maximize their field of fire. They built a sturdy yet low barrier out of whatever garbage, bricks, and wood had fallen onto the floor before hunkering behind it for the night.

Daniel checked his watch.

Aside from an underlying sense of foreboding, he could feel the boredom set in. He checked his weapons and reflected on the search. It had been a tedious stop-start affair, searching and rummaging through ruins, radioing Daryna's command post for the latest reconnaissance report.

From time to time, Daniel listened to German radio chatter, which he could tell displeased Daryna. She evidently had only a rudimentary grasp of her enemy's language and felt inferior. She hadn't complained, and he wouldn't have cared if she had. Despite honing his linguistic expertise back in England, this helped Daniel appreciate other Germanic inflections, dialects, and nuances.

Even though he had been in Russia only a few days, he was beginning to worry. He realized that no amount of training could have prepared him, or anybody else for that matter, for this experience. By every standard imaginable, he was a 'mission virgin'. He knew he had to feel the shock blasts, smell the freshly spilled blood, and believe there was the genuine possibility of losing his life. The tear-inducing stench of cordite wafting through the freezing air didn't help either.

He remembered Coventry. In many ways, this was the same and yet, different. Here, the sickeningly pungent stink of decaying corpses was everywhere. Daniel recalled fighting feasting dogs and rats so Daryna could examine each body they found. They had even searched the headless, but Yermakov hadn't turned up.

He shot her a sidelong glance. She rubbed the fingernails of one hand with the fingertips of the other and bit her lip. She looked more worried than him, and he was pretty sure it had nothing to do with what was going on outside and everything to do with not finding Yermakov. If the Red Army was willing to sacrifice its soldiers to make a point, then he couldn't even begin to imagine the kind of pressure she was under. Daniel figured she would be desperate enough to do anything to get the job done.

He laid his head back against the wall, removed his right boot, and massaged his foot. It was swollen and had stiffened right up. He couldn't remember twisting it, even after the jump. Maybe it was the cold and dampness. Maybe he'd turned it stepping on a brick or when he'd had to dive for cover. He scowled. This whole fucking place was horrible.

He glanced at Daryna between grimaces. Their missions were identical, but their endgames were poles apart. He knew he would have to ensure the bullet ended up in the back of Yermakov's head before she got him to safety. The logical move would be to remove her from the equation before finishing the job he had been sent to do. He wondered if she had any plans for him. He recalled what he knew of the NKVD.

Before the war, the Main Directorate for State Security had effectively two branches. It acted as the country's public police force: maintaining the international borders, sorting the rush hour traffic, it even extinguished fires. Then there was its more sinister arm, where political suppression was only one of its vices. It didn't take a genius to figure out that Daryna didn't drive a fire truck.

She may be his ally now, but he figured that if push came to shove, she would have no hesitation in eliminating him. Firmly wedged between two armies and a probable psychopathic roommate, he began to consider the sanity of saving her from the Waffen SS the previous day.

He glanced at her again, and their eyes locked. Her eyes sparkled an unforgiving black in the faint crimson glow of the burning city. He squeezed a smile as she inched closer.

'This is a dangerous place,' she said.

Daniel recoiled slightly. She drew closer still and placed a hand on his thigh. Her heat was like a morphine injection against the pain in his foot. He glanced down and then back into her eyes as her hand drifted towards his crotch. He clasped her roaming fingers and gently pushed away, but she was having none of it. She started to massage his groin, which stirred up all manner of sensations within him.

Daryna tugged gently on his zipper as she moved in to kiss his neck. She stood and slipped off her boots and pants. Gracefully, she swung a leg across his body and straddled him. Daniel's body secreted hormones by the bucketful, and every nerve tingled with nervous excitement. His stomach fluttered as she brushed her long hair across his face before moving her mouth to his lips. The tip of her tongue flicked at his as she drove her pelvis harder.

He would have liked it to have lasted longer, but it hadn't. And, he was sure it had been too quick for her liking, too. He might have felt the embarrassment of damaged masculinity were it not for this place and the potential for dying lurking around every corner.

They kissed for a few more minutes before she slid off and fixed her clothing. She moved away to where she had been sitting before and rested her head against the wall. With everything back where it belonged, Daniel listened for sounds of nearby disturbances, but all was quiet. The distant bombing had become less regular, and the crackle of rifle fire had all but disappeared. He tried to stay awake for the next few hours but failed miserably.

*

'Sir, I have to operate…'

'No…'

'But if gangrene…'

Daniel squinted, and two razors of bright light sliced into his retinas. The pain was intense. He shut his eyes.

'… foot… to relieve the pressure….'

He tried to open his eyes again, tried to focus. There were two people, two men, both blurred. One of them was shouting, the other not.

'It'll kill him…'

Daniel's stomach churned. He could feel his insides percolating. He started to gag. The arguing stopped. They turned toward him, and he passed out…

Daniel heard the voice, fuzzy, distant, vague.

'Hey there, sleepy.'

He mumbled. His head felt as though it had been rammed into a bulldozer. He turned toward the voice. He knew the voice.

'Dad?' His throat was raw dry. He opened his eyes.

'Don't talk,' Tom said. He touched Daniel's shoulder, gazing into his eyes.

'Where am I? What happened?' Daniel's voice cackled like a Thanksgiving turkey. He searched his dad for answers.

His dad dropped his head and looked the length of his body. 'You were caught in the middle of an air-raid.' He offered a cup and straw.

Daniel nodded gingerly, his face etched in pain. Recollection of the night began to emerge from the diaphanous mist of his memory. He touched his head and winced. One side of his face was covered with a bandage, as was his right hand.

'The others? My company?' Daniel asked, trying to ignore the aches.

Tom pulled a nearby seat closer toward the bed. He sat down, leaned forward, and cradled Daniel's hand in his own. His hands felt clammy like the air on a hot August night.

'Nine dead.' Tom's voice scoured across Daniel's skin like a rusty brillo pad. 'Some others injured.' He squeezed Daniel's hand. 'Including you.' He forced a smile.

Daniel's mouth still tasted like an Arab's sandal. He made a thick slackity sound as he rolled his tongue across his lips. Tom fed him some more water as Daniel glanced around the room.

It looked like a typical hospital ward. Thirteen beds lined each of the side walls. Every one of them occupied. Several nurses who looked as though they had been plucked from heaven moved between the beds, checking patient vitals, redressing bandages, and writing on charts.

'Germans bombed the city all night,' Tom said at length. 'Wave after wave.'

'As bad as London?'

Tom shook his head. 'Worse.'

'Why, Coventry?'

'They're targeting the industrial cities. Trying to break our spirit.'

'But the civilians?' Daniel's voice was becoming raspier.

'Unfortunately.' Tom said quietly. He offered more water, which Daniel declined.

'What day is it?'

'Monday.' Tom grinned. 'You've been unconscious for four days.'

That explained why Daniel's back was so stiff. In lying there for days, his muscles had cramped into the same position, a combination of that and his injuries, he supposed. He remembered the argument he had overheard after he had been brought in. He looked at Tom, his eyes flitting fearfully.

'My foot? They said something about my foot.'

Tom's face dropped. He glanced toward the bottom of the bed.

'Dad?'

Tom reached down and gently grasped the bedsheet. He pulled it back, and Daniel counted.

Two feet, ten toes.

Relief swept over Daniel like a fresh coat of paint.

'Any other damage?' He motioned to his heavily bandaged lower right leg.

'Well, you do look a state,' Tom said. 'You'd get seven years' bad luck if I showed you a mirror.'

Daniel tried to make a 'very funny' face, but it sent pain oscillating up and down his spinal cord. He touched the bandage on his cheek.

'You've some stitches under there. The doctor said you'll have that on for a few weeks. He doesn't know if there'll be a scar. We just have to wait and see.'

Tom stood and slipped on an overcoat.

'I've to get back home, tell mammy how you're doin'.'

'How long have you been here?' Daniel asked. His dad looked exhausted, his old face gaunt. He looked like he hadn't eaten a square meal in days.

'Since they brought you in.' He patted Daniel's shoulder. 'Now that you're awake and doing well, I'll be back at the weekend.'

Daniel nodded and watched as his dad made his way toward the ward doors.

'Dad. What about the girl I was with?'

Tom turned slightly and shook his head before disappearing out the door.

*

Daniel woke with a jolt. His muscles tensed, his eyes quickly searching the ruin in the gloomy morning twilight.

'Germans are attacking again,' Daryna said. 'Coming in from the northeast.'

He stared at her. She was wide awake and looked as though she had slept better than a hibernating bear. At least one of his niggling questions had been answered. If she had wanted him dead, she'd had ample opportunity.

He tried to draw a mental map of the city. 'The factory sector?'

She cursed them.

He could see the pressure building inside her.

'We'll move out when it gets a little brighter,' she said, 'I've radioed HQ. The Germans moved away from this sector during the night. We've left a small holding force to maintain watch while our men are redeployed to areas where they're most needed.'

They sat in the slowly growing light over the next twenty minutes before she got to her feet. She brushed a thin film of ice off her leather coat.

A single shot suddenly rang out. Daryna slammed back into the wall and screeched in agony. She slid to the ground and leaned against Daniel.

Daniel's waking weariness instantly vanished as his survival instinct kicked into gear. He stared at her and scanned her body for a wound, his eyes resting on a perfectly circular hole in her coat on her upper left arm. He slid across and checked behind to see if it had exited. He touched a slightly bigger hole and brushed his fingers off the wound. She let out a slight moan. There didn't seem to be any bone fragments, just blood.

'We're sitting ducks here,' he said, 'We've got to find a way out.'

She threw him an annoyed look.

'Since you radioed HQ, it must be a German. We're done for if he relays our position to a nearby patrol,' Daniel said, feeling his pistol and spare magazines in his coat pocket. He looked at the other weapons on the ground. If an attack came, they wouldn't be able to hold it off for too long.

He scanned the room and, using Daryna's position and the small gaps in the wall, worked out that the sniper had to be in one of the buildings across the street if, indeed, he was still there. That's what snipers did. Relocate to a new perch from which to crack off another round. Daniel knew it wouldn't do any good to look; it'd probably be the last thing he'd ever do.

But they were stuck. There was no back door and the only windows faced onto the street and the sniper lying in wait.

His mind whirred quicker than a Spitfire's propeller as he searched the walls for another way out; then, he saw it. It wasn't much – a tiny hole and an impact crater at the base of the wall to his left. It reminded him of what a burrowing animal might make if trying to escape from a pen.

'Wait here.'

Lying on his belly and using the mound they had built for protection, he crawled across the damp and grimy floor.

In less than a minute, he was at the hole. It wasn't as big as he had hoped and certainly not large enough for him to crawl through. Pressing his face against the wet floor, he peered out to the street. There were lots of rubble and timber, some in mounds a few feet high.

He grabbed the lowest brick and started twisting it from side to side. It didn't come away immediately, but it popped into his hand after a few tugs. Several more bricks followed the first onto the floor behind him.

Before long, he had torn a gap large enough to crawl through, but he hesitated. Even though the street on the other side was perpendicular to where the shot had come from, there was always the chance the sniper would see him if he went through. Was it a risk worth taking? Was there an alternative?

He closed his eyes and slipped his hand through. He held his breath as he waited for the excruciating pain of a bullet ripping through his flesh.

None came.

He pushed his hand further out, but still nothing.

Another moment of truth.

He paused, drew a deep breath, and, sucking in his belly, squirmed through. As he inched his way free, he braced himself, expecting to be picked off at any moment.

Once out, he squatted flat against the wall and looked at the buildings to his right. Either the sniper had already moved, or he was in a different building out of sight further down the street. His attention turned to the street itself.

That was a significant obstacle because it didn't offer any cover. It was about fifteen yards from side to side, of which Daniel guessed he would be visible for only the first eight or so. If he sprinted, he might make it.

He looked away to his left. That was another option. He could run and leave Daryna to whoever happened along. But he didn't consider it for long. She wasn't his enemy, not yet anyway. And besides, she may still prove useful. He turned back.

Sliding his back up the wall, he focused on the front door of the building on the other side of the street. That was his bull's eye. He retrieved the Lugar from his pocket, checked the magazine, and cleared the breach. He took several long, deep breaths, maybe his last, closed his eyes, and crouched.

One, two, three…, and he ran.

CHAPTER 34

Moments later, he dove headlong through the doorway, skidding face-first across yet another cold and grimy floor. He lay panting and wondered how he had managed to get across unscathed. He tried to recall what he had been thinking about as he ran but drew a blank. It was almost as if those few seconds had been wiped from his memory.

Daniel twisted his head and scanned the hall with his gun.

Bloody typical, there were plenty of doors in here.

He got up and walked cautiously to the back of the building, listening for any noise. He knew it might take a while to locate the sniper, but now the hunter had become the hunted.

Speed was essential if he was to get Daryna out safely. With the lower air temperature and her leaking blood, he had no idea how long she would last, especially if she went into shock. But he realized he couldn't just rampage through the ruins like an elephant stomping in a rowboat. Just because she might die didn't mean he had to. And so, a steady, methodical search was the key. Now that he was out in the open, he guessed that the shot had come from a second-floor window. But it was only a guess.

It meant he had to go up.

He found and frowned at a partially destroyed stairway at the back of the building he had entered. He could try it, but if one of the steps didn't support his weight, it could spell an ignominious end to an already far from glorious mission. He gingerly tested the first step, which surprisingly didn't yield under pressure, so he decided to risk it. Each step he took to the top was tinged with an increasing fear of falling until, eventually, he was relieved to place a foot on the first-floor landing. He looked to his right and rolled his eyes toward the second flight.

It looked worse than the first.

Heel to toe, Daniel moved silently to the bottom of the stairs. As he climbed, he hugged the ragged wall, catching his coat on flecks of chipped paint and brick as he edged his way to the top. He crept to the front of the house and peered into the room that overlooked the street. Aside from a bed frame, it was empty: no furniture, no books, no wallpaper, nothing, except a large hole in a wall. He edged across, snuck a peek, and slipped through to the landing of the building next door.

He checked the new building's front room, but it too was empty. This time there was no entry from it to the next one on the block. He blazed a scowl along the landing to the back of the building and the stairs at the far end. He puffed his cheeks and headed that way, realizing he had to go down and hope he could find another entrance to enable him to move into the next building. All the while, he considered the possibility that the sniper was on a completely different floor or perhaps gone altogether.

Before he got to the top of the stairs, he glanced into the back room and stopped. It, too, was empty, but thankfully, with a hole in one of its walls large enough to crawl through. That was the beauty of terraced houses. If the access was there, you could get from one end of a street to the other without stepping onto the pavement.

He thought back to the attic in his own house. It was, in fact, just one long attic that ran the entire length of terraced houses on his road. If he wanted, he could have walked from one end of his road to the other by merely moving above his neighbors' heads.

Just as he got to the hole, he heard something on the other side. His body tensed immediately. He strained his ears to make it out and smiled at the sound of fingers tapping a rhythm. Daniel peeked through.

A soldier squatted against the wall at the end of the hallway, quietly surveying the street below. Daniel watched as the guy tapped on his rifle in time to whatever tune he was softly humming. This time Daniel recognized the Russian uniform.

He shook his head.

They're shooting at each other.

He quickly considered his options and figured he was better an ally than an enemy.

He stuck his left leg through the hole and eased the rest of his body through. He strolled toward the soldier.

'You should take better care with your aim,' he said in Russian.

The soldier wheeled around, dropping the rifle on the floor with a clatter.

Daniel was surprised to see it was a woman, and a pretty terrified one at that. Her legs gave way, and she collapsed onto the floor. With arms and legs flailing like an upside-down spider, she scrambled wide-eyed on her backside, ramming the back of her head against the wall. Her body shook as her eyes searched for a way to escape.

Daniel forced a smile and put his hands up to try and calm her down. But she saw the German handgun and immediately dived to retrieve her rifle.

'No,' Daniel shouted, 'I'm a friend.' He took a step forward. It might have looked menacing.

She grabbed her weapon and swung it in Daniel's direction.

Without thinking, he aimed the handgun and called out again.

She seemed not to hear, her finger inching toward the trigger.

Daniel reacted before she could get a shot away, firing a single shot into her chest.

She slumped to the floor, almost in slow motion.

He held the smoking pistol for several seconds, his mind not registering what had happened. When he emerged from his daze, he hurried to her side and checked for a pulse. But he knew it was futile; his shot had been too accurate. The Germans had been right. What kind of war would make women fight on the frontline? He slipped her hat off her head and stroked her short, brown hair. She had a youthful but strained face, a teenager toughened from years of living on the streets. He looked closer at her, into her dead eyes. Maybe she was somebody's girlfriend. She might have been his in a different place or at a different time. A surge of remorse appeared from nowhere; it overwhelmed him, landing like a house on a wicked witch.

He hated himself. He hated this war. Hated what it had done to him, what he had become. He closed his eyes and wept.

Eventually, his thoughts drifted back to Daryna.

He covered the soldier's face with her soft hat and stood. He turned to retrace his steps, but something outside caught his eye. He hunched down and moved in for a closer look.

Two people stood in a doorway several houses down from where he and Daryna had spent the night. He was perplexed by their casualness, chatting as though the war were a million miles away. He watched them for a few seconds, his eyes moving between the two. Then he focused on the man. He leaned forward, squinting. Daniel's lips were caked dry, but every nerve lit up like an electric circuit board.

Running on automatic, he sprinted to the stairs, a euphoric exhilaration swamping him.

CHAPTER 35

'Don't go.' Nina gripped his shirt tighter. She was on the verge of emotional disintegration; Anatoly could see it in her watering eyes. She shook her head pitifully and stared back at him

'I have to.'

'Don't leave me.'

He placed his hands on hers.

'Then come with me?'

'I have to wait for my mammy and daddy. You *know* that.'

Anatoly looked at the ground between them and whispered. 'I don't think they're coming back.'

'But they promised.' Her voice croaked.

'I know, but look around.'

Nina's eyes flooded, and as her tears streamed, they eroded canyons through the layers of dirt on her face. She shook her head again.

'Please don't go.' She clung to him and squeezed.

Anatoly put his arms around her.

'It's not safe here anymore. The Germans are all over the city. You heard the fighting yesterday; it was the worst it's been. I… We have to get to the other side of the river.' He paused. 'I'll bet we find your mother and father over there worrying sick about you.'

'But you don't know that.'

'I know…' Anatoly started, 'I know a lot of things, and I know that when your parents see you again, their faces will light up, and your tears will be of happiness.' He smiled and wiped her face gently.

Nina began to open her mouth when suddenly he was ripped from her grasp and propelled through the hall door. Through bleary eyes and a dusty haze, she stared after him.

Daniel was first to his feet. He brandished the Lugar and pointed it directly at Anatoly's head.

'Anatoly Yermakov?' he asked, in a clear and steady voice, despite his nerve-endings shooting off like fireworks at an American 4th of July display.

Anatoly struggled to his knees. A dazed expression imprinted on his face. Blinking, he tried to focus on Daniel. He held his hands up to shield his face, then turned away.

'Don't shoot… please.'

Daniel's hand was unwavering.

'I asked you a question,' he said, although he already knew the answer.

On all fours, Anatoly stared at the hallway floor, unable to move, petrified.

This was it. Two months' intensive training and thousands of miles traveled had led Daniel to this moment. A blissful serenity engulfed him, despite the waging war swirling around him.

He took careful aim and pressed the muzzle against Yermakov's matted, greasy, blonde hair. His finger tightened on the trigger.

It would be all over in a second.

The Germans wouldn't claim their prize; their journey wasted. Russian atomic research would be set back decades, and he would return home a war hero.

His masters in London would be pleased.

London. Whitehall.

His father worked there. He thought of him… and then, oddly, his mother.

He shook his head. He had to remain focused. But Catherine's smiling face flashed into his mind. What would she think of what he was about to do? Would she understand this was for the greater good? Her smile melted away and became a look of disappointment.

Daniel glanced past Yermakov, at the floor, at the scientist's splayed hands; they were shaking, covered in blood as though he had been finger-painting with red ink. Daniel looked slowly along the hallway. The entire length was flooded with pints of half-dried blood, like a sticky, scarlet skating rink. His eyes moved up the walls and lingered there. More blood. Bits of bodies.

The place stank of death.

He looked back to Yermakov and jammed the barrel harder into the teenager's head. He tried to pull the trigger the last millimeter that would end it all. His hand started to shake and seep sweat. He re-gripped the gun and blinked his eyes.

His mother's face suddenly morphed with the girl he had killed in the building across the street.

Daniel's face contorted.

He pressed the fingers of his free hand into his eyes, wiped his sleeve across his face, and tried desperately to drive the images away. But the girl's face was replaced by the soldier he had strangled two days ago. He remembered the bulging red eyes, heard the last gurgling breath, and smelled the stench as the Russian defecated himself. If there was such a thing as innocence in this place, two innocent Russians were dead at his hands. His eyes refocused on Yermakov. Daniel's third Soviet victim.

After what seemed an eternity, he glanced sidelong at the girl. She hadn't budged. Her mouth was wide open, but no sound emerged, like Lot's wife after she had disobeyed the angels, while outside, the Russians and Germans traded blows in this modern-day Sodom.

He tentatively lowered the gun and stared at Nina

'Get off the street,' he said, 'There's a lot of fuckin' snipers out there.'

He walked deeper into the house and called back to Anatoly. 'And you, get off the damn floor.'

Daniel went into the kitchen and plonked himself on the floor. He slammed the gun beside him and brought his knees to his chest to hug them. Through the doorway, he watched Nina and Anatoly. Neither of them spoke as they followed, like children who had been summoned to the principal's office. They looked terrified, neither sure of what fate lay in wait. They stood before a scowling Daniel.

At length, he said, 'I came here to do a job.' He paused. 'But murdering an unarmed civilian isn't like killing a couple of Kraut soldiers. Mind you, whatever you've got yourself mixed up in, doesn't necessarily classify you as a civilian. All I know is that you're more bloody dangerous than the entire 6th Army, and somebody wants you out of the picture for good.'

'W-w-who are you?' Anatoly barely got the words out.

'That's not important.'

Nina threw Anatoly a frightened glance.

'You know that's why they're here,' Daniel said, beckoning to the street beyond. 'They've come to take you back to their Fatherland.' He sneered. 'We couldn't let that happen. We're hanging on by our fingertips back home. We had to try to tip the balance.'

He rubbed his unshaven jaw, the stubble making his skin itchy and dry.

'Now I've got a problem. What the hell do I do with you?' He motioned to the wall opposite, and Nina and Anatoly sat down.

He tapped his fingers off his knees. Nina and Anatoly didn't interrupt. He stared at the girl, who looked as though she was about to throw up.

'What's your name?'

'... Nina.'

'Well, Nina, relax. I'm not going to harm you.' He glanced at Anatoly. 'Nor you, it would seem.' He looked around. 'This your place, Nina?'

She nodded.

'Any water?'

She started to make a move.

'Whoa,' he said. 'Any food?'

She glanced towards the pantry.

Daniel looked into the cupboard but saw it was bare.

'Not much in there.'

'Downstairs.' Her voice was barely a whisper.

'Anyone else here?'

She shook her head.

Daniel believed her; the poor kid was scared out of her wits.

'Lead the way.'

Daniel and Anatoly followed her through the secret door behind the pantry shelves.

'Nice,' Daniel said in a low voice.

They walked downstairs, with Daniel taking up the rear. The last thing he wanted was to let Anatoly out of sight until he had decided what to do with him. He stared after the boy genius; he didn't look like much. Baby-faced, innocent, naïve, and blissfully unaware of the danger surrounding him, hunting him. How could somebody so intelligent not realize they were such a desired commodity by every civilized nation on the planet. Mind you, what the two armies were doing to each other on the surface could hardly be deemed civilized.

'Have you been down here long?' Daniel asked him.

'Almost a week.' Yermakov was still shaking.

'Judging by the mess, it looked like it was pretty busy upstairs.'

'We heard German and Russian voices in the house on different days. The frontline seems to move back and forth.'

'I don't think there is a frontline.' Daniel paused. 'Why didn't you go up when the Russians were here?'

Anatoly glanced at Nina. 'We didn't think they were alone. Sometimes we heard both at the same time. Besides, they may have shot at us.'

Maybe he wasn't so naïve after all, Daniel thought.

Nina went to the small cooker and emptied a tin of beans into a saucepan. She was about to light it when Daniel clicked his fingers.

'Don't do that. It'll smell.'

She suddenly turned paler than a chameleon in a sandstorm, realizing how stupid she had been. Daniel relented.

'You've gotten away with it so far. Best not to tempt fate.' He smiled.

She looked at him, clearly not understanding the idiom, which he didn't bother to explain.

'I'll take it cold.'

Daniel watched her empty the beans onto a twisted tin plate and fetch a canister of water from a cupboard under the small, slit window. He wondered how the two had met. He knew from Anatoly's dossier that the Ukrainian hadn't any relatives in the city. As for Nina, what was a child still doing in Stalingrad? Had they met by chance? They looked such an unlikely pair.

The growling in Daniel's stomach and the hardened thirst had withered away several minutes later. He sat back and watched the pair watching him. He looked at each, in turn, baffled as to what his next move should be.

Leaving Yermakov to his own devices could result in him falling into either German or Russian hands, an outcome that would gall his superiors and mean he had failed his mission. On the other hand, either side might complete his mission by killing the scientist by mistake, but depending on that outcome was risky. There were no guarantees. Then there was the reason he was here in the first place, but he had already decided not to add a civilian death to his rising body count. The three sat quietly in the cellar for over ten minutes while Daniel ruminated.

Outside, the roar of aircraft dropping their payloads on what remained of the battered city continued, shaking the ground and spraying the three of them with dust from the cellar rafters. The shriek of German 88s and the continuous crackle of machine-gun fire seemed to surround them and disrupt Daniel's decision-making process. He glanced at his watch; the killing had resumed, and it wasn't even what his mother would call breakfast time.

Then a thought struck him. A flicker at first, but as it fueled his imagination, it grew until it became a raging bonfire like the infernos blazing across the burning city.

He rechecked his watch.

He closed his eyes and tried to recall the distance and direction they would have to travel. Undoubtedly possible in peacetime, but traipsing about in a swirl of bullets and bombs bordered on the insane. Besides, he had no idea what lay in wait. It would be a hell of a walk through a Hell on earth. But it was an alternative, maybe the only one open to him.

He checked his watch for the third time. 6.22 a.m. That would give them just under ten hours to get to the airfield to catch today's flight. If they missed it, they would have to sit it out until the same time tomorrow, which didn't appeal to him. Every additional minute spent in the city was one more that might shorten his life. He just had to convince Yermakov, but how?

'My father fought in The Great War,' Daniel said quietly, without making eye contact with Anatoly.

'He fought in a war that didn't achieve much except kill a lot of his comrades. So many people died back then with nothing to show for it, and here we are, at it again. He was by the Somme…' He allowed his last words to hang in the air and raised his eyes until they met Anatoly's.

'We didn't fight on the Somme.' Anatoly said.

'True. Russia didn't, but the French, Belgians, and the British did.'

Anatoly eyed Daniel for several seconds. 'Who are you?'

'A friend.' Daniel smiled.

Slowly Anatoly nodded; Daniel could see he had started to put the pieces together.

'You have a problem, alright.'

Daniel laughed. It had been one of the few times he had done so since he had joined the army, and it felt good.

'I left my father in England to come here.' Daniel paused. 'You haven't seen your father or mother in how many years?'

'Almost seven.' Anatoly bowed his head.

'They've missed all your achievements. Your doctorates, your research–'

'What do you know about my research?'

'Why do you think I'm here?'

'It's supposed to be secret…' Anatoly said quietly, a tear rolling down his cheek.

Daniel stared at the young man. With slumped shoulders and an unshaven face, he looked a great deal older. The strain of his short life's work embroiled in this war had taken its toll.

'I've read your file,' Daniel said. 'Why do you think you were asked to move to Stalingrad?'

'Resources.'

Daniel shook his head.

'In this country, resources are plentiful. You didn't have to move from Kyiv. Besides, you're Ukrainian. I didn't think you got on with the Russians. There are stories of your countrymen fighting with the Germans against the Bolsheviks.'

Anatoly looked up. His eyes were swollen red, almost to the point of bursting. Daniel knew he had to seize the moment.

'The NKVD abducted your parents.'

Daniel waited a few seconds and then delivered the hammer blow.

'And what about Anya? You don't really believe she's still alive? With your parents gone, she was the only person keeping you in Kyiv.' He paused. He knew his next lines had to be delivered with the utmost precision if he was to convince Yermakov to abandon the country.

He inhaled deeply and said, 'The NKVD killed her as well. They had to make sure you continued your research. Murdering her removed any ties you had to your city. It made it easier for them to get you to come here. I wonder what they'll do with you once you finish your work. They don't consider human life to be all that precious.'

Daniel's words clung to the cold, damp cellar air.

'You've been manipulated all your life.'

In the time it took to breathe, the dam burst, and Anatoly erupted into an uncontrollable fit of misery. On the far side of the room, Nina looked on bewildered. Daniel let him cry before leaning across and putting an arm around him. Anatoly reached out and threw his arms around Daniel, embracing him tightly.

All outside distractions disappeared. Neither of them could hear, much less care for, the thundering battle being fought. Daniel could feel the anguish explode from Anatoly's body, almost as though he had known the truth all along but had refused to believe it. Now it had been released.

In that instant, they were simply two little boys.

After a while, Daniel spoke. 'I can try to protect you.'

Anatoly pushed back and rubbed his eyes with his palms. 'How can you—'

'You can come with me. There's a plane coming to pick me up in a few hours. I can get you on it.'

'And if I don't?'

Daniel shrugged. 'You'd sooner stay here? I'm offering you a way out, a chance to start your life over again, the opportunity to do what you want and not be told what to do like some organist's dancing monkey. Most people rarely get a second chance.'

His eyes bored into Anatoly's, hoping the teenager couldn't see how desperate he was to get him on that plane. Daniel didn't have the stomach for another pointless murder.

In the end, it didn't take long. Anatoly's firm nod caused Daniel's heart to skip a beat. He hadn't believed he could convince Yermakov to leave and, quite frankly, was amazed at his powers of persuasion. He stood.

'What about Nina?' Anatoly said.

Daniel looked across at her. A young girl tagging along would hold them up, maybe make them miss the plane. On the other hand, she gave credence to the fact that the three of them were civilian refugees.

'Okay, Nina, grab a couple of coats and get some food and water for the three of us.'

Nina looked shell-shocked; the second time Daniel had seen her that way. He went across and laid a comforting arm on her shoulder.

'That is if you want to?'

'But my parents?' She looked like a scared fledgling about to take her first flight out of the nest.

'I've seen a lot of dead civilians. They'd been out digging tank ditches, scrounging for food. Your parents may not be alive.'

Nina started to weep, and Anatoly reached out to hold her. He pulled her close to stifle her wailing.

'You could keep Anatoly company at least until the war is over. Maybe you could come back and search for your parents after. You never know. You might be lucky. They may survive. There are still civilians alive in the city; look at you two.'

She eventually stopped crying and searched Anatoly's eyes. He nodded a comforting smile. She shook herself and wiped away the tears, rubbing her filthy hands on her already dirty clothes. She turned away and began to scavenge the cellar for supplies.

Under Daniel's instruction, she packed three small bags with enough food and water to last the rest of the day.

The easy part was done. He had convinced Anatoly that his destiny lay elsewhere. The hard part was making sure he could get the genius there. He patted the Lugar in his coat pocket for reassurance and climbed the stairs.

CHAPTER 36

It was early morning when Cumming marched briskly through the narrow Whitehall streets; the unmistakable tinge of autumn carried on a crisp, easterly wind. Reconstruction work had already started on some damaged buildings as workers busied themselves with cleaning up following another night's raid. It was a never-ending cycle of bombing and rebuilding. Still, as Browne once said, 'it was essential that morale be maintained, by keeping the population's thoughts and activities fixed firmly on providing for the greater good'.

As the Colonel climbed the steps, a whistling breeze caught him by surprise, making him wish he had worn an overcoat. Having survived all that 'Jerry' had thrown at him, it simply wouldn't do to succumb to a dose of pneumonia.

Once inside, he paused in the lobby and checked the time. He didn't want to be late.

Several weeks ago, Browne had begun to host daily breakfast meetings. He even had a tidy round table brought in, especially for the occasion, where the only invitees were the Colonel and Sir Christopher.

Neither man ever disappointed.

Both men had noticed a change in their superior. He seemed to have aged quicker than everybody else, which worried them. It appeared he had grown tired of the war with its constant pressure to deliver. In truth, they were all tired. Hostilities on the western front had been a stalemate for months. The Germans bombed them, and they retaliated. Maybe it was the other way around – it all depended on your point of view.

Browne's apparent apathy for the cut and thrust appeared to have sparked when Miller stepped off the Portsmouth pier. If they didn't know better, they would have said he regretted the decision to send the young man away.

The fact was, they didn't know Browne at all. He didn't have any friends and never socialized. He never dawdled with the military brass or strategists after meetings, opting instead to head directly back to his office, no doubt, to re-immerse himself in some report or other. The only person who knew him was his secretary, and they doubted she was any more enlightened than they.

Cumming bounded into the outer office and nodded to a furiously typing Ruth Kendrick, who barely glanced in his direction. It seemed that administration waited for no woman.

He slipped his head around the door and spotted Browne and Sir Christopher, already seated before a breakfast of scrambled egg, toast, and freshly brewed tea. He glanced at the mantelpiece clock beyond them and smiled. Perfect timing. He took his seat, and the three men bowed their heads; so had become their ritual.

After a few seconds, they glanced at each other and tucked in.

'What of the plans for Europe?' Cumming asked nobody in particular. He scooped a blob of butter onto some toast.

'Progressing.' Browne poured tea into the three cups.

'Point of entry?' Christopher asked.

'We're reviewing options,' the old man replied.

Cumming sprayed a liberal dose of salt on his egg. 'Pas de Calais?'

'Too heavily defended.' Browne shook his head. 'Only a fool would attack there.'

'That'd be the least likely, alright.' Cumming cut his toast into several rectangular sections.

'But the shortest crossing point,' Browne said, immediately contradicting himself. He placed his knife and fork on either side of his plate and sighed.

The three fell silent for a moment.

'And the Germans in Russia?' Cumming pushed some egg delicately around the plate.

'At a standstill in Stalingrad,' Christopher said. 'Same as yesterday.'

'Same as every day.' Browne said. He planted his elbows on the table and breathed heavily, cupping one hand inside the other. It was the bloodiest custody battle the earth had ever seen; Fatherland and Motherland going at it hammer and sickle.

'The Russians are stubborn. They won't give it up.' Cumming threw Christopher a worried glance.

'I've been notified of a planned winter offensive,' Browne said, his mood suddenly brightening.

Cumming and Christopher stared back at him.

'Surely they haven't the manpower or the weaponry?' Christopher said.

'They have an abundance of both, and Herr Hitler is none the wiser. As he's pushed his 6th Army deeper into Russia and demanded that they take Stalingrad in search for young Yermakov, he's overextended his supply lines.'

'An elementary error,' Cumming said, with a pompousness that drew a dry smile from Christopher.

'It would seem so.' Browne sipped some tea.

'Judging by the communiqués we've intercepted over the past few years, it would seem Hitler has surrounded himself with counsel that is more likely to tell him what he *wants* to hear rather than what he *needs* to hear,' Christopher said, 'It's a pity really, he'd done so much for the country.'

Cumming shot him an angered glance but understood the sentiment. Hitler's rise to power had been nothing short of remarkable, albeit after a stuttering start. But, as with the most brutal dictators, his eventual descent into psychopathic paranoia inevitably led to him being surrounded by only the most loyal sycophants. The growing feeling in Whitehall was that history would soon prove it to be a recipe for disaster.

'Be that as it may.' Browne paused. 'What of our man?'

His intonation almost made it sound as though they had sent a schoolboy to fetch a quart of milk from the local corner store, but then, that had always been his manner. In Browne's mind, every question was simple, to which there was an even more straightforward answer.

'No news from Bletchley and no news from our other man over there,' Cumming said cautiously. 'But then, nothing of the Waffen SS sent in either.'

'Maybe he's blunted the German spearhead,' Browne said.

Cumming set his cutlery on the plate. 'Possibly. Or maybe the Germans have their man already. Communication between the squad and their command ceased around the same time as Miller's insertion.'

'Then why would they maintain their attack on the city?' Christopher asked.

'Why not?' Browne looked at Christopher. 'It's not the attack that needs to be maintained but the deception.'

The room descended into silence once more. While Cumming and Christopher played uncomfortably with their food, Browne tucked heartily into his.

'Of course, there is the other matter,' Christopher said.

Cumming glanced at him. He had been thinking of that too.

'There was a good reason why Miller hadn't been selected for the mission in the first place. Will that come back to haunt us?' Christopher looked between both men.

'I don't care what your amateur psychoanalysis proposes,' Browne said, 'Fear will override his natural tendency for empathy. As soon as he gets his hands on Yermakov, he'll blow his head off, which will be his ticket home. Do you believe he'd risk his own life pulling some other foolhardy stunt?'

'Have we done the right thing?' Cumming asked. A sudden and uncontrollable surge of guilt lathered his conscience. 'Or have we sent a young man to his death? I mean, it's not exactly France. We don't have many friends in Russia.' It was the first time he had questioned himself, and he couldn't understand why.

Christopher flashed a scowl in his direction.

'It was your plan.' Browne wiped a bit of egg from his lip with his tongue.

'And one that everybody bought into.' Cumming tried not to show it, but he started to regret the decision. 'It was the only viable option open to us.'

'There are always alternatives.' Browne slipped a fork of egg and toast into his mouth.

Cumming felt a red mist brewing but wasn't in the mood for an argument. He had toiled for an entire week on the operation, putting in twenty-hour days to fine-tune the detail. He had been precise in every aspect, but even he realized it was out of his hands once Miller had stepped aboard the submarine. Thousands of miles away, the warring armies would grip the mission and ultimately decide its fate.

He felt powerless.

'It's too early to tell,' Christopher said, coming to the Colonel's defense. 'He just dropped in a few days ago. It might take him days or weeks, or he may never find Yermakov. All we can do is await word from Cairo and continue to monitor communications coming out of the eastern front. We might get lucky.'

'Or Miller might get dead.' Cumming slapped the table. The china cups rattled in their saucers.

Browne and Christopher stopped eating and stared at the Colonel's face, flushed with agitation.

'You've sent men on missions before, knowing them to be one-way trips. They've known it too, yet they still go.' Browne stated flatly. 'We gave Miller the option of turning us down. He didn't. Nobody put a gun to his head. Christ, he practically begged us to go.'

Cumming was at bursting point. He knew Browne was right, but it didn't make it any easier. He sucked in an enormous breath and exhaled slowly, sulking at the breakfast. He sat back, pushed the plate away, and dabbed his mouth with a napkin, tossing it on the table.

Across the table, Browne and Christopher eyed him between nibbles and sips.

The war got to everybody, eventually. It drained the fight out of even the hardiest of souls. Nobody was immune.

*

Tom sat in his office in Whitehall, scanning the local papers for news of the war in Russia. He knew there would be nothing about Daniel, but he didn't want to miss anything. Even though his job allowed him access to classified war information that would never be passed to the media and would never become public knowledge, sometimes the simple truth in a broadsheet made the whole experience less intense. Even the odd journalist's perceptive commentary raised hope from time to time.

He had found it impossible to concentrate on anything except his son. Ever since he had waved goodbye, it had affected his life immeasurably. His productivity was down, and he knew his superiors were aware of it, but they had said nothing. Most of them had lost sons to the war. Some still had sons fighting overseas, in Africa and the Far East. They knew the pain he felt. They shared the pain. Sleep had been scarce, his appetite scarcer. He moped around the office during the week and the house at the weekend. He knew he was driving Catherine barmy, but she never complained. Sometimes, he floated into the local for a jar, only to leave an unfinished glass of ale on the countertop whenever the conversation turned to the war, as it inevitably did.

Hope and prayer had become his mantra, and he clung to both, believing that Daniel was still alive while he silently cursed the military for taking both his sons. He had been there. He knew the brutality of war and that the odds of a safe return were slim.

He stared at the paper, not reading, just reliving the horror of a lifetime past.

CHAPTER 37

ANATOLY HAD NO IDEA HOW Miller would get himself out of Stalingrad, let alone all three of them. But he seemed to have a plan, which was good because, for a genius, he had come up short. With the frontline seemingly dispersed across the city, hiking through it seemed a ridiculously dangerous proposition, but he had no other option. Miller could have shot him already but had changed his mind.

Why?

Why was Miller willing to risk his own life to save him? He had just met the man and now already owed him his life. On a more positive note, at least he was out of the stinking cellar. The air outside might not be much better, but at least the scenery had changed. He could feel his mind slowly change gear as the young synapses began to fire once more.

He felt alive again.

He grasped Nina's hand as they stayed a couple of yards behind Miller, who appeared to be leading them north-easterly. That made sense. The Germans would have approached the city from all sides, pinning the Russian army back against the river, so it was more likely that they would meet friendly faces by going that way.

He couldn't believe the level of devastation he saw around him. Not one building remained that didn't bear scars from the German bombardment. It was indescribable, almost as though he had lain in the cellar for a thousand years as the city eroded and crumbled above him.

He was delighted that Nina had also decided to tag along. The thought of leaving her alone in the city had torn him apart for days.

Their immediate destinies seemed connected, so if he could stay alive, then maybe, so could she. The surrounding mayhem didn't seem to frighten her, which impressed him. With squadrons of Junkers strafing not so far to the north and south and the grinding sound of tank tracks playing a discordant harmony against the constant backdrop of machine-gun fire, she had readily resumed her duty as unofficial city tour guide.

Miller seemed surprised too.

The deeper they went into the city, the more he noticed that the smaller link roads blended into one another, forming one enormous, vacuous blast crater. Great mounds of concrete, bricks, and splintered wood were scattered haphazardly all over.

It had occurred to him that their area had become very quiet and not as it had been last night. It was almost as though they were being pulled forward by an invisible force into some devious Russian trap.

But there was no alternative. All they could do was press on, albeit at a cautious snail's pace.

However, as the sounds of the battle gradually grew dimmer, the further east they went, Anatoly grew more confident of Miller's escape plan, guessing that any soldiers up ahead would most likely be Russian and that they wouldn't fire on three of their own. Of course, the soldiers had to recognize them first.

After a couple of hours of painstaking plodding, they paused for a breather inside an old, gutted warehouse. Conversation was non-existent while they rested. Anatoly could feel Miller's eyes scour his face, and he wondered if the Englishman might change his mind. Surely it would be easier for the man to kill him, leave Nina, and make good his escape. So why was he taking such a risk? What motivated a man to travel so far into such a hostile environment for the purpose of killing, only to have a change of heart at the crucial moment? How did such a man operate? He couldn't understand it. He also thought hard about what he would do if Miller decided to complete his mission as he'd been instructed.

Then again, what could he do against a trained killer with a gun pointed at his head?

Refreshed somewhat, the three resumed their journey, only to stumble upon a major intersection after a few minutes trekking. They stopped. Nina paused, seemingly unsure of which direction to take.

'This way,' she said, pointing right. 'The river isn't far from here.'

Without warning, they almost collided with a large, ragtag group of soldiers lurching toward them. The three froze and then relaxed once they recognized the Red Army uniforms. Anatoly reckoned there to be less than twenty in the group.

He glanced nervously at Miller, whose hand had slipped into his coat pocket. He imagined the man's fingers tightening around the pistol's grip. He caught a glimpse of Miller's eyes. The message was clear – not one false move.

As they drew nearer, Anatoly was surprised at how little notice the Russians took of them, almost as though they were an insignificant threat on a well-worn battlefield. He scanned their hanging and drawn faces, wretched in despair and disillusionment. He eyed their bloodied bodies, bits of them ripped off. Patches of dark, semi-congealed blood leaked from jagged holes, dripping on their uniforms, staining hastily applied bandages. Even if he wanted to give himself up, these men would be useless to him. They weren't even in a position to save themselves.

Memories of the scattered bodies he had seen on his way into the city a week ago flooded back. But those soldiers had been dead. These men were alive, even if only barely. Their methodical, swaying gait reminded him of the lilting 5/8 rhythm of Rachmaninoff's 'Isle of the Dead'. The only question was – would they get to pay Hades' ferryman, Charon, to cross the Volga safely?

He reached out to a soldier, the only one he saw with any command insignia. He could feel Miller's eyes bore into him as his hand moved slowly out of his pocket.

'How far to the front?'

Miller's hand slid back in. The soldier half-turned and half-mumbled a reply, which Anatoly deciphered as 'about a quarter of a mile'.

'Are we in full retreat?'

The soldier shrugged and continued walking.

They stood and stared as the walking dead tramped past. Anatoly glanced at Nina. Her face had turned a ghostly white. He put his arm around her and pulled her close. Miller, on her other side, looked equally horrified but also relieved.

Once the rabble had disappeared into the smoldering haze of ash, soot, and dust that continued to choke the air, Anatoly looked across at Miller. His mind was made up. He couldn't and wouldn't continue his research. He wanted no further part in whatever demonic creation he was capable of contriving. His life now lay in the Englishman's hands.

Anatoly nodded and grasped Nina's hand. She looked up at him, and his smile let her know they needed to do the right thing, which meant getting out of the city.

*

No more than a hundred yards behind, and ignoring the piercing pain in her arm, Daryna watched them pick their way towards the river. Her eyes barely registered the tattered company of soldiers winding its way northwards.

She had heard the single pistol shot and assumed that Dimitri had taken out the sniper. She hadn't cared whether it was a Russian or a German. What grabbed her was the sight of him charging across the street a few moments later. She had managed to glimpse Anatoly from her hiding place before Dimitri smashed him through the hall door.

That had left her feeling both delighted and perplexed. As Yermakov was only a stone's throw away, her search was finally over, and she knew Evgeny would be pleased. Maybe he would give her a promotion and a ticket out of Stalingrad. What intrigued her, however, were Dimitri's actions. Even as they had searched the ruined city, she had been careful not to discuss Yermakov; she had never once shown him a photo of the boy. So why did he attack him? If he was a threat, then why hadn't Dimitri just shot him? It didn't make any sense, and that made her feel uneasy.

It had crossed her mind that, if Dimitri did know who Yermakov was, he might claim her prize as his own. That idea hadn't sat well with her, either. It meant she had failed and so had become disposable. If that was the case, death was a possibility, the Gulags a certainty.

While she had waited for Dimitri and Anatoly to re-emerge, she had radioed back to Korolev. She needed him to contact Moscow and get as much information as possible on Dimitri. Between strings of swearing sentences, she had told him that he was to contact her as soon as he had an update. In the meantime, she decided to track them to see what developed.

Once her quarry was at a safe distance, she stepped out from the shadows and continued her pursuit.

*

Over the next half an hour, the landscape of tightly packed and ruined buildings slowly gave way to scatterings of abandoned and burned-out summer houses that overlooked a natural bend in the Volga.

The Englishman suddenly stopped and crouched low. Instinctively, Anatoly and Nina did likewise. Anatoly stared at him intently as Miller's eyes roamed the relatively flat terrain before zeroing in on a sound coming from the right. Anatoly watched Miller dive onto his belly and slide across the dusty soil towards a small stone wall. There, he inched his way up to a crack and peered through.

Anatoly yanked on Nina's hand, and they moved across to Miller. Once beside him, Anatoly copied Miller and peeked through another crack.

Less than a minute later, several trucks trundled to a stop near the riverbank, no more than thirty yards away. A couple of soldiers jumped off the back of each and threw back the tarpaulins.

Anatoly's heart started to race at the sight of the enemy so close. He glanced at Miller for a reaction, but the man was tight-lipped and deadly calm as he continued to watch. Anatoly turned back and looked on. Nina began to say something between them, but he gently placed a finger on her lips.

A mixture of terrified children, women, and old men flowed off the truck like lemmings off a cliff. Some women tried to calm their hysterical kids as the older adults looked on, their eyes frantic with fear. Several German officers appeared from the truck cabins, barking orders that the Russian peasants clearly didn't understand.

One of the officers pulled a Lugar from his holster and fired a bullet into the skull of the old man standing nearest him. Nina jumped as the man fell knees first into the sand, the rest of his body crumpling like a worn accordion. That had the desired effect of maneuvering the rest of the civilians closer to the water's edge, the children's wails intensifying beyond consolation.

The group of shivering Russians was lined up and forced to their knees facing the Volga. The German soldiers towered behind them, their weapons cocked.

Hidden behind the wall, Anatoly watched Miller withdraw his pistol, his teeth gritted. He looked as though he was about to make a move, but Anatoly grabbed his arm. Miller snapped his head around, his eyes blazing red. Anatoly shook his head; sadness painted across his face.

Miller tried to make another move, but Anatoly's grip tightened. The two stared into each other's eyes as the first volley of shots rang out. Huddled between them, Nina had curled into a ball. Her hands cupped over her ears.

The firing stopped soon after, and with it, the children's wails. The brief quiet that followed was disturbed moments later by the trucks' engines coughing to life.

Anatoly sat motionless with his back to the wall and watched as Miller fingered the pistol as the engine drones faded.

He felt numb.

Should he have let Miller do something?

He felt drained.

It would have been suicide if he had.

He felt powerless.

He looked across at Miller. His head bowed to his knees. Miller ran his fingers through his hair before thumping the ground. Next to him, Nina lay her head on his tummy. Her eyes clamped tightly shut.

Anatoly turned back and looked through the crack again. What he saw horrified him.

Over a hundred bodies sprawled, half on land, half in water; the gentle, rippling current rolling them from side to side, their blood leaking into the river, turning the water wine-red. A couple of smaller, younger bodies drifted away from the shore along with the steady stream of debris being purged from the city.

He scanned the row of dead, scarcely believing what had just happened. What kind of people would turn their guns on a city's most vulnerable?

It was unfathomable, unthinkable. All those things. His hatred for the Reich and all it stood for sizzled in his stomach. Whatever food he had eaten bubbled. He felt as though he was going to vomit. But then his eyes settled on a solitary figure hunched over some of the bodies.

Surely nobody could've survived. He eased his head over the top of the wall for a better look.

Sure enough, one person was alive, but he recognized the grey uniform. He turned towards Miller, but he had already hurdled the barrier and raced across the sandy divide.

Anatoly watched Miller's sprint become a trot before, eventually, slowing to a walk.

The soldier stood and turned.

Even at this distance, Anatoly could see tears stream down the German's reddened face. The soldier shrugged as Miller approached and dropped his rifle on the sand. At no more than three feet away, Miller raised his pistol, his face flush with fury.

CHAPTER 38

THE YOUNG SOLDIER STARED HELPLESSLY at his executioner, his eyes glazed over, his shoulders sagging, his hands hanging limply by his side. His hair was tossed and greasy, dust and dirt ingrained in his uniform like lice. But all Daniel saw was a German with the blood of millions dripping from his fingers

The soldier didn't cry out, didn't run, and didn't try to defend himself.

Daniel stared coldly at him and, for an instant, imagined Alex lying on the Dunkirk beach. Rage, borne in his subconscious, pumped through his arteries, propelled by his tortured heart. He would end this man's life here and now: another eye for an eye. He started to pull the trigger but hesitated. Somebody had shouted something. His finger drew back on the trigger once more.

'Stop, please!'

He shook his head and looked back to the wall. Anatoly stood with Nina, his arms wrapped around the child. Both stared at him, their expressions as dark as the soot-black clouds that choked the city. He turned back to the German, who hadn't budged. Something wasn't right.

He looked beyond the man at the lifeless bodies, their blood pouring into the already polluted water. His gaze shifted to the far bank a few hundred yards away. A couple of Russian officers stood staring through binoculars. There was plenty of activity over there as troops moved north, probably to the same crossing point he was headed toward. Daniel briefly wondered why the Russians hadn't fired on their enemy before he returned to the German. The man had started whimpering, but not, Daniel thought, because he knew he was about to die.

Daniel lowered his pistol without knowing or understanding why and slipped it into his pocket. He heard footsteps behind him.

Anatoly placed a hand on his shoulder. 'We should get to the ferry.'

Daniel nodded, still staring at the soldier. Without uttering a word, he turned and led Anatoly and Nina away from the butchered civilians.

They had walked no more than thirty yards when the sound of a solitary rifle shot pierced the relatively still and quiet air. Anatoly and Nina looked back. Daniel did not. He knew there was nothing to see except a falling corpse released of its anguish.

Instead, his eyes followed the river north as he focused on his own problems. He tried to work out how close the airfield was. He looked into the heart of the dying city to get his bearings, glancing at Anatoly and Nina.

'Have we far to go?' Anatoly asked.

'A few miles that way.' Daniel pointed directly across the river. 'Somewhere over there.'

Daniel wondered if the Luftwaffe hadn't already visited the airfield and carpet-bombed it out of commission. Without it, his escape plan was shot to hell, and what then? He didn't even want to think about that.

They resumed their journey along the sand before climbing back onto a narrow path that ran parallel to the river. As they walked, Daniel's head continually twisted back and forth like a broken lighthouse beacon. He had thought they were well on the Russian side of the line, especially having bumped into the Russian soldiers earlier.

He'd got that wrong.

He wondered if *anybody* knew where the battle lines were or if the whole place was just some giant smorgasbord with pockets of Russian resistance, besieged by larger pockets of invading German forces.

The place was a total fucking mess.

They had been walking for about forty minutes, spying Russian and German planes fighting for control of the skies like buzzards circling a fresh carcass. Daniel's attention was momentarily diverted to a familiar silhouette descending from the southeast.

The Dakota's landing gear was down and coming in fast.

He could make out muzzle flashes emanating from all sides as it defended itself on approach. Bursts of flak appeared indiscriminately across the sky, seemingly firing at everything and anything within striking distance.

The mission had been relatively successful so far. What Daniel didn't need was his luck to run out and for the Dakota to take a direct hit from a dozy Russian gunner drunk on more than his daily ration of vodka. He checked his watch and cursed. The plane was a full hour ahead of schedule, and he knew it wouldn't hang around the airfield a second longer than it took to unload its cargo, rearm, and refuel.

Time was running out.

He hurried to the river and looked frantically up and down the water's edge for a boat or something that might get them across. He glanced across to the other side.

Less than two hundred yards.

Anatoly and Nina looked on as he searched the scattered undergrowth. He pulled back bushes and lifted debris but found nothing. He started to panic.

So close.

His breathing shallow, he strained his eyes north along the riverbank. Amidst the smoke, gunfire, and explosions, he could see figures moving a long way off, but he couldn't be sure which army was entrenched up there.

Surely, they had to be Russian?

He glanced across the river again. It wasn't that far. Maybe they could swim. But he didn't know anything about the currents. Judging by the speed of the flaming wrecks that floated by, it was just too dangerous. His mind was made up for him. They had to plow on for the ferry.

Another couple of hundred yards further on, and the noise level had increased, in stark contrast to their rate of progress. They found themselves scouring the skies and diving for cover whenever a plane flew too close. With Swastikas emblazoned on their tail fins, their sweeping strafes cut the horizon to pieces; they were clearly closing in on the Russian lines.

Soon though, the Stukas and Messerschmitts disappeared, and the resounding thumping of the flak guns died away. Daniel figured that meant only one thing, the inevitable infantry assault on what remained of the Russian bridgehead. He nodded to Anatoly and Nina, and the three dashed for the lines.

They ran awkwardly with their hands in the air towards a row of blasted-out buildings that seemed to have borne the brunt of the attack. Now and then, Daniel spotted some movement through a hole or from behind a wall. His biggest fear was being shot by a punch-drunk Russian as they ran across the open ground.

The ground.

It was littered with bodies. German and Russian, men and boys, sprawled recklessly like confetti on a wet day. Some of them clung to the enemy with outstretched arms. They were so close. It was hard to tell if they had been fighting to the death or trying to save each other from certain death. The scene was disgustingly confusing.

Daniel's eyes continued to search the buildings.

'NKVD,' he shouted, his heart skipping beats. 'Let us through.'

Nobody fired as they approached and stumbled over the barricades. The Red Army soldiers were either suffering from concussion or were too scared to fire on an officer of the state's secret service.

He saw soldiers cowering among the devastation as they prepared themselves, checking ammunition and shouting orders. The deeper they went, the more men he saw mobilizing against attack, their numbers exponentially increasing as soldiers seeped like cockroaches from bunkers buried into the side of the hill.

They zipped through the rows of men who would soon defend the last few parcels of a city still under Red Army control. Daniel knew the battle could erupt at any moment.

Then, out of the haze ahead, he spied several ferries lumbering from the east, sagging to sinking point, carrying more troops to the city. The pounding in his chest was matched only by the sound of a far-off artillery bombardment. He broke into a jog and pressed Anatoly and Nina to pick up the pace.

By the time they got to the makeshift dock, the smell of sweat, feces, decaying corpses, and fear forced them to breathe through their mouths. Daniel raced to the closest ferry. All the soldiers had disembarked as blood-saturated medics frantically loaded some wounded for the return trip. There were guards all over, preventing everybody else from boarding.

Another moment of truth.

Daniel stepped forward, only for one of them to jab him in the ribs with the butt of a rifle. He crumpled at the man's feet and struggled to take in any of the putrid air. The guard snarled at him and was about to bury the rifle into the side of Daniel's head – he was too slow. With a speed that belied his exhaustion, Daniel unleashed a punch into the guard's crotch, causing the man to collapse into a groaning heap next to him. Daniel followed it up with a right cross that laid the Russian out flat. Some of the other guards watched and laughed.

Struggling to his feet, Daniel bellowed at the guard. 'Don't you know who I am, you idiot?'

Having been knocked unconscious, the guard didn't respond; his face scrunched into the bubbling mud.

Daniel glared at the other guards, who backed off. He held the upper hand. 'General Zhukov has ordered me to take this man and this girl back to Comrade Stalin.' He pointed a shaky finger at Anatoly and Nina before holding his ribs with a grimace. There was something broken in there. He motioned to Anatoly and Nina, who followed obediently, a look of utter shock plastered on their faces.

It took the medics only a few moments more to fill the creaking ferry before shoving it away from the jetty.

As if to compound the sickening smell, the ferry's pilot started up the diesel engines, which belched thick, toxic fumes into the barely breathable air. Daniel tumbled onto the deck and moaned. Anatoly and Nina rushed to his side and rolled him over, positioning him upright against the hull.

'At least I've earned my spot on this tug.' He forced a smile.

They had only moved a few yards from shore when all hell broke loose again. Another flock of ME109s roared in from the west, spitting bullets over the jagged rooftops. It sent those still on the riverbank scurrying for cover. Many were cut down before they had run more than a couple of yards. The ferry's pilot gunned the engines to an ear-bleeding scream, trying desperately to get the last knot out of the boat.

Daniel pulled Nina and Anatoly toward him and rolled over on top of them. Nina let out a slight yelp as his pistol jammed into her ribs.

A Stuka dive-bomber screeched from above and let loose its load, which missed and smashed into the river a few yards away, spraying an enormous plume of water into the air, and drenching the ferry's passengers. The men screamed madly, knowing they would be carried to the river's bottom if the boat sank.

Having obliterated as much as they could on the shore, it was the turn of the ME109s to have their fun with the retreating wounded. Time and time again, they swooped past, ripping bullets into the wooden hull and the men on board. Daniel could feel Anatoly and Nina contract under his body in a desperate attempt to make themselves as small as possible. Still, the pilot drove the ferry hard, with those still alive collectively willing it to the other side.

Then it came. Almost in slow motion and bereft of noise. Another Stuka landed a bomb plum onto the pilot's cabin, showering splinters, blood, and body parts over the remaining petrified passengers. The engines gurgled their last cycle, and the ferry began to tilt forward, taking on gallons of water by the second.

They were going down.

Daniel forced himself to look over the side. They were only about twenty yards from the riverbank, but he had no idea how deep the river was.

Decision made.

'We've got to swim before the suction pulls us down.'

Shaking, the three scrambled to their feet and practically fell overboard into the cold water, joining some of the other men who'd had the same idea.

The pain in Daniel's stomach was excruciating, but he wasn't about to give up. He bobbed his way towards the bank, dragging at the water with the one arm that wasn't clutching his abdomen. A few yards ahead, Nina and Anatoly made steady progress. He kept an eye on them and breathed a sigh of relief when he saw them stop swimming and begin to wade out.

But he struggled. He still couldn't feel the bottom, and the pain in his ribs was intolerable every time he tried a stroke. He could feel his body sink lower in the water as tiredness engulfed him. Waves sloshed into his face, and he found it increasingly difficult to catch a breath without swallowing half the Volga. He kicked his legs but felt as though his body was immersed in cement. He realized he should have at least taken off his jacket and boots. Another wave washed over him. He slashed at the water again, searching for something to grab onto, anything that would keep him afloat, but he was going down.

He knew it.

He tried one last kick, one last stroke before another wave buried him, and he sank.

CHAPTER 39

Daniel held what little breath remained in his lungs. He craned his neck upward, straining his body against gravity and the river's suction, but the light from the surface grew dimmer the deeper he sank.

His body, arms, and legs flapped aimlessly, like a beached whale struggling to return to the sea. His lungs seared with pain, gasping for oxygen, but he knew if he inhaled, then that would be it. Maybe it would be best to open his mouth and welcome the relief of death. The pressure intensified around his body, squeezing the air and life out of him – he had no more to give. He looked up to the surface one last time and breathed.

The pain was worse than he could ever have imagined as the rancid Volga scorched into his lungs. He immediately regretted his decision. Panic swamped him. His eyes flared and bulged as he kicked, dragged, and clutched at the empty water.

He was dying.

Then, something touched him and pinched his hand. It brushed his head, pulled his hair, it yanked his arm. He felt his body being hoisted limply as his soul slipped away. The scene around him brightened, and Daniel wondered if he was on his way to heaven. If he was, he expected to see St. Peter block his path before swiftly passing judgment; eternal damnation – punishment for the murders he had committed.

But it wasn't heaven. It wasn't even close. He was still in Hell.

Daniel felt himself being pulled along the river surface. He blinked his eyes, coughing uncontrollably, despite the pain in his ribs returning. He spluttered his lung's contents into the river. It was a common cliché that a drowning man clutched at straws, but he didn't have the energy. Not anymore. He allowed himself to drift.

He scanned the city on the other side of the river through bleary eyes. It was dying, cloaked in a dense, gray haze of smoke and dust. There were few fires now, as most things that could have burned already had. The sound of people shouting seemed distant, like children's delightful yelps in a faraway playground.

His dangling feet finally found purchase on the river bottom as he was dragged to shore, his body scraping along the bank. He twisted his head and saw Anatoly and Nina, both panting, fall beside him. He turned on his side and coughed up more of the Volga along with some undigested beans.

The three lay there for a while, among the others who had made it.

*

From beneath a burning truck, Daryna watched as Anatoly and the girl waded back into the river and hauled Dimitri to safety. From where she was, it didn't look like he was alive – that was one less thing she would have to worry about. But then, he turned onto his side and threw up.

She had been so close to catching them with the other NKVD soldiers around her for safety. Now, she cursed the Germans for their attack. She smashed her fist into the soil and gritted her teeth.

As Dimitri and the girl lay on the far side, she looked hurriedly for another ferry to take her across, but her search was futile. Several boats lay marooned on the shore or listing in the river, some of them exploding, all of them burning. Along with corpses, patches of flaming oil slicks floated past, smoldering like darkened logs on a fire.

Despite being so desperate, the panorama was captivating. Daryna felt like she could gaze at it for hours, completely enthralled by the chaos and destruction at its barbarous best. She sighed. She felt at home.

But it was short-lived. Beside her, the radio sparked to life. She threw it a furious scowl and snapped up the receiver.

'What?'

She listened for the next minute or so, her eyes following her prize, scampering up the far mud bank. As the caller spoke, her scowl changed to a smirk.

Without so much as a thank you, she slapped the handset back into its cradle and considered what had been said. She knew what she had to do. Her gaze shifted to the river. She was surprised at the current's strength. The ferry had made more of a diagonal journey as it had tried in vain to make the crossing.

Now, it was her turn.

She climbed out from under the truck and removed her coat. She winced when she touched the blood-stained bandage she had hastily applied while waiting for Dimitri. She tossed the coat into the truck's fire along with her boots.

Making sure her prey had disappeared into the undergrowth, she waded into the river, cursing its biting coldness. A month or two later and she would have been able to walk across its frozen surface.

As soon as she was up to her waist, she took a breath and dived forward. She almost choked as the freezing water shocked the air out of her lungs. She rose to the surface and gasped, her cold breath forming a small cloud that hovered briefly on the surface. The good news was that her wounded arm didn't hurt anymore, anesthetized by the glacial water.

With every ounce of strength, she began to stretch out, one stroke after another, until she found a good rhythm. At the back of her mind was the knowledge that if it were this cold in the river, it would be far worse once she emerged on the far side.

Breathing every second stroke, she could feel her muscles tighten. The cold was so acute that her back lapsed into spasm several times. She wondered how deep the river was but tried desperately to block the thought out. She knew she wouldn't be able to hold out much longer, which only made her more determined to get across. After all, there was nobody around to save her if she went down.

It took her more than five minutes of unimaginable torture before her feet touched the bottom. The woman who staggered out of the river no more resembled the beauty of the one who had dipped her toe in on the other side, but rather a disheveled geriatric with an overdue date with 'The Reaper'.

She wrapped her painfully sodden, uniformed arms around her body and climbed unsteadily up the verge before collapsing to her knees. She was exhausted but knew she had to keep her circulation going, which meant she had to keep moving.

Gritting her teeth, she pulled herself up and headed through the bushes to continue her hunt.

*

The three pushed through the torn undergrowth, leaving behind only a handful of wounded men, floundering helplessly on the riverbank, the rest having perished by bullets or drowned. Despite being soaked and uncomfortably cold, there was a spring in their step. Although only separated by a couple hundred yards, they were far safer on the eastern bank than in the battleground they had just left. Over here, they would meet only other Russians, which improved their chances of survival immeasurably.

And meet them they did, in their thousands. They stumbled upon a massive staging area with troops frantically preparing themselves – nobody paid them any mind.

Not only was Daniel's side hurting, but his right foot had started to ache. The ice water had caused it to completely stiffen to the point where he shuffled with an exaggerated limp. He could no longer feel his toes, and his ankle had swelled up and started chafing against the inside of his boot. It may have been his mind playing tricks, but he was sure that the numbness was creeping up his leg with each step.

As they hurried past the massing troops preparing to meet their fate, they were guided by a continuous blanket of flak that peppered the sky further on. Daniel figured it must be coming from gun deployments around the airfield. Bombing runs had all but ceased. The German planes had to contend with their buzzing Russian counterparts, each fighting for dominance of the skies.

But eventually, after a couple of kilometers of half-running, half-stumbling, the aeronautical activity overhead died away as both air forces broke from their killing. The grating sounds of war, too, had faded, with only some of the largest explosions heard. All three felt the effects of their journey, and their pace slowed to a sluggish crawl.

They found themselves in a lightly wooded area. Shafts of late afternoon sunlight streamed through the bare branches. Underfoot, their feet crunched on fallen leaves. It would have been a perfect place to picnic had it not been for the cold, the war, and their escape.

Very soon, they spotted a pair of Russian soldiers strolling around some open ground as though they were walking a dog in the countryside. Daniel knew the only way forward was to approach them with the same confidence he had shown at the ferry crossing. He would flash his soggy, fake identification and bullshit his way through the rest. Sticking out his chest as far as he could without passing out, he neared the soldiers.

'Which way to the airfield?' He started to withdraw his papers.

The bemused soldiers looked at him, then beyond, to a shaking Anatoly and Nina, before glancing at each other.

'Over that way,' one of the soldiers said, thumbing behind him toward a dense bank of tall trees. The other soldier simply stared, seemingly unsure what to make of the bedraggled trio.

Daniel was amazed at their naivety, which bordered on stupidity. He gave them a cursory once over. They wore spritely, clean uniforms, were clean-shaven, and had their rifles slung over their shoulders like they were carrying a couple of knapsacks. At a guess, he figured they hadn't been anywhere close to a battle, probably never been across the other side of the river (no doubt the sons of people in high places, people who made sure they were protected by keeping them out of the firing line).

'Don't you think you should check my identification before you disclose that kind of information?' Daniel's eyes burned brighter than a bonfire.

'Y-y-y-yes, sir.' One soldier reached for Daniel's papers, clearly shocked at the rebuke.

Before his fingers touched them, Daniel snapped his ID back and shoved the forgeries into his pocket.

'What the fuck are you doing?'

The two soldiers, their eyes wide open, took a half-step back.

'I could be anybody, and you're just going to let me roam around here, unchecked? Give me your names.' He was quite enjoying this heckling.

The two soldiers gawped at him, unable to speak.

'Oh, forget it.' He pushed past them. 'You didn't even ask who they were.' He indicated Anatoly and Nina, who had drawn up alongside him.

Anatoly and Nina followed a grinning Daniel as he stormed off in the direction the soldiers had pointed. He couldn't believe how easy it had been to get past them. If their performance were a measure of competence in the Red Army, then Hitler would have a free run to the Urals.

'Not so fast,' a sharp voice called from behind. It was female.

The three stopped and turned around slowly. The blood drained from Daniel's face long before he laid eyes on her.

'Where do you think you're going?' Daryna said with a crooked smile.

Beside her, the two soldiers had their rifles trained on him. Both looked as if they would crack off a round without any hesitation but equally looked as though they wouldn't be able to hit the side of the Titanic from an iceberg.

Daniel's mind clouded. He was so close to escaping. He could smell the airplane fuel and hear the fighters' engines scream as they revved for take-off. After all he had been through, to come so far, only to fail with a couple of hundred yards to go, would be devastating.

Despite the deepening depression, his mind whirred. This was what he had been trained for – to get himself out of these situations. His mind automatically clicked into gear.

'I'm taking this man back to Moscow,' he said, taking a step forward and pointing at Anatoly. He ignored the way her sopping clothes clung to her shapely body.

'Without me?' She dramatically feigned hurt. 'You knew I'd been searching for Anatoly.'

'And you failed. I got him first. I'm bringing him in.'

'I don't think so.'

In an instant, Daryna's smile vanished. She eyed Daniel like a Rottweiler would a 16lb steak; the only thing missing was the lip-licking. She slid a pistol from her trouser pocket and pointed it at him.

'You can't be trusted.'

'What do you mean?' Daniel forced a smile, even though his ribs and foot were killing him.

'The way you left me for dead back there. Not a very gentlemanly thing to do.'

'Time was against me. I couldn't risk the Germans capturing him.'

Her stare burrowed into his. 'I don't think it's the Germans I need to worry about.' Her sinister smile returned. She glanced at Anatoly and the girl.

For a moment, Daniel's heart stopped beating. Was the game up? Did she know who he was? If so, how? He hadn't time to think about the 'how'. He had to call her bluff.

'I don't know what you're talking about.' He took another step forward.

'Don't move.' She straightened her arm as if to emphasize the point. 'I'll blow your brains all over this field.'

'Stop.' Nina put her hands up. 'Don't hurt him. He was only trying to help us get away from here.'

Daryna fixed her eyes on the girl. 'And what's your name, dear?'

'Nina.'

'Well, Nina,' Daryna said, swinging her arm. 'Don't involve yourself in things that are none of your concern.' She pulled the trigger.

'No!' Anatoly screamed.

He started forward, but it was too late. Nina's body collapsed next to him. He dropped to his knees and plucked her off the ground. He hunched over her, pulling her into him. Nina's body hung limply in his arms like a piece of soggy cardboard.

'No, no, no.' Anatoly wept into her matted hair, 'Why did you do that?'

Daniel looked down at Anatoly, rocking back and forth, clutching the young girl. If he hadn't seen it with his own eyes, he wouldn't have believed what Daryna had been capable of. But then, who was he kidding? She had watched a dogged Waffen SS squad obliterate her team and then stood firm while he had executed each of them in turn. She had watched her comrades die in a firing line as an example to the rest of the men. She had even dragged him all over southeastern Stalingrad just to see out her search.

Now, this.

Daryna refocused her attention on Daniel. If anything, her smile had broadened.

'Look, Daryna.'

'No, you look, Dimitri, or wherever the fuck your name is. I've had it with your bullshit. I've checked. There is no Dimitri Guskov stationed in Stalingrad.'

'What? Do you think we keep accurate records of everybody who comes in and out of this place? There's a fuckin' war going on.'

'True.' She smiled. 'The regular army isn't as well documented as it could be.'

In a heartbeat, Daniel's expression turned from annoyed to smug.

'But every NKVD soldier is. And you're not on any list. In fact…' Daniel could tell she was enjoying this. 'Nobody's ever heard of you.'

'Most likely an oversight. Besides, I'm from Moscow. I don't know anybody here,' Daniel said. He shook his head in disappointment. 'I'm not surprised.'

Daryna laughed. 'If there's one thing we Russians are very good at, it's keeping records. You should know that. I don't believe for a minute that we've made a mistake. So, the only questions are, who are you, and what do I do with you?'

She cocked her head inquisitively. 'Actually, I don't think you're Russian at all, so… maybe German?'

Daniel tried to appear blasé, but his skin was crawling with fear.

'No.' She shook her head. 'Not by the way you executed that squad.'

Daniel forced a sheepish look.

Her smile returned. 'Too much pleasure in killing some of your own. I'm running out of nationalities. But then, I wonder why you're heading in this direction, to get to the airfield, perhaps? But why? Steal a plane? Where would you go? Any planes parked there have limited range. We don't fill them up because it'd be a waste of fuel if they're shot down. So, what then? What other planes going in and out of this particular airfield have a range longer than I can spit. Then it hit me.' Her eyes gleamed as she hissed.

'British.'

The two of them stared at each other for several uncomfortable moments. Daryna spoke again. 'Judging by the look on your face, I think I'm right.'

It was true. Daniel had tried not to let her glimpse what he was feeling, but inside, his nerves squirmed. It was one thing training for this, quite another pulling it off.

She had him.

'What do I do with you?' She waved the gun around like she was a schoolgirl with a lollipop. 'My superiors would be delighted to learn that I've foiled an attempt by our allies to capture one of our prized assets. They could use that information in their political games.' She spoke with a lyrical tone that belied her venomous eyes. 'But I wonder if they'd prefer you dead or alive?'

Daniel prayed she thought that they'd want him alive. Behind her, the two soldiers fidgeted and glanced at each other, their rifles bobbing limply.

'Of course, I'd be commended for taking you in alive. I might even get a promotion, but is it worth the risk?'

Without warning, the anti-aircraft guns behind them opened up, dotting the sky with deadly clouds of flak. Out of nowhere, several Messerschmitt 109s strafed overhead, skimming the treetops. Further away, Stuka dive bombers screeched their way towards the earth, their wailing sirens obliterating the quiet.

Blood drained from the two soldiers' faces, and they tore off, only to be cut down, having run only a couple of yards. Daryna launched sideways as bullets from a 109s MG131s laid a pair of parallel furrows into the soil behind her. Instinctively, Daniel dived on top of Anatoly and the dead Nina.

Explosions thundered away in the distance.

Amidst the chaos, Daniel knew the airfield was taking another pounding. The flak guns continued to pebble-dash the sky, trying their best to dissuade the Luftwaffe from approaching.

Daniel glanced behind at the 109 that had flown overhead. It banked steeply to the left as though it was returning for another pass. Unfortunately, he didn't see the second 109 steaming in after the first.

It dropped its payload right on their position, and everything went black.

CHAPTER 40

DANIEL TRIED TO MOVE. HE waved his arms through a sea of dirt and strained his neck towards the light, spitting out mouthfuls of mud. He spluttered and coughed, his face red, his eyes tearing up. He couldn't hear anything except low, dull vibrations, the sort generated by pressing the left-most pedal of a church organ. He was buried neck-deep in the ground on which he had been standing. He tried to wiggle his toes and move his feet, but they were either buried too deep or were gone.

He strained to search the small clearing for anybody else but had difficulty focusing his eyes. His head throbbed as though he had just woken up the morning after a thousand shots of vodka. He struggled to free himself, pushing the soil away with his legs and climbing out with his arms; it was like swimming in a bowl of rancid treacle.

It took him more than a minute before he finally managed to extricate himself from the mire, kicking away the last of his earthly restraints. He lay on the ground, his heart pumping blood to every muscle in his body, his lungs gulping in air.

Thankfully, the Germans had withdrawn their attack. He heard movement to his left and raised his arm to shield his eyes from the sun.

Behind him, Daryna struggled to her knees. She patted the ground in front of her as though searching for a pair of glasses. Then Daniel remembered – the gun.

Instinctively, he reached inside his pocket to retrieve his weapon but came out empty-handed. He glanced over his shoulder and saw Daryna crawling across to one of the dead soldier's rifles. He turned back to his patch, his eyes searching the ground.

He glimpsed behind again and spied Daryna rising to her feet, using the rifle as a crutch. Adrenaline swept through his body. He froze as soon he heard the double click of a cocked rifle.

Daniel turned around on his knees and faced her, his eyes red and drawn. He sat back on his heels and hugged his heaving ribs, gasping for air.

She stared down at him.

This was it, and maybe he deserved it. He had killed people and not just the enemy. He had murdered Russians, his allies, just to complete his mission. Had it been worth it? He didn't know anymore. His mind was numb. He just wanted a way out, and Daryna would give it to him. He had nothing left, no adrenaline, no fight, no flight.

Nothing left to give.

'Get it over with,' he said in English.

She raised the rifle until he could see her one open eye behind the gun sight.

A shot rang out.

His body bucked in response to the searing heat of the bullet, mining its way through his abdomen. But he felt nothing.

No heat, no pain.

Before him, Daryna dropped the rifle and crumpled to her knees in slow motion. She fell sideways onto the dirt.

Daniel stared at her for what seemed like an age.

She didn't move.

Out of the corner of his eye, he spied movement. He turned and saw a man about twenty yards away, a pistol cradled inside one of his palms. He dropped his hand to his side and threw Daniel a grim nod before looking away.

Daniel followed the man's eyes to Anatoly, who lay rolling around on the ground. Daniel staggered to his feet and hobbled over. He gave the Russian a quick once over, but aside from several cuts which leaked thin, red lines of blood, he seemed fine.

'Are you okay?'

Anatoly nodded weakly and glanced at the body next to him. Apart from her bloodied coat, Nina looked as though she was sound asleep. Anatoly rolled over and touched her face. Daniel saw a tear roll down Anatoly's cheek and decided to leave the two for a moment.

He looked back at Daryna and thought he saw the merest movement. He gingerly got to his feet and scampered across. Her eyes were closed, and he couldn't detect any breathing. He put his fingers on her neck.

A pulse. Weak, but there.

He picked up the rifle and flung it as far into the underbrush as possible. The other man drew up alongside him. His pistol gripped firmly by his side. Daniel glanced up at him. The man didn't look down but continued instead to scan the tree line.

'You should hurry if you're to catch the plane,' the man said with a rich, English, public-school accent. Daniel stood slowly and stared at him for several seconds.

'Igor,' Anatoly called from behind him. 'What are you doing here?'

Daniel could hear the confusion in his voice. He looked back. Anatoly was sitting on the ground cross-legged, cradling Nina in his arms. Daniel hurried across to the scientist, ignoring the sudden arrival, who looked as though he'd just stepped out of the silver screen.

Anatoly rocked back and forth and stared past Daniel at the other man. Daniel heard him approach and, spotting a pistol lying next to Anatoly, bent down, and casually picked it up.

'Hello, Anatoly,' the man said. His voice was warm and sincere, as though he was speaking to a grandson.

Daniel turned and faced him. Figuring the man would have killed him if he had so wished, he didn't bother to raise his pistol to defend himself. Instead, he stared intently, seeking an explanation, albeit a brief one.

'What are you doing here?' Anatoly said.

A coy smile slipped across the man's face. 'Making sure you catch your flight,' he said in Russian. He looked at Daniel.

'I had hoped not to have intervened,' he said, switching quickly back to English, 'but I knew what chased you.' He glanced at Daryna, lying on the ground.

Daniel could swear he saw a flicker of satisfaction flash across his face.

'She foolishly trusted me, didn't know who I was, what I was…'

Daniel decided to take a chance.

'Do we have a mutual friend in London?' Daniel asked.

'One with a limp?' The man said. The smile of a distant memory seemed to sweep through his mind.

Daniel nodded. That was all the confirmation he needed. The man was the double agent he'd heard about, the spy working with Sir Christopher. He wondered how much of his life he'd already given away to embed himself so deeply in the Soviet system – how alone and difficult it must be to become another person. He wondered if the man would be angry that he had had to reveal himself but, oddly, saw no emotion to that effect. If anything, Daniel saw what he believed to be relief as the man looked back at Anatoly.

'I'm happy you made the decision you did. I wouldn't have been able to go through with it myself. I'm not so sure those who sent you here will agree with what you've done, but then that'll be their problem to solve.

He looked around as though he was taking in a mountain vista. 'You need to get a move on. I'll tidy up here.'

Daniel nodded gratefully.

'You have to leave her,' Korolev said to Anatoly. 'I'll look after her.'

After a few moments that Daniel thought would never end, Anatoly laid Nina gently on the ground and got to his feet. He looked down on her one last time before going over to the man and throwing his arms around him.

'I really don't know who you are, do I?' he whispered.

Korolev smiled and gently patted Anatoly on the back.

'You get out of here. We'll meet again once my business here is over.' He shot Daniel a strange look that Daniel found hard to understand, but if he could have interpreted it, it would have been that of a man who knew he was destined to die on foreign soil. He stood back and stared at Anatoly proudly.

'It's been a pleasure to know you, Anatoly.'

With that, he leaned down and scooped Nina into his arms before turning and walking away.

Daniel took Anatoly by the arm and led him away. They shuffled across the clearing, Anatoly glancing back at Korolev several times until they had slipped into the small woods on the other side.

It was unusual to find any wooded area around Stalingrad, even more so since the Germans should have bombed every leaf off every tree to destroy or flush out hidden armory or regiments. In the end, the woods weren't that deep, and they soon found themselves on the far side.

They stopped and crouched.

Ahead lay a vast meadow of uncut grass, littered with pockets of bomb craters. It was surrounded on three sides by the woods, obscuring visibility to artillery spotters in the city. Over near the trees to the left was a large area covered by camouflage tents. Closer inspection revealed several steel containers.

'Fuel depot,' Daniel said.

On the opposite side of the field was another camouflaged tent under which Daniel could make out several people scurrying about, checking the sky with binoculars. Daniel figured that to be the control tower, although it wasn't much of a tower.

'Smart move, not having the depot near the tower. One direct hit and…' He mimed an explosion with his hands. 'I wouldn't want to be near it.'

Not quite what he had been working on for the past few years, but Anatoly agreed.

Batteries of now-dormant flak guns flanked the airfield, shrouded by similar green tents, their barrels pointing skywards in anticipation of another attack. Daniel completed a quick tally, totaling thirty-five. All were silent, but their crews were busy restocking their arsenals as several supply trucks leapfrogged each other on their delivery routes in what appeared to be a well-rehearsed routine. The closest to them was no more than sixty yards away.

Daniel's mind wandered to the aircraft. He searched the rest of the field for the Dakota he was sure had landed but couldn't see it anywhere. In fact, he couldn't see a plane of any description. That wasn't a good sign. Had the transport been and gone? He didn't think so. He was sure he would have seen or heard it taking off.

He broke into a cold sweat just thinking of the near impossibility of hiding undetected in the woods for another twenty-four hours. He groaned and gingerly rubbed his side again. He felt Anatoly's hand tug at his sleeve. He looked at the Ukrainian, whose eyes were fixed firmly on the control tower tent.

Anatoly pointed.

Two men dressed in pilot's uniforms exited and walked, quite casually, along the tree line before ducking into it and out of sight.

'RAF.' Daniel could barely contain his excitement.

The pair watched that section of trees to see if the men would reappear.

'Where have they gone?' Daniel said.

After a few moments, his question was answered. The sound of an engine sputtering to life filled the air, and his face brightened. The unmistakable whine of a single Pratt & Whitney R-1830 Twin Wasp engine swept across the field, followed by a second. But, still no plane.

They looked at each other, baffled.

Then, ever so slowly, a thin, vertical crack appeared in the trees where the men had disappeared. The gap yawned wider until it became an enormous, gaping, rectangular hole of blackness.

Daniel's jaw slackened as he looked on in disbelief as the nose cone of the Dakota emerged from the darkness.

'Incredible.' Daniel said. He quickly scanned the field for anything that might resemble a runway but couldn't make one out. Actually, he found it hard to discern any path that wouldn't have at least one bomb crater in the way, but it didn't matter. This was their only opportunity. They had to get on board.

Daniel turned to Anatoly, who looked at him expectantly.

'Are you sure you want to do this?'

'You haven't left me much choice.'

'You have a choice. You could keep heading east, although it's risky. I doubt the Germans will catch you now, and the Russians might not know where to look for you.'

Anatoly shook his head and looked back the way they had come. 'There's nothing left for me in this country.'

Daniel bowed his head. He was right. The NKVD had been so effective in isolating Yermakov that they had left him destitute. Daniel almost felt guilty for having played on his misfortune.

Almost.

'Okay.' He set his sights on the plane. 'We walk across the field towards the plane, not too quick, not too slow, somewhere in between. We don't want to let on that we're desperate to catch it, but at the same time, we don't want to miss it. Got it?'

Anatoly nodded, his eyes wide. 'Will it wait for us?'

'Yes. Once the side gunners see us, they'll let the pilot know. He should delay takeoff.'

'What if they don't?'

'They're under instructions. They've to keep their eyes peeled for me every day they come here.'

They looked at each other. Daniel could see he was scared, and if he were truthful, he would have said he was too.

Happy that he had allayed Anatoly's fears, he summoned his last morsel of energy and started to walk into the clearing, with Anatoly matching him stride for stride. Amazingly, the searing pain in his abdomen had been replaced by hopscotching butterflies.

They had walked no more than thirty yards before the Dakota had cleared the hanger and accelerated to taxiing speed. It was a magnificent sight.

Daniel's heart pounded at the thought that a little piece of England was within touching distance. With the pain almost completely dissipated, it took all he had to restrain himself from sprinting to the plane in a screeching, arm-waving frenzy.

That was when the shooting started.

CHAPTER 41

DANIEL REACTED FIRST. HE GRABBED Anatoly by the arm and tore off, half-pulling, half-dragging until the boy matched his pace. The ground around them sparked to life as bullets zinged past their bodies and over their heads.

Daniel could feel his heart thumping faster and faster, driving the oxygen and adrenaline in equal volumes through his arteries, powering the muscles in his legs and propelling him forward. He pressed on through the pain in his abdomen, his lungs gasping for air. He looked across at Anatoly.

For an academic, the Soviet gave him a run for his money, but Daniel knew that when the adrenaline spiked, people could become superhuman.

Less than twenty yards ahead, the Dakota swung its tail around, and its engines roared as it prepared for take-off.

The pitch of the bullets suddenly changed, and Daniel realized that the plane's gunners had spotted them and were laying down covering fire. He could think of far better places to be than stuck in the crossfire of the Dakota's machine guns and an unknown number of Russian rifles.

With every stride, they shortened the distance between themselves and the relative safety of the Dakota's hull. Still, the intensity of the firing steadily increased as they drew more fire from the soldiers in the artillery batteries closest to them. Fortunately, the flak gunners weren't nearly as proficient with their smaller caliber weapons.

As the Dakota guns blazed from all sides, Daniel and Anatoly darted past the tail fin and raced towards an open hatch a few yards ahead.

The plane started to move slowly forward, which had the effect of sending additional pulses of adrenaline surging through Daniel's body.

They drew up alongside the open doorway and grabbed at an extended helping hand reaching out from the inside. Daniel pushed Anatoly ahead. The young physicist flew, landing halfway in the door, his legs kicking out as he was dragged inside.

Daniel watched the plane inch ahead of him as it picked up speed. Panting and near collapse, he threw off his long coat and gave chase. Machine-gun fire from the Dakota mixed with sporadic rifle fire from the Russians spurred him on.

With aching legs and burning ribs, his outstretched hands flailed at the hatch's edge, his fingertips scratching wildly at the paint. Without warning, another pair of hands reached out and grabbed his wrists. Daniel put in one final burst and felt his feet leave the ground, the hands clawing him aboard.

He lay on the plane's cartridge-strewn floor, gulping the cordite-roasted air into his hollow, stinging lungs. With his surroundings beginning to swirl and darken, he last saw Anatoly's sweating but smiling face hanging over him.

*

Shivering at the far end of the airfield, Daryna coiled her arms around her body to protect against the cold. As she watched, the Dakota gathered speed and rose steadily into the sky, banking away to the south. She touched her bloodied head and wondered how she had come to be shot. After a few minutes, she turned and left to dwell upon her likely fate.

EPILOGUE

Late October 1942

The Wolfsschanze, East Prussia

The Adjutant snatched the note from the radio operator and, as had become his custom, gave it a cursory glance. His eyes widened, and his jaw dropped as a sudden paralysis gripped him. After a few seconds, the operator looked at him and snapped his fingers, flicking his hand toward the bunker. The Adjutant nodded absently and headed for the door. He stopped after a few steps and half-turned back before continuing. Behind him, the radio operator smirked. It was a message the Adjutant had hoped would never come and one he prayed he would never have to deliver.

Initially, the war in Russia had given him nothing but delightful messages of a rampaging Reich that he'd had the privilege of delivering to an increasingly enraptured Führer.

That had made him very happy.

But, with their armies' supply lines and resources severely overstretched, they had become bogged down at Leningrad and, as with Napoleon, been stopped at the gates of Moscow in anticipation of another long Russian winter. The battle for Stalingrad, though, had been, by far, the worst.

When the Swastika had been raised in Stalin's city less than a month ago, it had been reported to be as good as captured. But those damned Russians had been ridiculously stubborn and refused to yield. In scenes reminiscent of The Great War, when waves of men had been indiscriminately thrown against a hail of bullets, so too had the Russians wasted the lives of their young men against the steady German advance.

Since Barbarossa's fledgling beginning, nobody had dared dream of retreat, much less defeat. But the tide of military thinking had changed, and he knew that the message his beloved Führer would read in the next few minutes would copper-fasten an unheralded withdrawal. The Reich would be forced to scamper back to the safety of its homeland and pray to God the Russians did not follow.

The capacity for the German fighting machine to continue to wage war on two fronts had been a closely guarded secret, known only to the Führer's inner circle of confidantes. They had known for some time that if they weren't the first to develop the atomic bomb and use its ferocity as a bargaining chip in directing future world affairs, then the dream of a thousand-year Reich would fade into the realm of fantasy.

The message in his hand confirmed their fears – a Reich destined to implode in no more than a couple of years.

He stood at the bunker door, sweating, despite a cold gust from the east. He pulled on the handle and stepped in. He descended a couple of stairs and came to another reinforced door. There was shouting and screaming from the other side. With a shaking hand, he knocked politely, put on the bravest face he could summon, and entered.

He walked to a hunched figure, pointing haphazardly at different locations on a large map and barking orders at the glitter of Generals anxiously shifting from one leg to the other as they stood around the table. The Adjutant gave a slight cough, and the Führer turned.

The Führer's eyes blazed, his face and demeanor bordering on the hysterical.

With his hand shaking, the Adjutant passed him the note and took a step back. Hitler eyed the young man for a moment before lowering his gaze to the slip of paper.

The room fell silent.

As Hitler read, the Adjutant glanced at the other men. He could tell they had read his body language and determined that he bore only bad news. They all braced themselves for the inevitable uproar.

After a few seconds, Hitler turned and threw the note to the nearest officer. The man skimmed it and passed it on. It took only a minute for the room to know that the Russian theatre of operations was a lost cause.

Hitler remained silent.

One of the Generals cleared his throat and spoke. 'We need to get word to Paulus to withdraw his troops.'

Hitler tightened his lips and stared at him.

'He's right.' another said. 'We have to prepare plans for immediate evacuation.'

The group reluctantly nodded in agreement, but Hitler simmered, his eyes maniacally furious. They looked at him.

After several long and agonizing seconds, Hitler pushed past the Adjutant. He stopped at the door and said in a quiet, controlled voice.

'Paulus will not retreat. He will stand and fight.'

Without another word, he was gone. All ashen-faced, the Generals looked at each other in disbelief: the price for failing to capture the Soviet scientist would be the death of the Wehrmacht's 6th Army.

*

British War Office, Whitehall, London

Browne looked across his desk at newly-promoted Brigadier Cumming, who wore a grin wider than the Cheshire Cat. It had been a promotion that Browne had wholeheartedly endorsed but at the same time been one that had disappointed him. The powers that be could have skipped a rank and promoted him to full Brigadier General, especially given the outcome of the mission he had devised and led to success.

Sir Christopher sat next to him, also delighted. However, he didn't sport as broad a smile, primarily because he had been charged with deciding how best to handle the Russians from a scientific viewpoint, which he disliked immensely, and a political stance, which he detested even more. Although an expert negotiator and persuader of men, he was only too aware of the difficulties he would face over the coming months, maybe even years.

He had continuously found the Russians to be pugnacious at best and belligerent at worst, an ethos that had been cultivated by their leader who, it had been reported, had himself carried out several summary executions in the Kremlin corridors since he had learned of 'The Great British Deception'.

'Christmas has come early,' Browne said, regurgitating a well-worn phrase. He sipped a brandy.

Cumming and Sir Christopher nodded solemnly. They had heard many of those 'in-the-know' proclaim the same catchphrase as though they had been the first to coin it. By now, it had become tedious, but they weren't about to ruin it for the old man. The surprising outcome in the East had rejuvenated and re-energized the man, even if it lasted only a few days.

'What plans for our atomic weapon?' Browne asked.

'Scientists are split down the middle,' Christopher said. 'Some believe its invention is inevitable, so why not just get on with the job. Others, though, most notably Einstein, have been quite vocal in their opposition. They feel the world is not ready for such technology, that its very development will hasten the end for us all.'

Browne pursed his lips and pondered Sir Christopher's words before replying.

'He may be right, but I'd sooner we had it before any others. We're sitting at the big table now, the stakes couldn't be higher, and right now, we're holding the trump card.'

Both men nodded in agreement.

'That may be so, however….' Christopher said, 'I've spoken to Yermakov, and he seems determined not to continue his research.'

Browne sipped his brandy again. 'Can't say I blame him. He's been through the looking glass. He's seen what's on the other side.'

'But why come here if he isn't about to help us?' Cumming asked.

'Survival.' Christopher said. 'Given his options, living out the remainder of his life in exile far outweighs a bullet in the head.'

'There are those who would disagree,' Cumming said. 'They're called patriots.'

'They're also dead.' Christopher tapped his cane on the floor.

The three fell silent.

'Of course, it may not matter if Yermakov joins the project in the States,' Cumming said. 'My sources tell me it's a bit of a mess. No real leader has yet emerged.'

'I've heard a name being mentioned to run the whole thing,' Browne said. 'Groves. Rumor has it he's a one-dimensional character, completely driven and wholly focused.'

Cumming lit a cigar. 'Just the sort of man needed at the helm.'

The three fell silent once more. They knew the world was on the precipice of a dramatic change that would shape the global balance of power for decades to come. From here on, every step had to be calculated as nations jostled for their place in the 'New World Order' that would follow.

*

Somewhere in the Scottish Highlands

Anatoly looked out across the frozen waste. If it wasn't for the rambling, jagged mountains, he could well be in Russia. His gaze floated down the slight decline that sloped away from the bungalow, his eyes focusing on a solitary, snow-laden tree, a picture postcard. Behind it, the darkness deepened, covering Europe and, beyond, what was once his homeland.

Homeland. The place meant nothing to him anymore, and he wondered if it would ever again or if he'd ever feel the need to return. He'd left, not because of the fear of dying at the hands of some assassin, but because there was nothing for him there. All emotional ties had been systematically destroyed by the regime he now despised.

He picked up a handful of snow, molded it into a ball, and threw it at the tree. It disappeared on the ground somewhere in between.

His decision to leave with Daniel had forked his life down a path littered with unknowns, a trail where he couldn't see more than one step at a time. It terrified yet excited him in equal measure.

He pulled his cardigan together and hugged himself against the chill. He turned around and watched the sun dip below the mountain tops, its rays diffracting across the sharper edges and reflecting off other snow-covered slopes.

Although it was only late afternoon, he was tired. A cup of tea and a good book; that's what he needed.

He retraced his steps and shuffled towards the bungalow, his feet leaving tracks that night's precipitation would erase as though he never existed. He kicked the snow from his boots using a small step and entered.

In the kitchen beyond, a man looked up and pointed to a mug.

Anatoly nodded in reply.

He glanced into the room to his left and spied two more men engaged in hearty conversation. Some playing cards were scattered on a small table, their weapons sitting on the windowsill.

They didn't look his way.

He turned to the right and entered another room. It was neatly furnished with a bed, a partially filled bookcase, a table, a typewriter, a stack of unused paper, and many pens and pencils. He brushed his fingers along the spines of the small library. There was nothing there that he hadn't already read.

He sighed.

Was this to be his life? Living off the state that had rescued him, giving nothing in return? Although they hadn't said anything, they must surely want something.

He walked over to the desk and picked up an English reading book, the kind young children would begin to read. He flicked through it. He would have to learn the language if he was to survive, to contribute, to stop himself from going insane. Was there an alternative?

A tilted blackboard stood away to one side.

He walked over to it and picked up a piece of chalk. He raised his hand but hesitated. He put the chalk to his lips and cocked his head. He stood there, staring into the blackness.

'Tea,' a man said. It shook Anatoly from his thoughts. He nodded a 'thank you' and glanced out at the snowy waste one more time before scratching an equation onto the board.

*

Yorkshire

It was late evening when Tom stepped off the bus. He glanced across towards his local, debated with himself, but turned away. He had been traveling for the past five hours and was exhausted. It would be straight to bed, forgoing food or a wash. He began the comfortable stroll up to the Miller home.

Once outside, he puffed his cheeks and ran his hands through his hair. He leaned on the door and entered.

'I'm goin' straight-up,' he called as he began to climb the stairs.

'Can you help me with something, first?' Catherine called back.

He put his head over the banisters and, through gritty eyes, looked into the kitchen. She rarely asked him to do anything, and he had long since given up arguing with her whenever she did.

He trudged down the steps and along the hallway.

'What is,'

Daniel dashed across the room and threw his arms around his father.

Tom's eyes filled with tears.

They embraced like long-lost brothers. Behind them, Catherine shook and cried, overcome for the second time that evening.

'You came back,' Tom said with a hoarse whisper, '…no-one told me.'

Daniel nodded. He opened his mouth, but no words came.

The two men separated, and Tom looked into his son's eyes. He instantly saw what he had been twenty-five years before, a man who had returned, scarred by the full horror of war.

Tom's heart sank a little.

He had never wanted this for his sons. He had tried to protect them from reliving what he had been through but had failed. He could see in Daniel's face the terrible things he had witnessed and done and knew that his son would be burdened for the rest of his life, just as he had been. No matter how similar their experiences, he knew deep down, they would never discuss them. Like him, he knew Daniel would bury the memories that were too appalling even to contemplate.

But that wasn't all. His face betrayed not only the horrors he had witnessed but also signs of understanding, forgiveness, and redemption. He grabbed Daniel again and clung to his little boy as the kettle boiled behind them.

ACKNOWLEDGMENTS

LIKE THE JOURNEY UNDERTAKEN BY the novel's protagonist, writing 'Into The Lions' Den' has been something of a war of attrition. It took several years of continual redrafting and editing to get it to where it is today. During that time, the book has been dramatically chopped and changed as characters, motivations, and plotlines have wasted away on the writer's equivalent of the cutting room floor; I hope their demise makes for a more captivating reading experience.

It's safe to say that the book wouldn't be in the state it's in (whether that's a good or a bad thing remains to be seen) without the influence and direction of the staff at Cornerstones Literary Agency, who were thoroughly professional in their critique. Along with the 'too-numerous-to-mention-individually' beta readers, they provided invaluable guidance and advice, most of which was accepted, albeit with some initial reluctance. I thank them all for persevering with my initial sloppiness!

Along the way, there were sacrifices: a handful by me, the majority by my family, but especially by my 'writer's widow' Joan, who provided more than a cup of tea when I was stranded, with all hope apparently lost. In the darkest times, every writer needs a beacon of inspiration to light the way – 'thank you' doesn't seem to be enough.

Read on for an exclusive extract of **An Act of God,**
Stephen Francis' thrilling sequel to **Into the Lions' Den**

PROLOGUE

Temperatures soared and bathed Rome with a sweltering summer heat, bringing with it a tide of renewed hope, optimism, and opportunity that had displaced more than a decade of intimidation, fear, and hate, which had fed an ideology that had thrown at first a continent, and then the world into yet another war.

But Father Felipe Hernandez did not share the joyous mood that most of those who'd survived openly displayed. The dying declaration of a frail man's lifetime of experiences had haunted him since it'd been uttered. 'We are born without sin, a pureness that becomes eroded each day we live our lives.'

With the evening sun setting at his back, he hurried along the narrow, twisting streets, his feet sore from pounding the cobbled passageways. He stubbed his toe and stumbled slightly, quietly cursing his new shoes and tight-fitting cassock before quickly offering a penitent prayer. He pulled a handkerchief from his pocket and patted the dust from his sweating brow. He tightened his grip on the leather-bound envelope given him by his master and walked on.

As he made his way toward the river, he wondered how long this would continue and, more importantly, for him, the repercussions should he get caught. In recent times, an air of suspicion and mistrust hung heavy over the Vatican. He felt it every time he walked along the marble and parquet corridors. Usually, a quiet and serene place of tranquillity and thoughtfulness where the only sounds were respectful whispers; it seemed that the atmosphere had changed. Now, small groups of clerics huddled in corners, glancing warily at those who happened by, their fraught discussions abruptly ending whenever he strayed too close. They would nod reverently, pass on their blessings, and disperse quietly with bowed heads, their eyes fixed on the open prayer books resting on their palms. He wondered if he'd been reading too much into it; a consequence of heightened paranoia borne of what he had done in the past and what he continued to do.

The blast of a horn sounded, ripping him from his thoughts. His head jerked up, and he saw a large US Army troop transport barrelling toward him. Instinctively, he leaped back onto the path, scrambling for a safe foothold. The truck glided past only inches from his nose in a blur of green and white decal, billowing a plume of grit into his face.

He froze, his eyes clamped shut.

Sweat oozed all over his body, his claustrophobic garments sticking, making him feel muggy and breathless. He squinted through an open eye to the sound of an evaporating 'Sorry Padré'. He looked to his right and watched the truck bounce on without slowing down. It rounded a corner and was gone. He placed a hand on his forehead and let out a controlled sigh before blessing himself, the prayer he'd offered a few moments ago perhaps saving him this time. An old man passing touched his elbow gently and asked if he was alright. Hernandez nodded with a grateful smile and thanked him before looking both ways and scurrying across the road.

He arrived at a busy five-way intersection with the 'Ponte Principe Amedeo Savoia Aosta' off to his left. He looked across the Tiber toward the meeting point on the eastern side of the city. A nearby church bell tolled, echoed moments later by several others a little further afield – he had some time to spare. He spied a café nearby where a waiter gathered chairs from outside, tidying up after the day's trading. Hernandez slacked his tongue inside his parched mouth and slipped across the street to quench his thirst before the café closed for the night.

He sat on a rickety, wooden chair and watched the moisture droplets slide slowly down the side of a glass of iced water. He touched one and licked his fingers. Taking a sip, he sat back and listened as the Eternal City began to rest, closing its eyes for the night.

A young couple, in their late teens perhaps, argued a few tables away, their voices breaking the quiet in waves. He glanced across without trying to make it look obvious, trying to catch the tenet of their conversation. From what he could deduce, the young man was begging absolution for an indiscretion, the details of which Hernandez couldn't quite make out. But it sounded like there might have been another girl involved. At one point, the man threw his arms in the air and looked around as though seeking vindication from anybody nearby who agreed with his point of view. He spotted Hernandez looking at them and slipped the cleric a sheepish glance before turning back to the girl and continuing a quieter plea for clemency.

Hernandez smiled to himself.

After all, the Italians had endured over the past few years under Mussolini's dictatorship and the subsequent German occupation, the struggles of only weeks ago appeared to have been quickly forgotten and replaced by nuisances of far less importance. It never ceased to amaze him how his flock seemed to continually seek earthly torment when contentment through the divine was so easily attained, but then he wouldn't have much of a job if it were any other way.

His thoughts drifted to his troubles, and his face grew dark.

He had been caught. A Cardinal Sin and an abomination against the Church – worthy of immediate defrocking. Although he had always known that what he'd been doing was wrong on some basic moral level, such were his urges; he simply couldn't help himself. Sins of the flesh, it seemed, were not exclusive to those outside the Church. He had even heard of others performing similar acts with apparent impunity and assumed he was immune to persecution. Thinking back, maybe it had been a mere rumor, innuendo, designed to flush out and cleanse the Church of sinners.

He had been a fool.

But, he had been given a second chance, an alternative to a public defrocking, and that was why he found himself delivering the envelope on his lap. His hand brushed across the top of it.

It was smooth to the touch and identical to the others he had delivered, although he knew containing different versions of the same documents. He ran his tongue across his top lip and stroked his chin. Although a devout and obedient cleric and the possessor of many virtues, Hernandez struggled to control one in particular: curiosity. It had gotten the better of him on each clandestine trip that'd taken him beyond the confines of Vatican City. It teased and tortured, tempting him to sneak a peek into each of the unsealed envelopes he carried. What he discovered hadn't shocked him. In fact, he had half expected it. An assortment of official documents provided new identities to those who needed them most and, more importantly, were willing to pay.

But this envelope was different. It had been sealed, which was a first, not just by the slick flick of a tongue, but secured in place by a thick, burgundy-colored wax blob stamped with an embossed seal. Hernandez gaped at it now, struggling to recall where he had seen it before, which only heightened his intrigue.

Then it hit him.

He smiled and stifled a half-laugh. He looked at it again, rubbing a finger along the seal's circumference. It wasn't the most famous seal in all of Christendom, and, if he were to guess, he would say that few inside even the Vatican would recognize it, let alone anybody unconnected with the institution.

Realizing the envelope couldn't be resealed once opened, he sighed, tossing it on the table. He stole a glance at the couple as they got up to walk away, the woman snatching her hand away as the man tried desperately to take hold of it. Hernandez shook his head, still wondering what could have them so worked up.

He lifted his glass to take another sip, his eyes dropping to the envelope, and noticed the seal had inadvertently popped open. He stared at it for a moment, his heart beating slightly faster. Hernandez wouldn't have classified it as a miracle, but there it was: God had found a way to satiate his urge.

Unable to restrain himself, he reached forward and gingerly pulled the flap back, glancing around. He peeked in. He slipped his hand in and withdrew two documents, leaving what he knew to be a falsified passport untouched at the bottom.

The first was a letter, which he hurriedly scanned. It hadn't come as a surprise, as all the other envelopes he had couriered had included a similar introductory document, referencing the unknown holder to be of excellent character and standing. He turned his attention to the second document, four pages stapled in the top left-hand corner. His eyes sifted through an itinerary, a dossier, and what appeared to be a detailed set of instructions to be executed as soon as the recipient arrived at his final destination.

Hernandez drew a sharp breath, his eyes wide. He raised a hand slowly to his open mouth and glanced back at the letter, rereading the addressee's name even though he knew it to be an alias. His gaze darted to the signature at the bottom of the page. He whispered it with a gasp, his head shaking slightly. He had expected it to be that of the person whose family seal he had recognized, a man he had come to know very well, who had caught him all those months ago before placing him in this dreadful position. But, the signatory was infinitely more eminent.

His pulse quickened, and he immediately understood why this particular envelope had been so tightly sealed. He quickly dropped the documents back into the pouch and pressed down, praying it would reseal. He waited a few seconds before lifting his hand. It held for a moment but then popped back open. Hernandez grimaced, and a wave of panic began to fizz in the pit of his stomach.

He checked his watch – 10.07 p.m.

He only had a few minutes. Not knowing what else to do, he wetted the underside of the wax with his sweating fingertips and reapplied the pressure, hoping it would hold this time. He stood and looked around with his hand pressed firmly on the wax blob. He crossed the road and waited at the meeting point by the riverbank.

As Rome's magnificent architecture cast elongating shadows, the usually rampant city sounds had almost completely faded. Hernandez surveyed the length of the river. It had become the city's life-blood as it weaved its way from source to mouth. He peered into the rippling water that brushed against the bricked bank below.

The sound of an approaching vehicle followed by the screeching of brakes wrenched him out of his reverie. He turned and saw a U.S. Army truck nestle gently against the curb. The passenger door opened, and a soldier wearing a Military Police uniform hopped out. He walked around the front of the truck.

'You have something for me?' He glanced at the envelope in Hernandez's hand.

Hernandez nodded and handed it to the young man, praying the seal would hold.

The soldier took it without speaking, completed an about-turn, and walked briskly back to his side of the truck. Hernandez expected to see the door open and the soldier hop back in, but instead, he watched nervously as the MP walked back around the front of the truck again.

'Is everything alright?' Hernandez asked, placing his hands as calmly as possible behind his back. His eyes darted down to the envelope and the loose flap that the MP was flicking with his thumb. In one swift movement, the MP unbuttoned his holster, withdrawing his sidearm. Without hesitation, he aimed and fired a single shot into Father Hernandez's chest. The priest staggered back against the low wall that guarded the river, his hand over the bullet hole, blood oozing through his fingers. The soldier walked up and, placing a hand on Hernandez's head, gently pushed.

Father Hernandez's soul had already departed before his lifeless body hit the water some twenty feet below.

*

A Young Swiss Guardsman stood to attention before the Vatican Guard Commandant, having delivered the message a few moments ago. He could feel his skin prickle and turn pale and his mouth run dry. He watched

Michael Valent's face redden, his nostrils flare, and he prayed to be dismissed before his superior took his anger out on him.

Valent drove a clenched fist onto the surface of his teak desk with a force that made the office windows resonate.

The Guardsman's heart skipped a beat, his breathing quickening. He glanced down, expecting to see a crumpled hand such was the force of the impact, but instead saw only a few drops of blood, the glint of a ring, and the imprint of the same symbol that had sealed Father Hernandez's fate no more than thirty minutes ago.